A blind swimmer, seen. I have becon wanting to identify i. commonplaces into dramas revealing my most secret desires.

-Max Ernst.

The surrealist artist Max Ernst used the term "Blind Swimmer" to describe his own creative process: one in which he shut his mind off from the common everyday world around him then gradually re-opened it to a deeper hidden world in which irrational truths and revelations could be found.

Eibonvale Press came into being in the winter of 2005 in a tiny Slovenian mountain town at the hands of David Rix, who sat down one day and decided "Today I am going to make a book." The fact that he knew a lot about books but nothing at all about the book world somehow failed to make that dream flicker away like most dreams and the slow crescendo of Eibonvale Press continued from there and is still continuing. That quiet and lonely winter in the Slovenian mountains still doesn't seem so far away as the press continues its search for the bizarre, the unclassifiable and the strange in new writing, in the process working with some of the best writers in the UK and elsewhere.

Now, this new book provides a chance to look back a bit and define Eibonvale Press as an entity. Blind Swimmer collects together 11 stories, most never before published, by all the writers who have made up or will soon make up the Eibonvale Press family. The result is a book that is as varied as the press itself. Creativity in Isolation was the theme we set, and the results are as varied as the writers themselves. Different takes on what creativity is, what isolation is and whom we are talking to as we tell our tales in the wilderness. The stories stretch from classically tinged horror to urban strangeness to experimental fiction and surrealism. From short stories to full length novellas. From the wilderness of Britain and Sweden to the equal wilderness of the American urban landscape. Blind Swimmer is a unique and spectacular journey through the flip-side of contemporary writing.

Blind Swimmer
An Eibonvale Press Anthology

Blind Swimmer

Paperback Version
Publication Date: August 2010

Copyright of the stories in **Blind Swimmer** lies with their relevent authors.

You're On Your Own, Copyright 2010 Joel Lane
The Writer in the Wilderness, Copyright 2010 David Rix

Cover Art and Interior Design by David Rix

ISBN: 978-0-9562147-5-1

www.eibonvalepress.co.uk

Creativity

in

Isolation

Hi Paul.

Here is the anthology. Thanks for taking a look.

Best regards,

Foreword: You're On Your Own Joel Lane	9
Introduction: The Writer in the Wilderness David Rix	15
Bellony Nina Allan	21
The Flea Market Gerard Houarner	65
The Talkative Star Rhys Hughes	89
The Man who saw grey Brendan Connell	109
The Book of Tides David Rix	121
Flights of Fancy Allen Ashley	155
Pigs Eyes Jet McDonald	175
The Flowers of Uncertainty Douglas Thompson	187
The Higgins Technique Terry Grimwood	227
Far beneath Incomplete Constellations Alexander Zelenyj	259
Lussi Natt Andrew Coulthard	305
Author Biographies	353

Foreword: You're On Your Own
Joel Lane

What effect does human isolation have on creativity, and vice versa? That's an interesting theme. Someone should edit a book of stories about it. Hang on – they have.

Literary models of isolation – physical, social, psychological and cultural – abound in our fragmented and transitional society. Exiles, prisoners, outsiders and loners are iconic figures in the literature and cinema of the twentieth century, and real examples are all around us. The question is: how can this loneliness be shared and learned from without falsifying it?

Jean Genet wrote his first two novels in prison. They are inspired narratives of mystical visions, erotic fantasies and bleak memories. They create a world of bodies and voices whose underlying signature chord is the fact of solitude. When Genet's handwritten manuscript of *Our Lady of the Flowers* was destroyed by a prison guard, Genet simply began again. After his release from prison, he lived in a room with hardly any possessions – he bought many books, but friends kept them for him and Genet would borrow them a few at a time, as if from a prison library.

Writing in the 1970s, the Northern Irish poet Seamus Heaney described his own sense of isolation:

> *I am neither internee nor informer;*
> *An inner émigré, grown long-haired*
> *And thoughtful...*

In the same book, *North*, he advised writers to *Compose in darkness*. The loneliness of creative work, he suggested, offers a means of sharing the common experience of the dispossessed and the forgotten.

Heaney's phrase *inner émigré* echoes the phrase *internal exile* – a term used to describe the situation of many dissidents under oppressive regimes. As international awareness of human rights abuses has grown, such regimes have often made dissidents invisible by preventing them from either publishing or travelling – thus avoiding the political liability of exile or imprisonment.

Heaney was registering his own voice of protest in relation to British attitudes towards the 'Troubles' – and specifically, the internment of civilians. If you could be jailed for your political views, clearly you did not have freedom of expression – either artistically or personally.

In general, the experience of politically engaged writers in modern Britain is unlikely to be one of forced silence or imprisonment. Especially if they are writing genre fiction. Hardcore horror fans may equate the BBFC's insistence on a zombie film having its cannibalism footage trimmed for cinema release with the political censorship of the Third Reich, but their oppression is exaggerated.

What radical and countercultural writers in the UK face, regardless of genre, is being told that their work is irrelevant. The 'market' does not need their ideas. Any writer who does not buy into the 'affirmative culture' of forced optimism and competitive individualism is isolated by the indifference of the 'market' (a prescriptive myth shared by commercial publishers and booksellers).

In addition to cultural isolation, of course, many writers face personal isolation due to factors such as physical or mental illness or disability. The poet George MacBeth died from motor neurone disease; as his mobility deteriorated, he completed a superb final collection, *The Patient*. One poem comments on the 1976 power cut in New York that led to widespread looting:

> *I'm afraid of a boy*
> *With a television set*
> *Running out of my throat.*

When *The Patient* was published, one reviewer in a poetry magazine commented: "If sordor is your cup of tea, you may find this book worthwhile." In other words, the reviewer placed MacBeth's poetry outside the sacred circle of poetry culture. This kind of narrow and parochial thinking is responsible for the widespread perception that poetry is irrelevant to real-life concerns.

The short stories of Anna Kavan – a British writer who changed her writing name to express her identification with the alienated writers of eastern Europe – speak eloquently of the bottomless solitude of addiction and madness, a life gone adrift "among the lost things". By contrast, the junkie narrator of Alexander Trocchi's *Cain's Book* adopts a coldly arrogant stance: society is absurd, so why should he try to belong to it?

That's a mentality all too prevalent in a certain strand of weird fiction fandom that idealises the anti-humanism of writers such as H.P. Lovecraft and Clark Ashton Smith. Both writers have been praised for their 'cosmicist' perspective, their sense of the meaninglessness of human affairs in the greater perspective of the cold, dark universe. While the rhetorical force of such a perspective in imaginative fiction is undeniable, it hardly puts them philosophically ahead of their time – indeed, it was only by writing from an historical perspective that they were able to represent a Copernican and atheist worldview as a traumatic shock.

We would expect, given their lofty awareness, that Lovecraft and Smith viewed human affairs with Olympian serenity. It's a shock, therefore, to read their collected letters and see how small-minded their everyday concerns were. Lovecraft raged against the presence of immigrants in his home town, and used violent language to deny the humanity of "niggers". Smith said of Hugo Gernsback, a Jewish SF magazine editor who had underpaid him: "I wish Hitler had him." If people cannot speak with dignity and responsibility of their own social environment, do not trust them when they try to tell you about the universe.

It's important for any writer to embrace a dialectical relationship between inner and outer realities: not to withdraw into a narcissistic inner world of perpetual wound-licking, but also not to assume that the conventional norms of 'society' and the demands of 'the market' cannot be questioned. It's through human interaction that we develop and learn, becoming active members of society rather than autistic loners or blind followers. That interaction does not mean surrendering your own judgement or your own voice. Working out where you stand and who you stand alongside is a lifelong activity. So is the building of personal relationships. Trying to write stories does not exempt us from any of this.

It's important to keep the realities of a writer's life in mind, rather than talking in terms of 'pure' ideas (or even impure ones). Writers of fiction for books and magazines exist within a web of social and economic forces that trembles and tears every time the house of literary culture receives another blow from the wrecking-ball of corporate capitalism. For the most part, writers feel that they have no home in the new cultural environment. The shanty towns of the independent presses are crowded with literary refugees, all hoping that the future will bring them recognition, but knowing that it probably will not. The atmosphere is one of unease, loss and nervous tension – of voices unheard and books unread. Much of this spills over onto the internet, with consequences that are not always edifying.

Weird and speculative fiction raises the stakes, because the subject-matter cannot be taken for granted. Everything is open to question at a thematic level, which means that the role of imagination (and its prevailing delivery system, dreams) is stronger and more complex than in mainstream fiction. The writer has to balance the need to belong (by speaking a language that a fair number of other people understand) with the need to stay true to the "inner voice". That, too, is a dialectical process: you can't resolve it through introspection or writing a blog, you can only work it out through the ongoing activity of writing and living.

If you allow "the market" to tell you what imaginative metaphors are valid (for example, sexually naïve teenage girl meets emotionally conflicted male vampire), you will find it easy to belong and you will not be alone. Except that whatever part of you wanted to be a writer in the first place will be silently screaming from the inner chamber of your mind. You will be in the country of bad faith, where all the long-term residents have something to hide. Sooner or later, you will make an enemy there. It could be yourself.

On the other hand, if you stay with the secret stories of your childhood, with the intimate voices of the ghosts that visit when you are ill or in real distress, you may find that the world doesn't care very much. You may end up writing for a small and needy readership that corresponds to the most damaged part of yourself. Or you may simply end up with a collection of letters from publishers saying "the market has changed". You will have kept your integrity – but at the same time, you will have adopted a literary persona that is passive, negative and withdrawn. Can you do better than that? I would hope so.

Isolation teaches us that we need human contact in order to understand our world. But human contact teaches us that we also need to step back and keep our own counsel. Both are vital. But our culture encourages neither. Rather, it encourages a continuous drip-feed of pseudo-contact: instant access to push-button entertainment, vacuous messaging, Facebook friends, Twitter chorus, newspapers full of recycled bogus stories, the constant allure of 'real time' (in which nothing real happens) and 'reality TV' (ditto). For any writer, this offers a tempting way to feel less alone. The endless electronic chatter masks the loud silence of people who have nothing to say and nothing to feel.

We are unlikely, in Western Europe, to be exiled or interned for our writing – but we, like everyone else, are constantly being fed the only message of modern capitalism: *You're on your own.* We owe it to ourselves and those around us not to bow our heads in silent assent.

Isolation and social contact are not opposites. Learning how to be with people and learning how to be alone are interdependent processes. Equally, those who forget how to be with people are also forgetting how to be alone. In the haunted forest of the creative imagination – where everyone you have known returns in wingbeats and cries, shadows and flares, decay and growth – we have a chance to make some sense of it all. And go back out into the world with those ideas in our hands, our minds and our stories, ready to take flight.

Introduction: The Writer in the Wilderness
David Rix

So, who is reading this book? Who are YOU? As a writer, that is still a slightly strange thought. As a publisher, who attempts to make it happen for other writers, it is an even stranger thought. This is Eibonvale Press, publisher of experimental horror and slipstream literature – and of other strange stuff that is even less definable. It's been around for 5-6 years now (its start was a bit blurry, ok!), building up a catalogue of writers and books, and getting to the stage now when I am starting to look back and see an identity . . .

Things have progressed a long way since the early days when this thing first started – days when I was living in a little shared flat in the Slovenian mountains. Winter. Outside, the weather was ferocious – minus 23 degrees C and several feet of snow. Tramping to the shops in storms where you could hardly see more than a few metres in front of you. Astonishing the natives by tramping to the shed in bare feet to get wood for the little stove in the kitchen that powered the place. And I loved every minute of it (well – nearly every minute of it!). But somewhere in the middle of that, I just thought to myself "hmmm – why not make a book?" I didn't know how to make a book, of course . . . so I just sat down at my computer and began working it out. I bought a copy of Adobe Creative Suite and started learning how to typeset and do graphic art, while the snow battered against the huge picture window. The text was my own of course – no way was I negotiating this learning curve with someone else's work. That seemingly simple act of making my text into a book changed my own writing forever. But that's another story. It took months, but in the end – book existed . . . It existed. This physical object. I opened the parcel and held it in my hands, turning it over. I took a sip of the strong local Teran wine and wiped away a tear. And, in so doing, somehow this little press had started.

And then I thought to myself "Now what?"

Of course, the full story of the slow crescendo between then and now would probably be deadly boring to everyone. But fundamentally and no matter where the press has come or where it will go, the act of publishing will be forever defined by that one moment during that insane winter . . . when I opened the parcel and – book existed. It hadn't existed before – and now it did.

Ok – now fast forward by 6 years and over 10 new titles. Now Slovenia has been replaced by London – endlessly vibrant and inspiring. Now the Teran wine has been replaced by experimental home-made cocktails with the mystical power to make or break parties. Now the snow storms have been replaced by the London Grey – subtly different to any other form of grey I have ever seen – and the mountain wilderness by a chaos of ever-varying streets. The fact of a shared flat hasn't changed, though the victims of my company have. I no longer go out in bare feet. As I write, I am just ironing out the last wrinkles in the launch of Unpleasant Tales by Brendan Connell and struggling to meet the deadlines to get two more books out there in time for the 2010 FantasyCon. One of which is this one. Things have changed a lot, it seems. The isolation of the early days is fading away and I am in the mood to look back and take stock of the journey so far – and of the identity that is forming for the press. That was why the idea of an Eibonvale Press self-portrait anthology began to surface. It would be a book that would collect works by all of us, I thought, as I lay in my little room and dreamed wistfully. All the writers who had contributed to this strange happy family. I had never even met the majority of them face to face, yet many could now be considered friends.

But then – I dream a lot of things as I doze in this room that is my world . . . It had to wait for someone else to plant the seed before this anthology finally crystallised and acquired its theme. *Creativity in Isolation*. The idea was Douglas Thompson's – I remember that much. Unfortunately, that's about all I remember – the rest is a blur. The reason: I was leglessly drunk. *ahem* Honestly, I don't make a habit of this! The cocktails had made way for some quite agreeable scotch – London had temporarily made way for Glasgow – and here we were celebrating a recent book launch (Ultrameta, A Fractal Novel). The three of us,

Douglas Thompson, Andy Coulthard and myself, sat lazily around the table in Douglas's frighteningly neat home that evening talking for hour after hour about books and writing and the state of the world (as one does) and obscure areas of geology (as one does) . . . until it had all dissolved into a vague minimalist haze. A haze that lasted until next morning, when I woke up and thought to myself: "Wait a minute . . . did I just promise someone I would make a book?"

Creativity in Isolation.

I found myself thinking back to those early days when I held that first book in my hands, wondering what to do with it – and yes, the theme rang true. It's not just about being lonely and struggling to find ways to communicate with the world though (in itself a far too familiar feeling). It impinges very firmly on something that any and every writer – or anyone involved in creative acts of any kind – must think about at some point: The relations between what you are doing and the people who (in theory) will be receiving it. Creativity is not inevitably about isolation, but most people involved with writing will know the subject one way or another, as we sit quietly in our rooms writing our tales and fancies – maybe to be read by the tempestuous and (we are told) sheep-like public, or maybe not. As so-called slipstream writers – writers on the fringes who, either deliberately or not, have steered away from the 'mainstream' and recognised genres into more individual areas of exploration – maybe it seems even more close to home . . .

But isn't that rather . . . trite? What does it matter whether we sell a million copies or whether we are some unknown genius who has given away a few self-published chapbooks over the years? What difference does it make? Certainly the compulsion to create has nothing to do with best-sellerdom or fashions or wealth or its absence. All that is just extra junk that shouldn't even be in our minds during the creative process. In treating isolation as a worthy theme, we really need to define it in this context, which is inevitably complex. What do we mean by the term? The effect of the psychological state of loneliness on creation? Creation without an immediate audience? Creation without any audience? Creation with no one to get in the way with their expectations? What would all this lead to? Some kind of purity? Or madness?

Essentially, these questions were up to the individual authors to tackle, not for me to pontificate over here. Answers may be found later on in this book – or maybe you will have to find your own answers. Such

Introduction: The Writer in the Wilderness

is the nature of fiction. Each writer tackled the subject in their own, very different ways – some simple and straightforward, some (such as Rhys Hughes and Alexander Zelenyj) extremely abstrusely, with connections to the theme that may only become apparent after a little thought.

But for me, there is one last thing to say. My own take on this, which has been a guiding force throughout my own life involved in creative matters. And the germ of that lies with you, I believe. You, holding this book and reading these words right now. You personally – and how I am communicating with you, right now. Maybe you are lying in bed. Maybe you are sitting comfortably. Maybe you are riding on the train or sneaking a quick read at work. Maybe you are curled up in some tiny flat somewhere with the landlady hammering for the rent. Maybe you have a nice house and a certain amount of safety. Maybe you are in a specialist bookshop somewhere, sneaking a quick glance at the book to get a feel for it. But the point remains that we have touched – you, wherever you are, and me, sitting here. And right there, I think, is the definition of any creativity and the reason behind it. It seems to me that any act of creativity must have its receivers – for creativity is a communication. Even when there is no one physically there – there is still some kind of future audience. Some hoped for audience. Even some imaginary or delusional audience. Therefore the theme of the book is not about tracking down any mystical states of purity or absence, but an exercise in exploring the diversity of the receivers of art (of any kind) as much as the givers – and the ways of communicating with them. If you read a story, the isolation has been violated. If you see a picture, the isolation has been violated. If something made is seen, heard, experienced by just one other in the tiniest possible way – if some little doodle is left on a windowsill and elicits a smile – if some small graffiti causes a few new thoughts to flash through someone's mind . . . then the isolation has been violated. And the ways and paths for this to take place are as vast and infinite as the human imagination. It is up to you and all of us, as receivers, to listen.

- David Rix, London, August 2010

Bellony
Nina Allan

For Chloë Mavrommatis

It was further than it looked on the map. Even on a Thursday afternoon, when there was less on the roads than usual, even in Janet's new Audi the drive from London to Deal took her almost two hours. Terri left the car in the station car park, which was close enough to the centre and less expensive than the metered spaces along the front. It was a hot day. She walked down through the town, past the pedestrianised shopping area and then across Beach Street to the promenade and pier entrance. There were plenty of people about, and Terri guessed that many of them were on their holidays.

Like so many English seaside resorts the town was both charming and drab. There were a number of newer chain stores in the precinct, but the narrower side streets were mostly crammed with dismal-looking tourist shops selling the kind of cheap souvenirs you would never dream of buying unless you were killing time in a place like this. The once-resplendent Georgian terraces showed similar signs of wear and decay, the peeling paintwork and faded awnings a familiar outward sign of more general neglect. There was a resigned insularity about everything. People seemed to be enjoying themselves, but in a restrained manner that spoke of predictable pleasures, of aging relatives and wet Sundays, of a cloying tranquillity whose inevitable end was the claustrophobia of stasis and the need for escape.

Terri felt both exalted and frightened. New places excited her; no matter how unpromising they appeared on the surface there was always something to be discovered, a story that could be written. Terri believed that if you returned from an assignment empty-handed it was not the place that had failed but the imagination. It was this appetite for the seemingly mundane that had produced her initial successes at the magazine where until a week ago she had worked as a junior feature writer. It was only with hindsight that she realised the editor had made use of her, keeping her in line with vague promises whilst continuing to fob her off with assignments so outrageously turgid that no one else was interested in covering them.

She excelled at such work and even enjoyed it but she had come increasingly to resent the implications of being taken for granted. Now, in this small and faded town on the east Kent coast, she began to wonder if the editor had guessed her level all along. The Allis Bennett story was her first good idea for an assignment since taking the decision to go freelance. But now that she was here in Deal she feared that the town and most likely the subject had exactly the same qualities of dullness and parochialism as all the jobs that had been foisted on her while she was working for the magazine.

She did a turn of the pier then started along the promenade in the direction of Walmer, the smaller residential suburb that lay immediately to the south of Deal. Walmer had its own castle and its own history but the building developments of the nineteen-sixties made it impossible to tell where one town now began and the other left off.

Walmer had been the home of the children's writer Allis Bennett. She had lived there for thirty years, and then she had disappeared. Nobody had seen or heard of her since. Terri had told herself there had to be a story in that, that stories about missing persons always sold. Now she was starting to think the best thing you could do with a place like this was go missing from it. The thought made her smile, and all at once her spirits began to rise.

She was looking for a missing person. Even if she failed in her search it would make an interesting story. Perhaps she would go missing herself, at least for a while.

*

Terri first read a book by Allis when she was ten. The book was called *Bellony*, and was about a girl who finds a doorway to another universe. The girl in the story was named Vronia. Her sister Annabel had recently died, and Vronia invented a game with a door in her house as a way of being with her again. The door itself was ordinary – just a side door leading to the concrete passageway between Vronia's house and the house next door – but the act of passing through it was not. In Vronia's imagination, the world on the other side was always different from the world from which she emerged.

The book was unlike other books Terri had read, where children pursued adventures in magical realms full of vampires and talking animals. The worlds behind Vronia's door appeared at first to be the same as the world she had left. It was only gradually that the differences became apparent. Usually these differences were small but they coloured everything – everybody wore the same clothes, say, or speaking aloud in public was illegal.

At the climax of the book, Vronia became trapped in a world where no one recognised her. In this version of reality, her sister was alive but every time Vronia tried to speak to her she disappeared.

Terri found the story frightening but this did not stop her reading it. The book came into her life shortly after she went up to senior school. Her closest friend Melinda had been sent away to a girls' boarding school in Dorset, and Terri for a time felt very alone. She came to identify strongly with Vronia, who wore glasses and had few friends, and she searched for more books by the same writer, Allis Bennett. Those that she found she enjoyed. She liked the way that inexplicable things could happen in Allis's books and not be resolved.

When she was older she discovered that Allis Bennett had once been Alicja Ganesh and that she had been born in Poland. She had written ten novels for children altogether. Her one adult novel was a semi-autobiographical work, about a Polish writer who flees to England to escape the Nazis. The small number of critical essays that had been written about Allis all suggested that the darkness and ambiguity in her stories had its source in her childhood in Nazi-occupied Europe, and in the fact that her parents and sister had died in concentration camps.

Bellony, the strange-sounding title of the novel Terri had loved as a child, turned out to be the name of the street in Warsaw where Allis's family lived before the war.

*

Terri walked on along the promenade, taking note of the sights she had read about and was trained to look out for: the castle, the bandstand, the blue Art Deco dome of the old Regent Cinema. Once she was clear of the town there were fewer people. The tide had begun to go out, and the beach seemed to stretch for miles. Like most of the beaches on the Kent and Sussex coast it was notable only by being featureless, an unvaryingly flat expanse of shingle. But the landward edge, a strange, tangled hinterland of tamarisk and valerian, sea kale and exotic orange flare-ups of *kniphofia*, was interestingly wild, an unkempt no-man's-land between the coastline and the countryside beyond.

She looked out across the stones to where a small power boat was drawn up on blocks, surrounded by a chain of its rusting entrails. Just beyond it was a row of beach huts, painted alternately in yellow and white. It was like a scene straight out of *A Letter from Sabine*, one of Allis's novels that had been set on this part of the coast. A memory came to Terri then of the first time she had read *Sabine* and the pleasure and the mystery she had found in it. She supposed it was no coincidence after all that she was here. Allis's writing had first become important to her during a time of change, and this also was a time of change. She had resigned from her job and finally she had found the courage to end her relationship with Noel, her boyfriend for the past five years. She had known for eighteen months that Noel wasn't right for her. Leaving him had been the right thing but it still wasn't easy. She was on her own, as she had been alone before when Melinda had been sent off to Broadhurst.

It had been Allis's stories that had helped her last time. Now it was Allis herself she felt drawn to. Since making the decision to write about her, she had increasingly come to think of her as a friend.

Allis's house was on Wellington Parade, a little over a mile from the centre of Deal. The access to the houses was very narrow, over an unmade strip of raked-over shingle and sand. Some of the dwellings were new-build, uninspiring seventies chalets with red-tiled roofs and plate glass windows. But most of the houses here were older than that, a disjointed assemblage of post-war prefabs, colonial-style villas dating from the nineteen-thirties and clapboard bungalows with gently rusting cast iron verandah rails. They formed an intriguing spectacle and something wholly unexpected. In the mismatched incongruity of styles there was for Terri something almost dreamlike, as if each house was a concrete expression of its owner's fantasies.

Here at last she began to see what might have attracted Allis to this place and caused her to stay. She knew Allis had been attached to the town because she had set several of her books here, or at least in an imaginary place that looked exactly like it. It was a kind of miracle, the way she had transformed this rather tired seaside town into somewhere special. And yet even as she was thinking this it occurred to Terri that what Allis had done was not after all so different from what Terri was trying to do here herself. She was looking for the story behind the story. For Allis Bennett as for Terri, even the most ordinary things had the potential to become extraordinary if you described them properly.

It was strange to think that Allis had once walked where Terri was now walking, maybe even thinking similar thoughts.

Allis's house was right near the end, one of a pair of Victorian semis that had been built as mirror images of each other. The house on the left had a freshly-painted pink exterior and the flagstones that formed a path to the door looked recently scrubbed. The house on the right, Allis's house, was in a state of decline. The yellow paintwork had faded to a bleached ochre. Instead of a neat strip of lawn there was overgrown grass. The windows, long unwashed, were spattered with grime. Terri felt drawn to the house instantly. As she came closer she saw that the signboard of a local estate agent had been hammered into the ground to the right of the gate. The house was being advertised as 'To Let.'

She walked back along the front in a kind of daze. When finally she reached the car she called the agent, who confirmed that the house was still available, but on a short lease only. The long-term tenants had recently vacated and the owner was thinking of selling.

Terri said that would be fine.

"How soon could I move in?" she said.

"Well," the agent hesitated. "Normally we would expect references. And I should warn you it's a bit run down. Don't you want to see inside? I could drive you round there now if you like."

"I don't have time, I'm afraid. But so long as the roof is watertight there's really no problem. It's the house's position I'm interested in. It's perfect for what I need."

She told the agent, whose name was Cahill, that she was prepared to pay three months' rent up front if it would hurry the process along. "You're more than welcome to check my references but I'd like to move in next week if I can." She gave him the contact details for the magazine's finance office and the letting agency that handled her flat in Camden. She felt tempted to take Cahill up on his offer of showing her the house but made herself hold back. She did not want her initial impressions of the place muddied by the blandishments of an estate agent.

On the drive back to London she made a pretence of reflecting calmly on the day's events but in reality she was barely able to restrain her excitement. The idea of living in Allis's house was like a dream come true. It was not just that it would bring her closer to Allis in ways she had never previously imagined; she believed she might also find the peace and solitude she needed to help her work out what kind of writer she wanted to be.

She would be getting away from London, and away from Noel. Everything had happened so quickly it was hard to take in.

*

Allis arrived in London soon after the war. She was taken in by relatives in Highgate, where she met and married an Englishman, Peter Bennett. Peter Bennett was a keen weekend sailor, and it was his idea that they should move out of London. After a couple of months' searching and some minor disagreements they finally agreed to settle on the house in Walmer. Two years later Peter Bennett was drowned in a sailing accident.

Allis stayed on in Walmer, which she said she had grown used to. By then she had sold her first novel, which was published to favourable reviews and some small success. She could perhaps have made more of this, but her strong dislike of publicity made her a difficult author for the publisher to promote. She disappeared soon after her fiftieth birthday. Of those who were interested most believed that like her husband's her death had been from misadventure. Allis liked to walk along the foot of the cliffs, and it was easy to get caught by the tide unless you were careful. A small number of people suggested that she might have walked into the sea deliberately, but in the end the speculation died down. Allis's books had been popular for a time but she had never been famous. The quietly abandoned house, with its ordered rooms, left no hint of violence.

When seven years had passed and she had not returned Allis was declared legally dead. The house in Walmer was sold, and the money divided equally between the relatives in Highgate.

The new owner was a Turkish businessman based in London. Like Peter Bennett he was keen on sailing, and bought the house as a weekend retreat, but he soon found that he was too busy to spend much time there. It took longer to get to Walmer than he had bargained on, and he spent enough time on the road as it was. He decided the most sensible thing would be to rent the place out.

*

Terri moved in on the Wednesday. She had spent the weekend packing up her flat in Camden. Some of her stuff went into storage but most of it she found she was happier getting rid of. She wanted to make a fresh start. She arranged to sub-let the flat to Janet, who had been her best friend on the magazine. Once the six-month tenure ran out Janet could either renew it in her own name or let the flat go. Terri had decided she wouldn't go back there, whatever happened. The place would always mean Noel to her. If she wanted to return to London she would find somewhere else.

She travelled down to Kent by train. She had thought about hiring a car but in the end had decided not to. Allis had never learned to drive, and for the next couple of weeks Terri wanted to put herself in Allis's shoes. Knowing she would have to carry everything had made her selective about the things she brought with her. It was surprising how much she had been able to fit into a rucksack and two large holdalls. Walmer station was closest to the house, but there was the matter of the keys, which she had arranged to collect directly from the estate agent. It was only a short walk from Deal station to the agency office and even though her luggage was heavy Terri managed without too much difficulty but Alan Cahill reacted to her arrival on foot with a kind of incredulous amusement, as if she had just stumbled in from China.

"If you hold on just a moment I'll run you down to the house," he said. "You can't possibly walk."

He glanced again at the bulging holdalls. He looked to be in his early fifties. Terri noticed he was wearing cufflinks, and had the blandly smooth good looks of a host on a television chat show. Terri could tell that he was curious about what she was doing there, that for people like Cahill the very fact of her being alone and without a car would give cause for suspicion.

She wondered if people in the town had looked at Allis in that same way when she first arrived. Terri had managed to find a photograph of her from that time, a small, nervous-looking woman in a badly fitting plaid dress, her dark hair tugged back from her face in a bedraggled bun. Later photographs showed her looking more acclimatized, her hair clipped in a neat gamine crop, her figure fuller and her face less gaunt. She seemed altogether less foreign.

Terri's first impulse was to tell Cahill she would prefer to make her own way out to Allis's. But the thought of lugging the holdalls was not appealing and so she gave in. She was thankful it was just a short drive. She was uncomfortable with the agent, and had no wish to become more closely acquainted with him. She gazed determinedly out of the window for the entire journey, refusing to respond in more than monosyllables to his hopeful gambits about the weather, the comfort or otherwise of her train journey, the shortage of available parking.

"Would you like a hand with your stuff?" Cahill said as he brought his car to a standstill in front of the house.

Terri did her best to smile then shook her head. "No thank you," she said. "You can drop me here." She wished he would just go. She most emphatically did not want the agent inside the house with her.

"Well, you know where we are." He handed her the keys, four of them on a key ring, the house's number scrawled in bold indelible pencil on the cardboard fob.

She hauled her luggage out of the boot and on to the drive. Cahill backed his car and then turned it around, manoeuvring with difficulty in the narrow access road. Terri waved to him briefly, waiting until he was out of sight before approaching the house. Once the car was gone it was perfectly quiet. The tide was far out, the horizon blurred by heat haze. Now that she had returned here to live the place felt different, subtly enchanted, as if it had decided to trust her with some of its secrets.

There was no one at all to be seen. Suddenly she found it easy to imagine that Allis was close by, watching. She would be an old lady now, but that was no reason to presume that she was dead.

The front door would not open at first, and for a moment Terri thought Cahill had given her the wrong set of keys. But suddenly the lock gave way and she was inside. The hallway was stuffy with heat and the air smelled stale. Dust motes danced in the angle of light from the open door. There was a pile of junk mail on the doormat. Terri carried her things inside and shut the door.

There were eight rooms in total, arranged over the two floors: a sitting room at the front, with two smaller reception rooms and the kitchen downstairs, three bedrooms and a bathroom on the storey above. The place had been hovered and cleaned, but there was a down-at-heel air to everything and she could see at once that the house was in need of many minor repairs. The furniture was a depressing mix of nineteen-forties utility and modern flatpack. Terri went from room to room, feeling vaguely disappointed and wondering how much of this junk if any had been in the house when Allis was still living there.

As well as the front door key there was a key to the kitchen door at the back and another, smaller key that opened the gate to the side access passage where the bins were stored. There was a fourth key, which seemed not to fit anything. For the first time since deciding to rent the house she asked herself what exactly she had hoped for in coming here. The house was just a shell, after all; by itself it could tell her nothing. She wondered if she had invested it with too much power, if she had talked herself into believing it was the key to a mystery in order to give herself an excuse for running away from London and all the painful decisions of the last few months.

As if to press home the point, her mobile started ringing. The room's sparse furnishings made it sound aggressively loud.

She flicked it open and glanced at the screen. The caller was Noel. She felt immediately flustered, at a disadvantage. In her mind Noel had already receded into the past. The idea that he might call her here hadn't entered her head. She wished she had thought to block his number.

As it was, she picked up, knowing that if she didn't he would call again.

"Where are you?" he said. He gave no greeting, not even a simple hello, but Noel was like that. He said what was on his mind, regardless of whether you needed or wanted to hear it.

"It doesn't matter where I am," Terri said. "I needed to get out of London for a couple of weeks."

"Is it true that you've quit your job? I phoned the office first, but Janet said you left last week."

"Yes, it's true. I should have left ages ago." She wanted to say it had been him, or more accurately put her final row with him, that had finally given her the courage to hand in her notice. The prospect of going freelance had terrified her and she kept finding excuses not to do it. Splitting up with Noel had turned out to be easy by comparison. Once that had been accomplished she found she was able to take care of the other business as well.

"You're not serious?" Noel said. "How on earth are you going to manage?"

"I've got some jobs, pieces to tide me over. And I'm working on new stuff already. Anyway, I'll be fine." She felt angry at herself for answering his questions, for feeling she had to justify herself in front of him. She felt like asking him what the hell it had to do with him, but if she did there would be a row and as far as she was concerned that part of her life was over. She hated what he was doing, trying to make out that nothing had changed, trying to draw her back into his life by the simple expedient of ignoring everything she said.

It was what he always did, a kind of inverted bullying.

"Can I come and see you in your bolt hole?" he said. "I'm sure it's very cosy."

"No, Noel, you can't," she said. "Goodbye."

She broke the connection. Her heart was racing. The thought that he might find out where she was, was appalling.

After a couple of seconds she switched off the phone. If shaking Noel loose meant she had to cut herself off from the world for a while then it was a price worth paying. It occurred to her that Allis would not have had a mobile phone, and that if she was serious about trying to re-enter Allis's world then she should give up her mobile also.

For all her love of the place, as a foreigner and a writer Allis Bennett must have been isolated here. Had she welcomed that isolation, or had it been forced upon her? Did she have any friends in the town at all? One of the difficulties of writing about Allis was that no one seemed to have known her very well.

Allis had never remarried and rarely travelled. It was as if her life had been divided into two acts: there was before-Walmer, where she had lived in the world and terrible things had happened to her, and then there was Walmer, where everything came to a standstill and her life appeared to enter a cul-de-sac. There had been a third act also, of course: the event or sequence of events that had brought about Allis's disappearance from Walmer and whatever it was that had happened after that. Action, reaction, synthesis. Terri found she could hardly imagine what it must have been like for Allis, to arrive in a foreign country among a host of strangers who could have had only the shallowest understanding of what had happened to her. For most people the present becomes the past only gradually, but for Allis there had been this sudden and irrevocable division, potently symbolized by her final, one-way crossing of the English Channel.

Had Allis taken to writing as a way of coming to terms with her life, or had writing been a part of her life already? Terri had no idea. She hoped that this was something she would find out in time.

She opened one of her holdalls and took out the small folder of photographs and newspaper clippings that was all the material on Allis she had been able to amass so far. She dug around in it until she found the photograph of Allis as a new immigrant, the Allis of the plaid dress and untidy bun. She propped the photo on the mantelpiece in the smaller of the two back sitting rooms, the room she had already decided would serve as her office. The room overlooked the garden, and seemed private from the rest of the house.

She wondered which room Allis had worked in, where she had written her novels. Once again, Terri hoped she could find out.

She spent the next couple of hours unpacking her things and trying to give the house a feeling of home. There was a gateleg table in the front sitting room, sturdy enough to be used as a writing desk yet small enough to be easily moved. She dragged it through to her new office and set up her laptop, arranging her books and papers on the melamine shelves that lined the chimney alcove. Because of the problems of transporting them she had been forced to severely ration her choice of books, but the sight of those she had brought made her feel immediately uplifted. The room now had a purpose to it. She could even begin to believe she might succeed, not only in this assignment but as a freelance writer.

Once everything was unpacked she ventured outside. As she deposited her few bits of rubbish in one of the dustbins she noticed there was a side door in the access passage, an alternative entrance to the house that from its position should have led directly into her office. Terri knew already that no such doorway existed, at least not on the inside of the house. The door had a lock, and Terri tentatively tried it with the last key on her key ring, the odd fourth key she had been unable to find a use for. The key fitted but it would not turn. She decided that the door must have been sealed, the doorway bricked and plastered over from the inside. Such things were commonplace, especially in older houses. At least she now knew what the fourth key had been for.

The discovery pleased her. It was small and it was meaningless but it was something about the house she had found out for herself. At the very least it felt like a start.

It was getting towards evening. The sky was a mottled pink. The back garden was badly overgrown, a chaotic mass of blackberry thorns and nettles and seeding grasses. Among the waist-high scrub there were stands of goldenrod and speedwell and cow parsley, the same *kniphofia* she had seen on the beach. Terri smelled the scents of wild meadows, the dry-grass, pollen-rich aroma of so many lost summers. She thought of the way she and Melinda had drifted apart. There had been tears, and there had been letters, and then there had been the slow, cruel erosion of time. This gradual dissolution of their closeness was something Terri still found painful and shocking, even in retrospect. In it she could see everything she needed to know of transience and eventual mortality.

She remembered an image that often came to her when she thought about this, the image of two trains stopped at a station on opposite platforms. There was a girl looking out of the window of one of the carriages, catching the eye of a girl looking out of the compartment opposite. They held each other's gaze for a long moment, a moment in which worlds arose and possibilities extended. Then the trains moved off in opposite directions and they never saw each other again.

The image was from one of Allis's books, *The Hurdy Gurdy Man*. When Terri had first read it she cried, because it seemed to describe exactly what had happened to herself and Melinda.

She turned to go inside, thinking she should get herself something to eat. She saw with a start that she had not been alone, that there was a woman in the next door garden, taking washing off a rotary clothes line and placing it into a yellow plastic basket. The woman nodded to her briefly and then disappeared indoors.

Terri made supper then spent the rest of the evening going through her Allis file, arranging the material she had in date order then dividing it between four new files. Each of the files related to a different aspect of Allis's life. She hoped eventually to fill these files with new material.

At some point she realised she had completely forgotten about Noel's phone call. Thinking about him directly brought him no closer, and she found that to get any sense of him she had to conjure him up, like a character in a book she had read some time ago and mostly forgotten.

She went to bed late, choosing the main bedroom at the front of the house which had a wonderful view of the sea and that she felt certain must have been Allis's. She listened to the midnight news, the sound of the waves through the open window as constant as radio static.

It was a hot night. She tossed and turned for a while in the unfamiliar bed, then fell soundly asleep.

*

Arranging and rearranging the facts, Terri came to the conclusion that Allis's disappearance had one of three causes: she had met with sudden death, she had gone off with a new lover, or something unwelcome had emerged from her past.

Terri did not believe that Allis had been murdered or drowned; the former was too bizarre, and in the case of the latter her body would have been bound to come ashore eventually. The same was also true of the suicide theory.

It was more likely that Allis had met a new man, but this still did not explain why she had abandoned her home and all her possessions. The evidence showed that Allis had left the house suddenly and without preparation. There had even been a load of washing still in the machine.

Aside from a few book signings in London Allis had rarely left the town. Her life spoke of order and planning, not random impulse. It seemed unlikely to Terri that she would have altered her behaviour so radically, even for a new lover, unless some crime had been committed.

She entertained brief visions of Allis falling for a murderer, a bank robber, some man on the run, but then supposed her imagination was getting away with her. This left only the past. Terri made a list of the most likely reasons a person might have for wanting to disappear. There were many possibilities, but most of these could be categorized under one of three main headings: love, money, and fear. She had already discounted the man theory, and it was also a matter of record that Allis had not been in debt. It was one of the first things the police had looked into, and it had been shown that although Allis was by no means rich she was certainly comfortable. Her books brought her in a reasonable income, especially since the most popular, *The Carousel*, had been adapted for film by the Children's Film Foundation. She owned the house in Walmer outright. Her accounts all stood securely in the black.

The police had kept a track on her bank accounts for several months after her disappearance, waiting to see if there were any withdrawals. There were none. Allis's money, along with her house, had passed duly into the hands of the Highgate cousins.

What could have frightened or disturbed Allis Bennett so badly that she had made herself disappear without a trace?

It was true that Allis's past was filled with tragedy, that she had lost her parents and her sister at a young age. As she reread Allis's stories and studied her background it became increasingly clear to Terri that the loss of her sister Hanne had been the defining event of Allis's life, and that most if not all of her books were to some extent attempts to come to terms with it.

She had never spoken much of Hanne directly but there was a surviving photograph of her. It was in sepia tint, and showed a girl of about thirteen wearing a dress with a round white collar and metallic buttons. The girl's hair was cut in a pageboy, the front bangs secured with a tortoiseshell slide. The image was charmingly old fashioned, although Terri supposed that at the time Hanne's hairstyle would have seemed rather daring and thoroughly modern. The idea that this girl had been deliberately killed, swept up by forces beyond her control and beyond any normal comprehension, that she had been smashed on the rocks of history, was still dauntingly horrific. It reminded Terri that Allis had also been a victim of these crimes. Her past had haunted Allis all her life, but the worst had already happened and she was not to blame for any of it.

What more was there to run from? Terri knew there must be something. The very fact of Allis's disappearance was proof of this. She knew also that there would have been clues. The clues would have most likely been in the house, because this was the last place that Allis had been seen. The police had been over the house many times, but it occurred now to Terri that if they had missed something it would not have been through negligence, but because they hadn't known what to look for.

They would have been looking for signs of disturbance, of what was commonly referred to as foul play.

But what if the clues to what happened had been more subtle?

They needed someone who had known Allis better. Or another writer.

She decided she should telephone Alan Cahill. She knew it would have been more polite to arrange a proper appointment, to go into the office, but she found she still felt hostile towards Cahill and didn't want to see him face to face. She was aware that Cahill had done nothing to earn her dislike – if anything it had been the opposite – but there were things about him that annoyed and repelled her. His conventionality, his boring good looks, his particular brand of masculinity, subtle yet patronizing – in Terri's mind Cahill had become symbolic of everything about the town that was anti-Allis.

It was Cahill's secretary that answered the phone, but she put Terri through to Cahill almost at once.

"I'd like to know some more about the house," she said to him. "How long have you been the agent?"

"Is something wrong?" said Cahill. "I did warn you it was in need of attention."

"The house is fine," said Terri. "This is just some research I'm doing. Can you tell me how many people have lived here since the house has been on your books?"

She could sense him tensing up almost at once, as if the very idea of research, of anything that could not be accommodated on a spreadsheet, aroused his suspicion.

"I don't think I can help you. The information we hold on our clients is confidential."

"I'm not talking about your clients. It's the house I'm interested in. All I want is a bit of background." She wished she could come up with a harmless rationale for her enquiry, something that would satisfy the agent without her having to tell him about Allis. She did not want to talk to Cahill about her project. "I'm writing an article about the town."

This at least seemed to make some sense to him. Cahill told her that he had taken over the business from his father ten years before, and that the house had been on their books throughout that period. There had been three sets of clients during his time as manager. The first, a family of four, had been there since his father's time. The couple after that were Spanish, both teachers at a college in Dover. The most recent tenant had been a retired doctor.

"He was only there for a couple of months," said Cahill. "He needed somewhere to stay while he looked for a property to buy in the area. We found him a lovely little place in the end, just up the road on Prince Charles Terrace." He sounded very pleased with this outcome, and Terri suspected it had been his sale. A mad thought came to her, that he hoped she would include this information in her article.

"Do you think the doctor would mind if I had a word with him?" Terri asked.

"I shouldn't think so. He's a nice old chap, very friendly. But I don't think he'd be much use to you. As I said, he's new to the area. If you really want to know about the house you should speak to the lady next door to you. Judy Whitton, her name is. She's lived there for years. I know that because we employ her as a cleaner for our short-let properties. She's completely reliable."

"That's useful to know. Thank you." She ended the call. She was beginning to feel guilty about Cahill, who had been perfectly pleasant to her and more helpful than he could have realised. She guessed that Judy Whitton was the woman she had seen in the garden the first evening she was there, taking down her washing from the rotary dryer. She tried to remember what she had looked like, but could recall only the way she walked, the stout figure oddly graceful in its navy moccasins. Terri supposed she had been in her sixties, older than Alan Cahill but younger than Allis.

Terri went outside to the garden, vaguely hoping that the woman might be there again, but there was no sign of her or of anyone, not even a new crop of washing on the rotary dryer. She walked round to the front of the house and rang the bell. She waited on the doorstep for a couple of minutes, standing on tiptoe with her face to the glass, but when it became clear there would be no reply she went back inside. She felt disappointed and frustrated, as if information was being kept from her deliberately, although she knew that Judy Whitton was probably just out shopping.

She tidied the kitchen, washing up the plate and mug she had used for her lunch, then set out for a walk along the beach. She had grown used to taking a walk every day. She had developed the habit initially in imitation of Allis, who had stated more than once that her walks along the coastal path were essential to her working routine. But within a couple of days she found herself looking forward to the walks not only for the exercise but as a way of channelling her ideas and bringing her thoughts into order. She liked to think that this was how it had been for Allis too.

Also the landscape itself seemed to invite exploration. The level path, the glittering sea, the cliffs rising in the distance were for Terri an epitome of vanished freedoms, of the English summer and the urge to wander, exactly as they had been in Allis's stories. She walked south towards Kingsdown, taking the well-worn path that would, if she followed it for long enough, eventually bring her to the ferry terminal at Dover. It came to Terri that if she were to board one of the ferries it would in theory be possible to walk all the way from Allis's house in Walmer to the house on Bellony in Warsaw. The idea was fascinating to her and a little frightening. It gave the sense that if you walked long enough and far enough you might travel back in time as well as distance.

Terri smiled. She was beginning to think like Allis. She wondered whether Allis's unconventional cast of mind, her compulsion to stretch an idea to the very limit of its credibility was a tendency she had been born with, or whether the war had permanently altered her view of things. More than one critic had suggested that it was her marriage to Peter Bennett and the feeling of safety it provided that had given Allis the confidence and security to begin expressing herself in writing but Terri did not believe it. Allis might have loved Peter Bennett while he was alive but he had produced no lasting impact on her work. Allis's first subject was *being alone*, coming to terms with solitude and drawing strength from it. With his mousy hair and his clean shirts and his buttoned-up Englishness Peter Bennett had been a brief and incidental accompaniment.

She thought about the main character in Allis's novel *Orinoco*, a boy called Toby who loved ships and lighthouses, anything to do with the sea. He had fallen in love with an angelfish, and drowned. It seemed at least possible that Toby had been modelled on Peter, but far more than any superficial similarities with her dead husband, Toby Chowne resembled Allis herself, or rather the quintessential Allis character: a shy and lonely child marooned in some strange aftermath of loss.

Terri was beginning to realise that there was far more to Allis's story than could be covered in a single article. She thought there was at least the possibility that she could persuade a publisher to commission her to write Allis's biography. If this happened it could be life-changing. So much for Noel's sneering doubts about her ability to make a go of it alone.

She stepped off the path and began walking across the beach towards the edge of the sea. A narrow white line of surf flowed back and forth over the pebbles at the tideline, robbing them of their protective opacity. They emerged jewel-bright from the water, glistening in the harsh white sunlight, the pearlescent greys, veined greens and polished ambers of Murano glass. The stones tumbled and slid beneath her feet, their rolling clack and crunch as smoothly satisfying as the rattle of barley sugars shaken together in a jar. The sky was a vast blue vault. The surface of the sea flashed like tinfoil, its undulating meniscus a snare for the sun. The wind had dropped completely, and the rising heat of the day had begun to induce in Terri a mild euphoria. She had foolishly come out without a hat. She had one back at the house, a tatty green straw boater she had discovered hanging on a nail just inside the cupboard under the stairs. She had a feeling about the hat, that it might be one of the few things left in the house that had actually belonged to Allis.

At Hope Point the path divided in two, climbing straight on towards the head of the Down or turning left to thread its way along the foot of the cliffs. Terri did not like the lower path. The sight of the sheer white cliffs towering above her made her afraid. She came to a standstill, thinking how easily a person might be caught by an encroaching tide.

Could this be how Allis had died? She hated to think so. She could not bear to think of her terror, realising that she was trapped and there was no way round. She would have tried to swim of course, only the sea would have driven her back into the cliffs. From where Terri stood she could just make out the grey slate roofs of the first cottages on the road to St Margaret's at Cliffe. The skyline was blurry with heat haze, and to Terri it seemed for a moment as if the cottages were floating in thin air. Their roofs were sharply triangular, rigid as stage sets, flat as the cardboard façade in a children's theatre. There was a toy theatre in Allis's novel *The Carousel*. Terri mopped at her face with the back of her hand. The sweat was pouring off her, strands of hair were plastered to her forehead and neck. She turned back the way she had come, cutting diagonally across the shingle and heading for the cracked strip of asphalt that ran up from the head of the beach towards the Kingsdown Road. The road was shaded by trees, and was much easier to walk on than the shingle. She was back at the house in a little under half an hour. She went straight upstairs to the bathroom and stepped into the shower. She turned the cold tap almost all the way over, letting the fierce, hard jets bombard her skin with coolness. She leaned against the wall, her eyes half closed, listening to the sound of the water striking the tiles. The feeling of distance that had assaulted her at the cliff edge gradually receded. It was as if she was absorbing reality through her skin along with the moisture.

She dried herself and put on fresh clothes then made herself a cup of tea and went to sit in her office. As she pushed open the door she had the brief but strong conviction that someone was inside, waiting for her, but it was clear as she looked about her that the room was empty. She shook her head and the room seemed to spin. She supposed she was still feeling the effects of sun exposure. She opened the window as far as it would go, filling the office with the combined scents of bleached seaweed and exhausted buddleia. The afternoon heat was gradually beginning to subside. She noticed that the speedwell and ragwort she had placed in a jug on the windowsill had all wilted, and she felt a brief flash of annoyance at herself for being so thoughtless, for leaving the jug in the full glare of the sun. The jug was ugly, an Art Deco imitation she had found in one of the kitchen cabinets, its squat lines mitigated only by the modest presence of the wildflowers.

She wondered if the house was getting to her, the self-imposed isolation. Apart from Cahill and the girl on the supermarket checkout she had not spoken to anyone since her brief conversation with Noel the day she arrived.

She briefly considered ringing Janet but decided against it. Janet would be pleased to hear from her, but she would also see her call as an opportunity to bring Terri up to date with magazine gossip. Terri had no wish to hear it, at least not yet. To be drawn back into that world so soon after leaving it would only be a distraction. But neither did she want to talk to Janet about Allis. She felt proprietorial towards Allis, protective even. She had the sense that to talk about her to anyone else would be to betray her in some way, that it might even damage her ability to write about her.

She had felt that way about her subjects before, but never so strongly. She decided she would have an early supper then make an attempt at redrafting the opening of her article. She straightened the papers that were already on her desk, separating the photocopied cuttings from the handwritten notes. As she was doing this something slipped from between the pages and fell to the floor. When Terri bent to pick it up she saw it was the photograph of Allis's sister Hanne. The photograph of the girl in the white-collared dress was one of the few surviving images from Allis's life before the war, and Terri had made an enlarged copy of it before leaving London. The picture had been used to illustrate almost every known article on Allis, and had also appeared as an inset on the book jacket for her final novel, *East Wind*, which had also been her only novel written for adults.

East Wind was a strange book. It was presented as a novel, as fiction, but seemed to draw so heavily on Allis's own experience that it was a memoir in all but name. Yet there were certain details that had been altered for no obvious reason, and other things that didn't sound right, the way the uncle had joined the Nazi party, for instance. On the few occasions when she had mentioned them in public Allis had invariably portrayed her family as vehement opponents of everything Hitler stood for.

Terri had studied the photograph of Hanne so often she would have said she remembered it in every detail. Hanne in *East Wind* was characterised as a shy girl, but hugely intelligent, a mathematical prodigy who had already won a number of regional chess tournaments. Somehow this depiction of Hanne had never corresponded with the impression Terri drew from the photograph. The Hanne of the picture looked younger and less self-aware, a child with a Mickey Mouse watch and a tortoiseshell slide. The watch especially had struck her as odd. She had researched the detail, and discovered that the first Mickey Mouse watches had been manufactured by Ingersoll in 1933. It was therefore possible that Hanne had owned one, but now, as Terri prepared to return the picture to the folder where she kept all the other Allis photographs, something else occurred to her. The online article she read had informed her that there was not just one type of Mickey Mouse watch, but many hundreds, that the prototype had proved so popular that scarcely a year went by without Ingersoll, and later Timex, who took over the company, bringing out some new variant or design. There were enthusiasts who collected Mickey watches exclusively.

The article had included pictures of several of the most popular designs, ranging from the original Steamboat Willie right through to a digital model from the 1990s. Something about one of them looked familiar, and although Terri had meant to check it she never had.

She booted up her laptop and navigated her way back to the watch site. The photograph of Hanne had lost some of its sharpness in the process of being enlarged but the details were still quite clear, the design of the watch more easily discernible. With the photograph beside her on the table she scrolled through the various images, searching until she came to the one that had reminded her of the watch Hanne was wearing in the photograph. She checked it against the picture, clicking on it to enlarge it until she was sure.

The watch on the screen was a Mickey Mouse 'Mod' watch, with a white strap and oversized buckle. It was identical with the watch on Hanne's wrist.

The caption that went with the picture said that the Mickey Mouse 'Mod' watch first appeared in 1968. Allis's sister had died in 1944. Whoever the child in the photograph was it couldn't be Hanne.

Terri felt herself overcome by a feeling of unreality, of dissociation, reminding her of how she had felt on the beach in the glare of the sun. None of this made any sense. She looked at the photograph again, and the idea came to her that it was Noel, that Noel had found the photograph and doctored it in some way. It would be easy to achieve if you knew Photoshop, and Noel did. He could have altered the photograph to frighten her or ruin her article. Perhaps he had even discovered where she was, and was hoping she would run to him for help.

But that didn't make sense either. Even if by some awful chance Noel had found out where she was he knew nothing about her Allis project. So far as Terri could remember the subject of Allis and her books had never once been mentioned between them.

She needed time to think. She returned the picture to the file and went to make supper. Afterwards she sat and watched television.

Normally she judged television to be a waste of time, but on that evening she found some comfort in familiarity. The chat shows and sitcoms and home improvement programmes were inanely repetitive, but they were proof that the world was still out there, that she could rejoin it any time she chose.

Terri wondered if that was what Allis had done, after all: simply rejoined the world, in another place and using another name, bored with the life she had made for herself and curious to try out another.

*

She found it difficult to get to sleep. The house itself seemed wakeful, as if it too had been disturbed by her discovery. Terri had not looked at the photograph again before going to bed but once she was there it was all she could seem to think about.

If the child was not Hanne, then who was she? Had the photograph originally been used by mistake, with all its subsequent uses a simple repetition of that same mistake, or was there something more sinister behind it? Perhaps there was no surviving photo of the real Hanne, so a picture of a girl who resembled her had been used instead.

Perhaps there was no Hanne at all.

The thing that disturbed Terri most was the fact that Allis could not have been in ignorance of what had happened. Even if she had never read the articles she would surely have seen her own book jacket. She would have known the child in the photograph was not her sister.

But all the evidence suggested it had been Allis who supplied the photograph in the first place.

Terri felt certain that, however inadvertently, she had stumbled upon something important, that the photograph and Allis's disappearance were somehow connected. From the standpoint of the job she had come here to do the thought of such a breakthrough was thrilling. And yet there was something – a darkness – that made her uneasy.

The room was full of shadows. In her perplexed state of mind Terri found it was all too easy to start thinking of them as ghosts. The sea whispered through the open window, and when she got up to close the curtains she saw its surface was dancing with phosphorescence.

*

In the end she slept without realising that she slept, her conscious thoughts entwining themselves with the more lateral, instinctive thinking of her dreams. When she woke it was full day. Her first thoughts were of the photograph. She wanted above all to see it, to prove to herself that she had not been mistaken. She pulled on a T-shirt and jeans and went downstairs. When she entered the office she knew at once that something was different, but could not work out immediately what it was. Then she realised it was the hat, the green straw boater. It was lying on the table next to her laptop.

She reached for it cautiously, picking it up by the brim. She realised to her dismay that she could not say with one-hundred percent certainty that she had not put the hat there herself. She had been thinking about it after all.

The idea that she had left the hat on her desk and then forgotten having done so was after all less worrying than the alternatives. Which were either that the house was haunted or that someone had broken in during the night.

She remembered the feeling she had had the evening before, that she was not alone in the house. She looked carefully around the room, aware that her palms were sweating and that her breathing had become more shallow. When she saw movement outside the window her heart knocked in her chest and she almost cried out. Her first thought was that it was Allis, come to pay her back somehow for trespassing on the past and all the secrets she had intended to stay hidden. Then she saw it was the woman from next door, watering the roses in her back garden.

Terri dashed through to the kitchen, aware that she had not combed her hair and that she was wearing yesterday's clothes but determined she should not let it matter. She knew she had to speak to

Judy Whitton at all costs. She did not want to let her get away again until she had at the very least established contact.

"Excuse me," she called. She stepped out on to the overgrown lawn. The woman turned at the sound of her voice. She was wearing a blue-and-white striped shirt dress and the same navy moccasins that Terri had seen her wearing the week before. She was stouter than Terri remembered, the loose skin of her forearms mottled with liver spots. But her salt-and-pepper hair was neatly styled, and her lightly made up face looked alert and not unintelligent. She was as tidy and well kept as her house and garden.

"I'm sorry to disturb you," said Terri. "My name's Terri Goodall. I'm the new tenant here. I was hoping I could speak to you for a moment."

"How can I help you, dear?" said Judy Whitton. "Everything all right for you, is it? I know the place is in a bit of a state. The doctor had to get the plumbers in at one point." Her voice was clear and firm, with traces of an East London accent.

"Oh no, thank you, the house is fine." Terri smiled in a way she hoped was reassuring. "I'm writing an article about the woman who used to live here. I spoke to the letting agent, Alan Cahill? He seems to think you might remember her."

"Mrs Bennett, you mean?"

"Yes, Allis Bennett. She was a novelist. She wrote books for children." Terri didn't like to hear Allis spoken of in this way, as *Mrs Bennett*, an ordinary housewife, indistinguishable from Whitton herself. She felt anxious to establish at once that Allis was different.

"I don't know too much about that. My kids are all grown and gone. But I helped Mrs Bennett's nephew sort out the house, you know, after she left."

"Do you have any idea where she might have gone?" Terri felt like cheering aloud. Alan Cahill had been right: Judy Whitton had known Allis, had spoken to her. She had been living here at the time of Allis's disappearance. The fact that she knew nothing of Allis's writing might even be an advantage. She would have noticed other things, details that critical articles never mentioned. Her insights would be valuable and unique.

"Not a clue. I went through all that with the police at the time. You're not from the police, are you? If you are then I've got nothing to say."

Terri shook her head at once. She knew she had to calm down, that her rapid fire questioning was making Judy Whitton feel like a crime suspect. Much more of it and she was liable to clam up. But she sensed that Judy Whitton was the breakthrough she needed and it was difficult to restrain her excitement. "I'm not from the police. I'm a journalist. I read all Allis's books as a child. I'm interested in what might have happened to her."

"Just bored sick of this place, I reckon. She was never exactly what you'd call settled."

"Really? I've heard she didn't like to travel."

"I don't mean that. I mean in her mind. She didn't join in much. She preferred her own company. Once her daughter moved up to Nottingham she got even worse. I had a feeling she might have gone there, but the police said not."

"Her daughter?"

"Yes, Joanne. She married a chap she met at college. There was some kind of row between her and her mum, I reckon. Not that Mrs Bennett ever said, but sometimes you just know these things, don't you? It's hard for a kid though, growing up without a father. There are bound to be problems."

Terri couldn't think what to say. She felt stunned by what Judy Whitton was telling her. None of the articles had mentioned children. Terri felt she had been deceived in some way, although who had done the deceiving she could not tell. She had no reason to believe that Whitton was lying. What would be the point?

It was as if the world had divided in two: on the one hand there was the Allis she had read about, the solitary writer with the dead sister and the tragic past, on the other there was Mrs Bennett and her daughter Joanne.

Which of these women was real and why had Allis lied about her daughter? It came to Terri that both versions of Allis could be real, or neither of them, that the real Allis was the sum of the two. And just because Allis had chosen to remain silent about her daughter did not mean she had lied about her. Just because she had chosen to make some aspects of her life public in the form of novels did not mean that Allis had relinquished her rights to a private life.

The business of biography was complex, more complex than Terri had known when she started out. She had begun with the idea of uncovering a mystery. Now she was starting to see that the act of unveiling was also an act of destruction. She had wanted only good things for Allis. By writing her article she had wanted in some measure to repay Allis for the pleasure and comfort her books had brought to her as a child. But what was happening now was something else. It was like tugging on a piece of loose wire and bringing the whole house down.

She supposed she could stop now if she wanted to, but she knew she would not. If she cared more about the story than she cared about Allis that was something she would have to learn to live with.

"Do you think Allis felt isolated here? I'm sure you know about what happened to her during the war." Terri knew that in order to get the most from her she had to win Whitton's confidence. She hoped that by asking Whitton's opinion she might start to open her up. People liked to say what they thought, much better than they liked to answer a direct question. That was something Terri had learned from her very first interview.

"The little Jewish mite, you mean? I knew she was killed in the Blitz but Allis was only a child then. Lots of people were killed in the bombing, and it wasn't as if the girl was her real sister or anything. I don't see how she could have felt isolated. Her grandparents lived here in Walmer, you know. Allis stayed with them every summer before the war."

"But that's not possible," Terri exclaimed. The words were out of her mouth before she could stop them. "Allis Bennett was born in Warsaw."

"Not her." Whitton said. She laughed through her nose, a kind of snorting chuckle, as if she was trying to suppress her amusement at something vaguely illicit. "You must have got your facts mixed up somehow. It was the little Jewish girl that was from Poland. Allis's parents took her in just before the war started. They were running all kinds of schemes then, trying to help the children who had been transported. Allis didn't have any brothers or sisters of her own and

I suppose her mum and dad thought it would be nice for her, to have someone her own age to play with. Anyway, you see how it worked out." She paused. "If you're really interested you should look in the attic. She left the place just as it was, you see. All her clothes and furniture and things, no one knew what to do with it all. We gave most of her clothes to Oxfam and her nephew sold a lot of the furniture but there was a whole load of other stuff we just packed into boxes and stuffed in the loft. I remember there were tons of old letters. So far as I knew they're still up there."

"Thank you so much," Terri said. "This is just what I needed."

"No need to thank me, dear. I doubt you'll find anything much. She was just a normal woman, Mrs Bennett. She wasn't mad or anything, not like some of these ones you read about. She just kept herself to herself."

"Do you think I could come round and see you? Once I've had a look at the letters, I mean? It's so helpful, speaking to someone who actually knew her."

"That's fine by me, dear. Just remember I'm out Tuesdays and Thursdays. That's my WI."

Terri thanked her again and went back inside. She sat at the kitchen table, toying with a slice of toast and waiting for the kettle to boil. She made coffee then poured it away after only three sips. If Whitton was telling the truth then everything she had heard or read or believed about Allis Bennett until that morning had been an invention. Allis had treated her own life as one of her fictions: she had discarded the truth and fabricated a whole new past for herself based around the identity of the refugee child her parents had adopted during the war. Alicja Ganesh was just another character she had created, only this time with Allis Bennett's own face and body.

What Terri did not understand was why she had done this. Had the truth seemed so dull and inadequate that Allis had simply exchanged it for a story she liked better, stretching certain details to the limits of their believability the same way she did in her stories?

Or had she rewritten her past to make it fit with the image of herself she liked to present to her readers through her books?

She could not bring herself to believe she had done it for money. Terri realised she ought to boot up her computer and transcribe the conversation with Whitton, get the details down on paper before they were lost, but she knew she could not settle to anything until she had been into the attic. There was a set of steps in the understairs cupboard, pushed in against the wall behind the vacuum cleaner and an ancient wooden clothes horse. Terri dragged them out of the cupboard then carried them up to the landing and set them up beneath the loft hatch. She mounted the steps and pushed up the boards. The hatch was stiff, and made a dry cracking sound as it came away. Dust and small bits of debris cascaded down. Terri coughed, fumbling for the light switch on the central joist.

The roof space was hot and smelled stale, reminding her of the way the house had been when she first entered it. The thickness of the dust made it obvious that no one had been up there in years.

There were ten boxes in all, three wooden tea chests, the rest cardboard cartons from the local supermarket. It would be impossible to move them without help, the tea chests especially. Terri brushed dust from her hair and wondered whether it would be best to pay someone to help her or try and bring down the boxes' contents bit by bit. She opened one of the tea chests at random. The hardboard lid had been secured with tin tacks but was easy enough to work free. The chest was full of clothes: a paisley dress, a woollen overcoat with an Astrakhan collar, a wedding gown. They smelled strongly of the mothballs they had been packed in. Terri replaced the lid. The sight of discarded clothes always made her think of dead people. The second chest was packed with ornaments. They were wrapped in pages from the *Walmer Herald*, all dating from the summer Allis had been declared legally dead. Terri unwrapped a china teacup, a cigarette case, a model horse. The horse was about six inches high and made of tin. The brightly coloured paint had worn away down to the metal in several places, and there was a small dent in one of its flanks. Terri recognised it at once as the tin horse in *Bellony*. It had belonged to Vronia's dead sister Annabel.

*

She thought briefly of asking Alan Cahill to help her then dismissed the idea as ridiculous. Instead she called a man from the Yellow Pages, a number picked at random from the House Clearance section.

"I don't actually want a house cleared," she said. "I just need to get some boxes out of an attic." The man said it would cost her twenty pounds.

Two hours later the boxes were out of the loft and lined up neatly in one of the back bedrooms. Terri spent most of the next three days going through them. She went to bed each night feeling physically drained yet so mentally preoccupied she found it difficult to switch off. The whole of the upstairs floor was now covered with piles of oddments and paper and bundles of letters, the scraps and tag-ends of what had once been the life of Allis Bennett. Even after she had showered and changed, Terri felt filthy with dust and newsprint. She barely stepped outside for the whole three days.

Yet in spite of her exhaustion she felt triumphant. She knew she had found what she had been looking for: a story so remarkable that no one had guessed at it, let alone written it down. She also felt buoyed up with the knowledge that this was precisely the kind of writing she wanted to do. She had thought of the project from the start as the search for a missing person and at the time she had meant that literally but she now knew there was more than one way of going missing. Uncovering the truth about Allis was proving to be one of the most thrilling experiences of her life.

Three of the boxes contained books, many of them Allis's own first editions. Terri had purchased paperback reprints of those novels of Allis's that were still available but seeing the originals aroused in her a depth of emotion she could not have predicted. It would have been easy to lose herself in them for hours, but she forced herself to save them for later. The books and clothes and household effects were fascinating and they would add colour to her account but they could not tell her much. They told her that Allis collected Victorian paperweights, that she read Shirley Jackson and Elizabeth Bowen, that the spinning top and the wooden monkey in *The Carousel* had material counterparts. They could tell her what Allis had liked but not what had happened to her. Terri knew she had to press on.

There were more than two hundred letters from Joanne, a whole box of them. These ranged from the postcards Joanne had sent to Allis while on trips with her school right through to the brief notes posted from Nottingham after her marriage. These last letters were few in number and subdued in tone, entirely lacking the detail and spontaneity of the much longer letters written while Joanne was at college. The underlying tension was palpable, although its source was never specified. There was no mention of Poland or the war, or even of Allis's books. The Allis of Joanne's letters was Mrs Bennett.

In the box with Joanne's letters was a crumpled white envelope containing a tortoiseshell hair slide, a Girl Guide badge, one half of a return train ticket from Walmer to Tenby and a bunch of loose photographs. One of the photographs showed a young man with floppy fair hair cradling an infant. Terri guessed that this must be Peter Bennett holding his daughter. Another photograph was clearly the original of the photocopied reproduction she had in her office downstairs, the picture of the girl wearing the Mickey Mouse watch. The photograph was in colour. A caption scrawled on the back identified the subject as Joanne.

The other photographs were less interesting, snapshots of Walmer Castle and the bandstand at Deal. Like the books and ornaments, they told her very little. Terri had hoped there might be a picture of the Jewish girl, something that confirmed her existence, but all the photos had been taken long after the war.

Terri feared she had come to a dead end after all. She stared at the contents of the last of the boxes with a mixture of disappointment and perplexity. In contrast with the others which had been packed selectively and with care this final carton appeared to contain a random assortment of stationery and other inconsequential bits and pieces. Terri could not understand what had made Judy Whitton and Allis's nephew single out such rubbish for preservation. It wasn't until she flipped open one of the notebooks that she realised that what she was looking at was the contents of Allis's desk on the day she disappeared. Everything was there, right down to the last paperclip. Terri found it incredible that these things had remained in the house, that the police had not removed them long before. She supposed then that the police had not been much interested. There was no body and no sign of violence. Allis was an adult and had broken no laws; if she wanted to disappear there was nothing to stop her.

The notebook had been dated on the front cover and contained the draft outline for what was clearly to have been a new novel. The book was set in London and told the story of a girl named Linney. Linney's parents were unable to have more children of their own, and so decided to take in a child of the *Kindertransport*, one of the thousands of Jewish children sent to England by their parents to escape the Nazis. Linney resented the newcomer and did everything to make her life a misery. In the end the Jewish girl went missing during an air raid. The story had been left unfinished but there was enough for Terri to see that here at last was Allis Bennett's true autobiography. Far from loving her adopted sister she had disliked her intensely and wanted to be rid of her. It was only once she was gone that she realised what she had done. It was impossible to know what had really happened the night of the bombing, but it was clear that Allis had blamed herself for the girl's death and had gone on doing so. She had blamed herself so much she had relinquished her own identity. It had taken her thirty years to confess the truth.

Terri felt she could weep for Allis. The story itself was sad but understandable; most children feel resentful of strangers, at least to begin with. It was Allis's reaction that was extraordinary. From a private domestic tragedy she had constructed a whole new universe, a reality from which she had been prepared to exclude even her own daughter. Terri did not like to imagine how lonely she had been.

Still none of this explained the suddenness of her disappearance. Her fantasies had evolved over years and had survived every change in her life up until that time; she would not have abandoned them without a reason. Terri continued to sift through Allis's desk litter, her phone bills and old library cards, convinced the answer had to be there somewhere but as uncertain as ever as to what she was looking for. When she came upon the airmail letter in its slim blue envelope she almost discarded it, half-convinced that she had looked at it already. The letter was handwritten, in the angular copperplate script that was familiar to Terri from the letters of a German girl she had had as a pen friend back in secondary school. The envelope was addressed to a Miss A. Clowes.

It had been postmarked in Antwerp, just seven days before Allis went missing. Terri thought at first that the letter had been delivered to Allis in error, until she began reading and realised that Clowes had been Allis's maiden name.

> *My dear Miss Alice Clowes,*
>
> *I hope you will forgive me, but I have been to considerable trouble to procure your address! My name is Rosa Steen Ringmark and my sister was Hanne Steen. I believe that Hanne was legally adopted by your parents, Arthur and Marie Clowes, in the summer of the year 1942. Hanne and I were very close as sisters. When we were told that only one of us was to be sent abroad with the transport we were heartbroken. It was not the idea of war that terrified us but the idea of separation. Indeed it is still this parting from Hanne at the railway station that embodies the terror of war for me, more even than the things that came later.*
>
> *I did not hear of my sister's death until some years after the war. Until that moment I had always cherished the hope that we would be reunited. I found it impossible to accept that we would not be, and in truth, this is why it has taken me so long to go in search of Hanne's second family. However as I have grown older I have come to realise that I will never feel complete until I can hear Hanne spoken of by another, someone who knew her and was close to her during those final years when we were apart. Time is running out for all of us; if it is possible I would like to make recompense for my delay before it is too late.*
>
> *It is for this reason that I would like to invite you, as a sister, to spend some time with your second family. I know this letter will come as a shock to you and that it will maybe awaken memories of what must rightly be called the darkest time for all the peoples of Europe. But I can only hope most sincerely that you can find it in your heart to accept. Your acceptance would mean everything to me and might perhaps be useful to you also.*
>
> *Please write to me soon, if only to assure me that you have received this letter.*
>
> *With heartfelt greetings,*
> *Rosa Steen Ringmark (Mrs)*

Terri knew the letter would have horrified Allis. It was not just her guilt over Hanne, but the thought that the lie she had made of her life might now be exposed. The thing Allis cherished most of all was her privacy, the privacy she needed in order to write. Rosa's letter spelled the end of everything. She would have felt she had no option but to run.

The only mystery that now remained was where she had gone. Terri had no idea how she could discover this. She still believed Allis must have left clues but for the moment she was out of ideas. She had already searched the house from top to bottom. She wondered if it was worth looking in the loft again and went downstairs to fetch the ladder, wondering why she was bothering when she knew there was nothing to find.

The attic was as empty as she had known it would be, the dust already settling over the clear patches on the floorboards where the boxes had stood. She replaced the hatch and took the ladder back downstairs. It was then that she realised she had never searched the cupboard under the stairs. She leaned the ladder against the wall and began dragging the cupboard's contents out into the hall. The cupboard was stuffed with all the junk such cupboards usually contained: a vacuum cleaner, a broom, a mop and bucket, the gargantuan clothes horse. There was a plastic crate packed with tins of shoe polish and furniture wax, a food blender still in its box. Terri thought it highly unlikely that any of these things had belonged to Allis; rather they had amassed themselves organically in the wake of each successive batch of new tenants. In either case as evidence they were worse than useless.

When the cupboard was finally empty Terri wedged open the door with a folded scrap of cardboard and went inside. It was a large cupboard, larger than normal. It was difficult to see all the way to the back, even with the aid of a torch. She took a hurried step backwards, convinced for a moment that she had seen something move, but it turned out to be an old skipping rope, twisted about its handles like a dust-grey snake. Even once she had established it was not alive the skipping rope gave her a peculiar feeling. For some reason she was sure it had belonged to Hanne Steen. She left it where it lay and began backing out into the hallway, feeling her way along the wall with the flat of her hand. A foot or so from the cupboard entrance she felt a bump in the plasterwork. Terri shone the torch where her hand had been and saw that the paper that had been used to line the cupboard had started to peel away. The surface beneath looked like wood. Terri tore at the paper, which came off easily, peeling away from the wall in an intact mass.

There was a door in the wall, a gloss-painted, panelled door set flush with the frame. Clearly whoever had papered over it had done so on purpose. Terri found the idea fantastic and a little frightening. Why would anyone hide a door, unless it was to stop someone passing through it? Terri remembered that Vronia's father had done this in the end, with Vronia's door in *Bellony*. She saw that the inside handle had been removed. There was a square opening just above the keyhole where the shaft should have fitted. Terri slipped two fingers into the opening and pulled backwards but the door would not budge. She tried again, bracing herself against the floor and tugging more forcefully but the door remained immovable and she realised it must be locked. She imagined herself trying to cut out the lock with a hacksaw and wondered what excuses she would make if Alan Cahill had her in court for criminal damage.

Sorry, your worship, only I was trying to saw my way through to another universe.

It was thinking of Alan Cahill that made her remember the keys, the mysterious fourth key on the key ring for which she had yet to find a discernable purpose. Cahill had never explained what the key was for.

She fetched the keys from where she kept them in the kitchen. She tried not to hope too much but she could not help herself. She was already certain the key would fit the lock and she was right. The key turned smoothly and with a satisfying thump. Terri found she could use it as a handle. She pulled the door open and towards her. Light flooded in, its sudden and unexpected presence stunning her eyes and revealing the blacker depths of the cupboard as a humdrum arrangement of sloping walls and faded wallpaper, a predictable accumulation of cobwebs and dust. Directly in front of her Terri saw the two dustbins and coil of green hosepipe that were in the access passage to the side of the house. The key had been for the disused side door after all. For reasons unknown it appeared that the door could only be unlocked from the inside.

Old houses were just like that, they had quirks. Terri emerged into the daylight, feeling foolish and covered in dust. The day was as hot and bright as the days before it but a cooling breeze was blowing in off the sea and the air was heady with the scents of tamarisk and bergamot. Terri knew she should go back inside and tidy away the junk in the hallway but for the moment she couldn't be bothered. She'd had enough of trawling through rubbish. She needed a break.

She locked up the house and set off along the promenade. Instead of taking her usual route towards Kingsdown and St Margaret's she went in the opposite direction, towards Walmer Castle and Deal. She walked along briskly, enjoying the feel of the wind against her face. The tide was a long way out; children dashed about on the exposed sand, playing Frisbee or hunting for shells. The area around the bandstand was packed with tourists, but once she was past the pier the path quickly became less crowded. The coast beyond the town was completely unpopulated. The cliffs of South Foreland were more dramatic, but to Terri the featureless wilderness to the north of Deal was actually more beautiful. She felt glad to be out in the open. The wide landscape stretching before her made her realise how strangely she had been behaving this past week, as if her own self had been usurped, leaving her mind as a repository for the fantasies of Allis Bennett. The odd episode with the door had been like the breaking of an enchantment. It had literally let in the light. She felt better than she had done in days. Perhaps it had been a mistake to isolate herself so completely. She decided she would call Janet that evening and tell her the whole story. It would be good to have someone she could bounce ideas off, and Janet was someone she trusted more than anyone.

She walked as far as the edge of the golf links and then decided it was time to be heading back. She had eaten nothing since breakfast and she was starting to feel faint from lack of food. The tide was on the turn. A man was approaching along the coast path, walking his dog. The dog was a pot-bellied beagle with a greying muzzle. It moved along with its nose to the ground, stopping every couple of yards to sniff at the grass. The man was elderly and walked using a cane. Terri thought he looked vaguely familiar. She supposed she must have seen him in the town. The man came closer and began to wave to her. Terri waved back, although it felt strange to be greeting someone she did not know.

She came to a standstill as he approached her. The odd feeling of familiarity did not diminish.

"You're thinking you know me," the man said. "It's written all over your face." He smiled. His face was rubicund, weather beaten. Terri guessed he was a practised walker, in spite of the cane. She laughed, a little uncertainly, though she sensed no threat from the man.

"I don't know," she said, and laughed again. "I can't know you really. I know hardly anyone here."

"I'm Alan's father. Alan Cahill? We looked even more alike when we were both in our youth." He held out his hand for her to shake it and told her his name was Michael. Now that he had revealed his identity she could see the similarities at once. She guessed the father had been very good looking, his features less conventionally handsome than the son's but with a ruggedness that leant them extra appeal.

"You're renting Allis Bennett's old place, aren't you? Alan told me. I hear you're going to write about Allis."

Terri nodded and confirmed that this was so. She could not remember saying anything to Alan Cahill about her Allis project, indeed she was sure she had not. She supposed Judy Whitton had told him. She knew that small towns were notorious for their gossip. It came to her that Michael Cahill was the first person she had met who had talked about Allis without being prompted. A week ago she would have been eager to question him but now suddenly she felt too tired. The questions could wait. There was no reason to suppose that Michael Cahill was planning on running away.

"It was nice to meet you," she said. She turned to go, but Michael Cahill appeared not to have heard her.

"I remember her when she arrived," he said. "I was only just married myself then, but I lost my head a little, even so. I thought Allis was very beautiful, but it wasn't her looks that made me fall for her. She still had a foreign accent then, which I found attractive, but I'd met Polish girls during the war so it wasn't that, either. She had an atmosphere of tragedy around her. I think I had the idea that she knew more than other girls, that she would understand me better. I used to see her on her walks, and sometimes I would follow her, just so I would get the chance to say hello to her. We would sit together sometimes, out on the headland, and a couple of times we had tea together in St Margaret's. It was all perfectly harmless, and I knew from the start it would never go anywhere. She liked me, and I think she appreciated my friendship. But she wasn't interested in me, not in the way I wanted. I suppose I was lucky things never went any further. It would have made a terrible mess for everyone." He was staring out to sea, shading his eyes with one hand. The beagle snuffled and pawed at the long grass at the edge of the golf course. "It was as if she was really somewhere else. She talked to me about her sister, more than once. I don't think she ever got over the fact that she had survived the war and her sister had not."

Terri stared at him blankly. Her mind felt paralysed by shock, a kind of mental concussion. It was as if he was compelling her to believe that the earth was flat.

"You've got it wrong," she said at last. The words spilled out all at once, rebounding off the sallow grass like pellets of gravel.

"Perhaps," said Michael Cahill. He seemed unaware of the impact his words were having on her. "I didn't really know her all that well. I don't think anyone knew her properly, not even her husband. It was tragic that he died so young."

"What about her daughter? People say they were close?"

"Daughter? There was no daughter." Michael Cahill's eyes widened and for the first time he looked surprised. His eyes were larger than his son's and very bright, the colour of amber. "Allis never had any children. After her husband died she lived alone."

Terri found herself unable to speak. For a moment it was as if she could sense the world rotating as it spun on its axis. It made her feel nauseous, seasick. Her eyes filled up with tears. She quickly wiped them away with the back of her hand.

"I'm sorry," she said. "I have to go."

She strode off along the path, stumbling in her haste to get away. She knew her behaviour must have seemed rude but it couldn't be helped. Better for him to think that she was rude than that she was crazy. It was only when she came into sight of the town that she began to feel calmer.

The air was cooler now and the tourists had begun to disperse in search of food. Terri stopped by the seafront supermarket and inserted her debit card into the cash machine there. As it dispensed the ten pound note she had requested her bank balance flashed up on the screen. She had checked it online that morning and the two amounts tallied to the penny.

Whose world was she in, exactly, and did it matter? What had happened when she stepped through the door? Could it be possible that Vronia's door in *Bellony*, like the tin horse and the wooden monkey, had a counterpart in the world Terri chose to call real?

In Allis's novel the worlds that Vronia visited seemed just like her own, revealing their difficulties and dangers only with time. Perhaps the same would be true of this one. Or perhaps Allis's version of her life really had been the truth, all along.

Terri knew the first thing she had to do was get something to eat. Then she would call Janet as planned and talk things over with her. She did not know yet how much she would tell her but that didn't matter. What mattered most at least for the moment was to establish that Janet existed and still remembered her.

Beach Huts at Walmer - photo: Teresa Goodall

The Flea Market
Gerard Houarner

Derrick's fingers froze in mid-flip motion as the album cover flashed in his vision like a lightning strike's bright after-image.

"What the hell—" he muttered, steadying himself on the overturned empty plastic milk crate serving as his seat. He looked up from the row of record albums he'd been going through to see if anyone had overheard him.

The stall's proprietor was deep in conversation with a neighbor about real estate developers driving flea markets and vendors like themselves out of business. It was too early for Sunday browsers to be wandering through the aisles. Most of the stalls were still closed, anyway. Traffic on the avenue was light, and a hymn from a nearby church's organ carried clear and strong in the crisp Spring air. A song full of voices followed the organ into the morning, rising up with the sun, giving the new day a sense of peace, of sacred innocence.

The only other digger in the flea market was going through another dealer's crates of 50's and 60's rock and roll singles looking for the lost soul of Elvis Presley, or maybe just a 45 with a Sun label. Derrick knew him by face, but never had much to say to him.

He turned his attention back to the album he'd discovered, the cardboard cover cool against his fingertips. He was almost afraid to look at it.

The dense, complex collage of manically detailed drawings had jolted him with some kind of latent power, as if the assembled image had detonated a bomb in his unconscious. The piece first snagged his attention by its startling contrast to the other covers in the stream of 40 and 50 year old packaging styles he'd been glancing through, flipping with practiced rhythm as names and conditions registered in his head with their collectable values and the holes in his collection. Yeah, he had that James Brown in his basement, who didn't, and too bad this Lou Ragland was water damaged, the vinyl inside badly warped, or else he might have made some money today, and maybe he could get something on eBay for this Teruo Nakamura *Unicorn* reissue but did he really want to bother, with 10,000 other records at home waiting to be catalogued, many of which he was ready to let go. He should have been at the house working on his inventory, or the plumbing, or maybe dusting the place out pretending he was actually going to slap on a fresh coat of paint, instead of searching flea markets, thrift stores, and impromptu apartment sidewalk sales for more recordings left behind by changing fortunes, tastes and technology.

His mom would have said he should be in that church raising his voice in praise of the Lord. His father might have mentioned something about sleeping in a cold bed in what he'd have called an empty home – a house with no children. There'd have been nothing to say to his mother's accusation; he flinched at the thought of even trying, and bowed his head to her truth. For his father, he'd always had one word: Sarah.

His youngest brother, Clarence, would have laughed at Derrick's intensity, made fun of it, rifled through the records in a crude imitation of his oldest brother, and then been seduced by the collector's passion and ended up knowing more about records than Derrick. He'd certainly been the better soldier, though he could have avoided the draft by going to college on scholarship. But he'd wanted to see where Derrick had already been. Being the better soldier hadn't saved him; in fact, it probably got him killed.

Richard would have asked which records were worth the most, and if Derrick took them home, sooner or later they'd have disappeared. Like Clarence, he would have acknowledged that what Derrick was doing was a hell of a lot better than dying in Nam, or in jail.

Back in the day, a couple of Brooklyn aunts, and his grandfather on his father's side, used to say he and his brothers should have been in the church band or choir, or at the very least, in the band from the night before, making their own music – Clarence on drums, of course, because he'd always liked the noise, and Richard on tenor sax, because he'd picked it up for a year and blown a lot of pain through the reed. If everyone in Derrick's life hadn't died, they'd still be saying the same thing. Maybe, after all was said and done, they'd come closest to a truth more than one person could hold on to.

But here he was on Sunday morning, beating the crowds on a lonely, pointless quest. After years of carrying the weight of all the empty places in his heart, that's exactly what he damn well felt like doing. Only now, finally, he'd been shoved out of his routine and made to stop by a burst of unconscious recognition at what he initially took to be a mock-up of an early 70's soul album that was never issued.

In his initial appraising glance, he'd locked on the name of the supposed record and its label – All The Hated Peoples by Hated Peoples Records – and quickly dismissed the item as a kid's art project, or an uptown political manifesto from back in the day when politics meant something, slipped into the milk-case full of records. His hands had jerked, kicking into their automatic reject reflex.

But the cover's image stopped him cold, refusing to let him move on, as if all the tiny hands of the people caught in the hallucinogenic spider web spires dominating the piece had reached out and grabbed a hold of him.

He blinked, and this time only thought, *what the hell?*

The spires reminded him of the Watts towers, and the arresting electric neon colors arcing through the thick, crude lettering of the title design looked like the tracks of a wannabe Soul Train ad, which he supposed was why the album had registered as some kind of soul funk offering. But a more subtle range of colors, shades from the dawn and dusk of another time, colored the figures trapped in the finely cross-hatched latticework of the towers, from their skin to their clothes.

Derrick leaned into the picture, following the sometimes ragged, other times neatly trimmed borders of one sketch fragment pasted over another, trying to imagine the bigger images cropped and submerged one under the other, and to figure out how so many layers had been built up into the overall arresting image of four latticework towers of differing heights and thickness looming from the lower left corner to a vanishing point in the upper right quadrant of a rectangular piece of cardboard.

The title letters brightened into a surreal blaze, a neon road side sign carving electric lines into an empty night. The ridiculous name, the absurd detail of a catalog number, the figures, so small and yet perfectly rendered and differentiated by body shape and clothing style and even facial features, as if delivered to paper by a pen tip of infinite sharpness using an ink that could never run, all battered his sense of what was real and possible with a weight of meaning and import he couldn't quite capture in his mind. He felt out of place, out of rhythm, like when he woke up on bad mornings after drinking all night with the younger men who came through the garage for a few months or weeks before moving on to other jobs, or when he walked into the wrong store in the wrong neighborhood and became lost in the whites of the eyes on him.

The world spun around his head for an instant, at a stately 33 rpms. The diamond-hard needle of what he knew to be true slipped over reality's groove. Nausea choked him, smelling like the gas the VA gave him when they had to operate on a cancer he wasn't supposed to have caused by chemicals that hadn't been carcinogenic.

The sense of dislocation was as bad as coming home from war nursing a wound, a habit, and the title 'baby-killer' from a rich kid in poor drag at the airport. As bad as listening to his father tell him over tumblers of warm scotch that Sarah had been killed in a car accident on the Cross Bronx Expressway a few days before he shipped back home, in the company of her college radical boyfriend. As bad as watching the light in Mom's eyes fade like her heart in a hospital, while listening to a younger woman weep in the bed next to hers as if already mourning his loss.

He fell into the picture, through its layers and between its borders, head first, diving for the towers.

His lonely Sunday morning vanished and a new day washed over him, as if a strange sun was rising, summoned by organ music and church choir, called into existence by all the lost music in crates and boxes, on vinyl and tape and shiny disks, tucked into chips and cards and even scribbled as lines of notation on staff sheets. He fell into a sky lit by this different sun, into light that changed the values and meaning of familiar shades, broke the code of color he'd grown up with and into by rite of passage, heritage and revolution. He had no names for the new tints, but they made his heart skip.

Immersed in the palette of another rainbow, he shed the crust of what he'd grown into by living with firefight echoes and the whimpering of dying men. Chains of unkept promises made by others, and worse, himself, shattered and slipped away. Pits and gouges dug by hostile stares, craters left by sudden bursts of insult, all filled with the makings of a freshly reborn spirit. The new light changed the meaning of the code of color he'd known through silent years of death and pain and loss, when he'd had to bury the blood and bones of the love that had

The Flea Market

made him. Its touch transformed him, revealing and setting free what had always been, would always be.

His outstretched arms lost their scars, the thickness of muscle and fat, became smooth and wiry like they'd been in his 20's, his hands no longer worn from laboring with engines, but lean, capable of embracing a piano's keyboard like he'd always wanted. He wiggled his lively new fingers, thinking to discover in them rhythms and harmonies he'd absorbed from Oscar Peterson or Bill Evans aching to be released. They seemed capable of so much more than writing out repair estimates and parts orders and bills, working tools on unforgiving metal, flipping through records.

Flushed with excitement, Derrick wondered how far his metamorphosis might spread through him, if his hair could grow back, and if that extra chin might fall off along with those puffy cheeks of his, and if maybe his belly would shed fifty-eight years of too much rich food and beer, and not enough of other things that might have made him keep that weight off.

As he kept falling, his body did begin to change, as if he'd gained the power to make wishes come true. He fell so long, by the time he really was different he thought he was flying. The towers grew larger, came closer, soared with the intimidating indifference of mechanical marvels. He started paying them more attention, feeling their shadows converge on him like cross-hairs.

As one of the towers drew even nearer, Derrick realized that if he was flying instead of falling, he had no control over his flight path. He was heading straight for the latticework as if drawn by a magnet, right into the spider web, where the figures he'd thought so delicately rendered and beautiful now seemed horribly trapped, their arms and legs caught in a lattice of thin lines that had to be covered with some kind of glue, or else why didn't the little men and women just climb down, or leap into the air and fly away, as the rules of this place allowed?

Derrick began to flap and wave his arms and kick his legs, trying to change the direction of his fall like he'd seen skydivers do on television. He didn't want to be bound in place, set into a pattern serving whatever purpose the towers were designed to perform, like a bolt, strut, broken piece of ceramic or a lost shell or a piece of glass in a mosaic, like in those Watts towers. He wanted to keep his new fingers. He wanted to fly through a new light and a different world and –

Shadows moved through the spiderweb heart of the tower, a haunting of something long gone.

The strangers stuck on the web called to him using someone else's name.

His skin turned grey, then began sloughing off, revealing bone underneath, as if he was a snake shedding its hide without having grown another to take its place.

"Been looking for one of those," a voice like gravel crackling under the weight of passing semi said from behind and above.

Derrick smelled tobacco and freshly turned earth, rich and damp, like a field ready for planting.

Or like a new grave.

The sound and smell pulled Derrick back like an elastic cord, out of the picture and the light and the falling flight. Suddenly, he was back in the city, hunched over a row of old albums, hemmed in by buildings and streets and avenues, the flea market's grid of tables and stalls, stacks of milk crates full of records.

He turned, looked up into the eyes of a familiar face.

"You gonna buy that thing?" the old man said, pointing a crooked finger at the album in Derrick's hands. A smile crinkled the already wrinkled skin around his lips and eyes. A forest of white sprawled across his throat, jaw and half his cheeks. But his bald head was smooth and polished, like a black pearl, an obvious point of pride and masculine vanity designed to distract the eye from the leathery, weathered flesh clinging to the contours and hollows of the skull below.

Derrick opened his mouth to say, grandpa?

But, of course, the man wasn't his grandfather, who'd died over forty years ago, and whom he hadn't seen in probably half a century, a time so remote that Derrick was surprised he could even be reminded of the man by a stranger.

"No," Derrick said, embarrassed by being caught off-guard and day-dreaming, and still disoriented by his little trip into the picture and the reminder of a man long dead, and ashamed, somehow, to not be buying what he held in his hands.

The Flea Market

The old man picked the album out of Derrick's hands like a ripe apple left on a limb after harvest. He winked, and again Derrick thought of grandpa, and held out a hand – as if he was still a little boy and the old man had to hold on to him to cross the street to get to the candy store.

"Everybody got something to say, don't they?" the old man said, as much to himself as to Derrick and the vendor turning to make the deal. He clutched the album to his chest. "Everybody needs their time to dream."

A couple of dollars were exchanged, and the old man took his prize out of the flea market and across the avenue. The man had his mother's eyes.

Derrick stood, started to follow. A bus came by, squealed to a stop on over-used brakes, took off again with a roar. The old man was gone.

Derrick went back to the booth and searched through the rest of the crate, then a few more, before asking the vendor if he had any more items like the one he'd sold to the old man.

"Got a couple of cases in the warehouse," the vendor said, with a slight roll of the eyes. "Came out of a condemned school. God know what they were trying to teach those kids. I'll bring them in next week, if you're interested."

Derrick promised to come back and made his way home, the wonder and dread of his flight of fantasy dulled by the encounter with the old man. He wished his mother's heart was still beating, and that cancer hadn't consumed his father from the poisoned marrow of his bones. He yearned for an older brother or sister, an uncle, a cousin, somebody, anybody he could talk to about his grandfather and stir the ashes of old memories into vivid recollections.

Sarah would have met him, if she'd stayed.

What he had instead was an image from a visit to South Carolina: grandfather sitting on a stool on top of a table, guitar in his lap, singing and playing, foot tapping, head lowered and eyes looking out in a fierce glare while a smile played in the corners of his mouth. A roomful of people clapped and stomped and laughed, all of them just another instrument, grand and drunk and loud, being played by the man on the table.

Derrick blew on the sputtering flame of a memory with his life's breath.

He'd been little and the noise and music, all the big bodies and his grandfather's face, had frightened him, all eyes and cries and mouths open wide to swallow. He remembered people laughing at him, too, and his mother picking him up and dancing with him and scaring him even more.

The flame caught, leapt, bringing him to another time, maybe his family's last visit South, when his grandfather had taken him horseback riding on a Spring morning, chillier than today. They'd wandered through backwoods and side roads and open fields lost behind and between hills, scaring wild turkey and deer out from stands of oak, walnut and hickory while wrens sang and the scent of jasmine sauvage and dogwood drifted on the breeze. They'd talked about Willie Mays, and then Blind Lemon Jefferson, who Derrick had never heard of. Sitting with their backs to a tree trunk, they'd talked about heaven, and how it might look and feel a little like that day, peaceful and quiet and pretty. Maybe a little warmer. And a baseball game going on in a field right in front of them.

That had been long ago, before the reality of death had robbed the innocence from talk of heaven.

He hadn't thought of his grandfather, Mom or Dad, his brothers, or much of anyone outside his circle of drinking and card-playing garage guys, for a while. He hadn't felt that pain, long and thin and deep, like a bamboo spike from a Charlie deadfall trap going through him, since he'd heard his mother's last breath.

Right now, with the image of the old man clear and strong in his mind, a startling, bright flag that wouldn't stop waving, he couldn't even remember what his mother and father, or his younger brothers, had looked like when they were alive.

Not that he'd spent too much time trying to remember over the years. He never had days like today, when church music and familiar old men proved haunting. It was as if the long parade of the dead marching through the desert that was his life had raised too much dust. Long ago, maybe around the time he read the Army's letter about Clarence, he'd stopped trying to look through those stinging clouds. If he'd opened his mouth to wonder aloud if he'd brought death's shadow out of the

The Flea Market

jungle, or if he'd simply been cursed when he was born, he choked, so he'd learned to be quiet around his father and uncles as they drank their pain away. If an aunt reminisced during a family visit, he'd sit quietly and listen, her voice keening through him like a dry, hot wind. There was no point in listening because soon enough, he knew, she'd be gone, too. And he'd always been right.

He went home to Brooklyn. When he walked up to the house he'd lived in his entire life, he had to stop, bend over, hands to knees, and breathe until the nausea went away. So many lives tied to that old wood-frame farm house. He could almost see Dad and his brothers working on it, dragging the walls and floors and plumbing forward through time another ten or twenty years. He heard the old music, the laughter of birthdays and holidays and Saturday nights, the smells of pie in the oven and flowery perfumes.

That never happened, either.

Derrick brushed himself off, looked up and down the street to see it any ghosts were coming. He spent the day in his basement, digging through boxes of belongings left behind by various family members when they'd moved on while Sonny Rollins blew through the speakers on the floor above, the sound of the sax coming through the floorboards as distant as the blowing horn on a tug as it worked barge and river under the Brooklyn Bridge.

He glanced through pictures he'd never bothered looking at, before now, catching occasional sight of himself over the past nearly sixty years. Mom, Dad, Clarence, Richard. Cousins he still ran into occasionally and spoke to, thinking they were only old buddies. Kids from the old neighborhoods, people and places he couldn't remember from visits to the South. Old girlfriends who'd thought they could cure what ailed him, and gone away suffocating on dust.

Sarah.

The faces flashed before his eyes like rockabilly or British invasion records he didn't collect, irrelevant and vaguely irritating.

And then there he was, in Derrick's hands, the image of what he remembered, the reflection of the man he'd just seen in the flea market: a faded black and white picture, with a white serrated border, of his grandfather, short and frail, a bony figure hardly filling his clothes, yet standing tall and proud in his Sunday suit, head shining with his hat in his hand, which was often even though covering the head had been the fashionable thing to do back then.

What did it mean? Was he going crazy? Had drinking finally gotten to him? Was he going crazy keeping to himself, or were more strange, harmless chemicals that were never supposed to be used in war detonating like mines in his system, causing a kind of psychological cancer?

Derrick spent the night going through more moldy liquor cases, crumbling shoe and hat boxes, wooden chests, worn suitcases and trunks, moving cartons, plastic bins, all stacked along the walls, piled into corners, stuck behind the boiler and the oil tank. He'd never realized how much of the history of the people he'd grown up with or who had come before him had accumulated in the house over the years. Though nothing like it had ever happened, he had a vision of funeral processions stopping by and unloading possessions before driving off to the cemetery.

Desert winds blew, but grandpa's voice kept his vision clear.

He was surprised to find some old 78's, though most were warped beyond playing, and others cracked or broken. A few of the books looked like they might be valuable, but many disintegrated in his hands. There were dresses and suits, shoes and hats, for both men and women, neatly stowed in boxes, carefully packed in tissue, some in styles as old as black and white movies. Journals spilled forgotten secrets as pages fell open, filled with paragraph stacked on paragraph like bricks, written in a precise, flowing hand, punctuated by poetry. He found an oboe. A guitar. A cavalry sword. Toys, from tin wind ups to his old Lincoln Log set with half the pieces missing.

By morning, a buzzing filled his head that drowned out Rollins, still repeating on the turntable. Fragments of memories, the smells of old paper and musty clothes, grime and dust, overwhelmed his senses. He sat with his back against a wall, surrounded by piles of history, and allowed himself to be amazed at finding such a flea market in the house he'd inherited from his parents. He'd stumbled across strangers he should have known, rediscovered friends and family only to find them foreign to in his heart.

The Flea Market

For an instant, he considered peddling the goods stored in the basement. He could start his own flea market booth. Maybe quit working in the garage and begin easing into retirement.

But the thought of selling off the hoard of personal history, even the records he'd been so willing to get rid of upstairs, suddenly took his breath, pained the heart and even his head, from neck to the space behind the eyes.

Like a bamboo spear.

He ran the back of his hand across his cheeks and eyes, then stared at a set of pictures he'd drawn as if they were a hand of cards: his father, in Korea; his mother, dressed in her Sunday best, including a hat, speaking from a stage with one arm raised, finger pointing to an unseen audience; Clarence, rail thin, half-naked, laughing on a beach; Richard, smirking under a huge afro.

By now, he was getting used to missing all that he'd lost.

He called in sick to work that day and the next. The garage owner gave him hell. He didn't hang around the local bar for the rest of the week.

He returned to the market the following Sunday, and as he examined the crate of made-up records the dealer had brought in, he kept an eye out for the old man. Soon enough, though, he couldn't look up from the images and words passing through his flipping fingers.

The record covers came in various sizes and shapes, from the standard 78, 45 and 33 to larger, smaller and in-between squares, triangles, octagons, and more erratic constructions. A quick check of the sleeves revealed that they all held cardboard facsimiles of records, down to grooves drawn in crayon, paint, ink and even pencil, some even carved with a knife or razor into the paper, spiraling down to the center hole, though the platters themselves often mimicked their packaging with eccentric shapes.

Like the Hated Peoples' record, they had eccentric titles like "Under the Waves Over the Sky," and "Jakob's Jupiter Jump," and "Singled Out." False production details like production labels and catalog numbers were appropriately placed and, on the more sophisticated creations, looked real.

The art on the covers ranged from the rare professional-quality painting or photograph to hand-drawn pictures, mostly poorly executed, or the occasional collage. None were as bizarre as the one he'd picked up last week, but some explored a particular theme to a similarly provocative extreme, to the point where he was, for a moment, the torn and bloody man who looked nothing like the usual figure nailed to a cross by nails through hands and feet; or the singer curled into a question mark crooning to the microphone cupped in his hands while a sea of arms reached for him from below; or a panther, staring out from behind bars, hunger seething in its eyes and rumbling in its belly.

While all the records in the crate kindled some kind of reaction in him, a few drew him deeper into their vision, like the Watts towers creation, though their ability to do so had nothing to do with the designer's level of skill. The child-like portrait of a singer's head wailing made him short of breath, as if he was the one who'd held a note, while a polished, air brushed Chinese dragon only made his palms tingle. Derrick quickly passed over the more powerful images, not wanting to be drawn into their worlds. He was afraid of losing himself in some perfect little creation, cut off from real world, as if on a never-ending drunk, or riding an endless spike of heroin.

Derrick hesitated, hearing his mother's voice telling him, isn't that what you've been doing with yourself, anyway?

He checked his fingertips, sniffed and licked his skin, and searched for any sign of hallucinogenic drugs coating the paper stock, or in the ink or paint, or even the glue holding the constructions together.

Paranoia blew its cold breath down his neck, and he paused to survey the windows above and around the parking lot for observers, half-expecting to find his mother and grandfather waving at him. Or, more likely, men in suits pointing surveillance equipment at him.

He'd learned not to underestimate the powers of the world. He wasn't the kind of vet who experienced flashbacks or psychotic breaks. If anything, war had tuned him into the reality of the here and the now to the point where past and future were irrelevant. War had been helpful to him in that way.

No one watched him, not even the dealer. He was alone in the middle of the flea market with the collection of made-up records. In the here and now, he let himself feel their covers, imagine the music their creators thought they might represent, experience the hours of passionate work that went into their making. There was something fascinating, enticing, even seductive about the imaginary recordings. They spoke, through all the different styles of music and artist they represented, about the people who had made them.

But the effect they had was also disturbing. It was wrong. Art, no matter how inspired, didn't do what he'd experienced. Nothing was supposed to make him forget where, when and even who he was.

Nothing was supposed to bring the dead back to life.

He finished going through the crate. His grandfather did not make an appearance.

He took the lot, surprising both himself and the vendor.

He spent the rest of the day laying out the records side by side on the first floor of his house. They filled the living room, where he left a passage so he wouldn't have to walk on their covers as he studied them one after another, trying to find a pattern in their assembly, a secret message of freedom in the motley quilt of their imagery. Maybe they were pieces of a puzzle, a cry for help, an answer to a question.

It wasn't until night had flooded the living room, throwing darkness over the cover images, and Miles Davis' Sketches of Spain had finished playing for the third time, that he thought to take one of the cardboard records out and put it on the turntable.

It was a ridiculous idea, of course. He couldn't afford to ruin a needle. There was no way to play them, they weren't real records.

But standing in the dark, it seemed a better idea than turning on the light and studying the images more closely, crawling down among them, putting his face up against the ones which called to him, and perhaps falling into one or another picture and never coming out.

He put the record on. Heard the needle drop, the speakers pop.

A horn called, announcing its presence in a rich and mellow tone resonating with the timbres of flesh and blood, bone and brass, a sound that was a word in an unwritten language, a patois of feeling and logic, a creole sensation. A simple tune followed, a story that was a gospel of sound and emotion, bolstered by a bass, accompanied by a piano.

Derrick's fingers ached.

The darkness thickened. A draft rose from the floor, as if each record was an empty pane in a window looking out on a mosaic of a world.

Something crashed in the basement.

Derrick jumped, nearly lost his balance. He went down on one knee. His hand brushed the floor, touched cardboard, and then nothing. Warm air blew against his skin, air whistled from the edges of closed doors, comfort smells as sweet as cinnamon-perfumed baked pie and savory barbeque mingled with burnt plastic and rotten meat. Light from every season and time of day shined from the windows onto the floor, painting the walls in colors from forlorn winter sunset to bright summer noon.

Derrick made his way gingerly to the basement door, teetering occasionally on the brink of other worlds, and went downstairs.

"Hey, there," his grandfather said, sitting in an old rocking chair that hadn't been whole the last time Derrick had seen it. The old wood creaked as the chair rolled back and forth on the hard concrete floor.

Derrick tried to answer, but his throat closed up, his mouth dried out. There weren't any words in him, anyway.

"Yeah," his grandfather said, "this is all quite a sight." He pointed to clothing Derrick had unpacked earlier. "That dress there? I bought that for my first daughter Ethel when she was sixteen. And I wish you'd taken better care of those records, son, because – "

"I didn't do anything, I got them like – " Derrick began, then stopped, embarrassed by making excuses. "What are you?" he finally managed to ask.

"You know," his grandfather said.

A chill passed through Derrick. He wasn't sure what he knew, but suddenly he wasn't certain if the apparition was only the ghost of grandpa, or something more. "Are you the devil?"

"Do you believe in the devil?"

"I don't think I ever have."

"Why don't you ask me if I'm God?"

Derrick didn't want to know. Instead, he asked, "Why are you here?" And suddenly he thought to look up, to see if the record jackets had opened their windows through the floor to let strange light shine down on them and offer entry to other worlds, to places that might be heaven or hell. He was relieved to find the ceiling intact.

"You called," his grandfather said, eyes fiery. He pressed his lips into a smile, like he was getting ready to hum a song from a long time ago.

"I did?" Derrick glanced around the basement, back to the chair. He closed his eyes, opened them again.

"Why don't you pinch yourself?" the old man said.

Derrick did. The old man remained, perhaps his grandfather's ghost, maybe more.

If he'd finally gone crazy, there was no way he could tell. "How come no one ever answered before," he said at last, remembering lonely times, and times of terror, when he'd called on all kinds of people and entities for salvation. He hadn't thought on all of that since his last brother died. He didn't want remember such things, but he didn't want to go back to what was waiting for him upstairs, either, so all there was left to do was deal with what was in the basement with whatever came to mind.

"You don't have the conjuring way. You needed the help your hands got you to find."

The impossible record still filled the upstairs with its unnamed melody. "Is that you playing upstairs?"

"No. That's someone else's dream, banged up, lost, left behind, waiting for someone else to pick it up, give it a cleaning and call it their own." He stopped rocking. "What happened to yours?"

Derrick found himself fixed in his grandfather's gaze like the figures stuck in the dreamworld latticework. There was no flying off, no way back down from where he'd put himself.

Derrick opened his mouth to ask a question, but instead surprised himself by saying, "It died."

He couldn't recall ever dreaming about doing things other than what he already did, though his fingers tingled, and he caught his breath as his heart raced with a rhythm he wanted to hear as a song.

Maybe as a child, sure, there'd always been music, and a piano in an aunt's house.....

"People die," his grandfather said. "Dreams don't. They float on peculiar currents, drifting like seeds until they land in the odd, desperate places where they're needed or wanted."

The old man reached behind the rocking chair. A guitar appeared in his hands. He leaned forward, stomped his foot on the concrete floor in a slow, easy rhythm. A progression of chords commanded attention, then a run of notes winding and bending their way around the foot-stomping rhythm announced a direction taken, a journey begun.

The old man faded slightly.

"If I ever did have dreams," Derrick said, "they've been gone a long time. I don't know if I want them back at this late stage of my life."

"It's never too late," the old man said, lowering his head and bobbing his head to what he was playing. "Ain't nothing more of a fright than a dream. Especially when you let one grow and take you places you didn't expect. Like those kids did, long ago, with those records upstairs."

Derrick flinched, as if an enemy round had just whizzed by his ear. "What do you want from me?"

"Peace."

"Go on, then," Derrick said, dismissing the apparition with a wave of a hand. "Leave me alone. Take those records with you – "

"You found something that brought me here. Now you've got to give something else up to let me go."

"What?" Derrick asked, impatient with a house lost to other people's dreams, feeling helpless in negotiating his release with what had to be a figment of his imagination.

The old man's playing grew louder even as he faded a bit more. "You've got to make something, son. Build it, play it, make it up, tell it. Anything, as long as you put yourself in what you make. Make way for a dream, and it'll come."

Derrick's hands twitched. He envied his grandfather's playing. "I don't know how."

"You don't have to know."

"What if I don't want to find any dreams," Derrick answered, thinking about who might decide to drop by next and not liking the possibilities. He was afraid to see Clarence in a corner behind a drum set, Richard on the stairs holding a tenor sax.

Sarah, leaning on a piano where boxes of records used to be stacked, smiling as she tickled the keys, humming a tune like her last name might have been Vaughn.

The Flea Market

If they'd been there, the temptation to join them would have pulled at him too hard.

"You've always got a choice of which way to go when you move on from the crossroads."

Derrick turned away from the rocking chair. The man sang something that might have been an old traveling blues song, though Derrick had never heard it before. The names of living places rose up from an all-too-human throat, couched in growls and grunts:

> *I found a heart in New Orleans, but I knew it wasn't hers.*
> *I woke without my heart one night, she threw it out for me to find.*
> *Back up the road I go, back up on my feet.*
> *Back up the road I go, running from the tears.*
> *Angola had me to itself, for three long years in stone.*
> *She didn't have it coming, under stone in earth so cold.*
> *Back up the road I need to go, back up on my feet.*
> *Back up the road I need to go, running from the tears.*

His grandfather's song rolled on, wearing at Derrick like the dirt and rocks from a hard path on old leather soles. It drowned out the music from upstairs, becoming all Derrick could hear.

Photographs he'd pulled out called to Derrick. He gathered them up, and the voices of people he knew in them rose up in his mind. Snatches of forgotten conversations, tall tales and bursts of laughter worked their way into his grandfather's song and filled his head. Derrick found himself ripping pages from journals, swatches of material from suits and dresses, beads and feathers from hats. He picked up watches that had long stopped working, a cracked glass, a broken ceramic bird. In his hands all these fragments came together, and he worked both blind and all-seeing, snatching pieces of the past, mementos of the dead, bringing them together into a construction that didn't make sense, like those Watts towers, but was part of something larger, too vast for him to see, which did have meaning and gave him comfort and encouraged him to go on, keep trying, don't worry about looking foolish, join in, join us, dream, dream and play and let go and be.

The old man was gone, the rocking chair still, but his blues played on, louder than before, as if Derrick was standing in a steeple while a church bell rang loud in his ears calling people to service. And in his basement, the remains of what his family had been came together into something new: a tiny house, a fragile, twisted, insane model of the one he lived in. A crypt for dead things. A cocoon for new life.

He crawled into the model and sealed himself in, so that no light or sound, not even his grandfather's music, could penetrate the womb he'd made for himself.

And in the darkness of that place, he broke a wall he never knew had been there, and stumbled, then fell into a new world.

He landed on soft earth that yielded to his weight, like snow. The sky hung over him in purple drapes, so low in some places he could reach up and touch its velvet smoothness. Pools of blood bubbled across the ground, and in the distance, past skeletal trees dotted with brightly colored blooms, streams ran to rivers which emptied into a sea, all filled with blood. And as he watched, dead men, women and children rose from the blood land, stepped out of the ocean, fell from tree blossoms like ripe fruit, alive and walking.

The sun rose, turning Derrick's skin golden. He wept, and others came to comfort his sorrow for what he'd lost, and what he'd let go to waste, and after a while he saw a host had gathered around him. He spoke of his country, his world, of death and loss and shame, promises and hope, and they listened, and when he offered to lead them back to show them what he said was true, they said yes, and followed. And he led them back the way he came, through his house, and his neighbors and countrymen and the people of other countries reacted with terror and revulsion, until their skins turned golden, too, and they saw the world through his and each other's eyes. Together, the people Derrick had found and the ones he'd left behind tore down the old, and from the ruin they re-built a new homeland, without kings, empires, wealth or sadness.

And then Derrick was tired, and he lay down and went to sleep, dreaming of what might happen the next day.

When he woke up, he was flat on his back in his basement, resting on a bed of family keepsakes and pass-downs. Empty pizza and Chinese food cartons and soda cans also littered the floor. There was no music or grandpa, and for a moment he thought he'd had too good a drunk the night before.

But there was no taste of liquor in his mouth, no hangover, no empty bottles. Upstairs, the pretend-records he'd bought from the flea market were spread out on the living room floor where he'd left them, to him, the night before. A perfectly good needle had embedded itself into a cardboard platter he'd foolishly set down on the turntable.

He climbed upstairs to the bathroom, checked himself in a mirror. His beard had trapped bits of food and sauce, and his skin was ashy. The stink from his stained clothes quickly filled the small space.

He moved to the bedroom and looked out the window to see if anyone on the street had turned golden. He half-expected to see Richard shooting craps with some kids, and Clarence on a bike, maybe Mom and Dad taking a walk arm in arm, or some of the guys from the old platoon sprawled out under a tree, chatting with neighborhood regulars long gone between tokes.

A church bell rang. It was Sunday morning. He'd been gone a week.

A couple in their church-going finery passed by on the sidewalk. Teenagers going the other way ignored them as they laughed, lost in their own world.

Derrick sat down. Listened a while to the silence in the house while counting the shelves of records he'd collected over the years, as if in a graveyard adding up the tombstones. "Is this real?" he asked. "Was that real?" No one answered.

But something brushed his lips, while a whiff of sweet perfume made his heart race. He'd been an innocent the last time he'd caught that scent, and everyone had been alive.

"Sarah?" he called, turning, but saw only the outline of a slim body in the rumpled linen covering the mattress.

He looked at his hands, and then the sky, and remembered dreams.

I left my life in Brooklyn, the day I went to war.
I found my death in Brooklyn, the day I came back home.
Back up the road I need to go, back up on my feet.
Back up the road I need to go, running from the tears.

Sitting on the edge of the bed, he sang a while to himself. People's names came tumbling out, instead of cities, along with tiny pieces of the hurt he'd felt when they'd left. His voice grew hoarse and finally he stopped, but the truth he'd found for himself didn't fade. He tapped thick fingers against his thighs, and remembered what ivory keys felt like under them a long, long time ago.

He tapped fat fingers against his thighs, and found what he'd left behind.

The Talkative Star
Rhys Hughes

Curtains

The setting sun eventually became paranoid. "Why does everyone keep staring at me? They never scrutinise me in the middle of the day – only when I'm going to bed! I think I'll draw the clouds tight from now on and get some privacy!"

Waiting for Breakfast

A boy sat on the beach with a toasting fork, holding it up to the sun. "You need to light a fire with driftwood," the sun told him, "because I'm not hot enough to toast that slice of bread."

"You will be when you turn into a Red Giant," answered the boy.

The sun considered this and said:

"Yes, I'll swell up and engulf the innermost planets and boil into steam the oceans of Earth, and any bread lying around will toast nicely, but that won't happen for billions of years!"

The boy laughed and shook his head.

"Don't you know that one day I'll have children and entrust this task to them, and that they too will have children and do likewise, and so on until the necessary time has elapsed?"

The sun was amazed. "That *is* a long wait for breakfast!"

The Fable

"What are you doing in there?"

"Nothing, I assure you."

But the sun wasn't convinced. "Are you writing fables again? You'll grow pale and unhealthy if you stay indoors all day; come out and bask in my beams instead. If you must continue writing, you can do it in the fresh air. There can't be much to write about in a dark room anyway! I wonder what inspiration you find in gloom?"

"Sometimes," I responded, "it's easier to write about a subject when I force myself to avoid the real thing."

"Ah, so the new fable is about your wife?"

I said nothing; I'm not married. But I looked down and to my surprise saw that my fable was finished: this one.

Passing the Light

The moon reflects the light of the sun; and the frozen lake reflects the light of the moon; and the coin held between the thumb and forefinger of the assassin reflects the light of the frozen lake.

"If this is genuine, I'll do what you ask," he tells a hooded figure who stands in the shadows of the tallest tree.

Then he puts the coin between his teeth and bites it.

And on the other side of the world, the sun screams…

The Free Spirit

The sun has a large brood of planets and Earth is just one of its children and not even the favourite. "Saturn's the one that makes me most proud and I wish the others would try equally hard to be so distinctive; I don't mean by copying his rings but with some other original approach to the question. It's not for me to specify what."

An astronomer overheard this and said, "But Saturn isn't really the most unique world in your family."

"How are you able to understand my words? They should be inaudible to you; I have already set on your locality."

"But I'm standing on a high mountain and although the land below me is blanketed with the shadows of twilight, up here you are still visible and will be for another minute at least."

"Fair enough, but won't you grow cold up there?"

The astronomer pulled on thick gloves and knotted a scarf around his neck. "I'm a professional and used to it. Every evening I wait here for you to go down, and then I enter my observatory."

"Tell me why you disparage Saturn," the sun demanded.

"Because it's just as timid as the others: they all refuse to go off and make their own way in the universe. I left home when I was seventeen! And yet once, many aeons ago, you had a planet that took the brave step of leaving its orbit and going travelling; it wanted to establish itself as its own master in this difficult cosmos of ours!"

"Ah yes, I remember Scruffy, the old rogue! But he never came back, never kept in touch. Do you have news of him?"

"Last night my telescope found him. He is herding lost comets near Alpha Centauri and seems happy enough."

The Sun Lamp

Two merchants approached the sun and said, "We have something to sell you that we know you'll find very useful. In this box is the latest kind of sun lamp! It's powerful and projects a light similar to your own. So now you'll be able to read books or comb your hair or search for dropped pins or squeeze your spots at night."

The sun frowned. "I don't know what you mean."

The merchants smiled indulgently. "Which part don't you understand? The books, the comb or the pins?"

And the sun answered, "What is night?"

Sayings of the Sun

Some of the sun's favourite sayings:

"I yearn for nostalgia!"

"Second guessing is my special talent. I know what you're going to say about that… but it really is!"

"My apparent arrogance is always tongue in cheek, but it's a wonderful tongue in a most super cheek!"

"I'm a tautology lover and therefore love tautologies!"

"Bring back atavism!"

"A business question about Mephistopheles: was he ever incorporated or did he remain a soul trader?"

"Is the San Andreas Fault all it's cracked up to be?"

"Standing on the shoulders of giants to see further is a fine tactic, but not when they have big hair!"

"This is only the second time I've had déjà vu!"

"The word 'chortle' always makes me snigger; but the word 'snigger' mostly just makes me guffaw!"

"My mind's an open book, but I've cracked the spine so it always falls open on a pre-arranged page!"

"Despite the pain it always causes, a contradiction in a sentence never hurt anyone." And ultimately:

"Excessive understatement is so over the top!"

Making a Request

"Why don't you ever come to Wales?" asked the people of that country, through a gigantic megaphone that penetrated the thick endless layers of low grey cloud. "Not once in living memory have you visited us; but we have many attractions for you to shine on! There are castles and hills and forests and secret valleys and little offshore islands and ancient megaliths and the ruins of abbeys and quaint piers and narrow-gauge railways and rousing choirs and coracles and odd hats. Take a copy of this guide book and read about them for yourself!"

"Don't be silly!" came the muffled reply. "How can I read anything if I have no eyes? How can I hear what you are saying, or respond to it, if I have no ears or mouth? I'm not even a sentient being but an unimaginably vast ball of seething hydrogen and helium atoms. So go away and leave me alone. Your request is foolish!"

The sun will use any excuse to avoid Wales.

Misplaced Comfort

The explorer was lost in the desert and now he sank to his knees and his bloated tongue protruded from his gaping mouth. The sun sighed. "I reach down to stroke him continually; but it doesn't seem to help. I don't even think he's grateful for my attention!"

The Labyrinth

The girl smiled and said, "My name's Ariadne and I'm a direct descendant of the Ariadne who helped Theseus find his way out of the labyrinth after his encounter with the Minotaur."

"I know the story," admitted the sun, "but there's no point giving *me* a spool of thread to unwind; I'm far too hot and it would burn up in a blink. You'd better try something else…"

"There are many kinds of threads," she said.

And she whispered something.

The sun entered the labyrinth, he really had no choice: at every bend there was a mirror angled to project him in a new direction; and before he knew it, he had reached the centre of the awful stone maze. The grotesque Minotaur that sat on the rotten bench there was also a descendant of the original and doubtless he would have roused himself enough to stand and confront the intruder with his club.

But many centuries of degeneration, of living in shadows without the benefit of fresh air or true exercise, of loneliness and boredom, meant his mythic bloodline had degenerated. Centuries of semi-bovine melancholy had turned him into an albino parasite. In fact he was a vampire, or rather his human half was. He glanced up and almost immediately the sunlight caused him to wither, shrivel, char.

The sun turned to escape the labyrinth, and he recalled Ariadne's wise words. "Follow the motes!" And that's what he did: those specks of dust, of airborne flakes from the hybrid monster's skin, enabled him to find his way back to the narrow entrance.

"You slew him!" cried the girl.

The sun nodded. "Accidentally. I didn't have time to introduce myself or offer a tip and I regret that fact."

"What a peculiar idea! Why offer him a tip?"

"Because this labyrinth is a hotel as well as a trap, isn't it?"

"How did you arrive at that conclusion?"

"He was a bullboy, wasn't he?"

On the Windowstill

The sun wanted to complain about a trick that humans kept playing. "I'm intrigued by the magnifying glasses they leave lying on their windowsills; but every time I peer into one, all I can see is a rapidly expanding charred circle and wisps of smoke. I'm certain that's not the same as what humans see. There's something funny going on!"

The Dungeon

The sun poked its nose into a prison cell and saw a depressed prisoner on a bed of rotten straw. "What's wrong?"

The prisoner pulled his matted beard and said:

"I shared this grim cell with a man who kept me entertained with tales of distant places and through him I lived vicariously as a traveller, but he has been moved to a different room and I am bored again. The bubbles of illusion he created have all burst."

"Tell me about *your* life," prompted the sun.

"It has been a long and exciting one, that's for sure! I was born in Pisa in the tumultuous 13th Century and became a professional fabricator and embellisher of romances at a young age. I was captured by the forces of Genoa at the Battle of Meloria…"

"One moment. I'll write down everything you say. Maybe a book can be made out of it; a bestseller!"

"Do you really think so?" blinked the man.

"Sure! What's your name?"

"Rustichello," came the answer, spoken in a resigned tone, for many readers wouldn't recognise it.

But *you* will, because you're clever.

The Tribal Philosophers

The people of the remote island said to each other, "The light of the moon is more important than the light of the sun. This isn't hard to believe! The light of the moon appears at night, when it's most needed; but the light of the sun appears only in the daytime, when we can already see everything clearly, and is therefore superfluous."

And they added salt and pepper to the missionary.

The Dagger

The two merchants approach the assassin and say, "We offered you that dagger on a trial basis only. It's a Damascene blade, very finely tempered. Did it meet expectations? The trial period has just ended, and unless you return the item, you must pay in full."

The moon reflects the light of the sun; and the pub window reflects the light of the moon; and the stiletto held in the leather glove of the assassin reflects the light of the pub window.

"But I haven't had time to use it yet!"

A hooded figure hisses from the nearby shadow of a tall tree, "Hurry up! Hurry! Get the job done quick!"

The assassin snorts, "Everything's under control." And he reaches into his pocket for the coin it contains. He cuts this coin in half with the blade and gives a piece to each merchant.

And on the far side of the world, the sun frowns and gasps, "Suddenly I feel like an amoeba. How curious!"

Confusions of the Sun

There are particular metaphysical problems that bother the sun from time to time. Although he turns these problems over and over in his own mind, he doesn't ask anyone for advice about them. He's afraid of looking like a fool and being mocked by sages.

So when he passes over philosophers and other wise fellows he calls a brisk, "Hello there!" and dashes behind the nearest cloud; or if there aren't any clouds in the vicinity, he makes other kinds of small talk, about sport, politics or taxes, maybe, but never about the weather, because he dislikes giving away all his trade secrets.

He enjoys shining on Buddhists, but there's a paradox in one of their beliefs that he can't get to grips with. If you are a person who believes in reincarnation, surely it makes sense to work hard to improve the general condition of the world, so that living standards rise for everyone? This way you can be certain of improved comfort in your next life, no matter where you are born! In other words, if you are very holy you need only care for yourself in this life; but if you are sinful it's in your own interest to be good and improve the world. So good people should act in a selfish manner and bad people selflessly…

The sun isn't ready to convert to this faith yet.

Baking Hot Day

Intrigued by his contact with Rustichello, the sun decided to pay a visit to Pisa, the town of the taleteller's birth. He saw that a cunning arrangement of concave mirrors had been set up on the roof of a house. "What's going on down there?" he mused aloud.

"This is a solar oven," answered a stout woman.

"You expect me to slave in a kitchen for you? No chance! I work only for myself; all stars are aristocrats!"

The woman laughed. "You have been my employee ever since you got here! Don't you know your beams are bouncing off these mirrors onto the baking tray inside my brick oven?"

"Am I baking a loaf of bread for you, then?"

"Not bread, no; the flour contains honey and raisins and apricots, and I used wine instead of water to mix it."

Much later, the moon asked the sun, "I heard you did your share of the cooking today. Was it difficult?"

"Nah," replied the sun. "Pisa cake."

Creativity in the Wilderness

I want to be serious just for a few moments and talk a little on the subject of Creativity in the Wilderness. The fact is that I need the sun to facilitate the proper exercise of my imagination.

I don't mean that I don't get ideas in the wintertime – some of my best work (if any of it is actually good) has been done in low temperatures, but never through choice. When it's dark and chill I wish to hibernate, and so *forcing* myself to work is a perverse form of retirement, of hiding myself away from the cold sky: a way of taking my mind off the gloomy present moment. But this doesn't work well…

When I'm cold all my muscles contract and I feel hunched and stooped like an old man; I lack only a corncob pipe, hobble and liver spots. I can't wait to be warm again, to uncurl and unfurl and to live the outdoors life. I take my empty notebooks with me when it comes, and pens, and though I do less work, I'm happier in my soul.

The wilderness for me must be sun-drenched. Otherwise I can't feel its beauty deep down; I succumb to bleakness instead and mope from cliff to cliff, or over pallid dunes, searching for a cave mouth where I can huddle around a fire of frosty driftwood sticks.

No thanks. I love the sun far too much! My creativity ripens in the sun and ferments into the wine that will keep me from despair in winter. Once I walked across the Alpujarras in midsummer, writing at odd moments as I went: the result was a novella full of inventors, explorers, mermaids and minstrels across which daily crawled large ants to greet, or challenge, the scrawl of black multi-legged words.

Jumping into Summer

Two hikers, one male, one female, stopped for the night in a forest glade. The sun was low in the west and its ruby beams slanted almost horizontal between the rough trunks. A hooded figure watched from the shadows of the tallest tree and grimaced ferociously.

"I feel a little uneasy," said the female.

The male hiker nodded. "I know what you mean. Spending the night in a forest is always unnerving. Not like sleeping on the beach or in dunes; there's the constant feeling of being watched and of being at the mercy of predators or paranormal forces."

"I'm not sure I can last until morning!"

"Very well. Here's a solution. Night is about to fall and will probably endure for the whole of the next paragraph. If we both take a long enough run up, we should be able to jump right over that paragraph and end up in the one after it, which will almost certainly describe tomorrow morning. I think we should hold hands and do this together. Are you ready? Let's run as far as that log and then leap…"

The sun vanished over an unseen horizon. Dusk gathered itself rapidly and the stars were very dim when they appeared through gaps in the thick canopy of rustling foliage. Owls hooted, rodents scurried and bright eyes glowed in the undergrowth; twigs snapped and the very trees appeared to unfreeze from some paralysis and move their branches like arms. Hours passed slowly, fearfully, chillingly.

Very slowly, the sky grew lighter. The night was finally coming to an end. The sun came up and climbed higher; and the character of the forest changed completely; the eeriness was utterly dispelled and now it was a cheerful place, a paradise of wild flowers and birds. The sun reached its highest point, began to descend, sank lower and lower and its ruby beams slanted almost horizontal between…

"Damn it!" grumbled the male.

"What's the matter?" asked his companion.

"We jumped too far. We cleared not only the paragraph containing the night, but also the one describing the morning after, so we're back in late afternoon – of the following day!"

The female considered this. Although unaware that the hooded figure had been left behind in yesterday, she said, "I don't have the same uneasy feeling. Let's camp here anyway."

"I agree," the male said, "and nothing has been lost by the jump. We're one day closer to summer, in fact!"

The House of the Lying Sun

There is a House in Old Orléans they call the Lying Sun… That's how a song might begin. Except that *this* Orléans is pronounced Or-Lee-On and the house in question is a café rather than a brothel. Inside this café there are steps leading down into a cellar and in one corner of this cellar, which has been converted into a private room for patrons, the two merchants are trying to turn on each other. One of them said, "Why not purchase off me this bronze Ptolemaic model of the solar system? It depicts all the planets and stars in their correct positions!"

"No, it doesn't; it shows the sun going round the Earth! And where are Uranus, Neptune, Pluto and Scruffy? I don't want it. But you ought to like my efficient solar-powered torch…"

"Don't be inane! That's a joke, not a product!"

The other merchant gritted his teeth. "You misunderstand: it works off artificial light too! A real bargain!"

"Tell you what: why don't we leave each other alone and go back out to search for some proper victims?"

As they climbed up the steps and then left the café, the sun shook his head and clucked his tongue. "Wine is bottled sunlight, so they say, and that cellar was full of rare vintages, so I overheard everything! Don't they realise that Pluto is no longer an official planet? It was demoted in 2006 for an unspecified misdemeanour!"

The Beach Ball

The sun passed over a crowded beach in the middle of summer. He saw that people were throwing a yellow beach ball back and forth, yelling in joy as they caught it in outstretched arms. The sun studied the likeness of the ball and was highly flattered. They hadn't included any spots. "That's me, that is!" he announced proudly.

The Sun Bed

The two merchants approached the sun and said, "We have something to sell you that we know you'll find very useful. In this box is the latest kind of sun bed! It's very comfortable and perfect for tired suns. After a tough day crossing the sky and sharing your life-giving energy with plants and animals, you probably need to put your rays up and take it easy. There's no better place than in this bed."

"I don't need much rest, to be honest," explained the sun. "Just a few minutes of shut-eye every now and then; I get my winks during eclipses. Your product doesn't interest me."

"Don't you ever take a siesta?"

"Only if the heat of a nearby star gets too much for me to continue my work. And that hasn't occurred yet."

"Then we'll come back after the next supernova."

"Sorry, I don't buy *that* either!"

The Jeweller

There was a girl who took crystals and wrapped them in wire and twisted the wire into elaborate patterns, so the crystals could be hung from little chains and worn around the neck.

In the sunlight, these crystals shone with many colours.

"What are you up to?" asked the sun, as it passed overhead. "What are you doing with those sparkly things?"

"I'm making pedants," answered the girl.

"Pedants? I think you mean *pendants*," corrected the sun.

The girl smiled. "Yes, those too."

The Music Shop

The sun poked its nose into a music shop and saw a depressed prisoner in a cobwebbed corner. "What's wrong?"

The prisoner said nothing in reply. Nothing at all.

"Let me guess," pondered the sun. "Did you share this grim shop with a friend who entertained you with tales of distant places, through which you lived vicariously as a traveller? But now your friend has been moved to a different shop and you are bored again. The bubbles of illusion have all burst. Is that what occurred?"

The prisoner remained silent, unresponsive.

And so the sun said enticingly:

"If you speak to me, I'll write down everything you say. Maybe a book can be made from it; a bestseller!"

Still no answer, no enthusiasm, nothing.

A gust entered the abandoned shop through a crack. The strings of the neglected instruments sang badly.

"What has happened?" cried the sun. "Don't you recognise me? Rusty cello! Rusty cello! My old friend!"

The sun often makes linguistic mistakes.

According to the moon…

The Sundial

"I wonder what time it is?" the sun said as it passed over a land where trees were dropping fruit. There was no one to ask; but then it spotted a sundial in an overgrown garden. "I just need to consult this delightful contrivance and then I'll know."

But it came away frustrated.

"Typical! The part that holds the information is the one part that's in shadow and I can't see a thing!"

Time Gentlemen Please

In fact it's time to wind up this set of absurd little stories and explain that the sequence is supposed to be a microcosm of a book I wrote that itself is a microcosm of my stated project of writing one thousand linked tales. I call that project my 'Grand Wheel' and I've been working on it for many years. I'm busy on it right now but it's still far from completion. The book I mentioned is entitled *Tallest Stories* and is a sample or preview of what the finished project might be like.

Provided I do get to finish it, of course... There are forces out to stop me. I am standing in the pub known as the TALL STORY and slurping my pint of stout at the bar. Unlike most other pubs, this one tends to migrate from place to place, sometimes on wheels, sometimes not. It wanders the universe like a nomad; and on one occasion it even became the universe. Next to me is the girl who makes crystal pendants. She also happens to be the female hiker; and I'm the male.

She is drinking red wine. We have just returned from a camping trip in the forest. Abruptly the front door opens and the hooded figure strides in, his cloak spattered with mud and encrusted with leaves. He gazes around and spots me. Then he cries, "There he is! What did I pay you for? Do the job now, you incompetent buffoon!"

From a table in the corner rises a man: the assassin. The long dagger in his hand glimmers in the firelight.

"No hard feelings. I'm just making a living."

"But what have I done?" I wail.

The assassin can't tell me; he doesn't know why I must die. But there's no doubt in the mind of the hooded figure, who throws back his hood and reveals himself to be... The reader!

Yes, it's you! You out there!

But you're inside here now... And you say:

"Yes, it's me! I'm tired of your whimsical nonsense and I want to shut you up. I began reading this story in the hope of learning a sensible thing or two, but almost immediately I realised I had been deceived. You must die and stop writing it; and I have arranged precisely that destiny for you. What do you have to say to that?"

"You're too late. The story is over!"

The door opens again and all the characters from all the sub-chapters swarm in, their work finished. The merchants; astronomer; boy with the toasting fork (he toasts the bread on the open fire instead); the explorer lost in the desert; Ariadne and the dead vampiric Minotaur; Rustichello; the tribal philosophers and the missionary they ate; the woman from Pisa; and the entire population of Wales.

The pub is very crowded now and when I reach the door and look out, I notice the reader walking away along a winding road, the sun casting his shadow right out of this page and onto the wall or floor next to the chair you are sat in at this very moment.

New Year's Resolution

"If sunbathing is so dangerous and can cause skin cancer I'd better stop setting in the ocean," mused the sun to itself one day, "and only set over mountain ranges from now on."

The Man who saw grey
       Brendan Connell

"Not now," she said pushing him away. "I'm cooking."

"So am I," Greg laughed, kissing the back of her neck.

She twisted. "If you need something to do, why not change the burnt out bulb in the living room. You said you would do it two days ago."

"I said I would do it yesterday."

"But you didn't."

"I was painting."

"Still."

He sighed, opened one of the lower kitchen cabinets, took out a small spare bulb and put it in the pocket of his khakis. He watched his wife, Cassie, and noted how sexy she looked, poised in front of the stove, stirring the spaghetti sauce, her blond hair done up in a bun. She often got on his case about not performing chores; but he considered his painting to be far more important, and the little time he had, when not at his job, he tried to dedicate to it.

"So I'll go change the bulb."

"You do that."

Greg Schwegler went into the living room and turned on the reading lamp. He glanced at one of his paintings which hung up over the couch. It was an expressionistic work, which made use of slops of yellow and red in a slightly adventurous way. He considered it to be a good painting, and it very nearly was. Though he had a decent job as an administrator at the DMV, downtown, he considered himself to be a painter at heart. He had had his first showing the year before at which three canvases sold.

"It would be wonderful to be able to make a living off my painting," he had told Cassie.

"Sure, but the money from those three paintings wouldn't keep us going for more than a month."

"Still, it is a nice fantasy."

In order not to frighten her, he told his wife that it was a fantasy; in reality it was an ambition. Though he was but a mediocre painter, he thought he had talent. It was perfectly possible that, with time and labour, he might have become a true artist, – A thing more rare than a two-headed cow.

He smiled slightly as he looked at the painting and thought of the one he had going in the garage. So far it was not as good as the one over the couch, but with some work he might be able to make it happen.

Greg took the three-legged stool from in front of the bookshelf. He placed it in the centre of the room, climbed onto it and then reached up to the lighting fixture, which was a faux-chandelier with four, flame shaped bulbs. It was a high ceiling and he had to stretch and balance on his tiptoes to reach the fixture. He unscrewed the burnt out bulb, stuck it in his empty pocket, and then fished the new bulb from the other pocket. He stretched out and began to screw it into place, shifting his weight somewhat too near the edge of the stool as he did so. The stool, which was poorly built and unsteady, fell over. In falling, Greg hit his head against the edge of the coffee table and cursed loudly.

"What is it?" Cassie cried, running in.

"I hit my damn head!"

"Oh, poor baby!" She bent down and kissed him on the forehead. "Are you alright?"

"I feel dizzy as hell."

"It's just a bruise. Does it hurt?"

"I said it did."

"You want me to get you an ice pack?"

"No."

"Let me get you an ice pack."

"My eyes are all screwed up."

"You need an ice pack."

Cassie got up and went to the kitchen, walking with the quick, deliberate steps required by a minor emergency. Greg sat on the floor with his legs spread out in front of him. He rubbed his head, though in truth it did not hurt much. What primarily distressed him was the fact that everything in the room seemed incredibly dark. He remembered the burnt out bulb in his pocket and checked. It was unbroken.

"Turn on the light," he said when Cassie returned.

"The reading light is on."

"I feel sick."

"The spaghetti is ready; you want some?"

"I feel sick."
"Lie down on the couch."
"I'm going to the bedroom to lie down."
"I'll get you some Tylenol."

Greg took three Tylenol, undressed and lay down in bed. He felt nauseous, strange and disoriented; and in that state fell into a deep sleep.

When he awoke the next morning he felt for Cassie, but she was not there. He opened his eyes. The first thing he saw was grey; a disgusting eerie grey. It was like a strange apathetic nightmare, but he did not in the least question its reality. There were subtleties to the world around him that could not possibly exist in any dream state. Through the window came a mushy, bland dullness, somewhat different in tone than everything else, but not the least felicitous. He felt its warmth through the blankets and touched it with his hand. It threw a murky patch on the blanket.

He was appalled.

"Damn; it's the sun," he murmured.

He climbed out of bed, saw two morbid limbs attach themselves to the floor, and then ventured to the window. The spectacle outside was so dreary, that Greg, who was by no means an emotional man, felt like crying. Giant fluffy mounds protruded from a monotonous, colourless earth. The sky was a depressing slab, heavy and joyless as prison concrete. The flower garden was nothing but a mass of grim wands. There was occasional ambience, but what it offered was callous and dead. The raw images of the world were there, but they were grey and raped of spirit.

"Oh good, you're up. The coffee has been ready for an hour; should I make a fresh pot?"

He looked over. It was Cassie. She stood in the doorway, a featureless mass.

"You ok honey?"
"I'm sick."
"Does your head still hurt?"
"I'm sick Cassie. Take me to the hospital."

*

After being run through a number of tests in the emergency room, Greg saw a doctor, whose words he hung on with agitation.

"Well, the good news is there is nothing wrong with your eyes, and you don't appear to have a concussion; – The bad news is that we don't know what is wrong with you."

"But there is *something* wrong with me," Greg said, looking at the gloomy splotch that was the man's face.

The doctor shrugged his shoulders. "I recommend seeing a specialist."

"I'm not crazy." (Desperately.)

The doctor laughed. "No more than the rest of us I imagine. – I meant a neurological specialist, not a psychiatrist."

He wrote down a name on a slip of paper and handed it to Greg.

"He can help me?"

"I would think so; – He can at least give you a proper analysis."

As they walked out of the hospital, Greg handed the number to his wife. "Call him," he said.

"It's Sunday today; – He won't be in his office."

"Well, call him anyway. I want to have this thing resolved right away."

"Does it really hurt that bad?"

"It doesn't damn well hurt at all; but I can't see; – I can't see a god damn colour!"

She called the number, but, as she had predicted, no one was in the office. She could see that Greg was beside himself, so she looked up the specialist's name, which was Arnold Meek, in the phone book, called him and made an appointment for the next morning.

Greg spent the day in the bedroom with the blinds drawn and only came into the living room when the sun had set and even then he insisted on having the lights kept low.

"The light bothers you that much?"

"Yes – it shows me what I am missing."

Cassie, in an attempt to take her husband's mind off his sight, had prepared a wonderful meal of lamb chops and a green bean salad. She opened a bottle of champagne and poured two glasses. Greg drank the champagne off in three swallows and began to cut his meat, while Cassie filled his glass again.

"Is the lamb good?" she asked.

"Yes. – Yes it is."

The lamb was good. It tasted good; but it did not look like food. It looked more like stone and he was surprised when his knife slid so easily through it. The taste, aroma and the tenderness were perfect; but the fact that what he saw was so utterly bland thoroughly disturbed him. He drank heavily of the champagne, in a frank attempt to get drunk. He fancied that insobriety would be easier than reality.

"Are you getting tipsy?" Cassie laughed. "I am."

"I'm a bit drunk," Greg said, draining his third glass.

Cassie leaned over and kissed him. He closed his eyes and the experience seemed enjoyable.

"Should we go into the bedroom?" she said. "It's been a while."

She took him by the hand and he followed her. It would take up his attention; and he thought it might be just what he needed. Two minutes later they were in bed together.

"Turn off the light," he said.

"Shhh." She bit his ear and tried to please him.

He wanted the light off. He found the sight of her thoroughly repulsive. Her skin reminded him of a rat's; all her faults suddenly became glaring; he could see how her bones protruded from her flesh and her chest, with its small, coarse breasts, made him feel as if he were pressing up against the living dead. She kissed him madly and pushed her tongue into his mouth. He pushed her back and gasped for air.

"What is it darling?"

Her smile was grotesque; the shading was hard and ruthless; she was like a phantom.

"I'm sorry," he said. "I have an awful stomach ache."

"Poor baby!"

She put her arms around him and he pulled away.

"I feel sick," he said. "Sorry, but I feel quite nauseous."

"Is it me?" she asked, her face becoming suddenly set.

"No, of course not; it must have been the champagne."

He found his feet on the floor and quickly made his way to the bathroom. He turned on the light, closed the door behind him and gazed in the mirror. He looked like a sordid old man, his own lacklustre eyes staring coldly back at him. With a moan he flicked off the light, sat down on the toilet seat and felt the salty liquid oozing from his eyes.

"Damn," he murmured. "Damn it! – That doctor better do something for me tomorrow."

*

Doctor Meek sat opposite him, twisting a pen in his hand. "The fact is," he said, "that the human machine is something we don't altogether understand. People assume that doctors and scientists know everything, that we have all the answers – But that is simply not true."

"So you don't know what is the matter with me?"

"I have a pretty good theory on what is the matter – I believe that somehow that section of your brain which controls 'colours,' that part that differentiates colour, has been shut down or cut off from the rest of your brain – Somehow in the fall it must have been jolted out of place; turned off like a light switch."

"Can you fix it though – can you turn the switch back on?"

"Well, as I was saying – us doctors and scientists don't know everything. Many of our most basic functions, such as smelling, hearing and seeing we are still not totally clear about. We know how the nose and eyes work, but we do not altogether understand how the brain transforms smells and sights – and colours for instance – into particular sensations."

"So – So what does this mean for me? It is absolutely hell to live without colour."

"I am sure it is. Unfortunately I can offer no immediate solution to the problem."

"So?"

"Your case really does fascinate me though. I have never come across anything like it and I would like to continue working with you."

"Then you think you might be able to – You might be able to find a solution?"

"I can offer no promises, but I think it is possible."

There was a brief silence.

"Naturally you are upset with the situation," the doctor said presently. "That is perfectly understandable, but hopefully you can continue leading a relatively normal life – Unless – Until we can find some sort of cure."

Greg did not answer. He stared at the doctor's left hand, which was wagging a pen. It looked like some kind of cruel instrument of torture.

"What is your work?" the doctor asked, with a sudden softening of his voice.

Greg paused.

"I . . . I work at the administrative department at the DMV."

"Well then," the doctor smiled, "at least this problem should not much effect your ability to work. – Now, if you had been something else – a botanist or artist let's say – something where your livelihood depended on the ability to discern colours – Well, then it would have been a bit of a disaster. – As it is though, I don't see that the lack of colour can affect your ability to do paperwork."

Greg left the doctor's office. He was appalled at the man's callousness. He was even less understanding than Cassie. It was obvious that no one could appreciate his state – how incredibly painful it was to be without colour. They seemed to think it was something equivalent to being short sited, but for him, for Greg, it was an absolute horror.

His entire life changed. The doctor was wrong about it not affecting his work. He took an indefinite sick leave, as he could not bear to go out in the daytime. He was dreadfully depressed, slept throughout the day with the shutters closed, and only rose at night. The world seemed have been transformed into a vast ghost land – a place deserted of feeling. While at night streets and buildings were tolerable to view, at no point could he stand the sight of natural or living things. Parks and trees were simply dismal; animals, such as dogs and cats, were genuinely frightening. The sight of mountains, forests and oceans filled him with a terror that was unparalleled. A meadow without colour was far more desolate than the driest desert. A stream, when reduced to a sickly colourless trickle, was simply ghastly. The sight of humans turned his guts.

Greg, due to a good employee benefits package, was able to receive half pay for up to six months. Cassie, who was disappointed, at least saw that the situation was not an irremediable disaster.

"You'll see," she told Greg. "The doctors will make you better. – And in the meantime, at least you can work on your painting. You have been wanting to spend more time on it."

Greg could hardly believe his ears. Was his wife really that out of tune to what he was going through? Paint? How could he paint without colour! Red was grey, yellow was grey, blue was grey! Life was simply a mush – an exasperating, vomity mush.

"I don't think I can go on with my painting," he told her, just barely restraining his anger.

"Not go on with your painting?" She gave him a startled, annoyed glance. "Well, just what do you plan to do then? You can't stay shut up in the house every day without employment. I think you're going overboard with this whole thing. You have been sulking for weeks now and its time to stop it. Plenty of blind men live full, happy lives, and you're not even blind!"

"No – No I am not blind. I see grey."

*

He prowled along 25th Street, smoking cigarettes. The clouds of smoke that came from his throat gave him some comfort – at least they were meant to be grey. He watched the prostitutes linger on the corners, haunting as ghouls. He walked by a few, eyeing them nervously. No, – They were simply disgusting. In his condition, relationships with women, even the most sordid sort, were out of the question. Greg was living in a world neither black nor white; it had none of the charm of an old movie. It was a world both ugly and twisted that filled him with pain and repulsion.

He gently caressed his eyelashes, feeling their fine feathery texture with his thumb and forefinger, and then ran his thumbs over his eyeballs. They were moist, somewhat slick, and the touch made them water. Everything he saw through them was grey; he was unable to detect pigmentation of any sort.

"These damn eyes," he murmured.

They were really the cause of his suffering. He remembered Cassie's words: 'At least you're not blind' she had said. It was easy for her to talk that way – but it was quite clear that she did not realise how much he suffered. He could not even make love to her any more – love to a woman who he had previously found incredibly sexy and attractive. Now when he saw her, she looked like a giant rat. She did not realise how precious colour was.

"Sight without colour is worthless," he thought. "These eyes are a torture. I *would* be better off blind."

'Blind men live full, happy lives.' Those were her words.

He touched his eyeballs with his fingertips and felt their slick softness. A cruel thrill ran through him. Sliding his forefingers behind his upper eyelids, he began to dig; feeling the hot circles he began to gouge. Like fingering peeled grapes; dipping behind the cornea. Panting, groping back towards the optic nerves, he damned those lenses, those partitions that refracted, perverted dreary light.

With a little cry, a moan of joint horror and satisfaction, he had them. He felt the oozing down his cheeks, the pain, and then, as he clenched his tongue between his teeth, the ecstasy of blackness.

The Book of Tides
David Rix

On this lonely Scottish beach, it was rare to see people of any kind and those few who did pass by were usually heavily loaded walker-type wanderers tramping through the hills – a certain breed of people distilled by the distance from anywhere populated. But now the ragged girl had been sitting there for three days and when he finally approached her, he realised that she looked different somehow. A different species of human. She seemed too lightly dressed for long walks in the wilderness.

He approached her, realising that he was treading softly though he wasn't sure why. She hadn't moved much since she had arrived – always just sitting or lying there in the sand looking dejected. She was curled up now in a tight human comma and she gave him no response as he approached, so he put down his bag and knelt beside her. She looked young – scarily younger than he was. Was she even alive? he wondered. She wasn't moving and, now that he was up close, he realised that her face was terribly pale – the sort of paleness that almost looks transparent and makes any skin blemish show up like a wound. This thing was never living, surely, he thought. She was an empty husk, the wind whipping sand over her and playing with her hair. He shuddered at the implications of a death on his doorstep. People would come – wanting to talk to him. The police would have to clear the mess up and his isolation would be shattered.

Maybe he could at least haul her down below high tide level or something, for the strong currents here to take away somewhere else.

He remained looking at her for a long time without reaching any conclusions. He realised that he was going to have to touch her instead – to see if there was any ghost of warmth or pulse in her flesh. And as his fingers touched her neck, he realised that her skin was cold and wet – seemed as cold as the sand in which she lay. And he sighed.

But then she gave a sudden twitch and he flinched away, aware of two eyes staring at him. He felt a wash of panic and the immediate reaction was to leave right then. Just jump up and walk away. He had solved the riddle, after all – she was a living person. What more interest was there? But he hesitated, his brain ticking over.

"Ok," he said reluctantly after a long pause, in which she just stared at him in motionless silence. "I had better take you home, hadn't I? You – you need to be warm? Right?"

She made no sound.

"Um . . ."

She blinked.

He didn't want to touch her again but there was no alternative. As though trying to work out how best to pick up something very exotic and unpredictable, he took her shoulder and gently shoved her into a sitting position. Her eyes were staring a question at him, he realised, which he didn't know how to answer – so instead he just concentrated on what he was doing. He got an arm under her legs and the other round her back, then lifted her up bodily, dimly aware of her hand fastening onto his jacket. She looked lighter than she was and the reality of her weight surprised him. But even so, he was easily strong enough to get her up in the air and her arms went round his neck like an exhausted child. Up close, he could smell the reek of sea and the human body on her together – brine and cold sweat. It was a puzzling smell coming from someone unfamiliar.

Slowly he made his way towards his home, occasionally pausing to shift her weight and trying to ignore his racing thoughts, which chattered in panic at what he was doing. Trying to convince him that he should be far away from all this. His home was a lonely looking old building set a few metres above the sea. It sat there slightly surreally within a small walled off area, surrounded by wild brown hillside. It looked like a discarded toy that someone had thrown there, a simple square brick of a structure with a few outbuildings and a small boathouse down on the beach. There was no road to it as such, just a rough rutted track leading away inland. There was not even a car waiting in the drive. The only means of transport here were a battered old bicycle and his small boat shut carefully away from the weather. The house really did look as though it had no right to be there. A few rather stunted trees kept him company, but most of this land was bare.

Even from a distance though, the strange forest of poles that surrounded it stood out. It was a forest of elegantly twisted driftwood and spars, raised upright and set in the ground, then festooned with oddments that the sea had cast up. Each one like a surreal tree. Choice artworks from the various tides he had read and recorded suspended there as mementoes – all given a uniform aesthetic by the processes of the sea. It was a strange patch of art in the wilderness that few people ever even saw.

Getting the door open and her through it was challenging but he managed it eventually and then she was sliding from his grasp onto the sofa in his impossibly cluttered front room. Her eyes were closed again now and he realised that she had begun to shiver. She hadn't been before, he registered. Her flesh still felt far too cold to be living. He stared down at her, his mind turning like clockwork, trying to compute all the things he would need to do now. And in which order. Kettle. Coal. Hot soup. Kindling. Drink. Newspaper for the fire. Perhaps she would want to get out of those freezing clothes. And if so, into what? If she showed any sign of moving at all, that is. He bent to the fireplace, hastily and clumsily shovelling the ashes out and rebuilding the fire. Balled up newspaper was shoved in there, followed by a scattering of kindling, and he lit it quickly. Then he just came to a stop, and continued staring at her as though, for all her stillness, she was putting on a performance for him.

As the fire began to take hold and radiate, she finally began to open up to it. Her shivering faded a little and she finally stretched out her hands towards it and gave a huge sigh.

"Is there anything I can get you?" he asked.

She shook her head.

"No – thank you," she managed in a low voice. "If I may – I will just go to sleep for a bit and warm up. This fire is amazing."

And that was her first verbal communication, her voice so quiet it was almost a whisper, yet light and clear.

"Of course," he whispered. "I wont be – I I mean, I will be here . . . if you . . . if you need anything . . ."

But she had already closed her eyes.

Looking at her, he still couldn't shake off the feeling that he was looking at a corpse. Now she was on his sofa, he could see her chest rising and falling, but her pale skin and lank hair still looked dead. However, a few minutes later, she was actually snoring quietly.

Outside, the day was progressing and he suddenly remembered the bag he had left on the beach. He gave a low laugh, realising just how much this unexpected visitor had thrown him into confusion. He hurried urgently outside again on a mission to fetch it, then settled down, idly going through the stacks of material it contained.

- Intact light bulb – clear glass – how gentle the sea could be if it chose
- A wooden ruler
- A length of steel cable, snapped and with the strands trailing viciously at the end.
- Swimsuit bottom with a thread tied roughly to the waistband – that was a mystery.
- A battered old floppy disk
- A fragment of some kind of dial containing a circle of measuring increments on a weathered metal face.
- A sodden pencil
- A bird skull
- A necklace of shell fragments, almost intact though with a few missing pieces. Taken from the sea. Constructed. Then back into the sea. And now washed up again for him.
- A piece of bright purple cloth – thin silk – maybe from a head scarf.

He laid them all out on the table and examined them, one by one. He tested the strength and flexibility of the metal cable, which was immense, then fingered the swimsuit thoughtfully, a frown on his face. Something about this went far beyond its simple appearance, he could tell that much. It was iridescent blue and quite small. Whoever had worn it had been quite willowy. It was also quite skimpy, just thin bands of material that would have shown a fair amount of arse. It was just a simple bikini bottom. But with a long chord attached to the waist in a neat knot and ending with a frayed twist.

Finally, he put it to his face, not sniffing it for that would have been little use after its time in the sea, but instead feeling it. Trying to read it.

And he winced and put it down sharply, shaking his head. It wasn't a violent pain he felt or a panicked pain, but a leaden one. A pain that clouded inside him like a cold mist. And he knew what that meant.

At last he crossed the room, sat down at his ancient looking beige computer and began to write.

The girl is in the water. She swims gently. The water glows faintly with phosphorescence. Behind her trails a thread and what she has tied to it. People like to judge in life and people like to judge in death. People said of her afterwards that she was selfish. Her mother never realised that she was a poet. Secret texts. Loneliness and helplessness. You can't change the world around you. Feelings of guilt and cowardice. The razor tied to her swimsuit. She stared up at the moon and stars and the distant lights of the shore with nothing clouding her eyes now. The night is beautiful. Warm air. Water that flickered faintly with reflected light. The falling tide. Floating gently on her back. Cuts wrists in a T shape. The first good, the second less so as her wounded hand trembled.

What force lies behind this event?

He sat back with a deep sigh, then glanced at his visitor again. He was not used to having someone with him when he worked but she was totally dead to the world on the sofa, mouth open, one leg flopped out onto the floor, still snoring gently. There was something unexpectedly cute about that snore that made him pause and stare at her with a small frown. Under the influence of the fire, her skin was already flushing and looking healthier and, under the ruined clothes and seaweed-like hair, she had a distinct sharp-edged beauty, which he couldn't help registering.

But even as he stared at her, she seemed to feel it for she shifted abruptly and opened her eyes.

"How are you feeling?" he asked awkwardly.

"Better . . . thank you," she said, her voice slightly less hollow than before. She sat up with an effort, holding her head, and turned towards the fire eagerly.

"So, who are you?" he asked at last.

"I am Feather," she said.

"Just Feather?"

She nodded and he accepted it with a smile.

"I didn't expect this," she said at last, gesturing vaguely at the window. "I'm not used to such wilderness. There's nothing to eat out here, except for a bit of shellfish. And it is all so exposed. I'm not surprised no one lives here."

The fire was at its hottest now – the coals a heap of glowing orange, and she stretched out her feet towards it luxuriantly.

"Yeah," he said. "Not many do. There are . . . well, it's a long way to anywhere from here. Where were you trying to get to?"

She shrugged, with a faint ironic grin. "I wanted wilderness," she said. "But I didn't expect it to be quite so inhospitable. Believe it or not I am basically a city girl. I come from London."

"Right," he said. Words felt like alien things in his mouth and he struggled to think what to say next. But she spoke first.

"Do you mind if I take these clothes off? They stink."

"Of course not," he said. "I have a robe you can use. And – and I will get some dinner ready maybe?" A look of hunger came to her face. "What do you – like to eat?" he asked and she gave him a crooked smile over her shoulder.

"Anything – seriously. If it wont kill me or make me see green goblins then it is fine." She sighed. "And at the moment I might even take the goblins."

In spite of himself, he found himself grinning shyly. She leaned down and fumbled for her shoelaces.

"I am not sure I ought to do this near a naked flame," she murmured and he was surprised to see a flash of real humour on her face. "There might be some sort of explosion . . ."

"I'm sorry?"

"Been wearing these for rather a long time," she said, tugging off a shoe.

He caught a faint hint of the smell of it and she gave an awkward smile.

"Um," she murmured, "I await your instructions."

"Yeah," he murmured. "Just dump it all straight in the washing machine in the kitchen if you want – or rather, I will. Leave them here. I mean . . . and I will . . . do them . . . for you."

She nodded and kicked off her other shoe, followed by her socks. Then she began undoing her trouser belt and he hastily exited the room, vaguely aware of her dry glance following him.

*

"I sense things going on here," she said.

He quickly swallowed another mouthful of their simple dinner. "I'm sorry?"

"You are a collector?"

"Sort of, yes," he muttered. "I'm a . . ."

He hesitated, then gave her a stubborn look.

"I'm a writer."

"So what do you write? Do you tell stories?"

He shrugged awkwardly. "I suppose."

He felt increasingly uncomfortable though. It was hard to answer this kind of question – partly because nobody had ever asked it before but also because it meant actually defining it – and defining things could sometimes be a sure way of killing them. He waved vaguely around at the room and the vast array of odds and ends it contained.

"Those," he said. "Every tide. Rubbish, I suppose. But if you look hard enough, you can read rubbish as clearly as any great literature. And . . . it all has stories to tell if you can find them."

He sighed uncomfortably. But Feather was staring at him curiously – a gleam of interest in her eyes. Finally she gave a small nod. "You tell the stories of the sea," she murmured, as though there was nothing strange about that.

"Of the tides," he said. "Of all the tides. Two stories every day."

"Wow," she murmured, staring round at the piles of materials. He followed her eyes, trying to read her expression. Feeling the prickling sensation you get when something familiar is being examined by someone else, leaving you with an unexpected sense of the alien.

"Every tide has a story to tell," he murmured at last. "Stories from somewhere, somebody. I just write them down."

"From the tidal debris?" she asked, wondering. He nodded and she continued examining with her eyes the seemingly endless array of rubbish that the sea had cast up. Finally she returned her attention to him. "And what about me?" she said with another flicker of that wry humour. "Am I now a part of this . . . rubbish?"

She sat back from her empty plate and he gave her a curious look. That aspect of things hadn't occurred to him.

"You picked me up on the beach after all," she said, grinning quietly. "What story did my tide tell? Is it about me?"

"I . . ." he hesitated. "I don't know. I don't think I read that tide yet. I – I will need to read properly." He hesitated a moment, realising where this was leading. He was reluctant because this was supposed to be something private, not through any conscious decision, but because that was the way it always was. He was reluctant because he already felt tense all over at the presence of another and how could you read like that? He felt reluctant because he didn't know what to do or what to say that could actually explain any of this. But Feather's eyes were gleaming with interest and there was a curious twist to the corner of her mouth that wasn't a smile – and he could find no reason not to continue. He gave a sigh, then stood up and crossed to his desk. He looked around vaguely for a second chair for her, which he knew wasn't there, but it didn't matter for she simply settled behind him, leaning comfortably on his. He quickly opened up *The Book of Tides* computer file and started skimming through it towards the present, while Feather stared at him and it curiously.

"All this?" she asked. He nodded. "It's huge," she murmured as page after page of small texts flashed passed on the screen.

"Each one is a separate story," he said. "And together they make up one . . . big . . . novel."

The file reached the end. She read briefly: *The girl is in the water. She swims gently. The water glows faintly with phosphorescence.* But he cut her off and backtracked a few pages until he reached an empty one. His eyes wandered over to the stacks of material, neatly arranged tide by tide – and picked out the pile he wanted.

"This is your tide," he said. "The tide you came in on three days ago."

- Military Jacket – shredded.
- Distress flares x 6
- One male shoe
- A fragment of cloth
- A girl's hairband
- A broken flower pot
- A cardboard carton that had contained cheap wine
- A length of rope with a knot in it
- A worn plastic warning sign – explosive
- A bulldog clip

He picked up the shoe and held it thoughtfully. It had once been smart, made of black leather – very businesslike – but it was well worn even before it ended up in the sea. The leather was bulging and split and deep indentations had been left in the heel. It had also been burnt somehow – there was a certain charring to it. Had it just been discarded as a cast-off? Or was there something more lingering in this shoe? There was something about it that stirred him. He sniffed it curiously and flexed it in his hands. A sense of pain, though not quite like the swim suit – and he felt his heart sinking. There was a scream somewhere – not a groan of despair, but a full throated scream.

Then the hairband came to hand – a sad piece of garish purple and black elastic cloth adorned with a small metal skull. When he unfolded it, he found the word 'fuck' hidden deep within its elastic folds – soon followed by 'the world'. It had been a young girl piece – the stroppy and rebellious goth with a score to settle with the world. He put that to his face as well and abruptly flinched away with a grunt.

"What is it?" Feather asked. He glanced at her, his heart beating heavily. He wondered for a moment how to put that hairband into spoken words, before immediately giving up. There was no way to express the almost bottomless rage it had contained, except by writing it down.

And then the length of rope. It appeared to have been cut and sealed to this short length, not frayed, and this also sent a little prickle down his back. He glanced up at Feather in silence. What the hell was all this stuff? He felt an uncomfortable sensation in his stomach and on his skin and gave Feather another heavy stare.

"What is it?" she demanded. "Why are you looking at me as though I murdered your first-born son?"

"I . . . don't . . ." He couldn't explain though. Spoken words were never much use. "The plant pot is corporate," he said, as much to fill the silence with words as anything. "No question. A pot that sat in an office or bank housing some plastic twigs. It reads dead to me."

"Is it?"

He nodded, and quickly typed a note to that effect.

"Cheap wine," he said. "And an explosive sign."

"Meaning?"

"A burnt shoe," he said, "and . . . and a lot of rage. Something has happened. Something more extreme. Are you angry, Feather?"

"Not really," she said blankly. "Are you really reading these things? Are you a fortune teller?"

"I am just trying to find the stories in them," he muttered, putting down the last items.

"What do you see in me then?" she asked.

"I . . ."

He paused.

"You read all those – what about me?"

"In you personally?" he asked, almost formally. She nodded. Trying to forget that this was a person, he reached out hesitantly and touched her shoulder, then leaned in close up against her robe, while she stared down in silence.

"Sorry," he said at last, "I must write it down. I – I cannot . . . talk."

He quickly turned to the computer.

Fugitive. On the run as a misfit. Never matched the normal units of measurement. Far from normal life. Physical pain and emotional misery and confusion. Wandering – always."

She stared at him with wide eyes. "Fugitive?" she stammered. He winced.

"I don't mean you committed a crime," he muttered urgently. She nodded slowly.

"Why did I come out here?" she murmured. "I wanted the wilderness – I wanted to escape . . ."

She drew a long heavy breath.

"And . . ."

She suddenly lifted up her robe, revealing her upper legs. He stared for a moment before picking out the faint network of white lines of scar tissue that traced there. He stared up at her – feeling some large emotion rolling inside him. Something he was completely unequipped to deal with or express. He could say nothing, but Feather didn't seem to mind. She let the robe fall again, then fixed the screen with a piercing look.

"That's about right," she whispered. "But – did you just deduce that . . . or?"

He swallowed. "I'm not sure," he said. "Let me carry on." He picked up the shoe and the hairband for a moment and gave a groan. "There is something really frightening in here," he said.

"Um . . ."

But he was already typing.

So much rage. But you have to know it from within. From without is blind and you see nothing. I see exhilaration. I see the misfit finally lashing out at what squashed her and tried to shape her world in ways it could not be shaped. The exhilaration of extremity and of the final escape.

"This is too easy," he said, trying not to catch her eyes. The expression on Feather's face was unnerving. "Ok," he said softly, "this is the story of your tide."

White light. No pain. Just a white oblivion that obliterates everything – both you and that which squashes you down. A room where many many people sat working, spinning the nets of lines and angles that are the world. They surrounded her, with eyes of glass and hands of wire. Until they realised what she was. She stared round the room, taking in the fleeing figures, and those cowering in corners, too scared even to move and attempt to get away. Their eyes were wide. Maybe this wasn't so futile after all, she thought. Maybe this would instigate some thought and questioning. But then she gave a sigh. Why? That had never happened before.

"No politics," she whispered. "No religion. No race. No ideas. No stories. Just truth . . . and reality."
White light. No pain. Just a white oblivion . . .

He surfaced from that, becoming aware of Feather behind him, staring blankly.

"Are you saying I'm a . . ." She shook her head. "I don't understand. What does this have to do with me?" she asked guardedly.

"That's the story," he murmured. There wasn't much else that he could say. He drew a deep breath and again pressed the hair band to his face. So much rage. Dull, helpless rage. Then he glanced at the text again, as though seeing it for the first time – wondering where it had come from.

"No stories?" he quoted, puzzled.

She gave a shiver. "I don't like stories."

He gave her a sharp look, feeling a touch of dismay at the words. There was a look in her face that frightened him. "Why not?"

She gave him a wan stare. "Maybe because they have too much power in people's minds – to start distorting reality."

"But . . ."

He broke off – his limited powers of speech deserting him completely. She finally stepped away, looking cloudy and unhappy.

"Is any part of this true or are you just telling tales?" she asked at last, sounding almost fierce. "Did some girl really blow up a building? It is just stories, isn't it?"

"What part of a story isn't true?" he asked, feeling puzzled and helpless.

"Um – the part that is unreal?"

"I don't know what's real or unreal," he muttered. "It's all the same . . ."

"I . . ." Feather shook her head. "Stories have wrecked the world," she cried dramatically. "People thinking things that are not. Fucking fantasies."

He stared at her in amazement.

"You told me that physical pain and emotional misery and confusion were my foundation in my life – and I can thank stories for that. People telling stories and expecting me to just believe them. What to do. What to think. What fucking religion to believe in. Even what to eat. Singing fantasies at me. It's all stories. And my confusion when the world I saw had nothing whatever to do with any of that? What am I supposed to make of that?"

He was silent. Then Feather suddenly sagged and gave a smile, looking very tired. "Sorry," she said softly. "You scared me a little. For a moment there, I thought you really were trying to be a fortune teller. And I am still not quite my usual bonny self."

"Of course," he murmured uncertainly. *Really trying to be a fortune teller?* What the heck was the answer to that? "Don't worry. Just . . ." He gestured vaguely at the couch. "I think I need a rest as well," he muttered, glancing sourly at the materials beside him. His heart was still beating with frightening speed and, when he rose to his feet, he was startled to find his legs week and trembly. He gave her a long look, aware of some form of pleading in his eyes, but unsure what he was pleading for. To make the world simple again? To not exist?

135

To restore the isolation that was the basic tenet of his life? Feather sat down with a sigh, staring at the floor and he slowly began clearing away the remains of the dinner.

    In the kitchen, he ran water with a sigh of relief and slowly washed up – enjoying the fact that he was alone again. He leisurely packed all the utensils away, then forced himself to re-enter the living room, only to find that she seemed to have fallen asleep now. Either that or she had simply curled up and shut her eyes to close herself off. He wasn't sure. After a moment, he slowly tramped upstairs and grabbed the quilt from his bed, then draped it over her, tucking it nervously around her face. She gave a sleepy murmur and squirmed into it gratefully. Finally, after a last long look down at her, he stepped outside into the cold night wind and drew a deep breath. He could feel his face relaxing for the first time in several hours and he sighed, feeling the night air cutting into his cheeks. A mist had drifted in and was covering the hills but there was enough moonlight to see that, and to make out the vague shapes of the land across the water. In the midst of that darkness there were just two lights showing – shining out from the scattered buildings. The stillness here was absolute and even the gentle wind in the heather and the soft sound of the waves on the beach couldn't break that. This really was a lonely place, he realised, and now he felt a sharp appreciation – Feather's presence had reminded him of that somehow.

    Finally he stepped back inside, stood for another long moment staring down at her sleeping face, then finally tramped upstairs to find his own bed, trying to put images of his guest from his mind.

*

City. Night. London. Tall, cramped buildings clustering over narrow labyrinthine one-way streets. Shops of many kinds and many languages. Grim apartment blocks. People crowded together in a desperate attempt to exist within the shimmering stench of the city. Camden. Soho. Brick Lane.

Anywhere where the roads were narrow and murky and where neon flashed and glimmered. It was silent, however. No cars or buses moving. Only Feather – running. Running. Head down. Exhausted. Casting dark glances round her. Cliffs of stone and glass and narrow cracks of sky. But even here, impossible to lose yourself in.

Then there are figures ahead and Feather darts to the side. Black and fluorescent yellow jackets that spoke of the official. Feather running down a corridor of low red lights against black. Obviously frightened. Gazing round with wide eyes.

"Stop telling stories about me," she screamed.

"Feather," I call, wanting to help but unsure how. She flinches and gazes at me with fear in her eyes. Why is she frightened of me?

Running again. Away from me down the corridor of red lights.

And I am running after her. I have to. Something here needs clearing up – I don't understand. But others are running after her as well, I realise. I finally see her pursuers and they all look like me. I am an older man after all – and she looks so young.

Then the lights suddenly end in a place where something big lurks. Gleaming metal and heat. Dead end. Feather stops in despair and the pursuers swarm over her. Feather down. Vanishing under hands. And mine are among them. My fingers are on her leg. Tearing fabric. My fingers pushing into her flesh, which parts for me like dough. There is a thin scream.

Then my hand on her face holding her down on the tarmac. No struggling. Then the knife going cleanly across . . .

He woke up with a jolt and a gasp, gazing into the faint dawn light of his bedroom with eyes that felt huge. His heart was throbbing and prickly cold ran all over his body, his leaden limbs barely able to move.

For a long few minutes he just lay there, breathing deeply and slowly smoothing the nightmare away. The window was a dull grey square in the almost blackness of his room and he focussed on it, willing his mind to imagine the soothing wild shoreline outside. Trying to imagine the harsh pounding of the waves sweeping like tongues – tongues filled with stories. Of those stories, he could be the master. At that thought, his heart began to slow, the ache in his limbs fading. He quietly pursed his lips and produced a long whistle – just one note that continued until his breath died. Any desire for sleep seemed to have completely faded now. There seemed little point just turning over and closing his eyes, so instead he got up and tramped downstairs. Feather was an inert heap on the sofa and he found himself staring down at her, his eyes prickling with unexpected tears. She did indeed seem so very young somehow – though in reality she must surely be somewhere in her twenties. This was a mystery, he decided. The mystery of the stranger – the other person. A mystery that his brain seemed unequipped to fathom. Those were feelings that he had tried to escape from before when he first came out here, but now here they were back again.

After a while, Feather gave a small sleepy shift and sigh under the quilt and he turned away unhappily, heading for the door. Now that he was up in this time of dull pre-dawn light, he might as well catch the night tide. Sleep was over today and maybe there would be something interesting on the beach. Something to continue this bizarre novel.

And the first thing he saw when he stepped onto the strand line stopped him in his tracks. It was strewn with passports. He found sixteen of the sodden documents scattered along the beach, tangled up in seaweed. Still somewhat haunted by the feelings of his nightmare and by Feather herself, he felt a prickle of amazement. He thoughtfully added them to his bag – the foundation stone of the pattern of this tide – and began looking around for more debris that would give them context and help unlock their stories. But he felt an uncertainty that he had never felt before. He gave a sharp and rather humourless laugh. The turmoil Feather had induced in him, and which he could sense in her, seemed to be reflecting in nature. There was something unnerving about these passports and the sea seemed to be filled with tales of violence and suicide everywhere he looked. For the first time that he could remember, he felt reluctant to read what the sea was telling him.

Finally, his bag weighted down, he made for home again, scrambling over the rocks and grassy sand at the head of the beach. He tramped into his garden, through the forest of driftwood, then paused in the doorway just as the first hint of a pale sun appeared, cutting through the milky sky. There was a faint mist drifting over the ground now and the many flotsam-decked poles of his garden loomed out of it like surreal ceremonial objects. Like a pathway of totems. From here, he could see the whole of the remote sea inlet that he called home. The familiar pattern of hills that enclosed him. The familiar islands dotting the sea in the distance. This was where a mountain range fell into the sea, after all, he thought with a smile, and it did indeed seem a safe distance from anything human.

Then the stillness was cut by a sound behind him and he glanced round, realising with a slight flinch that he wasn't alone. Feather had joined him in the doorway, leaning against the frame, and he gave her a sleepy but welcoming look. She stared out at the garden.

"Good morning," she whispered.

He watched her. He was subtly proud of his show of marine debris here, even though there were few people to ever really see it. Just the occasional passing walker. And now the perfect melding of art and morning – sea and mist – somehow stifling any desire to speak. It was the sort of morning that reminded you of the power of silence and of the bleak magical inhumanity of the world.

"It is so quiet here," Feather said at last. "So far from any of the noises of life."

She paused for a moment and the silence came back.

"Funny," she said at last with a tiny giggle, "how we always associate sound with humanity."

"Hmm?"

"It isn't silent," she said. "And yet – it seems silent."

"What can you hear?" he asked and, though he still felt wary of her, he was pleased to find that the atmosphere between them was relaxed and comfortable.

She shrugged against him. "The sea on the beach," she said in a drowsy monotone. "I can hear it on the rocks and on the sand separately. I can hear the wind – calm, but its gently shaking the grass. I can hear it in the bushes and I can hear it in your stuff there. Your sea stuff. Things are moving. I can hear it on the roof and in the walls. And that's it. That's silence?"

He grinned. "That's one of the beauties of isolation," he said.

"What are the other beauties?"

"No one to see or hear you in return, perhaps," he said. "You can make a racket at any time and nobody cares. You can do what you please really. Be what you please."

She gave an enthusiastic smile.

"I like that," she said. "Yes. You really can do what you want. You can flop out naked on the beach and nobody will get scared. You can go running round screaming your head off and no one gives you any disapproving looks."

"Um – yeah," he said, unable to avoid smiling and finally moving to go indoors.

"Yeah," she agreed sleepily. She glanced at the bag in his hand. "Another story?" she asked curiously.

"Yes," he said, briefly shaking it. He stepped inside and spread the pieces out with practiced hands. "A very strange one," he murmured.

- Passports x 16
- The stock from a shotgun
- A black leather belt with metal-reinforced holes and a missing buckle
- A mangled bird cage
- A length of thin chord
- Three non-matching children's shoes
- A cracked plastic dinner plate
- Thirteen wine bottle corks
- A length of electrical cable with a standard three-pin plug
- A hair band – pale blue and cute this time
- A half of eggshell
- Shreds of soft fabric – underwear-style maybe

He stared at them for a while, then glanced over his shoulder at Feather, who was watching curiously.

"This is really an unusual tide," he said at last. "I have never seen a horde quite like this – and . . ."

He spread his arms in a dramatic shrug.

"It's frightening. I'm not really sure . . ."

Feather made a questioning noise.

"I – I – I am not sure . . . What stories are these? What is . . ?"

It was, as usual, hard to articulate anything though and he forced himself to shut up and concentrate. This was just another tide after all. Just another story to be found and recorded. He grabbed the passports impatiently, examining them – feeling the small thrill that they sent through him. The faint hint of the unnerving. He tried to feel them in more detail, but he wasn't sure. All he could feel was Feather's eyes on his back.

"Nationality," he murmured. "Nationality . . ."

He quickly counted them off.

"All British," he said. "Nothing strange there. Except," he murmured, "yes. They are all young. Like students. Your sort of age."

He put them down heavily with a sigh and reached for something else.

"Look," Feather said, coming up behind him. "I still don't really understand . . ."

He glanced up at her, feeling a twinge in his stomach. Please don't ask me to explain any more, he begged silently. To cover it, he quickly picked up item after item and felt them carefully.

How the hell could a birdcage make its way here? He shook it sharply. "Restraint," he said softly.

"Or . . . cherishing – cherished pet? Protection?" He glanced at her, looking confused.

"Really?"

She shrugged. He quickly continued. "Look – shotgun stock. Leather belt. Electrical wire."

"Hunting for food – electric light – keeping your bloody trousers up . . ." she murmured, but he ignored her.

He picked up the tattered knicker fabric – just flaps of very soft cotton hanging on a thread of elastic. He fingered it and felt it

141

carefully, then sat back and clasped his hands behind his head. "Rape?" he wondered aloud. "There is violence everywhere."

"The sea is violent," she said softly.

"Yes – no – I mean, maybe."

He sat back and gave a huge sigh. "The world is a rotten place, isn't it," he said heavily. "I get the feeling that you know that . . . all too well. Wherever you have come from. Right?"

"I really don't understand," she said earnestly, sitting down on the sofa. "How does this work?"

"What?"

"I mean – what about everything else on the beach that you didn't pick up? What about other beaches?"

He spread his arms, suddenly trembling slightly. "I – don't really know. I just tell stories – like everyone else."

"Yeah?"

He drew a deep breath.

"Look – I know you don't like it," he stammered. "But – but . . . I have to . . ."

He suddenly flung the fabric down.

"What is this," he yelled suddenly, painfully aware of the almost whining tone in his voice. He jumped to his feet and glared at the latest piles, trembling. "What am I reading in this thing? It feels like there's a bloody war on," he muttered. "I can't stop trembling. And all this mess – it never used to be like this."

"Um . . ."

"There's just so much violence – so much . . ."

She jumped up and rested her hands on his shoulders, rubbing gently.

"Please relax," she said with a smile, but he tensed violently and pulled away wih a gasp. Feather stared at him in dismay.

"Hey," she murmured. "What is it?"

"Sorry," he said. "I just – can't . . ." He drew a deep breath. "Look – um . . . would you mind leaving me to it for a few minutes. I can't really concentrate . . ."

Even as he said it, he hated himself for it, but there didn't seem to be any choice. All he felt was confusion.

"Um – sure," Feather said with a slight frown, backing away. "I'll go out for a bit."

"You don't need . . ."

She gave a sigh. "I think you've spent way too much time on your own," she said. "I am not an alien, you know."

"What?"

"I am not an alien. I may be younger than you but I am just a person. You are looking at me as though I was another species."

"I know what you are," he said, trying force himself to calm down.

"Yes," she muttered. "I know – you're the Fortune Teller."

"Look," he managed. "There's something very strange going on in all this stuff. In this novel. Something serious. And whether you like stories or not . . ."

She gave a little sound of discomfort.

"Suddenly I am not sure what is real any more," she muttered, rubbing urgently at one eyebrow. He gave a wan smile.

"Welcome to my world," he said.

She stared at him again for a moment.

"I am going out for a bit," she said at last. "You are making me nervous."

He stared after her in dismay as she slipped out with an uncomfortable half smile. Then, glancing back at the passports, he punched the wall hard, realising that any reading was now further away than ever. There was a savage knot of guilt inside him now and a bitter wish that she hadn't gone at all. What the hell was that about? It was ridiculous that he could possibly want here there – or anyone for that matter. But he felt a bizarre tingling sensation in the pit of his stomach – a brief wash of sex – and cringed in despair. He gave a long groan and sat down heavily at the dinner table. The tide pile almost seemed to grin at him from the desk – nothing more than a confusing mass of malevolence.

*

In the end, Feather wasn't gone long. Less than an hour later, she slipped back in with a curious look in her eyes that sent a prickle over his already nervous skin. She gave him a hesitant stare.

"How's it going?" she asked, absently curious. He shrugged dismissively.

"Nothing . . . much," he stammered. She sat down and stared into space for a moment, while his heart felt heavier and heavier. Whatever was hanging in the air now was very bad indeed.

"Um," she said at last.

"Yes?"

"You, er – you were out searching earlier, weren't you?"

Why did she want to know that?

"Yes," he grunted. "Very early."

She hesitated. "Where did you go?"

"Not far."

"Then you haven't found the bodies yet?"

Whatever he had expected her to say, that wasn't it. He watched her in astonishment, trying to work out what she meant.

"The what?" he asked at last.

She sighed. "I had better show you," she murmured, rising to her feet. She shook her head blearily. "You're going to like this."

"Ok," he managed. He followed her to the door.

Outside, she set off on a quick wordless tramp along the head of the beach and, about ten minutes later, they scrambled over a small ridge of grass and rocks and he glimpsed a huddled form – then a second. And he finally realised that she had been speaking literally. He stared blankly at the two bodies, then hurried after her down to them. Both were young men, dressed in ordinary clothes – both had their hands tied behind their backs.

"There's another on the other side of those dunes," she said. "Come on."

He silently followed her and now a teenage girl was laying face down, legs half buried in sand.

"I have found five altogether," she said. "Scattered along the beach. Washed up here. I don't know what they are. Is this another part of your tide you were trying to read?"

He shook his head, feeling utterly unable to place all this.

"I am going to search them," she said.

He gave her a startled look. "Why?" he asked stupidly.

"If there is anything interesting on them, you can put it in your novel. Right?"

He winced silently as she crouched down beside the sodden form and began going through her clothes. Her zipped trouser pocket produced a wallet and she examined it quickly.

Sodden money. Business cards. Credit cards. Misc pieces of paper.

"Catherine Bennet," she said, reading a small piece of plastic. She handed him the wallet and he took it reluctantly. There was a photo of a young man in one compartment, now almost obliterated by the sea.

Then Feather started going over her body, probing it, apparently looking for injuries. And eventually she found it – a single neat knife wound in the back of her neck.

"Any ideas?" she asked. He shook his head dumbly. "You are the reader," she muttered. "Tell me what these are."

He sighed, trying to remember the feel of the items on his desk and reluctantly staring around the beach, hoping for more clues. Presumably this was all a part of the same tide. But the detritus here also just seemed meaningless. Just fragments of rope, plastic and paper. He was seeing things through Feather's eyes, he realised. Just the familiar world. He turned his back on her and tried to recapture the sense of violence he had felt earlier. The ropes used to bind . . . the sticks used to beat . . .

Then something unnaturally round caught his eye and he leaned over to investigate. It was a button – a large one. Just a plain brown disk with four holes and a ridge round the edge. He picked it up and felt it curiously. There was a shred of cloth attached – just a dull brown and rather coarse. He wasn't sure, but it might have been tweed.

"How old is she?" he asked. "Any idea?"

Feather glanced at the card. "Seventeen," she said.

"And the rest?"

She shrugged. "All the same. All as young as she is – I think. Can you read something?"

"Let me see that," he said, reaching out for the card. He fingered it uncertainly, trying to work out what it was for. It wasn't a credit card and didn't seem to be a travel card. It was labelled *Youth ID* and bore the logo of the home office in all its deceptive innocence – but that was all. *Building a safe, just and tolerant society.* On the back was a magnetic strip. There was a cloying and slightly stifling feeling about it, but even that didn't make much sense.

Or did it?

He stared bleakly at Feather. What war was being fought here?

He turned his attention back to the beach and scanned around again, strolling further down the strand line and feeling the sentences coming together in his head. He stared round at the sea, always so comfortingly inhuman, for all the stories it told.

The heart raced at the sheer impossibility of knowing what was happening coupled with the urgent need to understand it before it was too late. But it could never be understood, Catherine thought, her muscles taut against her bonds. There was nothing to understand. And everything anyone had ever said on the subject of humanity, life and death was wrong.

So what should you do? With your life-time measured in seconds. What could you think about? Just a storm of memories, none of them relevant to the present.

Outside came the distant sound of gunfire – just three shots – and the murmur of voices. The sound of a crowd. But she ignored it. Then there was a whimper and a twisted breath beside her as Steve fell forward on his face. Then the prickling awareness of someone behind her – her neck suddenly an agony of exposure. Someone had said something, but she wasn't sure what. She was shoved sharply.

"Well?" the voice demanded.

"I am not listening to you," she said dreamily. "You don't make sense."

For that, she found herself shoved forward onto her face and pinned down with a knee in the small of her back – the feel of something cold at the back of her neck.

"I wish there was a hundred like you," he said sharply, in a voice that would have been farcical if he wasn't the one carrying the knife. "Right here. Why do I have to work so effing hard at this? Have you no respect?"

She glanced round at him, just a dull and shabby man with an anonymous face behind her. The face of an old man, lined and set in a permanent sulk. Brown tweed – worn and torn and marked with blood spots.

"Yeah," she managed. It hurt and her breath was short, but even that didn't matter much now. "When I was young," she began hesitantly.

"You are still young," the voice muttered contemptuously. "Well?"

"When I was young, I used to escape into the fairy tales – where curious creatures lived under mushrooms and where stupid kings could be bested by cunning bards. Where magic was possible and where you could fly with the clouds – where you could achieve things. And you know what? That makes perfect sense."

There was silence.

"That was real – somehow. You aren't real – you can't be."

The man gave a dismissive grunt and there was a needle-sharp pain at her neck, sending an electric shock sensation right through her entire body. Then paralysis and complete shutdown . . .

"That makes perfect sense," he echoed sadly, glancing at Feather with some kind of expression on his face. He wasn't even sure what the expression was, but it made her frown uneasily in return.

"What does?" she asked carefully, kicking at the sand.

"Fairy tale," he said. He drew an intense sigh, realising again that there was far more that he wanted to express here than he ever could in words. "It's all we have," he said at last. Feather stared at him and suddenly he felt as though they were speaking different languages entirely. "You hate stories, yet without stories, none of it makes sense. Look at it," he said.

Feather was silent.

"Just a dull dreary horror? The world has – has . . . hiccoughed again and the sea is full of torture implements. Full of death . . . It is a war, yes. I was right. There can be no more doubt. Generations are fighting generations I think. As far as I can tell. There's more difference between generations now than there are between countries. That's what it's all about . . ."

He felt strangely dreamy, almost hallucinatory for a moment. It felt strange for so many words to be coming out of his mouth, and he was not even totally sure that he understood or believed them all – but he didn't stop them.

"Is this really a war?" Feather asked carefully. "Somehow broken out since I came out here into the wilderness. Do you really mean that? The generations have always hated each other but surely you don't mean . . ."

He sighed. "Maybe I should have been writing fairy tales instead."

"Huh?"

He glanced at her.

Then Feather suddenly gave a grating growl. "What are you talking about?" she demanded. "It's ridiculous."

He flinched.

"Do you seriously expect me to believe that this country has suddenly declared war on itself in the few days since I wandered away from it? You're living in a fantasy land."

That silenced the words in a moment and he stared at her in silence, feeling frozen. But it's true, he wanted to cry. Of course it was true. But he knew that he could not speak again.

"It's a fucking story," she cried. "Can't you see that? Why don't you go and see what's happening if you want to talk about the world?"

She stared at him intensely, waiting for an answer, then pressed on – in a softer voice but still with an icy glimmer in her eyes.

"You live out here – you never have any contact with anyone or anything. You never hear much . . . any news – so you start making up your own. Right? And then you forget what's real and what's just make-believe. Right?"

No, he wanted to say – but how could you ever explain something? How could you ever formulate an argument containing everything that clamoured in your head? It was impossible. Instead he just stared out to sea.

"Right?" she repeated.

Then he exploded.

"What do you know about stories?" he shrieked at her, feeling every muscle in his face suddenly twisting. She stepped back sharply, then accidentally trod on the hand of the dead girl behind her and gave a wild flinch, loosing her balance and sprawling out in the sand on her back. "If you're so clever, you try and tell me what makes them. And where they come to an end. And . . . and what they have to do with reality? Do you know that? Do you really?"

"Hey . . ."

"I just tell them," he whispered. "It's what I do."

Feather was silent – her eyes large.

"Please," he muttered at last, turning away. "I think you had better go."

"What?" she said, her voice unsteady.

"Please," he repeated. "I need this isolation. You'd do much better elsewhere. Back somewhere less wild and cold. Back in London. And with someone less insane."

He turned away and stalked towards the house, trying not to tremble. Then he paused. Surely he should at least give her some food and drink for the journey. He glanced back, but she was already pulling herself to her feet. He watched her brush sand off herself, then turn away, looking crestfallen and heavy. He wanted to call after her, but his tongue was tied again and, just a few moments later, she scrambled over the rocks and vanished. She had come with nothing, and she left with nothing. He just stared at where she had been, then back at his distant house and its poles of sea debris, now all seeming sinister and foreboding. Then he glanced down at the body in the sand and shut his eyes in despair.

"The world is at war," he whispered aloud. "Who cares what happens now?"

*

- A round wood pole with the remains of white paint on it
- A fragment of fishing line and the decaying seabird attached to it
- A plastic bottle marked shampoo
- A discarded plastic wallet containing a sodden rail ticket – destination obliterated
- A fragment of tire rubber
- A half-burned wooden plank
- A plastic flower
- A broken doll – naked

The tide had been and gone again now – the old storyteller leaving one more chapter for him to read. As he tramped home along the beach with his heavy bag, still making himself pick up items that caught his eye, there was a dull roar and an arrow-shaped grey jet passed overhead through the dull and undramatic afternoon light. He paused and stared after it tensely. That was not such an unknown event, even out here in the wilderness, but now it was only another confirmation.

There was no doubt – no doubt at all.

As the train raced towards London, there was surprisingly little to see of the city. The rails passed through deep cuttings, behind high walls or in half-tunnels under buildings. The decrepit and grim railway architecture seemed just as usual and it wasn't until she was well into the city, when the tracks suddenly emerged onto an elevated section, that she caught a glimpse of the smoke. It hung over London in a pall of dull haze, with a few rising pillars on the skyline, rearing up over the buildings like serpents. Down below, the streets were unusually empty and many were strewn with debris. And Feather stared with a sinking heart – a sudden realisation . . .

He sat back in his chair and began skimming through *The Book of Tides*, wondering whether this novel was anywhere near finished yet. Or maybe it had only just started. Maybe everything so far had been building up to this epic conflict in the world outside, which he would now have to chronicle. He would need to concentrate, but it was hard. He had the feeling that Feather's name would be deeply woven into everything the sea had to tell him now. And in what roles? Feather the fugitive? Feather the outlaw? Feather the freedom fighter? Feather the terrorist? He closed his eyes, her form suddenly vivid and the memory of her presence – the presence of another – sending a tingle through him. A restlessness.

Quietly, he got up and inspected the sofa, where she had slept for the few days she had been there. After a bit of searching, he found what he was looking for. Three hairs – long and brown. He knew that it was the only trace of her that would remain here, but it was sufficient. He quickly twisted them together into a loop and tied them with a small scrap of white ribbon. Then he looked for her tide. As of now, he decided, he would have to name this one 'Feather's Tide' and it deserved something more than the eventual clearout that was the usual fate of most tides.

In a prime place in his garden, he dug a hole. Then he tramped to his shed and studied the stacks of wood that it contained – wood for the fire, and other wood. Driftwood. One of the largest pieces was dragged out into the grey evening. It was an impressive chunk of branch, as tall as he was and splitting into two substantial stems with several twisted knots in various places. Barkless and cracked, it seemed to reach out, though he wasn't sure whether it was in agony or exultation. Maybe both. Dragging it back to the hole and setting it firmly upright was the work of a few minutes, but he spent the rest of the evening armed with twine and wire, slowly building the new flotsam tree. The single shoe was suspended, toe-downwards, at the bottom and the broken flowerpot nailed above it. The cloth and the rope twined round loosely and were fastened. Then the military jacked was added scarecrow style over all and, within that, the three hairs were hidden, carefully nailed to the central junction where the branches divided. The distress flares and the warning sign studded the tree like fruit. It was a simple arrangement, but it didn't really need to be anything else. It was the objects that were important here and nothing should get in the way of that.

Finally he stepped back to study his work. The sun was long gone now and the grey was deepening. His world bordered by the familiar shapes of the hills and a stony sky – as comforting as always. As lonely as always.

It looked good.

Around him, people bustled. The endless stream of faces that was London. Glancing round, he seemed to be the only person who wasn't moving. He stood as a still point in a storm of people. Feeling horribly exposed.

"Well?" he cried out at last. The passers-by took no notice, carefully avoiding eye contact. Overhead, the roar of a jet made him look up anxiously, but it was just a 747 passing low overhead. Nothing more. And in a few moments it was gone, hidden above the buildings.

Flights of Fancy
Allen Ashley

Friday

Josh and I have managed to prise open the tiny cell skylight so that we can peek out at the grey waves breaking on the pebbly beach to the west – or else gaze up at the squawking birds wheeling in spiralling searches for food and thermals. We triggered no alarms with our handiwork. And if we were to somehow miraculously escape through this impossibly narrow window, what then? The government's new policy of locating all prisons on remote, mostly Scottish islands means freedom would equate with freezing and starvation in the unlikely event of any breakout.

Josh is the perfect companion in this place. Muscled, streetwise, prone to outbursts of violence, but fiercely loyal to me.

He even insisted on seeing the governor to back me up in my request for an MP3 player and microphone or even an old-fashioned Dictaphone on which to record all my thoughts and ideas.

"Fucker asked me what you'd had published, Kris," he reported. "I couldn't remember nothing, pal, apart from a couple of reviews on eBay. 'That don't make him Dan Brown, does it?' he said. I coulda twatted him."

To be fair, the governor has allowed me a pen and pad of paper. I'd expected a mere pencil but maybe he was worried about us poking one another with its sharp point or slipping the tiny blade out of the sharpener and drawing slits across our wrists.

*

Saturday

I've been in worse institutions. Boarding school was more violent and more prone to attempted buggery. The saving grace here is that our masters sometimes intervene and break up the disturbances.

I know that the traditional route would be to invent an imaginary world where I was king or else a prince crossing the wilderness or whatever: dealing with overpopulated incarceration by imagining its opposite. Maybe that will come later. At the moment, I'm writing like a novice by simply starting this diary and keeping everything personal and first hand. "My body in chains but my spirits soars"? Not quite yet. Leave that to the birds for now; let me first make sense of the present situation.

*

Later on Saturday

But would I really want that seclusion? Well, yes, actually. I don't need the crowd to bounce off from – give me isolation in an ivory tower any day of the week. Even Josh has a touch of this need, rabbiting on at night about fishing trips he took as a youth.

"One guy, a rod, a line, nature all around. Perfect," he proclaims.

*

Monday

We have a visitor at our open window. A bird – I think it's a herring gull but I'm not a hundred percent. Josh and I have taken to secreting bread crusts up our sleeves to feed our perky visitor. Is life imitating art – as usual? Are we convicted criminals to be become the birdmen of McNulty's Correction Centre?

*

Flights of Fancy

The troubling dreams were still plaguing Sirk but, in other ways, he supposed that he had adjusted to the hermit's life quite well until the warrior J'sshsosh arrived at his cave entrance. Sirk had considered his course of action for the next five or ten years, intending to devote himself to theological and necromantic studies upon his return to the city of Doub-lay. He would make enough to get by from selling the occasional potion or invoking a binding spell or curse. Nothing too tragic, though: that was behind him. He wished to get closer to the gods, to know their ways and histories, the better to tap into their secret knowledge.

"Mage, you are needed. I cannot complete this quest alone," the warrior implored.

"I'm beyond all that youthful nonsense, friend. Now it is my wish to be thoughtful, creative, studious... alone."

Ah, but the knight-errant was clever as well as fierce and brave in all fights. The pack on his horse was loaded with the finest sweetmeats known to this civilised half of the world. After existing on a diet of dry biscuits, boiled water and what little fruits or berries he could scrounge locally, Sirk felt his visitor's offerings to be the greatest manna he'd tasted in a decade. As the dry twigs and branches crackled and sent smart yellow sparks up to join the white stars in the heavens, the mage felt his head itself starting to spin like the celestial orbs themselves.

"He who holds the Golden Key," J'sshsosh repeated, "holds the whole kingdom. Come on, sage, one last great adventure."

One last great adventure then, sire....

*

Thursday

I must have a special talent, an empathy with our feathered friends that had lain undiscovered until I got here. I was out in the yard ambling around, watching the flocks swoop and swoon above our heads like a giant airborne net exacerbating our incarceration. Suddenly one of the components lost its poise and plummeted to earth, breaking its fall with a few frantic flaps just before hitting the concrete.

Smart black and white feathers – it was a wagtail. I recognised it from holiday camp when I was a kid. I picked it up, feeling its frantic heartbeat beneath my cold fingers. I spoke calm words like you would to an injured child. Some of the guys watched me with mild interest; a few others threw minor insults along the lines of. "Oi, Bill Oddie!" or "Look at old Bird Brain!" I cared not. I wanted to take the frantic creature back to my cell, feed it up for a couple of days, release it eventually through the skylight we'd secretly prised open.

No joy. One of the warders let me take it to the door of the refectory where the cook sorted out some crusts and a saucer of stale water for the poor little mite. Then I had to let it go. It bobbed its tail several times, stuttered in its approach to the makeshift runway. Finally, it was airborne, ascending slowly into the dotted sky to rejoin its kin.

The warm glow of satisfaction kept me beaming all evening, despite the shit food and the cold cell and the block I was experiencing with my tale of the wizard Sirk.

Writer's block, eh? I'm halfway to becoming professional.

But that wasn't the end of the story. At breakfast we were all given a stern lecture by the governor along the lines of don't touch the wildlife, one of the guards and three of the inmates have already succumbed to the new strain of bird flu. Indeed, we were now to be confined to our quarters for forty-eight hours.

I clocked several hateful looks arrowed in my direction.

Given so much time with his own thoughts, Josh would doubtless be quietly masturbating on the lower bunk. Meanwhile, I had a literary quest to try to unravel.

Flights of Fancy

*

After two days, the soldiers had tired of torturing the two travellers and had merely resorted to keeping them chained to the stone wall of the dingy cell. Soon the floor was stained with piss but, mercifully, no excrement. That had all departed their bodies when Goven's henchmen had run the blades of their daggers slowly across the goose-pimpled skin below their exposed belly buttons.

"No, sire, I do not have the Golden Key upon me or hidden away. No, please tell his imperial majesty that we do not know where the key is to be found. Please stop twisting my arm and squeezing my neck and pulling out my toenails."

Later: "Kill me if you must. Any knowledge or skills I might possess which could help you will then be lost. The Golden Key will not be liberated by ghosts."

Waiting. Hungry, thirsty, injured, exhausted, slightly delirious, spirit close to leaving the body. All previous thoughts of higher intellectual study now reduced to a desperate clinging on to mere survival. Sirk had thought that his time as a hermit had prepared him for so much privation but that was mere nursery school compared to the ordeal Goven's evil guards had planned whilst he still breathed.

Woozy, weary, wounds festering, muscles twisted and beaten into near-submission.

"J'sshsosh, I cannot stand any more," he croaked.

"Mage," he responded, "we die as men… as warriors."

The metal clasp on the door clanked once more and five soldiers entered, including the evil captain with the barbed trident. Sirk prayed to every god of the pantheon that either they would soon die on the excruciating rack or be simply put to death by the sword or the rope. But no –

"His imperial majesty wishes you to reconsider helping us and offers you the comfort of the west tower. Come with us, scum."

They were taken through the courtyard with its ripe smell of market stall fruit and horse manure, up a flight of cold stone steps that almost proved too much for their lacerated legs, then deposited in a new cell which held a jug of spring water, a hunk of dark rye bread and two animal skin blankets. Most incredibly, there was also a barred window giving a view out across the fields and streams so diligently tilled and fished by the king's obedient serfs.

"Better to die," J'sshsosh whispered once they were alone.

Sirk nibbled at the food, knowing not to rush the filing of his desolate stomach. After a time, his companion supped lightly, too, perhaps having decided that poisoning was not one of Goven's preferred methods. The wizard stood awhile at the window, watching flocks of birds wheeling in the clear blue sky, wishing stupidly for freedom.

*

Tuesday

The daily routine has changed recently. They have started to rouse us much later, which means that I lie here in bed for hours listening to the raucous gulls and gannets encircling the jail in their search for scraps. I can even make out the distant crash of waves on the quieter mornings.

They are only feeding us twice a day. The initial rumbles of hungry protest died down pretty quickly when they compensated us by increasing the tea and biscuit ration and lengthening the free association period. Now we can spend even more of our day grumbling together about the injustices of the justice system or playing poker for broken matchsticks and sordid favours.

Lights out now comes a mere thirty minutes after supper. Having barely flexed my muscles all day I am, of course, nowhere near ready for slumber. This is my most imaginative time, when I can let my thoughts fly and believe that this prison tower is instead an ivory tower in which I have chosen to creatively isolate myself.

Fortunately, I have learned to scribe in the dark. Josh jokes that my handwriting is no messier for it.

I realise that we are quite literally cut off from British society here at McNulty's but the recent withdrawal of newspapers, radio and television privileges can surely only build a swell of paranoia. Wouldn't it make sense for them to censoriously show us all the great, positive facets of the culture we are excluded from? The overpaid prima donna Premier League players tickling the too light leather ball to each other; the home ownership and makeover shows with their Spanish vistas and heated Jacuzzis; the endless talents shows full of wannabe singers, dancers, one-legged tightrope walkers and blind bird trainers... Here, boys, look what we're missing through our enforced incarceration!

*

Wednesday

It all looked like kicking off today. A whole bunch of us inmates had been marched down to what passes for a gym here. OK, it is a gym of sorts, but the sort that you'd associate with a rundown secondary school. From the last century. The screws stood around making sure nobody tried anything serious with the metal disc weights or the rigid medicine ball. The murmurs about being kept inside – I mean, literally inside, indoors – would not die down this time. All we wanted was a little stroll in the open air; maybe a kickaround with some balled up socks. But no – the yard is out of bounds. And for why? Some of the more intrepid inmates were about to find out.

I suppose it's come to something when the prisoners don't make a break over the wall but simply for the outdoor association area. Burly bastards in black uniforms blocked our surge. But we could see beyond their tensed arms. The small square of concrete was filled with birds. Squabbling, pecking, screeching, squawking, bickering bloody birds. I saw one crow take to the sky with a telltale white-red string of gut in its beak. It flew as high as ten feet before its mates mobbed it for the booty. I couldn't see what was on the ground to cause such a commotion. I didn't want to think.

"Nothing to worry about, fellows," the governor's typed note informed us later. "Just some idiot left the rubbish and the food recycling in the wrong area."

Sure, and my name's Einstein Machiavelli.

*

Friday

At least the water still flows and the showers are passably warm. The routine has slipped, though, and we strip and gel only twice a week now.

"Oi, little dick!" a hard-faced lifer said, "I 'ear you been writing stuff about us." I avoided looking at him below waist level but did take in the powerful, clenched fists before attempting to hold his stony gaze. "A fucking la-di-dah diary, if you please. Well it don't please me, cunt, an' I think you're trying to sell us out to the screws."

Shit, where was Josh when I needed him?

"It's... it's... escape plans," I replied. My acting wouldn't have convinced a bunch of children high on fizzy lemonade and yet –

"If it is that, piss-face, you'd better copy them to me. But I reckon it's just some flight of fancy, some poncey choirboy poetry about flowers. Eh?"

I was spared having to answer him by the thunder crack of a rough towel being flicked sharply against a wall. Josh, thank fuck.

"Leave him alone, Sharkey," Josh called out from the side of the stalls, "he ain't doing no harm."

"He ain't doing no fucking good, neither." Sharkey spat messily onto the stone floor, lazily wrapped ribbed white cotton around his midriff and muttered, "I wandered lonely as a bird" as he solemnly exited.

*

Shun Day

Chicken is off the menu. There is the occasional scrag arse gristly bit of grey tasteless mutton but the meals have started to become mostly vegetarian and very starchy – loads of cheap white chemical-tasting bread to fill us up with its bulk.

When was the last time we had visitors? I can't actually remember. Sure, this remote island is, uh, remote but during the first month my mother and twin sister managed to get a train and a ferry to the old fishing port before piling onto the rickety coach for their two hours of familial hand-wringing.

This isolation, this loss of the last contact with society and, if not sanity, at least normality has become the only topic of whispered conversation whenever three or more of us huddle together in a corridor or the mess hall. We have sullenly submitted ourselves to a succession of the expected indignities, such as a thorough search of all bodily orifices in order to find all electronic equipment, in fact anything that might bring news from outside. We have stopped caring about the lack of outdoor space, light and exercise. But if our long-suffering loved ones can't ever come along to alleviate our cramped loneliness for a couple of hours every so often… there will be trouble. Serious stuff. The seesaw has tipped too far.

*

Allen Ashley

Lose Day

I have abandoned the piece I was writing. It was to be my island of calm, my escape into fantasy, the discovery of the better person inside of me. My opus will likely now lay unfinished on its scraps of grubby finger-marked exercise paper. Just another half-completed masterpiece.

Life is stranger than any Tolkienesque art I might strive to create. The rumour mill has gone into overdrive. We are temporarily confined to cells. Unfed since morning. Wound up, unable to relax. Ears assaulted by the screeching and squawking of the too numerous birds dive-bombing the bleak area surrounding the prison. Minds whirling with the pace of the apparent catastrophe befalling the world we have been exiled from.

No time for cosy lands of knights, magicians and quests for magical objects that might save us.

*

Lags' Day

We are all banging whatever objects we can find against the walls, doors and floors of our cells. Deprived of air, nourishment, freedom and, lately, even face to face contact with anyone other than our cell mate, we have found our true creative spark. Welcome to the premier performance from the McNulty's Correction Centre Symphony Orchestra. The music of the downtrodden, the underclass, the deprived, the desperate...

Let us out, let us out, we will even fight on your side.

If it's man against mutated bird, make use of our clenched fists and firm boots. Together we shall beat the winged enemies.

Shouts of apparent news fill the gaps in our primitive percussion. End the rumour mill, give us facts, you bastards! Full knowledge will make us fight more effectively. That's what I learned in the cadets.

Before they kicked me out for trying to nick our tutor's campaign medals.

If just one of us could get the golden key that unlocks all doors, we could be out, a liberation force together showing we are not a burden on society but instead its saviours.

And when we tire of our homemade cacophony? Then we must listen to the abominations of creation outside the stone walls and barred windows. The evil birds circling, waiting to pick us off, or peck us off, with their quick breeding numerousness and mob mentality. The failed flu vaccine has released their dinosaur heritage.

Humankind could be fucked.

*

Towards A New Day

One tiny spell of quiet in the darkest, coldest moments of the night. Is it the lull before the final conflict, the battle they are calling Bird-mageddon?

The soft days of not so many weeks ago are now forgotten. We are reduced to the basics of survival. The notion of writing some sort of escapist quest fantasy novel and taking it to the governor with a view of getting my work published, noticed, read as an inspiration or a way out… pipe dreams! A flight of fancy. You don't come to a prison to be inspired, to create, to find the solace to draw out your inner spirit. No, you come to the prison to die. And even if you don't die within its actual walls, upon release you take the prison with you to what used to be the outside world and you still operate within its confines. Forever.

Not that there's even a viable outside world left from what I hear shouted along the corridors. Someone's got a smuggled phone or has heard something or has conjectured plausibly. Birds are laying eggs faster than previously. Their wings are getting bigger, their gestalt intelligence – the force that keeps the flock flying in the same direction towards migratory lands – has taken a chemically induced turn and now they are acting in concert against Earth's oppressors. Us. And they are ravenous.

*

Screws' Day

Ask any lag what their favourite flick is and you will only get one of three answers. Firstly, some gangster piece where the forces of law and order sustain casualties on a massive scale and the hero is fit, quick and cold-bloodedly cool in his penchant for violence. Or else, they might go for some big budget blow up every building on screen type shit that appeals to the less developed mind. Lastly, the more self-reflective will name "*The Shawshank Redemption*". That could be me up there having my wrongs righted!

At least fifty per cent of the inmates will tell you, "I am innocent, I shouldn't be here, it's a complete miscarriage of justice." Me? I'm one of the thirty percent who agree they have committed the crimes for which they have been jailed but don't accept the level of punishment. Like the rest of them, my gripe is that my sentence has been unduly harsh. I didn't kill or even punch anybody.

It was a theft at the local manor house. The idea was to nick the William Blake manuscripts, the John Constable sketches and a couple of wildlife paintings from their well insecure safe. Our plan was to take the stuff, store it discreetly, stay schtum for a while and then get a go-between to do a deal with the insurers, with the ten percent working out to perhaps several tens of thousands each even when split three ways. Nobody hurt, no real damage to the art, a victimless crime by my reckoning.

It all would have gone well except for Lord Bittern's malarkey of Mynah birds screeching and raising such an alarm that I had to open their cage and throttle the raucous bastards. Black feathers, peck marks, artworks carelessly dropped on the floor, part-time old pensioner of a night watchman callously kicked in the guts by my accomplices; all of us rugby tackled and arrested by the filth on the croquet lawn. Laughable really, if it wasn't for the fact that the old fucker later died of his wounds in the local hospital.

    Ten years. For a farcical fifteen minutes.

*

Shattered Day

What was that old story about Emperor Nero playing his fiddle while Rome burned? Have I become like that historical character – sketching out a creative fantasy while the world goes to shit all around me? Sitting in my shared cell scribbling away at whatever I can conjure out of the interior… because the breakdown of the exterior is too horrible to contemplate any further?

    Where have all the warders gone? Gone to bird feed everyone.

    And where is yesterday's paper? Because we dearly need to hear yesterday's news. Not the punny cricket reports: "*England get the 'Ump*" or "*Hey, Aussie, Stop Tampering with our Balls!*" No, the front page world and political stuff, the lurid, screaming capitals declaring "*BIRD WORLD WAR*": the truth about this bird flu vaccine gone wrong, the truth about the collapsing society beyond our still locked doors.

    We are surely right to be concerned that we will be trapped in our cells forever as the warders are called off to fight the war to save humanity. Come on, guys, these are changed circumstances: If this is a war, surely you need all us inmates, whatever we have done before, to be out there battling away for Great Britain?

    Don't believe everything you read online. Turn your nose up at Facebook and see beyond the pale corona of Sky News. But that dropped mobile on Block B had Twitter tweets aplenty about the failure of the mass avian inoculation. The birds are having a war with each other and with humans and other creatures. They have all gone feral. The vaccine to beat bird flu has reacted with the virus in an unanticipated, world changing way.

We don't have much evidence except what little we can hear of their flocking and screeching outside. The gulls, the magpies and the pigeons that litter our island all seem to be affected but who knows about flamingos or hornbills or emperor penguins? Is this truly a worldwide problem or just a local difficulty? How can we tell from this confinement?

We dream of a simple walkout, a calm and bloodless escape. All we need is someone to turn up with a golden key.

*

Sirk had taken a chance that they would have at least a further three days grace in which to recover their strength before facing King Goven's inquisition again. The routine was to bring them victuals and fresh straw for their toilet in the morning then to leave them in this cold eyrie for the rest of the day and dark, unlit night. He believed that he had time to weave a way out.

Remembering much that he had learned at the Magisterium, he called to the birds and they came. He asked them to donate feathers and they did. The eagles and falcons found small mammals for him and neglected feeding their chicks on the nest to instead chew, swallow and then regurgitate the partially digested flesh into a paste that would serve his purposes. He knew this to be a race against time. J'sshsosh proved remarkably adept at weaving the quills, mouse guts and glue into acceptably sized wings to facilitate their escape. But would they work?

Did they have any other choice?

The sharper beaked birds had done wonders

loosening the cylindrical metal bars from the aperture. The necromancer crouched there now, barely daring to look up or down, frozen into breath-holding immobility. He might have remained there until the end of creation had not a frightened series of squawks from the avian helpers alerted him that the guards had rumbled their plan.

He stepped... fell... flapped... arms hardly strong enough to hold the makeshift wings... flapped again, caught a lucky updraft... somehow soared and moved away from Goven's hateful hell hole of a castle, with the flock of birds around him shielding his ungainly form from archers on the ground.

He had discussed heading for the mountains bordering this evil realm but they seemed a million miles away at present. It was merely a matter of pulling his aching arms up and down, up and down...

He chanced a look behind him and his friend was airborne and soaring a little higher than he was. There was no time to hang around admiring the view. Move on, ride the wind... and hope.

He touched down on a grassy knoll several leagues beyond Goven's angrily massing army. He said a spell of thanks to his assistants and bade them farewell. He and J'sshsosh would continue on foot.

Except that the journey would now be for Sirk alone. Maybe his cell companion flew too high and the sun's rays licked him dry or at the very least melted the glue holding his contrivances together –

The warrior plummeted like a stone thrown by an angry sky god. Sirk didn't see where he landed but was sure that he would not have survived. He honoured his memory and knew that he should offer him a decent burial but dared not search for the body as, callously, he knew that would endanger his own continued safety. There would be time to mourn or celebrate his brave memory later. For now, on with the quest.

When Day?

Josh has been gone for nearly half an hour now whilst I sit with the cell door open. We could have relocated to different quarters but something holds me here, some belief that this is where I have finally found my creative spark. Or just that one cell is much the same as any other.

The noise from outside is extraordinary as the feral birds squabble over the latest pickings. All they seem to do is eat, these new masters of both the earth and sky. In fact, they gorge – on us as well as each other. If only we had as much as a fraction of their manna. But our cupboards are bare, the supplies looted or rotten. The tap water has become a stagnant dribble. The electricity is off. All our communication devices are struggling to boot up and present the human point of view in face of the new world order. The energy crisis has hit with sudden impact as we are down to battery power only.

I read a story once about people eating the fabric of their clothes in order to survive another day. Quite what nourishment a prison issue sweatshirt will offer the human stomach, I can only conjecture.

At last, Josh returns with a laptop, its cable severed and its screen partially cracked.

"Still dreaming of a better world, Kris?" he smiles.

"Better? Probably. Different, certainly."

The computer sputters into life. The tinny speakers are full of screeching and twittering. The birds have hijacked our tools and are using them for their own purposes. And now they are starting to bombard us with their propaganda.

The leaflets we found in the governor's office advised us not to use speech when out in the open but to communicate by hand gestures, although that is surely too akin to the hypnotic motion of the wing.

The birds' shrill cries are confusing our minds, turning us against each other. We are fighting for scraps, squabbling over the crumbs. Do as your masters command.

Flights of Fancy

Who's a lovely boy, then?
Pretty Polly.
Pieces of eight.

*

The dreams came to plague Sirk again last night, no doubt a reaction to the drama of his escape from Goven's castle. Or maybe the cause was more immediate: the nocturnal cold and discomfort of sleeping in the forest at the foothills of the mountains.

In the dreams, the birds were not his allies but instead were humanity's sworn enemies. And his persona was as a younger, weaker man trapped in a castle of sorts – a prison, certainly – with little prospect of release except into the pecked to death bloodbath that awaited beyond the grey stone walls. He stayed his hand. He waited…

Strange visions indeed. He took them essentially to be worries that he might not find the all-solving Golden Key.

Stay strong, sage. Do not falter in this quest.

Pigs Eyes
Jet McDonald

●

Elizabeth Stanford worked for a company that made peanuts out of pigs' eyes. She found herself reflecting on the fact that it was only the slaughter of thousands of sows that paid for the company car she was now driving. Ten years ago, such an irony would have been impossible but the rapid spread of Islam had spelt the death knell for the pig farming industry and one by one lights had been turned off at pig rearing complexes across the world. It was only when a pig labourer from Holland, the now famous Sven Dortmuller, returned to collect his tools that the pig industry refound its direction and so, by consequence, Elizabeth Stanford's career.

Ten years before, Dortmuller had visited a shuttered and abandoned piggery near Stockholm. He found that the starved and night blind animals continued to produce litters, living on mushrooms and the dregs of the grain silo. The pigs had no rump but their eyes, in compensation, had grown fat and protruding. Dortmuller selected a runt, cut its neck and later that night fried an eyeball in the company of his wife Frieda. It was the most delightful thing they had ever tasted and 'Dortmuller's Pig Eyed Peanuts' was born.

The Islamic governing bodies needed some persuading, but once pounded and pulped and chemically modified into a peanut like protein pignuts were declared sufficiently un-pork-like to bypass any particular holy doctrine and it was with gay retail abandon that Dortmuller rained them down on the strip malls and corner shops. Delicious, addictive, cheap. They were the truffle of the common man. There were even peashooter clubs in Soho where pig eyed nuts were fired into the mouths of willing punters by ladies with tassels on their nipples for less than the price of a bottle of Cava.

With such a profoundly marketable product, Elizabeth's job as a middle ranking marketing manager for Dortmuller's Pig Eyed Peanuts (UK) wasn't difficult. Indeed, she spent much of her time trying to dissuade small rural grocers from overstocking to a level they clearly couldn't afford and so it was with a deep seated sense of irritation and boredom that she found herself travelling up the M5 to meet the winner of the Dortmuller (UK) 'All You Can Eat Pig Eyed Peanut Prize.'

Toby Switz hadn't wanted to win, in fact he thought he was applying for a cruise to the Bahamas. He had other matters to contend with. He was an agoraphobic and a writer. He had long ago decided that every fey author deserved a phobia and it was their authorial duty to identify which neurosis suited them best, much as a calligrapher might choose the best quill. Having settled on a pretty even-handed fear of wide open spaces, he found himself living in a village in the middle of the Yorkshire Moors. He would never leave his two bedroom terrace unless forced to by lack of food or printer paper. It was all Emily Bronte's fault. He had tried to be a romantic novelist; the spitting rivers, the desolate skies, the heathen moors like ripped purple petticoats, but it had all been too much and he had retreated to his two up two down and a bespoke fear of the larger world. Paradoxically, he cultivated an interest in travel writing, more specifically travel to the archipelagos of the Caribbean. When he was a child, he had been taken on a package holiday to Barbados and he often found himself at his desk overlooking the frozen moors re-imagining that single trip in exquisite detail like the miniature silver crab that had negotiated the creases of his ten year old palm. In fact, so all consuming had this interest become that he found himself writing about nothing else as he stuffed himself with pig eyed peanuts. His inner journey wasn't a narrative, more a reimagining of the world he had long left behind and there were stacks of prose to bear witness, towers of laser printed sheets filling every room, finally fighting for space in the bathroom, so that he was no longer able to bath and showered with a tarpaulin over the residual piles of paper. In fact, the only things that competed for space were the half empty sacs of Dortmuller's Pig Eyed Peanuts.

Switz, Elizabeth decided, was a porker. He was on the right side of forty but unable to fit into his porch and had to stand in the doorway sideways.

    He peered past her.

Pigs Eyes

"Miss Stanford," she said offering a hand, "Dortmuller's Pig Eyed Peanuts. I've come for the feature..?" He continued to peer past her "...for the "advertorial?"

"No thanks." Well versed in doorstepping, Elizabeth stuck her leather boot in the closing gap.

"It's in the terms and conditions Mr Switz," she smiled tightly and pointed at the facsimile of the coupon.

He backed away, as they always did, and she negotiated the listing stacks of printed paper to gain entry to the lounge. There were further yellowing reams of type on the sofa and he had to balance these on stacks on the floor, making them lean one upon the other ever more precariously.

"Some light perhaps?" She didn't wait for his answer and pulled the curtains back so a shaft of sunlight fell across his face, picking out a two day stubble and flinty grey eyes. Switz's hand went instantly into a brown sack beside him and he pulled out a shiny foil bag.

"Pignut?"

"Mr Switz..."

"Toby." He flicked a pignut in his mouth.

She opened a ring notepad. "So... Toby... what is it that you do exactly?"

"Do?"

"Yes, you know. What's your occ-up-ation?" She enunciated it in case he was learning retarded or whatever they called it nowadays.

Switz's larynx bobbed up and down as he swallowed and this seemed to make his eyes bulge as if one were connected to the other by a sinew mechanism.

"I write," he said, finally.

"So you're an author?"

He blinked at her with his bobbing grey eyes "Well it's more I just... write."

"But *what* do you write about...?"

He nodded at the stacks of papers, the empty mounds of Dortmuller nut packets and the segregated motes of dust drifting through the sunlight. "The Caribbean."

"So you're a *travel* writer?"

179

He looked down at his hands but they were partially obscured by his girth. He let one search out, crablike, for a packet of Dortmuller's but found the bag empty and tossed it into the air. They both watched the packet float down through the dust, silvering the sunlight.

An hour later and Elizabeth Stanford was no further. She wasn't sure if Switz was being evasive or if he was just truly empty headed. He had a tea cup tipped to his face and was examining the bottom like the screen of a digital camera.

"So, let me get this straight, you write about the island of Barbados. Day in day out, day after day after day?"

"Mmm-"

"And that's what you want me to put in the advertorial?"

"I don't really care what you put in the advertorial." He lowered the cup so all she could see were his closed eyes and those fine feathery lashes.

She snapped shut her notebook and Switz's eyes opened, obtuse and bloodshot. And then he placed his pulpy liverspotted hand on hers. "When I close my eyes," he said, "I see sharks. Toothless. Basking. Sharks."

She tried to convince herself that the trip had been uneventful. But the more she prodded at the silver film of her Sat Nav, plotting her way back to the motorway, the more she saw those grey eyes, the red capillaries reaching towards the dilating pupil. And that night, in her tiny studio in Hoxton, she dreamt she was lying naked with Toby Switz on a beach in the Caribbean and the sea covered their bodies with gold and phosphor.

After the woman had left, Toby spent two hours writing about the spiral patterns on the back of a spiny starfish. But that night he dreamt only of her. She was curled on her side on the bottom of the stream than ran through the moorland behind his house. Her breasts were an earthy brown. He lay down beside her on the stream bed and felt its movement through him, as if the veins of granite in the moor now ran through them both and into water and the river and beyond.

When he woke, he went to his writing desk and tried to conjure up his Caribbean utopia. But it was gone. He stared across the moorland and listened for the garden gate. It swung weakly in the draft of the dusk.

Elizabeth Stanford tried not to think of him. But her dreams sang to her through the night. She found herself drawn to the swimming baths and spas of the city. She would not swim there, just float, letting the thermals quiver through the web spaces between her fingers. With her eyes shut, she could mask out all the sounds, the squeals and whistles and shouts, diminish them to a single hush until it seemed there was only a single slow sine wave that vibrated through the tiled walls of the baths and led on through the macadam and the starved soil and the underground water tables to his moorland home.

She took her Sat Nav from her car and smashed it on the point of a fruit squeezer. When she fixed it by its sucker above the television set, it blinked into Toby Switz's eye, granite grey and astonishing.

Toby Switz found that he could just about force on his misshapen old boots and he walked through the overgrown garden and into the moor. At first, the gorse was high and he felt as though he was wading through it, but then he was released into the open moor and his gut rose and fell as if it was its own being, and he saw himself like some kind of monstrous 'Sound of Music' production, screaming with his arms wide as he galloped over the brow of the earth. Below him, the stream coursed in its silver spindles, ferocious and alive. He fell into it and lay on his back and stared up. A bird of prey made an apostrophe in the sky. Hovering. And then he held his breath and closed his eyes and let the petrifying water rush across his face. And in the darkness behind his eyes he saw the bird still hanging there, waiting for the words to begin again.

Two days later she knocked on his door.
"I've come," she said, "to be with you."
"I know," he said. He had cuts up his arms and on his cheek.
They undressed and went to the bathroom and stood facing each other under the shower. He closed his eyes and turned his head and lay his cheek upon her breast. She put her hand on the back of his neck and held him to her so he could better hear the wash of blood through her vessels.

Elizabeth cleared out the house. The bags of pig eyed peanuts were taken away by a man. A bonfire was made in the garden and thousands of sheets of Toby's imagined utopia burnt through the night and their ashes carried across the moor. Toby still wrote – occasional journalism, a short novel about rural Yorkshire life, but no more did he pour over his childhood. He slimmed down. He ate salads. He went for long walks with Elizabeth.

She left Dortmuller's and worked in a local cafe as a waitress. She painted in the afternoons. Together they lived a quiet life without demands.

Sometimes you could hear the stream across the moor, a distant burr.

Pigs Eyes

And then, ten years later, Toby Switz came home with a coconut. He had not gone with the intention of buying one but there it was in the corner shop, leaning incongruously against a rack of plastic sunglasses. He would make Elizabeth a coconut sponge. She would like that. Balancing it on the kitchen table the coconut regarded him with its singular bruised eye. Toby took the nut down to the lean to shed at the end of the garden, put it on a shelf next to some garden tools, and waited. The nut blinked.

Weeks passed and he did not tell her. He would say he was going to do some woodwork or a bit of potting, wander down to the lean to, close the door and then gaze at the nut for hours until it blinked. And increasingly, within that moment, he saw glimpses of his old utopia; flashes of surf, pink sands, tentacled coral...

On Christmas Eve, with the whisper of the stream lost in a gale, he wandered down to the shed, wrote a short note for her and waited for the time to come.

When the nut blinked he held it open with the thumb and forefinger of his right hand and pushed the eye inwards with the pad of his left thumb. His thumb was drawn in by the coconut. He then allowed his whole arm to be sucked in after it. He raised his left leg till it was level with the arm, in the manner of a man trying to renter the womb, and then this was consumed also. His torso, right leg, arm and head followed, so all that remained, just poking out of the coconut's eye, was his nose. He took a sniff of the damp winter air, laced with turpentine from the local DIY store, and disappeared.

Elizabeth returned home from the cafe to find a dripping tap. She wasn't angry. She just wanted an answer. The relevant authorities were contacted, the bills were stacked in a dresser and some tears allowed into the restless night but it was only some weeks later that she found the note.

It said that he loved her and he would see her soon. A coconut was balanced next to the rusting tools. The nut was old and there was a musty growth on its brown threads, the bruise of its single eye already beginning to fade.

She wrote him love letters everyday that she never mailed. She wrote about the stillness of her life without him but she also wrote of the moor; the perishing mists, the carcasses of the fox-ripped sheep, the rust dappled bellies of the fish in the stream. In exquisite detail, day in day out, she scrawled and the letters piled up in the dresser.

The village called her 'The Hermit', bow-backed as she was with her task. Words spilled out of the wooden drawers and frothed into the house and, in the spaces between, she collected coconuts, huge piles of them, with their black unblinking eyes, their hearts of souring milk, delivered in carrier bags by a distant supermarket.

It was Christmas Eve, twelve months later, the house drafty and perishing, that she lit a fire in the grate with a single love letter. And it was then, as she coughed into the grate, that they opened their eyes. With a sound like a yacht's sail snapping full, a hundred astonished shiners flashed into aqua blue.

She backed away from the fire and the hundreds of blue coconut eyes followed her and then flicked up towards the ceiling. She followed their gaze to the rumbling sound from the first floor bathroom. She stepped backwards up the stairs and the eyes followed and those coconuts on the landing turned to watch as she went to the closed bathroom door and saw a turquoise light from the gap between the wood and the hinges. She opened it to find an ocean, a sea that was a rippling window within the frame. And within that sea, sharks swam in slow languid circles, one pushing with its nose into the transparent film of the door's entrance so this layer flexed outwards. She stripped off her clothes to the sagging skin, walked through the wall of water and into the ocean.

It was the stench of rotting coconuts that forced the neighbour's hand. They did not find her body but they were not particularly interested and the council went on to fill two dumper trucks with lined paper and rotten coconuts. As per the department's recycling policy, the love letters and coconuts were pulped together and added to the food waste collection system. The waste was made into livestock feed and this was used to supplement the grain poured into the underground silos where Dortmuller reared their ball eyed pigs for harvesting and processing.

    Soon enough these runts were ripe, their eyeballs tumescent and needy. They were funnelled into the overground abattoir where halogen lamps were sequentially flashed into their faces. And though there was no one there to hear, they did not squeal as they were funnelled towards the bolt gun. They chirruped, like high summer swallows in a cloudless sky, escaping out the Winter's dark.

The Flowers of Uncertainty
Douglas Thompson

> *"In praise there is more importunity than in blame"*
> -Friedrich Nietzsche,
> *Beyond Good and Evil.*

A solitary figure slowly makes his way on foot through a vast green landscape of cliffs and moors. The last time this scenery changed was probably during an ice age, and therefore it gives out no clue as to the fate of humanity at this moment in history. The sun clears the clouds and sends a shaft of quasi-religious light down on Harold Swimmer like a wandering mystic, a knight on a penance, a self-flagellating monk in a hair shirt. He talks to himself as he walks his long journey of return to rejoin the human race.

The disappearance of Sharon had been as confusing to Harold as it was disappointing. After thirty years of loyal service, where was the logic in her disobeying his very last command? His clear instructions had been for her to bring a national newspaper and an up-to-date encyclopaedia of modern literature, to their last meeting, together with contact details for his surviving family, and some spending money and contemporary clothes.

Instead he had found himself locking up the beach house for the last time on his own, without the slightest clue what to expect in the world that awaited him, except a two-day hike across the hills to reach his now antique car, which Sharon had assured him had been maintained in working order through yearly check-ups.

But now Harold was all at sea. If she could betray his final trust before terminating her contract, then how was he to be sure that all the previous trust he had placed in her over the years had not been secretly abused? He tried telling himself that perhaps she had been too emotional at the prospect of them parting, but the idea seemed risible. She was as cold and emotionless as he was, or as they had both gradually become through the necessarily abstract pattern of their interaction.

At first she had only been hired to bring him food provisions every month, clean the house, take away the bins and very occasionally, yearly at best, take away a copy of a new manuscript to his literary agent. All of this business had to be conducted in total silence. Had he been some Roman emperor or decadent sultan from history, perhaps he would have had her tongue cut out at the start. She had played her part well, as far as Harold could tell, until now. Unless she had been secretly selling her story to a national newspaper, ridiculing his eccentric isolation in a public arena. This unlikely thought irked him more now, after this infuriating last-minute no-show. But this was paranoia talking. He had always known that paranoia would be one of the chief dangers of this experiment. There was no way of knowing whether anyone out there even remembered who Harold Swimmer was anymore, never mind wanting to read salacious gossip about him from his housekeeper. Was her departure some kind of statement though? A calculated insult? A foretaste of what was to come? -Of some terrible wave of horrors he was going to encounter as he sought to re-make his acquaintance with an estranged world?

Harold stopped to get his breath back as he gained the high ridge and soaked up the view, hoping the good weather would hold up for a dry night in his tent. He was fifty-five now, he told himself again, not the fit young man anymore who had turned his back on the world to everyone's astonishment, at the height of his new fame and fortune. He had suddenly been someone then, or had thought he was. And it was that very feeling that had frightened him. The egotism, the megalomania he had felt unable to resist as it ran through his veins every day and multiplied. The compliments from critics and publishers that all quickly began to feel like dirty handprints on his mental clothes, veiled demands that he should be what they wanted, say what they wanted, fit into their mould. That, he remembered, was why he had come out here. To forget all that and to remember instead how to be nobody again. What was that phrase of TS Eliot's again? The *"intolerable shirt of flame"*... here he had managed to take it off again at last, and breathe easily.

He sat down on a rock and got out his sketchbook and jotted down a few notes before he could forget them. All too soon, he realised, the actual world out there would erase all his strange half-formed postulations of what it might have become now, and he was scared to lose those elusive, fragile concepts: the fruits of his life's isolation, a unique literary experiment.

*

The Flowers of Uncertainty

A bright summer's morning, the twittering of birds and the gentle sobbing of the waves on the beach. The patio doors lie open, a few grains of sand blowing in across the polished wooden floor, a patch of blazing sunlight edging across the room to rouse Harold where he lies on a mattress on the floor under a pleasantly dishevelled pile of different-coloured blankets.

He crawls out from under it and puts the kettle on at the kitchenette, then shuffles out onto the sand. The light blinds him with its swaying diadems. He breaks into a run, then walks into the sea and swims back and forth, a few gulls spying him and circling above, mocking him with their cries. *You, prisoner of your own ideas...* they seem to laugh *...can never be so free as us.*

Harold hears the outboard motor turning the promontory and just for a second tenses, as he still always does, at the vague prospect that some unbidden stranger should accidentally stumble into his remote bay. But it is Sharon of course, he quickly sees. Her long black hair blows out behind her in the breeze, obscuring her face like a veil of mourning.

Distracted, Harold suddenly notices that something has snagged under his feet. The effect has been gradual, but Harold could swear that marine pollution has increased over the decades. It is some kind of empty plastic canister, with writing on it, even a skull and bones. He picks it up in disgust, planning to take it to Sharon's bin bags, when something in his brain sounds an alarm bell. This is the defence mechanism that Harold has disciplined himself with over the years. There was something in the glimpsed writing and symbols that he knows he mustn't read, the danger of some fragment of knowledge breaking through from the outer world, and he panics. Almost running to meet Sharon, and in a parody of the joyful embrace they will never share, he thrusts the plastic canister urgently into the bags in her left hand. Caught off guard, Sharon nearly speaks, and Harold raises an eyebrow and puts a finger to her lips.

Indoors, they silently unpack Sharon's provisions together. He cuts melon and fresh bread and cheese for her and takes it out onto the veranda. She signals to him and he hands her the notepad, her only permitted form of communication. She writes on it: *I brought the costumes that you asked for, what do you want, for what price?*

Harold takes the sealed sacks of money to his study and puts the bulk of it into a locked drawer, takes a handful of twenties back out and returns to the living room with it. He hands half of it, along with a red swimming costume and an owl mask to Sharon, then says: *change into them and join me outside.*

Harold keeps no mirrors in the house, so Sharon has no firm conception of her appearance, probably exotic, as she comes out to join Harold under the parasol. As they eat in the usual silence, her owl's head cocks from side to side occasionally, its lurid red feathers blowing in the wind, those merciless round eyes seeming to scrutinise him.

Scarcely has the last dripping piece of melon left her mouth, than he asks her to stand, as she passes his chair he cuts the strings of her bikini with his knife, drawing a little blood from its serrated edge. She lets out a little shriek and he kisses the blood, drinking. The gesture is one akin to dining rather than a gesture of love. She walks to the sea, as the bikini drops, and he admires the perfection of her form in the twisting sunlight, her footsteps adorning the sand as she moves, sinking in deeply. At the water's edge, the naked red owl cocks its head at the noonday sun and seems to open its beak to heaven, as Harold's vision swims, uttering a silent scream.

He takes the remaining twenties from his pocket and rolls them tightly. When she returns he turns her around and tries to put the money inside her. She slaps him and holds his throat then turns to the table and writes on the pad: *More... money, that is.* He gives her the rest of the notes and she takes a white scarf from his chair and ties it around his head, blindfolding him...

When breakfast is over, Sharon knows she must leave. Another month before the current manuscript is finished, he tells her, and writes its title and number of words down, and passes the note to Sharon, who hoists her backpack and heads for the jetty. As she starts the motor and round the bay, Harold returns to his chair and begins writing, the red mask's feathers blowing among the sand at his feet. He writes: **Harold closed his sketchbook, and resumed his long walk...**

The Flowers of Uncertainty

*

Harold closed his sketchbook, and resumed his long walk, pleased with his jottings. His old gifts had not yet deserted him, perhaps. The prospect of how his seventeen subsequent books had been received in his absence made his mouth water at times. Surely they had each been even better than that fateful first novel? –which although it had spawned much controversy, had made him enough money to set himself up for life. Or could his star somehow have faded? Fickle fashion turned its back on him? Ah, but then surely he would be due a revival by now? Or think bigger. He knew the Nobel rules did not permit a dead author to win, but a self-exiled one would certainly have remained gloriously eligible. There had been comparisons to Joyce and Beckett. It was not a ridiculous hope.

His first book, the cult novel *The Flowers of Uncertainty*, had been acclaimed for its philosophical ideas as much as for its mind-bending descriptive sequences. Not since *de Sade* or *Nietzsche* had there been such a sense abroad of the potency and danger of words and ideas. Some social commentators were afraid there would be copycat activity by the young and impressionable, of people taking the book too literally and applying it to their own life. The description of casual suicides, of sex between humans and animals, had appalled the conservative lobby and kick-started the beginnings of a backlash. Harold's agent had laughed and said this was the surest formula for more sales he could possibly imagine. Literary immortality would be assured. Make the next one even more offensive if you like, Harry. Just pick a taboo and blast it. The man's smarmy grin and reeking cigar over dinner at his London club that night had sickened him at that moment, and haunted him ever since. That taste of the last cocktails he had ever tasted was with him still, like a thirty-year hangover. Drawing back the blinds on the Notting Hill skyline the next morning, he had realised he had to escape and never come back. Until now. Until he was ready. Until all the rest of the extraordinary unfolding of his written world had completed itself, unpolluted and just as he wanted it. No huckster or hawker or hack to slave-drive and slobber and fawn over his shoulder, trapping him in a fairground of mirrors, turning him into a circus clown, a performing bear.

Yes. He was clean. He had been clean out here in the wilderness. Beautifully free of every compromising influence. Sharon had been only his housekeeper at first, and his courier. The one necessary point of contact, a non-return valve to control and constrict his access to the world. Voluntary self-imprisonment. A paradox. The only way to be truly free.

He had found her through various anonymous ads in the paper. Then through a series of letters in advance, in which he vetted and prepared her for the need for absolute secrecy and discretion, and the necessity of never daring to speak. Harold had thought it through. Verbal conversation was too impulsive, too throw-away. It would have been only a matter of time until Sharon let slip some clue to a critical world event, some crisis or startling new discovery, and then in some casual but hideous moment: Harold would be subtly rejoined to humanity, brought up to speed with all their petty squabbles and tribulations. That was what he needed to avoid. His books, his thoughts, might influence the world. Hopefully they would, and had. But never vice versa. Whatever money he might be making, Sharon was authorised to bring only regular set amounts of it back to Harold.

He had everything he needed, or so he thought. A small collection of the greatest books ever written, to read and re-read for inspiration, several encyclopaedias and anthologies. Food and water and time.

But he was only twenty-five when he shut himself away.

Later he would tell himself, rather lamely, that Sharon had brought it on herself. -That her turning up increasingly late had meant her carrying out the housework in front of him, that her stockings and skirts had become more and more calculatedly alluring. But he was probably imagining all that. Was it her scent on the air? Pheromones, the imperceptible gravity of evolution working its nefarious sorcery behind everyone's back? He had been both surprised then astounded when he found himself pressing himself up behind her on some sleepy pretext, to find that as one hand went on swishing with the cloth, her other hand merely reached back and held his thigh there like a natural and necessary addition, a welcome extension to herself. This was the

The Flowers of Uncertainty

only time she had found herself permitted to make noises, although they could scarcely have been called words. As things rapidly escalated, the expression on her face, her rosy cheeks and parted lips, were like a kind of animal exasperation that seemed to mirror his own: as if an insatiable and inconvenient itch was finally being answered with a remedy that could not be administered quickly enough.

They had parted afterwards in a condition of mutual shame. He had been relieved when, some months later, she seemed to respond without insult to his suggestion that money should be involved in any future sexual transactions. She had merely responded by passing him a note: *how much?* Somehow this seemed the masterstroke. The businesslike atmosphere from then on, stripped away all possible connotations and dangers of romance. She, he imagined, although of course he would never have asked, could continue a relationship with her boyfriend or husband, emotionally intact and watertight (since they always used protection), while Harold could view her merely as a sexual care worker.

The arrangement carried one special danger however, that Harold had mostly managed to avoid since. If his proclivities led him to request too much or anything untoward, and thus to offer Sharon more money: then the spectre would loom in his mind that Sharon knew something he didn't about how much money his books were making. It was one of Harold's golden rules of course, that Sharon must never impart such information to him, since it might inevitably give an impression of how his last book had been received and influence unconsciously what he wrote next.

Mostly the sums of money exchanged for sex were small, fifty or sixty pounds, but if for instance Harold were to ask to bugger her and she were to write "five hundred pounds", then a line might be crossed. Would that mean she knew he could afford such a sum? Could he? The price of oral sex seemed to fluctuate like stocks and shares. Harold didn't want to know if this "movement" was linked to the world economy or the Federal Reserve, or worst of all: to his own success.

*

It was midsummer, fortunately, as Harold had always planned, so that this journey, at this latitude, would involve a minimum of darkness. He pitched his tent at ten in the evening and lit a small fire on which to warm some tinned soup. The cool evening breeze picked up and ruffled his hair, as the watchful stars slowly emerged overhead amid the deepening blue, a glittering shawl to wrap around his solitude, a mother he was content not to know.

Afterwards, climbing into his sleeping bag, he looked at his diary then wrote a few more words: ***Harold's old Mercedes, Bessy, sprang miraculously into life…***

*

Harold's old Mercedes, Bessy, sprang miraculously into life. So then, Sharon must have been getting it maintained, and that much of her promises had at least been kept. But perhaps this only made her recent disappearance all the more mysterious: why that last minute betrayal?

After some evening rain, it was another mercifully bright morning, and after a shaky start and numerous stalls and bumps, Harold found that the part of his deep memory dedicated to driving had taken up where it had left off, after three decades. He drove and sang to himself for the first time, then remembered the radio. But when he switched it on he found there were no transmissions, no stations. This seemed odd to him, but he dismissed it as some kind of misconception on his part. The radio mechanism, simple though he knew they were, might have corroded over the years, from condensation on metallic parts inside. He switched it off again, a little disturbed by the strange sound of emptiness.

After the second hour of driving, he began to see buildings, barns, isolated houses. But as he slowed down he saw that some were boarded up, some derelict, but none were occupied any longer. Disconcertion, then fear, began to prickle at his neck. He saw no livestock in the fields. Had he even seen any birds for the last fifty miles? What if…. What if? His mind raced. Where was the nearest nuclear reactor? Was it possible there had been an accident? Surely Sharon wouldn't have let him head off into the middle of a Chernobyl-style wasteland without a word of warning, even a word technically against his own ground-rules?

Then he drove over a rise and felt his unease slacken: he could see people working in the fields, spread out, dozens of them. Then his unease returned, redoubled. There was little or no farm machinery, these people were dressed in curiously shabby greys, headscarves and ragged overalls. A shot rang out and his left windshield shattered and another one blew out one of his tyres. Some gaunt figures, hollow-eyed were turning towards him, lumbering towards the road as his vehicle slid helplessly to a halt. He panicked and felt in the glove compartment, looking for some kind of weapon, the tension and sickness rising in his throat.

*

Her name was Naomi and all her clothes, as well as her hair and eyes: seemed to be in shades of brown, their gently dissonant tonalities the only relief amid this blighted landscape. Even the wheat they tried to live off seemed off-colour. Most children died in infancy, it was whispered. Harold recognised the pattern: these people were returned to a medieval peasant's existence, with the added burden of an infertile earth.

They had a name for their plague, a strange word, which when they were forced to speak it, made them avert their eyes from each other's gaze so as not to amplify between them the force of their recollected horrors. Everyone had lost someone: parents, their children; children, their parents; brothers, their sisters; lovers, their irreplaceable companions. All walked with the walk of dead men to the gallows. No longer slaves of bosses and timetables as they had been before, they were now slaves of life itself, in the form of a God they no longer recognised, so random and unremitting had his punishment of them become. Dreams of golden hopes were banished from their heads, such was their power to break the heart. The safe thoughts now were of the eternal peace of the beloved and departed and the hope of a painless death.

Saratogen. A biological agent devised to improve crop yield, had incorporated nanotechnology, genetic modifiers with self-replicating ability. Once released into the air and carried on the wind and insect wings, plant life and the entire environment had gradually succumbed over six months. The pathogens had evolved and entered human lungs through airborne spores. The symptoms, even among the survivors, were deep lacerations and pock marking of the skin like premature aging. Naomi was no exception, as he saw when she lifted her sand-coloured veil for him in the dusty evening light. The dog she kept in the yard outside had two fully-functioning heads, both trying to bite him.

She was only twenty-one, born during the height of *the distortions* as they had become known. He asked if she could give birth, and she said she had a few times, but never to anything recognisably human, or that had lived for more than a day. She tried to forewarn him, but when she undressed in the dark for him and came to embrace him, he felt between her legs and found her labia swelling to reveal something like a pair of insect mandibles.

She, nor most villagers below the age of thirty, could read or write. The few survivors in their forties were considered old and revered. Harold would sit with them around the campfire at night in the ruins of their church hall and read to them from the one copy of his book he had with him. Gradually over coming days, he found they were surprisingly receptive to his ideas, as they grew to respect him for the physical work he put in, out in the fields, during the day. He showed them how to build a wooden suspension bridge and irrigate their fields using an Archimedes' screw, and at night read from *The Flowers of Uncertainty* about the protagonist's philosophy of interconnected fates and the chains of causality.

Many present seemed suitably comforted, intoxicated even by these revelations once he had elucidated them adequately. He urged them to consider themselves as expendable units of group consciousness, linked invisibly, across space and time, one with their ancestors and descendants. He taught them to discount the burden of freewill by refusing to admit the reality of time, and therefore to recognise creativity and inspiration as the points where time was weakest and the future leaked back. Once he had read his book through to them seven times in as many months, the village elder led him to their secret store of artefacts from the remembered world and presented him with a fresh ream of paper and a fountain pen. Now he would write his next book, his first since his isolation ended. How differently, how much more poignantly, would he see his relationship to the human race now, after such long absence and such calamity?

After another long day in the fields, he finally sat down in his meagre timber hut and began writing: **Sharon walks across the sand in a long black dress and veil...**

*

Sharon walks across the sand in a long black dress and veil, twirling a parasol. Parisienne period dress. In her left hand she holds a long samurai sword, dripping with blood, and in her right hand the severed leg of a goat.

After Harold has photographed her, she brings the leg back and hoists it onto the brazier to cook above the beach fire.

They dine among the waves at an elaborate Edwardian table set with tablecloth and silverware and crystal glasses and decanter.

Later, Sharon knows she must leave an hour before darkness falls. She cuts the living room chandelier down with the sword, so that it plunges down into the floor and impales itself there with a satisfying thud.

He takes her from behind over the kitchen worktop and thrusts their clenched hands into a bucket of ice at climax.

She releases a recently purchased cage full of twenty yellow canaries into the living room then turns to go. Excited by the birds' confusion in the growing gloom, Harold runs after her as she approaches the jetty. Catching her shoulder, she turns and the evening breeze lifts her veil to reveal, to his horror, the deep red pocks and lacerations of the

Saratogen virus. She punches and slaps him and he cries out and falls back onto the sand.

As the sound of her boat motor leaves the bay, he lifts his head up to look back at the house. In the windows of the lit rooms, tiny black shapes dart about amid the glowing yellow lamplight. While outside his way back is lined with a dozen elaborately framed Victorian mirrors, each half-buried at different angles in the sand, all orientated towards him now, the jetty, the direction of the setting sun.

*

Harold woke up with a start. He was in his tent, cold, limbs stiff after a night on the ground. A bad dream. And all nonsense of course. He hadn't reached civilisation, or even his old car yet… if it still worked. Still another day's walking to go. He stretched, then knelt to relight the fire. Exercised to warm up, set a pan of water to boil for coffee.

Outside the day was clear again, as he hoisted his pack. He wondered if the pattern of white cirrus above contained some dissipated contrails, but found it hard to say. With a flash of paranoia, he wondered when the last time he had seen an aeroplane pass overhead was, then dismissed the thought. Perhaps he just stopped noticing them at some point over the years.

*

It stood to reason that development might have moved further into the wilderness over the years, but even so, Harold was surprised to encounter some houses before he reached what had once been the road end where his car was parked.

In daylight, he was uncertain if anyone was inside the houses, but they looked well-maintained. One had a car in the driveway: the

The Flowers of Uncertainty

design of which was alien to Harold, but not excessively so, as if the future has been no leap forward, just an aimless improvisation on past themes.

At last he saw a small shop ahead and resolved to buy some water. As he approached however, he was confused to see crosses either side of its signboard and a crucifix above the door. The building didn't look like a church. In the window display he saw books, and beyond that: shelves and fridges of drinks and snacks and thus emboldened, he walked in. An electronic voice was triggered and said into the air above him *Good day, sir, and may the blessing of Jesus be upon you.* Harold was slightly startled by this technology, and stopped and hovered at the books, and was relieved to see they were not all bibles and pamphlets.

Can I help you? – a voice asked from behind him, the first living voice other than his own, that he had heard in thirty years. He turned around to see a middle-aged man with close-cropped white hair and beard, in a black polo-neck with a silver crucifix around his neck.

Startled, Harold asked: *Oh... good morning, is this a church shop or something, charity, salvation army?*

The man laughed half-heartedly and shook his head, as if dazzled by Harold's faulty logic. *A what?*

You know, a religious bookshop, a charity shop... except these books aren't second hand, are they?

A charity shop... the man repeated to himself, scratching his head. *That is a strange and old-fashioned expression, brother. You want to buy charity? You want the books for free?*

Harold was thrown by the *"brother"*.

Are you an outlander or a voyager?

A what?

The two men stared at each other in increasing perplexity, even hostility. The tapestry of common language that both presumed they shared seemed to be beginning to unravel before their eyes under the pressure of misunderstandings. Harold felt the foundations of cultural assumptions starting to shake beneath his feet, the façade of politeness cracking. He knew how colloquialisms encode and enforce a way of life, and he was starting to feel like a trespasser across some invisible assault course.

You seem confused sir, shall I call your wife for you?
I don't have a wife.
Oh, I'm sorry for your loss, sir.
Sorry?
No, I'm sorry, like I just said.
Why? She's not dead, I mean she doesn't exist. I don't have wife, I've never had one.

The man's eyes darkened gravely at this, his cheeks coloured and he retreated to his back counter to make a telephone call.

Harold muttered *Jesus Fuck* under his breath as he looked for some crisps and lemonade, the brands all new and incomprehensible to him, but a moment later was grabbed from behind and physically shunted out of the shop by the seat of the pants and thrown onto the pavement.

How dare you profane against the saviour's name in public, you pervert! –the man bellowed at him and tossed some tepid liquid over him from an elaborate glass jar.

What the fuck is that? Holy water?! Harold wailed, and the man crossed himself and vanished inside and barred the shop door behind him, closing for the day.

Further on, Harold came to a petrol garage, and while he was smart enough this time to remain almost silent while buying his provisions, he was dismayed to see that the staff here were also dressed ecclesiastically with crucifixes at their necks.

After this good behaviour, Harold was in disbelief when a police car slid to a halt in front of him and two officers emerged dramatically, aiming some sort of weapons at him. *Are you kidding?* -he laughed, then one of them fired an agonising electrical pulse over his right side, while the other one tripped him up and kicked him in the groin.

Before he blacked out he heard the words *Pervert! Pervert!* Being chanted, as more kicks came in.

*

Harold woke up in an interrogation room, with a jug of cold water being thrown over him. The man in front of him was in black uniform, and insisted on being addressed as *Father Inspector*. As Harold's eyes adjusted he saw to his disbelief that this man had small silver crucifixes on each shoulder, amongst his other quasi-military ribbons bars, and a white dog-collar around his neck.

Your name please.

Harold Swimmer.

His henchman leaned over and punched Harold off his chair, head-butted him then sat him up in the chair again. Harold noticed the crucifix around his neck. *How can you behave like this and wear a cross?* Harold moaned, wiping the blood from his swollen face.

The thug slapped him and said: *You will always address his grace as Father Inspector.*

Your name please.

Harold Swimmer, Father Inspector.

The thug moved to punch Harold off the chair again, but to his relief, *his grace* raised a hand in mercy.

Sir... I'm going to give you the benefit of the doubt for a minute. I'm going to assume, incredibly unlikely as it seems, that you were actually christened with the name Harold Swimmer, and that in an attempt to be honest you are repeating to us this unfortunate moniker. One must presume, however, that to have survived to this age... how old are you?

Fifty-five...

An eyebrow rose.

Fifty-five, Father Inspector.

Then you must have gone under another name for most of your life, a second name, your mother's maiden name perhaps.

No... Harold shook his head in confusion. *My name is Harold Swimmer. I am Harold Swimmer. What's wrong with that?*

The atmosphere in the room chilled with his last sentence, into something approaching shock.

What's wrong with that? -His grace mused, finally breaking the silence. *Well, let me see... Would you call your son Adolf Hitler? Guy Fawkes? Genghis Khan?*

I don't understand. I am Harold Swimmer.

Everybody knows, every child is brought up to know, that there was no Harold Swimmer, any more than there was ever a Ned Ludd of the Luddite movement. Both were invented names, mythical figureheads, masks for a variety of scoundrels, who in the case of Swimmer became the name for the movement of Swimmerites.

The Swimmerites?! No way! Look, there's something I ought to explain.

The thug moved towards him, truncheon drawn. *You must never interrupt the Father Inspector when he is in mid-sermon, you unmarried perverted cunt.*

Again however, the hand of mercy was raised and the muscle withdrew. *Continue...*

I have been away. Living in isolation, for thirty years. I have had no knowledge of how the world has changed while I've been away. Do you understand? I am lacking all thirty years of recent history. It's not my fault if I am confused and confounded by your customs, and hitting me won't make any difference, other than killing me eventually. Please try to understand: I am an outsider to this, you need to explain things to me slowly, not hit me. Please.

His grace sighed and leaned back in his chair and reached under his desk and brought out a large black leather-bound bible and placed it on the desk and began leafing through it. Eventually he left it open at a particular page and turned it around for Harold to read. Harold leafed back a few pages and saw the chapter heading *The Third Testament*.

Read this section, out loud, please... the Father Inspector instructed. Harold began, as the thug tapped his truncheon menacingly at his shoulder:

Every century has its abominations and its abominable books. Hitler's **Mein Kampf**, *de Sade's* **Hundred Days of Sodom**, *Rushdie's* **Satanic Verses**. *The Swimmerites' profane and obscene book* **Flowers of Uncertainty** *was a call-to-arms for morally-flacid and corrupt liberals everywhere. Their leader, Marcus Vermont gained power in the aftermath of the World Currency Wipeout and the third devastating Oil*

War. Blaming all of society's ills to date on the political right-wing, he enacted as an antidote the deranged policies expounded in the Flowers of Uncertainty. He held a referendum on hanging, then publicly hanged everyone who voted for it. He rounded up all the holocaust-denialists and put them in a concentration camp to be starved and worked to death while telling each other it wasn't happening. He proclaimed, by use of a spurious, supposedly watertight argument from the book of Swimmer, that every fundamentalist Christian who condemned homosexuality as a matter of choice rather than birth, must in fact be themselves homosexual to think like this, and were thus condemned to wear pink poof hats and armbands for the rest of their life. Under Vermont's deranged rule (akin to the medieval Feast of Fools led each year by an Abbot of Unreason), all racists were injected with a variant of Nelson's syndrome, to alter their skin pigmentation to black. The Swimmerites called their political movement "The Poetic Justice Party" and by the time they were done, half a million innocent men, women, and children had been brutally put to death just for harbouring supposedly right-wing views.

Fortunately, after the ensuing civil war, sanity and Christianity were restored, in the pure and morally unassailable fusion of state and church that we all prosper under today. At last the institution of Family is safe and in safe hands. The Book of Swimmer, The Flowers Of Uncertainty, is one of a number of extreme, profane, and banned texts, preserved for scholarly study, by appointment only, at the Christian Regional Institute of Military Ethics (C.R.I.M.E). Like spores of Smallpox, the recipe for Artex plaster, and the museum at Auschwitz, it has been deemed only wise to preserve certain obscenities such as this, as moral warnings to the future generations of Humanity, and constant reminders of the depths to which we can all stoop in an age of moral decadence without appropriate spiritual guidance from government. Never again must these corrosive ideas be unleashed to corrupt and intoxicate zealots…

I've read enough, Harold sighed, and slid the book back across the table.

Just before the incident in which you publicly blasphemed against our holy saviour's name, you told a Christian brother that you were unmarried. Is that so?

Yes.

So how long have you been a sodomite?

Sodomite? Swimmerite?

Same difference.

I'm not one. But I've never understood why God is supposed to lie awake at night worrying about men's bottoms. I mean, what's wrong with the guy?

Chairs are thrown back in shock at this profanity, and the thug prepares his truncheon for duty.

I think, then, the Father Inspector intones piously, closing his bible, standing up and bringing his "sermon" to a close, *-that the Reverend Sergeant should illustrate to you now exactly why God worries about men's bottoms…*

*

Of course, the foregoing was all just fantastical conjecture from Harold's diary, filled out at his midday rest, as he ate a sandwich on a mountain pass, looking down over the long valley. He would have to walk for another half day before hopefully finding his motor car intact.

As he set off and walked downhill, his limbs were pleasantly tired, his mood fair as the good weather continued around him. He felt buoyed up by the prospect of perhaps reaching civilisation by nightfall and getting a comfortable bed for the night.

But he was to be disappointed. It was with growing disbelief as he approached at last the location of the remote wooden lock-up shed for his car at the road's end, that he saw signs of black sooting on the landscape around it.

He felt like weeping when he stood at last before the scene, at close quarters: the acrid smell of burning, only diluted slightly by recent rain. Someone had used petrol to burn down the entire garage and destroy the car, disturbingly recently. It was hard to escape the unsettling suspicion that Sharon had somehow been involved. But why and how?

Harold kicked his way for a few minutes through the twisted debris, looking fruitlessly for clues or fragments of consolation, some kind of explanation.

There was nothing for it. Harold would have to walk along the road now, as far as he could before nightfall, then pitch his tent by the roadside.

Somewhere ahead soon, tomorrow perhaps, there would have to be a phonebox or a cottage, a car to flag down for assistance. He kept walking. Angrily.

*

Next morning, after a cold and sleepless night, running low on fuel for his stove and provisions to eat, Harold came at last to a road junction after four hours walk, and flagged down the first passing car.

He was too overwhelmed at first to take in the design of the car or the clothes of the driver, but once he was settled in the passenger seat and hurtling along happily at sixty miles an hour, making his first inconsequential conversation with a stranger in thirty years, it began to dawn on him how unsurprising and un-different everything was. Mrs MacAteer was a local teacher on her day off, a plump woman in her early fifties, in frumpy Arran tweeds and boots. Her car was some sort of Ford or Honda, its proportions distorted, but not drastically so, in some new direction dictated by the arbitrary and ultimately entirely meaningless whims of fashion. Design, he suddenly saw, in every field, with all its restlessness and self-seriousness, had no more moral validity than sexual perversion. Indeed, it was all a form of fetishism.

The engine was surprisingly quiet, and he wondered to himself if it was petrol or diesel or some new elixir that he would have no knowledge of.

Soon enough, as they approached the nearest train station, his questions about train times and fares led Mrs MacAteer to ease off in her monologue about her own trivial affairs and pry instead into her passenger's background. *Have you been away a long time or something? You don't seem very prepared for your journey. Are you returning from a holiday?*

I've been on a remote farm, for many years, without television or radio. I don't even know who the Prime Minister is.

You're joking! -she exclaimed and eyed him in awe, nearly failing to pay attention to the road. *How many years exactly have you been out of contact?*

By the time she dropped him at the quaintly painted Victorian country station, Harold was quite depressed by the discovery that, in thirty years, so very little of any importance had happened. There were new names, unfamiliar individuals in power, a few minor scientific breakthroughs but, particularly when described to him by such a mundane-minded individual, Harold had the extraordinary sense that the glitteringly exotic "Future" he had so looked forward to and longed for, for so many years, was just a mirage, a fantasy. -One rapidly being replaced in his mind now, minute by dreary minute, with the utterly sterile grey boredom of a present much the same as the one he had left behind.

It was with some relief therefore, reaching Inverness a few hours later, that he began to see some new glass and steel buildings, new bridges and highways, signs that progress and development had set about turning an old country town into something resembling an emergent city. There was a buzz about it, and as he alighted from the train, he hurried with some excitement, through the altered and thriving streets towards the newest bookshop.

He walked between the aisles and puzzled, with some irritation, over the proliferation of headings and sub-headings, new genres and sub-genres. He wondered for a moment if people weren't writing books anymore, just new genre categories. He found nothing under Swimmer in the literary section, nor under Fantasy, Horror, or Sci-Fi.

In increasing perplexity and dejection, he turned at last to the pretty young assistant behind the information desk and tried to speak to her calmly without being distracted by her bizarre clothes and tattoos that she and everyone else seemed to think entirely normal.

We have nothing here under Swimmer, oh... hold on a minute, one Penguin Classic, now out of print, "Power of Uncertainty".

The Flowers of Uncertainty, he corrected.

Whatever. Yes, we can order it for you, but it may take up to six weeks to arrive.

What about other titles, by the same author? The Smiling Precipice? Fugitive Dreams of the Enslaved? Destiny's Lips? Under the Glacier? The Thorns of Vanity?

Mmm... it looks like we have some of those titles, yes... the assistant smiled, light from the screen flickering over her face as Harold's heart leapt, *...but under the name Sharon Sullivan,* she finished.

I'm sorry?

Here. She rotated the screen to show him, and Harold felt the blood rushing to his ears, his vision beginning to pixelate and dissolve under the onslaught of sensory malfunction. *There must be some mistake...* -he was stammering and stuttering so badly now that other customers, particularly those in the queue behind him, were getting agitated and impatient, showing little respect for his seniority. He struggled to focus his mind, before acquiescing to this pressure to give in and retreat. *P-please, c-can I o-order some of th-those th-then?*

No need to... -the assistant smiled, assuming her best painted expression of patience for a senile lunatic. *There on the shelves there behind you.*

With disbelief, Harold turned and walked like a dead man towards the *Sharon Sullivan* section of the bookshop and the ten to fifteen colourful bestselling paperbacks there, with their covers adorned with all kinds of praise from critics and celebrities.

With difficulty, and the aid of an in-store cup of espresso going under some bewilderingly exotic name like Brazilian Negress (the request for *just a coffee* had been met with amazement and laughter at the counter), Harold managed to still his shakes somewhat and sit down to read from one of "Sharon's" books.

What he read there only deepened his outrage and confusion. To have stolen his identity would have been one thing, perhaps reversible by a string of lawsuits, but with the exception of the odd recognisable sentence here and there, Sharon appeared to have completely altered his work into a kind of schmaltzy *Women's Weekly* parody of itself. It was all incredibly readable, incredibly popular supposedly, but in Harold's eyes at least: incredibly shallow froth.

Re-reading the review comments on the covers, he saw now that praise came from other authors of similarly populist and lightweight "romances".

On the back cover of each book he found a synopsis that closely resembled his original plot outline, but inside he found that every idea and subtlety of narration and description had been replaced by clumsy and moronic infantilisms, every character reduced to a cardboard cut-out of a media stereotype.

In the inside sleeve of the hardback edition of "Sharon's" latest book, he found a photograph of her faintly smiling face, with bookish looking spectacles on, and a studiedly intellectual expression.

What began as a nervous spasm and cough in Harold's throat, unexpectedly followed through into an urgent need to wretch and suddenly, too bereft of hope to care and too exhausted to stand, he sat and vomited over the books in front of him, while the other café patrons looked on helplessly with expressions of dazed horror only pale imitations of his own…

*

No. All of the foregoing was mere paranoid speculations of course, written in a tent by the roadside in failing daylight.

What Harold actually came to first on his long walk of that morning was an emergency telephone box, from where he was able to call, with the aid of Directory Enquiries, his brother in London. To his amazement, the display showed him his brother's face, who seemed to be actually able to see him also. Of course, his credit cards were no longer valid, even the money in his pocket no longer legal tender. Victor would have to come to meet him, if he was to have the slightest chance of quickly finding his way back into society again without being apprehended as a suspected madman or illegal immigrant.

In the background, behind Victor's face, children were running around and when one of them came to the phone, Harold was able to marvel at the hereditary likeness of an unknown nephew looking back at him wide-eyed. He felt like a space-traveller just returned from a thirty year voyage around Saturn.

*

It was with astonishment, followed by delight, that Harold saw that the taxi coming to meet him an hour later, ordered remotely by his brother, ran on neither wheels nor petrol. Its design was low, curvaceous and sleek, extremely fast, but making only a slight electric whistling noise as it moved, not unpleasant.

At last, Harold marvelled, here was reality, more surprising and unexpected than any of his postulations in his diary. Here was the real future, arrived at last, thrilling and unimaginable.

The car stopped suddenly yet gracefully beside Harold and, to his astonishment, went on hovering. He waved at the driver but circled around the vehicle in awe, kneeling down to look right under it. The chassis didn't even feel that hot. When he looked up again the driver seemed to be regarding him with a mixture of worry and puzzlement, his brow furrowed.

You alright, mate? he asked, in a jokey sort-of off-hand taxi-driver manner, and Harold smiled at the familiarity of an old archetype in new clothes. No doubt, he would talk to Harold about football for the entire journey with a liberal smattering of right-wing views about immigration thrown in.

The door opened for him, not overhead or any other ridiculous sci-fi notion, but sideways with considerable grace and economy, as natural as the wing of a fly.

The driver's smile was genuine and relaxed, and for a moment Harold felt like embracing him, simply for existing, and appearing such a straightforward and unproblematic example of the human species.

As it turned out, the man wasn't interested in football, but instead regaled Harold for most of the journey with his reasonable understanding of the missing history of automotive engineering that explained the vehicle they were driving in. He, in turn, was delighted by the novelty of Harold's tale of self-isolation, although perhaps not entirely convinced he wasn't being wound-up.

Retaliating needlessly against this imagined spoof perhaps, the driver even tried to tell Harold the Prime Minister was now a dog, before relenting and confessing that this was just a current joke based on some kind of pun on his name. *Hey, you won't have heard about the moon base then will you? Or the Centauri signal? No? Well, it just looks like a huddle of portakabins to me, but I fig it's a start thing, frere. They say it's going to be a low-grav lux hote for mega-richers in ten years.*

Harold tried to ignore the words he didn't understand. *What was the other thing you mentioned?*

Centauri Signal? Alien stuff they say, just looks like a load of crap to me, but the big brains say they've part deciphered it.

What do they look like? Did they send pictures of themselves?

Yeah, sort of a bit crab-like in a boring sort of way. It's no big deal. Some experts say their world is vanishing into an expanding star, and their signal is a kind of calling-card to us to ask us to be ready for them when they evacuate to here in a few centuries. Yeah, right. Let's be ready for them with a large interstellar machine-gun, that's what I say. Bloody aliens, coming here and stealing all our jobs…

When the driver dropped him at the station, Harold was surprised to see that what he thought had been some kind of taxi-driver's uniform was in fact a widespread form of clothing, a fashion perhaps, worn by almost everyone. The weave was curiously broad and open, a kind of synthetic mesh in whitish shades of pale blue and yellow, it seemed to shed water and stains instantly. To Harold, people almost looked liked they were wearing shell-suits, as if the whole world had become social security claimants on sink estates, but with a leap of imagination he realised they must be high fashion and shuddered at the mystery of how his clothes might appear to them. He was beginning to feel out of place, sartorially cast adrift, a cultural interloper.

He suspected the train was hovering too and wanted to inspect the curious housings that were clutching the rails, but was warned off by a platform guard muttering about magnetism. The luxury inside was impressive, with video screens on the back of every chair that somehow projected sight and sound into a focussed beam where he sat, but became invisible and inaudible as soon as he moved away. He nearly cried out in fright when he saw that the luxurious cushions of his chair used shape-memory, and he left an embarrassing little bass-relief of his own bottom behind him when he went to the toilet.

He was amazed on reaching Inverness to discover that it had become, in essence, Tokyo. Moving display signs unfolded in every direction on buildings of a height he had never expected to see in an erstwhile modest country town.

When his brother arrived to collect him at the station and they embraced in tears, lamenting each other's aged appearance, Harold had a thousand questions to ask. First of these was why the station staff had locked him in a room and made him put a white shirt on.

Ah... -Victor sighed, and pressed a bracelet on his hand against the lapel of Harold's shirt, until an array of musical notes rang out.

What the hell was that? –Harold gasped.

Your train fare, encoded in your clothing, and me paying it for you.

My shirt is a credit card?! -he laughed, astounded.

Pretty much I fig, frere, and a 'puter, phone, and a few other things, I'll show you later.

Wait! What did you just say there? The taxi-driver did that too, "frere" or something? And "fig"? Why do I keep hearing that?

Oh, Harry, language has changed, I suppose, in lots of silly little ways, mannerisms, tics and idioms, don't worry about it, you'll pick it up. I suppose "frere" is from French for brother, though nobody thinks about it anymore, European integration and all that. But I'm guessing. What the hell did OK mean when people used to say that?

Beats me. I seem to have forgotten, but what do they say now, instead?

Cool, of course, or Sweet, or Hot. And they never say "beats me" now, so you can drop that one first up.

*

After a short ride in Victor's car, he was overcome with emotion at his first sight of Victor's wife and children waiting for him in a hotel restaurant. His wife was so beautiful and kind, their children Dean and Maggy wonderful little semblances of each of them, so healthy-looking and well-adjusted. He found himself crying with joy until his brother started to become embarrassed. *I thought Directory Enquiries said you all lived in London, how come you're all here?*

We've come up to meet you, Harry, a little away-day. It's only a few hours journey these days, we'll stay overnight, make a holiday of it. Maybe we should go look at your hideaway, the kids might be fascinated to see it.

Shit. I've just left there, Vic. I never want to see it again.

Why did you do it anyway? You look like you've been through Hell. Why on earth did you ever do this to yourself?

Harry looked down at his feet in the restaurant where they sat and felt something approaching shame. *Oh we went through all that at the time, in the weeks before I left. What's done is done. I got some amazing books out of it though, didn't I?*

There was a curious, embarrassed silence for a moment, which puzzled Harold, which he felt compelled to break: *But guys, I have a thousand questions for you... like how did you meet and where? Where were you married? What do you both do for a living?*

Harold enjoyed himself so much in the company of his closest surviving family, being shown amazing "Puter Games" by their children, many of them stitched into their shirts and trousers, that he somehow almost forgot his own erstwhile chief obsession in life: books.

The first bookshop Victor took him to looked like a computer games shop to him. Victor had to explain that books were virtual now, and the shelves only held focussed data streams of each book, which touched your senses one after the other as you walked by. To buy a book, you merely downloaded the data streams onto your "puter" or of course your clothes themselves, where the pages could be turned at will, or narrated into your ear as audio files.

The Flowers of Uncertainty

Harold felt quite disorientated and sick in the midst of this, and prevailed upon Victor to lead him instead to an antique bookshop where he could find old-fashioned physical volumes bound in paper and even leather. Needless to say, when he got there, the shopkeeper was old, and Harold was immediately in seventh heaven (not an expression, incidentally, that anyone used any longer).

The works of Harold Swimmer? No.... The bookseller was quite adamant, there had only ever been one book by Harold Swimmer. The cult classic *The Flowers of Uncertainty.*

Then it's still being read?

Oh yes, on every literature course in the country, and many others across the globe. A unique classic of early twenty-first century literature, it sparked off a string of imitations at the time, continues to influence writers today. The writer went missing I believe, a tragic loss to the world.

Harold closed his eyes, took a deep breath, and nearly blurted out some deranged response to this, but thought better of it and restrained himself. *But you're certain he didn't write other books like "The Smiling Precipice" or "Under the Glacier"?*

The kindly old gentleman entered the names into his computer again, just to humour Harold, but confirmed what he had already established. *As far as I can see, these titles have never existed, never been in print, and my databases are fairly exhaustive. Where did you find references to them? Are they mentioned in some journal somewhere?*

The man seems genuinely intrigued now, but Harold walked away downcast, muttering under his breath: *Maybe I dreamt it, then.* Before he reached the door, he turned back and suddenly asked, shaking: *Have you anything by an author called Sharon Sullivan?* But of course he hadn't. All that had just been a bad dream, one of his paranoid postulations, but now he was uncertain whether reality was necessarily going to turn out any better.

*

Later, when Marla and the kids had gone up to bed, Harold sat with Victor in the Hotel bar and Harold worked through his dark mood, sharing his perplexed fears with Victor.

I don't understand it, Victor. I'm struggling to come to come to terms with the enormity of what must have, might have, happened here. I hired this woman Sharon, I trusted her completely, to pass each of my manuscripts on to my literary agents and get them published and place the royalties into my trust fund. If she wasn't doing that then where on Earth was all the money coming from?

Have you got other copies of each manuscript? –Victor asked suddenly.

Of course, of course, back at the beach house, and on my computer.

What was your Agent's name?

Strutter and Giraud, Harold said.

Allow me, Victor said, and turned Harold's shirt into an interactive screen, on which he dialled up the world wide web and scrolled through numerous websites and databases. *Folded ten years ago, taken over by Watkins, Maller and Fulton of New York. Who did you deal with personally?*

Jacques Giraud.

Here we are. Retired from the firm, it looks like, five years ago, now resident in the United States. The States are eight hours behind, right?

What are you doing?

Phoning him up of course, it's afternoon there, and it says here he still runs his own little consultancy from his home in Los Angeles.

No. Vic, wait... too late.

Good morning, Mister Giraud? You won't know me, but I have a former client of yours sitting here with me. A mister Harold Swimmer. Would you like a word with him?

What? Harold who? Swimmer, you say, that's impossible...

Victor switches the screen over onto his own chest so that

Harold and Jacques can look at each other, and both men's eyes widen in recognition and sadness and the ageing of their appearance.

Harry?! Is that really you?! How can this be? What happened to you? Did you run out of ideas? What happened to all those books you were going to write? Where the hell have you been hiding?

Listen, Jacques, this is really important. I wrote, I have written, seventeen books over the last thirty years. Are you really telling me that you never received any from my appointed go-between Sharon Sullivan?

Sharon who? Harry? I've never heard of her, and I never heard a word from you after the day you left, blabbering all that stuff about how you were going to lock yourself away from the world to keep your art pure and free from contamination. Harry... what did you write? I'd love to read it!

Don't worry, Jacques, it's all safe. All seventeen books, ready to see the light of day now at last.

After thirty years!? But Harry, that would be sensational, a literary earthquake. I don't get around so much these days, health's not been so good, but you should get yourself over here and I can put you in touch with some of my old contacts in New York.

Jacques, I'm tired tonight. It's been great to talk, but I'm kind of bleached out from travelling, in time as much as space, or that's what it feels like. Can I call you in the morning?

Sure, Harry, sure. You do that. Wait until I tell Mary-Ann. Harold Swimmer... after all these years...

Victor's shirt flickered and blanked down, and Harold's eyes drifted up to meet those of his brother and the look of fear and sadness and doubt that hung now in the air between them.

Harry, what did you say that woman's full name was? Do you have any photographs of her? A friend of mine used to be a detective, he might be able to run some police checks on her and find out some background. How did you meet her?

Harold's eyes were staring off into the distance now, the walls and ceilings of the bar around him a kaleidoscope of flickering colour and light from the hundred other transmitting and receiving shirts. He spoke slowly, in a trance, some strange cold fear taking hold of him.

I found her through an ad in the paper, Vic. The local paper here. It might not even be her real name. I know nothing about her. That was the whole idea, to preserve anonymity and prevent intimacy. If Jacques never got those manuscripts then she must have faked the letters she showed me early on. We're talking major fraud... clever, devious stuff, over decades. What kind of a person...?

Oh Harry... Victor looked down at the floor, shaking his head, ashamed again for his crazy big brother: *What on earth have you gone and gotten yourself into?*

*

That night, Harold had a nightmare in which he was trapped inside one of his favourite oil paintings: *The Isle of the Dead* by Arnold Böcklin. Indeed, Rachmaninov's symphonic poem of the same name seemed to be playing as a soundtrack as he found himself bound and gagged in the bottom of an ancient rowing boat sailing towards the infamous and sombre island: gloomy cliffs and cypress trees, hints of classical ruins and entrances to caves and crypts.

At the head of the boat, he knew of course, the white hooded and cloaked figure must be Sharon, commanding the oars, carrying them both forward across the rippling waves of the deathly black water. He tried to cry out. He kicked his heels against the sides of the boat, and she slowly turned her head a little to reveal that she was wearing the mask of a skull.

On the approaching shore, a wild pack of black dogs burst out of their home among the caves and began barking and yelping in anticipation of their arrival, racing back and forth across the the shore, howling in mourning or hunger: he wasn't sure.

*

Even in his now disturbed state of mind, Harold was able to sleep in late the next morning, such was his physical exhaustion after his long journey on foot. Victor more or less burst into his hotel room around eleven o' clock and shook him awake. *Harry, my friend called me back, you better take a look at this...*

Not opening the curtains, instead Victor turned the entire far wall into a video display at the flick of a switch and set off a data stream of newspaper cuttings and newsreels there. *Her real name is Sharon O' Brien, she was a promising medical student from a wealthy family, but she gave it all up the same year you went into isolation.*

B-but wh-what? -Harry stammered.

Her brother; they were very close. He committed suicide. She was devastated by his death.

Oh no... Harry winced... *why?* His head sinking.

She claimed it was because he had become obsessed with your book, the cult novel **Flowers of Uncertainty**. *Its numerous references to suicide sought to glamorise the subject, she claimed, and led directly to her brother's death. He killed himself in the exact manner of one of the most shocking scenes in your book, like a re-enactment. She campaigned for the next three years to have your book banned.*

And failed? Harold whispered.

Yes, but there's a few book chains became a bit shaky about stocking it for a while. She made a bit of headway with public opinion, founded an organisation called Bereaved Relatives of Suicides, BROS.

And at the same time, she was visiting me once a month. Unbelievable.

You see, Harry? You didn't find her by that ad in the local paper. **She** *found* **you***, she sought* **you** *out. But why didn't she kill you or poison you? Would anyone ever have known?*

Harold suddenly stood up out of bed and began pacing, then almost running back and forward around the room. *Oh God, oh God, Victor... I've got to get back to the beach house. How quickly can I get there?*

I thought you said last night you never wanted to see the place again?

Don't you see? That's where she'll be right now. This whole thing has been one big diversion, a decoy. How quickly can we get there?

*

It cost a lot of money to hire and Victor was a little wary of the controls at first, but by the time they reached the bay by turbo copter, a long plume of black smoke was already emerging from a jagged hole in the roof of the beach house.

Harold could see that Sharon's speedboat was moored at the jetty, and presumed she was therefore still around. Filled with terror at the prospect of the destruction of his writing, he rushed across the sand towards the house, while Victor powered down the chopper.

Inside, he found Sharon waiting for him, presiding, smiling, over the melted ruins of his computer and a charred stack of manuscripts on a makeshift bonfire in the middle of the room. Scattered across the floor were scores of Harold's colour photographs of Sharon in obscene sexual interplay with various fruit, vegetables, and animals. She lifted and aimed a rifle at him from the other side of the room, and there was nothing hi-tech or futuristic about this gadget: it was just a plain old-fashioned shotgun loaded with bullets designed to maim and kill. She spoke for the first time to him, and he was startled and astonished to hear the strength and vehemence of her voice:

Too late, Harry... -she said.

He fell to his knees and began to sob, raising his hands in supplication. *No, Sharon... no... why? Why? What have you done to all my books? My books,* he pleaded, *my life...*

Destroyed them all, over the years, very thoroughly, and now all the original files. I'd say I've done the world a favour, really. No more profiting from sick ideas and spreading the corrupting virus of your perversions throughout the planet. You killed my brother, you sick, twisted little fucker...

I didn't, Harold whispered, *I didn't,* in tears, shaking his head.

Sharon fired a warning shot into the wooden post beside him and a sheet of burning roof sarking fell across the room between them.

My brother Paul had so much potential. He was only twenty-two, you know... a gifted artist... a sweet, sensitive young man, shy, but impressionable. My beloved brother, he doted on me. Your book fascinated then obsessed him. He kept it by his bedside, re-read it constantly, gradually stopped seeing his friends, withdrew from the world. What was that phrase from it he always used to repeat? The silver ones and the sweetness of death...

The silver ones, drunk on moonlight... Harold completes it for her, his own words cutting him like a hangman's rough rope closing around his neck *-***taste sadness on every mouth, among the fountains and the broken statues. The sweetness of death is their nectar, the cold solitude of empty spaces their prize, beneath the falling stars**.

There you go. Wallowing in sadness, suicidal narcissistic rot. Just before yet another pointless suicide scene lovingly described on the page. You killed Paul as surely as if you'd set that chainsaw going and kicked the chair away yourself, you vile, diseased man. And you fucked me up the arse. And photographed me having sex with goats, and all the other abominations.

But I paid you... You could have resigned at any moment.

Harry... love and hate aren't so different. Not for the twisted ones like us. At some level I've enjoyed watching you all these years, having power over you and your pathetic little world, while you thought it was the other way around. Drawing out of you all those perversions and confirming the worst about that sweaty cesspit you have for a mind. Harry, I've loved hating you so much....

I paid you... Harold repeated again, helplessly.

Yes, Sharon smiled bitterly, *and now I've paid you back.*

Suddenly, Victor stormed into the room and froze at the sight of the loaded gun.

Who the fuck is he? Sharon spat.

I'm his brother... Victor blurted out before Harold could stop him and, absorbing the information in a second, Sharon shot him in the chest.

Oh no, no... Victor, Victor.... Harold wailed and knelt over his brother, as blood poured from his mouth, and his eyes began fading away. *Why, why, why?*

Too good an opportunity to miss... Sharon sighed slowly, reloading. *A chance for me to see which upsets you more: the loss of your books or the loss of your brother.*

But I haven't seen him in thirty years! Harold cried out, *He has a wife and young children...*

So would Paul have had by now probably, if it wasn't for you. Life's a shitter, isn't it? But you're not fooling me, you cold-hearted creep. The books still top it for you, don't they?

Is this your justice? My brother for yours?

*Listen to me, you fuckwit. You don't think you have a responsibility for the ideas you expound? I know you think that you don't, because I've still got those press-cuttings, the interviews where you said that. Here is your experiment, Harry, here is your answer. I hope you like it. You don't exist in a vacuum, you **can't** exist in a vacuum. You have a responsibility to Humanity. Without them, you're nothing, you don't even exist anymore. You've erased yourself, for thirty years.*

You've erased me.

While you paid for the privilege.

At least I fucked you, then.

I think we've just firmly established who was fucking who, don't you? How does it feel to be buggered?

So what now, shoot me?

No... Sharon breathed out and pulled up a chair and sat down and relaxed. *First of all, you're going to take that pad of paper over there and start writing. I'll give you an hour or two, to write down the whole story of what I've done to you. Then, after I've made you bury your brother, I'm going to shoot you in the knee caps so you can't run away, then shoot off all your fingers so can never write another word again. Then I'm going to keep you as my torture slave. Remember I trained as a surgeon, you won't bleed to death.*

You're joking?

Try me… -Sharon grinned. *I'll tell you a joke. The masochist says to the sadist "hit me", and the sadist says "no". D'you like it?*

How did you ever get so twisted and insane?

You tell me. You're looking at your own sick work, Harry. You made me. Now reap what you've sown.

Harold took off his jacket and laid it respectfully over his brother's face where he lay, surreptitiously switching his blood-stained shirt to transmit-mode, calculating how many hours it might take for Victor's wife to send the police, if she got the message.

Then with the shotgun still trained on him, he shuffled sadly across the floor and crouched down in the corner with pen and paper and let out a despairing sigh. *Well, I suppose I better make this a good long story then,* he said at last, wondering how the uncertainty would affect his imagination. He began writing:-

A solitary figure slowly makes his way on foot through a vast green landscape of cliffs and moors. The last time this scenery changed was probably during an ice age, and therefore it gives out no clue as to the fate of humanity at this moment in history. The sun clears the clouds and sends a shaft of quasi-religious light down on Harold Swimmer…

*

Harold Swimmer stopped writing and put his pen down. Had he made the character of Sharon too violent, the ending too trite and predictable? A little perhaps, but nonetheless the whole masochistic idea made him shiver pleasurably. He put his hand to his chest pocket, where he kept his paranoid DVD back-up of all seventeen of his novels with him at all times. He would have to seal this manuscript with wax to stop the real Sharon from reading it, he laughed to himself, in case it gave her funny ideas.... about him, about herself. Fantasy is harmless, until it's about people we know. He should stick to inventing strangers.

Before opening the patio doors, and going for his morning stroll along the beach, he turned over a new sheet of paper and started a brand new story, as was his custom, to make sure he was always in the midst of something:

The reclusive rural Scottish writer Douglas Thompson opened and read the letter of acceptance from his eccentric London publisher:

What a freakin' mindfuck! Where the hell does fantasy end and reality begin? Presumably nowhere or everywhere and where the hell do you draw the line between them? Layers beyond layers - and you at the heart of them as the bottom-most layer of all. You are playing a game with yourself as much as with anyone and anything, am I right? I love that type of work where you never know what is real and what isn't and where, in the end, maybe none of it is. But I don't think I could have resisted the urge to have some form of reality check at the end, if I were working that same narrative.

I did find the very end of the story just a touch over-dramatic for my tastes - but just a bit and of course, that in itself provides a tremendous dose of unreality to the conclusion, thus continuing the loop Harold is stuck in. He still seems to be orchestrating that grotesque finish very distinctly - as if he's still telling the story, or you are. I am unsure what possible hold she could have over him with that shotgun, all things considered. It could just be my romantic imagination, but it seems to me that there was some sort of unspoken agreement lingering over things that they both knew about... something the reader is never quite shown.

I do have one final question though... what kind of silly writer would start a major journey like that without at least some form of backup of the texts on his person? Unless he had really trusted Sharon over the years... but trust seems to the one thing he lacks, the key in fact, to the prison Harry has built himself. Or am I missing the point?

- David Rix

~

The Higgins Technique
Terry Grimwood

Geoff

I make stories.

For men, mostly.

Films, photo-strips.

I'm sick of the crap I produce. I want to change it. What to? Something worthy? Art? That's a fucking laugh.

This contract is for the same old shite. Money, that's what matters to the nasty gentlemen who've hired me, getting the punters to enter their credit card details so they can sit all alone in front of their computer screens and wank their fucking brains out.

Tonight I had to interview a new model. It doesn't happen very often. The people I work for usually send me the women I'm supposed to use. I worry about how young some of them are. I worry about the bruises and needle tracks on their arms and ankles. I worry about where they actually come from. Half of them don't speak English, I'll bet most of them don't have a UK Passport and sailed in via Dover or Felixstowe on the Luxury Container Line.

But, every now and then, someone answers the *Call for Models* ad on the websites I feed my work into.

My work, another fucking joke.

Usually they're not suitable, they're too nice or too stupid. They couldn't, and wouldn't, put up with what they have to do for me. They see it as an easy way into the world of modelling. Easy, it is not.

This one though.

I don't know what to make of her.

MaryAnn (yeah, that's how you spell it) thinks I should leave well alone. As we sat there in the snug at the *Hammer and Nails*, I could feel her dislike of the woman, I could feel claws unsheathed. Although why MaryAnn should be jealous is beyond me.

We're not lovers, she works for me, looks after the girls, gives them a slap when needed and a hug when it all gets too much for the little dears. But we stay out of each other's underwear. It's a professional relationship. Not that MaryAnn isn't screwable, Christ, she looks pretty good for forty-eight, a bit lined and hard around the edges but those Ava Gardner cheekbones and those dark, dark eyes of hers can still do a lot of damage.

The woman said her name was Emerald Stone. Yeah, right. She had red hair and green eyes. Her skin was pale and she looked delicate somehow. She must've been in her early thirties, and gorgeous. Not in the usual air-head way, no, she was…I don't know, interesting, yeah that's the word.

Which made the rest of it wrong.

Her make-up, smeared on with a trowel, panda eyes, false lashes, blood-red lipstick. And her clothes, a fluffy sweater with a vee-neck so low it was the most pointless article of clothing I've seen in my life and a skirt so short I thought she had forgotten to put one on before leaving home. There was a fur on the seat beside her, fake and cheap.

She was like a caricature, everyone's idea of a porn model.

When she opened her mouth, out came a load of fake estuary, which slipped every now and then to reveal something softer, though far from upper class.

When the interview was over, and the woman on her way, MaryAnn told me that Emerald Stone, so-called, must be a police officer. I told her not to be so fucking stupid. Undercover would mean a crash diet for that scrawny, wasted look, forced sleeplessness just to finish off the eyes and perfect the wan complexion, it would even mean a trip to the police doctor for some needle-mark tattoos.

The accent would be right, the slang unforced.

The clothes downbeat; scruffy, tee-shirts, short skirts and big boots.

They would not present us with a female Lionel Blair look-alike.

An exaggeration, by the way, she was still pretty fine, despite the Polyfiller and pantomime whore-wear.

"Don't go near her," said MaryAnn. "Take the girls they send you, play it safe."

She was right, of course, she's always right. But I couldn't help myself. It's the boredom I think, the crushing, pointless, sordid sameness of it all. This woman is different, a mystery, and perhaps, just perhaps she'll help me create something *I* can get excited about.

Emma

Okay, first entry, audio diary of a what? A desperate woman I suppose. This had better work. I'm scared shitless but if Jack Higgins could do it, could take a boat out onto the cold, cold ocean then throw himself in to feel what it was really like then so can I.

I write. But I can't write what I don't feel. Jack Higgins told the story of the boat trip on a *Wogan* chat show. I never forgot it, because I know why he did it. I call it the Higgins Technique and it's taken me to some strange places. .

But this time the water is deadly cold.

I'm in a bedroom in a house somewhere outside Barnet. I've only been here for a few hours and I've already been working, that's what they call it, working. I'm shaking, I feel, grubby and disorientated.

It's hard to believe that I'm actually here. I thought I'd blown it. They always say dress the part when attending a job interview, well I did. Jesus, I must have looked ridiculous, like a blow-up doll. Odd sort of interview mind you, no one said what the job actually was, but we all knew.

The woman, she calls herself MaryAnn, didn't like me. She sat and glared at me and said not a word. I felt as though she wanted to empty her Southern Comfort in my face.

The man, Geoff apparently, was friendly enough, gruff, rough-edged and hard-eyed, but affable and considerate. He's stocky, but not flabby, hides his baldness with a head-shave and comes across as a cheeky chappy, a sort of Bob Hoskins, gangster-with-a-heart.

I went through the motions, tried my best and left the pub planning how I would do better next time.

Geoff phoned me in the morning and suddenly it was on and I was terrified and I still am.

"Oh and drop the accent love," he said. "I don't need to know who you are or why you're doing this but perhaps you should just be yourself, yeah?"

Yeah...I mean, yes.

MaryAnn came for me at about five-thirty this evening. I was in the Kilburn bedsitter I've rented for the part. It serves two purposes, one it's the kind of place a woman like Emerald Stone would live and two, there's no way I want these people to know my real address..

"You ready?" MaryAnn asked.

She looks life-beaten but beautiful. There's a sort of aging hippy-ness to her, the way she has her thick, black (dyed?) hair, her clothes, the bangles clinking on her arms. There's film star as well. She reminds me of some Hollywood goddess of the forties or fifties.

I nodded in answer to her question, and felt like a non-speaking extra, but my mouth was too dry to trust for speech. So, charity shop, faux fur draped over shoulders made bare by my tiny, too small black dress, I locked the door of my room and led the way along the badly-lit landing.

Muse accompanied us down the curving, ill-lit staircase. Even though the song's finer points were muffled by sheer volume, I recognised "Stockholm Syndrome". I like *Muse,* but I prefer to listen to them in the privacy of my own room, not have them blasted into my consciousness by some thoughtless bastard who believes that his musical tastes should be shared by the whole world.

The coat didn't have any buttons so I had to pull it tight about myself to keep out the December cold. A bitter east wind slapped at my legs and dug through the false fur and useless dress until it found skin and bone.

MaryAnn took me to an illegally parked, BMW sports convertible, thankfully with its soft-top up. She opened the door for me, but offered no smile or word. The leather seats were low and not entirely comfortable. My coat tangled about me under the seatbelt.

The radio, loud with some techno-dance-trance-whatever, was quickly muted so MaryAnn could speak as we drove.

"Just do as you're told," she said. "You're an unknown. You have to prove yourself. Geoff likes his models to have a track record, likes to be able to look at their work before deciding whether or not to use them. He invests a lot of energy in these shoots. They're specialist stuff, only certain girls can cope with it. Some of them get scared and the whole thing turns into a fucking waste of time and Geoff gets pissed off. You don't want to piss him off, believe you me."

We found and followed the A1 out past Apex Corner, then left it soon after. I thought we were travelling back into Barnet, instead we headed into the countryside. It was bloody dark out there. I'm a town-girl, I like light, any light, darkness makes my flesh crawl, darkness is like grave soil.

Hedgerows flashed past, grey-stark in the headlights, caught-lost-caught-lost. A few cars blazed at us from around hidden bends then bled away behind us. Not many though. Not enough.

Suddenly there was a driveway and a run-down looking cottage. Light glowed from behind its curtained upstairs windows. The ground floor was in darkness.

Adjacent to the cottage was a barn and when MaryAnn sounded the horn the barn doors were opened. A light went on. We drove inside.

By the time I was out of the car, the barn doors had been closed and bolted by a tall bearded and ponytailed man.

When we went upstairs, to the studio as they call it, I discovered that the bearded man is Billy the cameraman. He isn't very friendly. In fact he hasn't spoken to me at all since I got here. I suppose I'm just another lump of meat for him to photograph

The cottage is okay. It's clean and warm. The kitchen, like the rest of the house, is very 1970s. The studio (once the master bedroom) however, is painted bland magnolia and is cramped, crowded and made hot by the stark photographic lights. There's a double bed, covered by a new-looking duvet.

"About fucking time." Geoff was sprawled in a cheap-looking Director's chair. Suddenly the gangster had no heart. "Time to talk cash," he said. "We'll give you a grand for three day's work."

"Sounds okay."

"Too bad if it isn't. You'll fucking earn it. We're doing stills, a photo-strip, yeah? We'll call it *Emerald's Torment*. I want Part One up on the web tonight. We'll finish on a cliff-hanger so the wankers will be desperate to come back for more tomorrow. Okay let's make a start. Leave the coat on."

Tony

I need stories. It only works if there's some sort of narrative. It can be as simple as you like, unsubtle, contrived, two-dimensional, but context is everything. Build-up, anticipation.

The law of diminishing returns I suppose. I mean an image used to be enough, but not anymore.

I need stories.

Aha, here's one, *Emerald's Torment Part One*, new on the *Dirty Trix* site.

Geoff

She bothers me.

She does it well, after a wooden kind of start; hands to mouth, wide-open eyes, struggling and screaming. Good set of pics.

Same old story though.

Same fucking old story.

I think I could make something different with her. A real film. She understands. She created a story out of the same old shite, she *felt* the story.

She bothers me.

Emma

"It doesn't sell anymore Emma." Caroline, my agent, is a large woman who isn't fat. "I'm sorry."

"So what do you suggest? Chick lit? Another bloody serial killer taunting another bloody cop? The Tracy Emmin Code? Oh, there's always ghost-writing. There must be some ten-year old X-Factor winner out there who hasn't had their autobiography published yet"

"Emma, you know as well as I do that literary fiction just isn't moving at the moment -"

"Moving? Oh yeah, I forgot, we don't write books anymore, we manufacture units. Units that have to move."

There's a plate of food in front of me, uncooked steak, the latest fad from New York apparently, comes with a salmonella-flavoured raw egg. Oddly enough I've lost my appetite. Caroline is glancing around the restaurant, embarrassed by my too-loud, unreasonable anger.

"Basically Emma, yes, books are units and we do have to move them because publishing is a business." She softens. "It'll change, it always does. Books are like fashion, they come and go then come back again."

"So what is moving *at the moment?*"

I feel like crying.

Perhaps I should switch the Dictaphone off - no, crying is part of the deal, part of the *feeling*. And why *do* I want to cry anyway? Come on, the real reason Em. Is it really the humiliation? The degradation? Think about it, pick it open, gouge it out. I have to know.

I can't write without *knowing*.

Lilly....

No, don't go there. Come on, the room, this room.

Fuck the room...

This room, my room for the duration. Small bedroom, mould around the windows, dingy curtains, light bulb with no shade. The bed seems clean though. There's a bedside cabinet, some bland piece of tat from Ikea or somesuch. It's even on-suite, though the bathroom is tiny; shower, basin, mirror, a selection of cheap toiletries and a jumble of make-up. Some of it is half used, by the last woman to stay here I suppose. The skin-and-bone blonde? The raven-haired goth? I've seen them, on the *Dirty Trix* web site, empty-eyed, wasted, going through motions and trying to convince the observer that the motions are glorious and terrifying all at the same time.

Pleasure *or* pain, pleasure *and* pain?

So what did they do to me in there? Can it be crushed into vowels and consonants?

Lilly I'm sorry...

I sat on that bed, shaking so bad I could hardly move. The bedroom/film studio, whatever they call it, reeked of maleness, the worst kind, uncaring, sweat-hard, and brutal. I couldn't cry out or speak or run and that was a revelation in itself, if this had been a real, I would've just sat, frozen, waiting for it to happen to me.

It was Geoff who snapped me out of it.

"Fucking scream, come on, some bloke's just broken into your bedroom, wants your flesh. He might have a knife. What are you going to do, make him a cup of tea?"

I struck a pose, slowly, awkwardly. I opened my mouth the way Skin-and-Bones and Goth-Girl had opened theirs and let out a hoarse, unconvincing squeak. Geoff scowled at me but nodded to Billy to press the shutter button.

I flinched back, raising a hand to protect my face, silent movie style. My arm was heavy, it ached. I could barely lift it. I smelled charity-shop mustiness, stale perfume and a hint of cigarettes in the sleeve of the fake fur – and why the hell would I be wearing my fur while sitting on my bed anyway?

Snap, snap, snap went the camera, the sound as fake as my coat, an electronic approximation, a pretend shutter like the smell they put in odourless natural gas.

The Higgins Technique

"Okay, okay, take a break." Geoff crossed to Billy who showed him the photographs, presumably scrolling them across the screen on the back of the camera. Geoff grunted. "Emerald, try to relax, yeah? We're all friends here. Try to imagine this is real and that Paulie -" *He* was leaning against the wall behind the camera, tall, skinny, dressed in rapist-black, complete with balaclava. "- really is coming to get you and hurt you. I mean, really hurt you."

Was he? I looked at him, and he stared back at me through the balaclava eye-holes. His eyes were dead. Blank. God, I've never seen such soulless detachment, like someone who could do *anything* and not think twice about it.

I nodded then forced myself to say yes. My voice was hoarse again. I swallowed, not easy when there's nothing *to* swallow.

"Yes." Louder this time.

Geoff sighed and went back to his Director's chair.

Scream (not bad), snap-snap-snap. Cower, snap-snap-snap. Arm over my face, snap-snap-snap.

Then Paulie moved in.

He smelled too, mustn't forget that. He smelled of aftershave, sweat, and something animal. He grabbed my hair. Jesus he moved fast. He touched me, he grabbed my hair, he meted out violence. No one has ever done that to me, no one, ever. It was terrible, terrifying, it was a car crash that shattered everything inside me.

He *touched* me.

"Good," said Geoff. "Stay like that for a moment. Billy, see if you can get that from a few other angles."

Billy picked up a second, portable camera.

And there I sat, looking up into Paulie's corpse-flat eyes, his hand in my hair, firm but not painful, the grip of an expert in fake abuse. He blinked and swallowed. My neck ached. The camera worked.

"Bit further back," Geoff growled, God, he sounded bored. "Em, put your head further back, that's it."

Me? I have to put my own head further back? What sort of assault is this?

"Okay, down onto the bed now, just lay back, that's it. Paulie, crawl onto her...stop, stop. MaryAnn, sort her leg out will you, and she's lost a shoe. Okay, Paulie get your cock out. Oh for fuck's sake Em, scream, come on, make some noise…"

Yes, he got his cock out and it was big and veiny and all the usual, but he didn't put it into me. My knickers stayed in place, hidden by my carefully arranged legs. Everything was carefully arranged, the way my skirt rode up over my thighs, my messed-up hair.

Apparently I fake a good orgasm.

Tony

Story, story.

Okay, she's reading her magazine. She's, uh, she's a detective, yeah, that's it, a detective, working undercover. She's pretending to be some sort of gangster's girlfriend, that explains the fur coat (I bet it's gorgeous to hold and feel, I wouldn't know, my wife never wears fur, fake or otherwise) and little back dress, *tight* little black dress. She's waiting for her driver to take her to some party. Someone's coming in. Not her driver, oh no, definitely not her driver.

He's a heavy, sent to sort her out by the gangster she's investigating. Her cover's blown and now it's time for her to learn a hard lesson.

That's it, oh God, yes…

She's looking up, scared, the heavy moves in. She's scared but there's also a thrill, a little electric shock, she knows what's coming.

Oh God…Oh God…Hurry up, come on, download before I do…

He's on her, grabbing her hair, tight in his fist. It hurts, it really hurts her. What's she feeling? Is she scared, God she's so scared.

He pushes her down onto the bed, skirt up, stocking-tops showing.

That's it…Oh God…Oh GOD…

Geoff

Cut off her head and put on a thousand others and it's just the fucking same.

But the pictures look nice and I suppose that's what the punters want. Nice clear pictures of rape and suffering. This Billy is a killer with a camera. I wasn't sure about him when he arrived, too surly for my liking. I wanted one of my own lads, Tom or Ced, blokes I can trust to do the business, but my employers, whoever the fuck they are, wanted their man Billy, so Billy it was.

What the hell am I doing?

Smoking a joint and drinking whisky at this present moment.

Very funny.

Where did this start? I wanted to make films, to write scripts and screenplays. Okay so I do that now, but it isn't art is it? Just licking and shoving and stroking and biting and now slapping and punching and strangling as well.

It's And's fault. That's And, short for Andy, short for Andrew, which is short for fuck knows what, Andronicus? I met him at an amateur filmmakers convention in Brighton. He was talent spotting, or so he claimed. He was dressed sharp, was all charm and ooze, even had some pretty bloody smart looking business cards.

He watched one of my short horror flicks. No zombies or vampires, but psychological drama, a *story*, the terror in the imagination of the beholder.

I was twenty-five, already wondering if it was too late.

"I can get you work," And said. "It may not be exactly what you want but it's a start. I mean, Michael Reeve made 'adult' films before he created *Witchfinder General*."

"So it's porn," I said.

"Glamour work, Geoffrey, specialist films. Artistic."

It *was* a start, or so I thought. I believed I could make artistic porn, muck with filmic integrity. Fat chance, but at least I made money, lots of it, and the work kept on coming. I tried to make the back stories interesting. But in the end it came down to visitor/workman/neighbour, attraction and clothes off – or on in some cases, uniform and leather on.

I managed to shut my ears to the voices yammering away in my head. I tried to drown it out in real filth; animals, strangulation fetish, shit fetish. Like I said, the money was good, the women, willing to do anything to get work, even this sort of work, so what the hell was I worrying about?

I became known as the filmmaker who didn't care what he filmed.

I have a saying, entertain the Devil and he'll return the favour. Well he did. My work came to the attention of some very dangerous people.

Porn always dances round the borders of the law. What's acceptable and what isn't seems to depend on the whim of the police or some ancient old judge. Suddenly, however, there was no doubt about where *I* was. But the money. Fuck me. All I had to do was take photos and make short films for internet download and the readies came rolling home. As long as I didn't think about what I was seeing through the lens, the heroin-addicted women submitting themselves to humiliation and violence, the obese, the skeletal, the dogs and kids.

But something was dying. I tried to blot the stink of my own shrivelled, rotting soul out of my nostrils. I drank I sniffed and popped and injected but the smell wouldn't go away. That sort of medicine costs a lot of money and it really fucks up your creative juices.

Just as quickly as I struck gold - a grubby sort of gold I grant you, but gold nonetheless - I fucked it up and the work stopped coming my way. I was probably too difficult and unreliable to work with. The people putting the money up are not the sort of people who want to piss around with temperamental, permanently stoned prima-fucking-donnas like me.

So this is redemption time, a last chance by all accounts. That's probably why MaryAnn is being so bloody pissy about everything, Nice to know she cares.

The job is relatively soft, conventional, brightly coloured and mildly rough, par for the *Dirty Trix* course. It's called a Damsel in

Distress site, relatively mild stuff, not one of your BDSM torture sites. Now *they* are a challenge, well, they were once.

I never see the money men. They have a go-between for the sordid business of communing with sick bastards like me. He's a fat, shaven-headed fucker who calls himself John but talks like a Yuri or Sergei. He smiles a lot and tells me what a great artist I am.

Emma

My first whole day. I think it's Tuesday,
Why am I here?
I write.
Why am I here?
Because of the Higgins Technique, boat-and-icy sea.
Why am I here?
Because good writing doesn't sell. Because difficult doesn't sell, Because literary art doesn't sell. Because I want to rub their (my readers or my publishers?) noses in what the great book-buying public apparently want; sex and pain and damsels in savage distress.

I went into W H Smith's when I walked out on Caroline and that plate of oh-so-trendy raw steak mince and raw eggs. I pored over their bestseller shelves and tried to work it out.

I have to write. Do you understand that? If I don't write I start to think dark thoughts studded with razor blades and dead babies. Writing is a shield that deflects everything from myself, my soul, the inner, rotten, dissolving core of me.

The books I saw in Smith's made me tired. I have no desire to research police procedure or explore war torn London where feisty young women fall in love with brave, square-jawed servicemen, I'm not interested in glamour or the film industry or the music industry. Who cares which vampire is in love with which werewolf.

And I can't write from a child's perspective because my child…

Lilly, that was her name.
Other books.

Up there on the top shelf, slim volumes with monochrome covers decorated with semi-naked feminine curves and in some cases leather cuffs and gleaming chains. They have titles like *Captives of Sin* and *Slave Den*. I grabbed a handful, I don't know why, reaction perhaps. You want trash, I'll give you trash?

I blushed when I paid the pleasant middle-aged lady on the till. She pointedly ignored the books themselves and dropped them into a branded plastic bag and asked me to enter my PIN then smiled and bid me good day.

Erotica, that's what those pulp-sized novels were apparently. I'd heard of them, of course, but had never actually read any. Some of it was very good, some of it abysmal.

Most of the titles I picked up were sado-masochistic in a soft-focus, afternoon TV movie sort of way. They involved women in some sort of captivity, often at a fantastical gothic academy or harem where they learned the arts of seduction under the strict tutelage of some fearsome dominatrix. Disobedience and failure were punished thoroughly (though seldom with any blood being split, these were not the works of the Marquis) and detailed and explicit descriptions of these punishments seemed to form the main meat of the narrative. The heroines seemed to be semi-willing, always innocent, unsure and afraid, and derived an odd sensual enjoyment from their trials and tribulations.

Aha. You want moveable units Caroline, you'll get moveable units.

But there can be no writing without application of the Higgins Technique. I was fairly certain the training centres described in the books didn't exist, so where was my boat and cold ocean?

The internet of course, God bless it. Where would we be without its infinite helpfulness? I filled the search engine box with such words as *punishment*, *bondage* and *training*.

Yes, I was shocked by some of it and not convinced that all the girls were acting. It didn't take long for me to feel stained and depressed by the parade of images, women, always women, brutalised, humiliated and degraded.

Why the hell did these people allow themselves to be displayed like this?

What the fuck was going on here?

It took a while to translate the patois. "Call for Models" was apparently what I was looking for.

So, now it's Tuesday and I'm a Captive of Sin and it's raining outside the Slave Den. The room is warm though and the bed surprisingly comfortable. No one has called me, no one told me what time I'm supposed to make an appearance. Perhaps I should just wait.

Which allows me to think.

Lilly...

There is no Lilly. Lilly is gone. I am gone. This is the shell, the outer hard coating that was left when the soft insides dissolved away.

What do I feel?

It is dull grey, soundtracked by the rain beating at the window (will they beat *me*?) I'm shaking a little, my stomach is clenched and my bowels are filling up. My heart is beating fast, not hammering, thundering or pounding, just beating fast enough to make me breathless.

I am afraid.

Will they let me go home when this is finished?

That thought is a bad one. I don't know these people. As far as they are concerned I am little Miss Alonesome. No one will miss me. I know too much...

Oh God, help me.

I can't swallow, I can't move.

Okay, okay, I have to calm down. They are not going to kill me. They are going to make me do horrible degrading things then pay me and send me on my way.

Let's think about fear. What is it like?

Physical, a weight on my chest, my joints and muscles ache from tension, I feel as if I have flu, my skin is sensitive and sore. My mind is in a...whirl, corny, poor choice of cliché but a true one. It won't stop working, it spins and creates images and scenarios, half-formed, smoky horrors. The whole thing roars, on and on.

Someone's knocking at the door. Jesus switch off, where's that bloody off button, Jesus, Je –

It was MaryAnn.

She brought me coffee and toast and told me, snapped at me in fact, to be up and in the studio at eleven. I am to wear the same clothes as last night. She has brought some new underwear, all black lace and silkiness and still in the wrapper.

A sequel then. The further perils of Emerald Stone.

Geoff looked ill, white-faced. He smelled unwashed and the stink of him made me feel sick. When he lifted his coffee mug to his lips I noticed that he was shaking. So was I. On time though, dead on eleven, made up, fragrant and stifling in the dress and fur coat.

"You ready Em?" Geoff growled.

"Yes." Was I?

"Good girl. Today's epic then. That bastard who assaulted you last night has kidnapped you and brought you back to his lair to have his wicked way with you."

"Is that it?" I asked.

"What do you mean is that it?"

"Well…"

He sat back and I assumed that he meant for me to go on.

"Well, does she try to escape, or fight back?"

"Fucked if I know," he said and laughed his wheezy cigarette-drenched laugh.

"Sorry, but, well, tell me if it's none of my business but can't we create a story out of this?"

He sat forward, suddenly, and glared at me with bloodshot eyes.

"You're right," he said. "It isn't any of your flicking business. Now, stand over there by the door. Paulie grab her arm. Em, put your hands behind you back and pretend you're tied up."

I did as I was told, struggling as best I could without giving the game away. It was difficult not to use my hands for balance. Geoff was irritable. He made us re-pose some of the shots two, three, even four times. I was overacting, under acting, he could see my hands.

Paulie's grip was tight. He said nothing, didn't look at me even when he had his hands round my neck and was staring into my face. His eyes were locked onto mine but the creature inside was asleep, or looking elsewhere.

The entrance completed, I was ordered to sit in a straight-backed chair in the middle of the bedroom. This time the tying-up was real. MaryAnn did the work though Paulie would step in every so often to pose over the knots. MaryAnn was not gentle and when she had finished my arms were crushed against the sides of the chair back and my ankles brutally cinched against the two front legs.

Paulie went through the motions. He kissed me, no tongues, his mouth a mint-breathed, fleshy hole. He grabbed my hair for a couple of photographs then faked a slap complete with my own dramatic swing of the head. Do I sound bored? There I was bound and helpless and I'm talking about it as though it's just another day at the office.

Perhaps bored isn't the right word.

Being trussed to the chair drove me to the edge of panic, I felt claustrophobic, I wanted my arms free, I wanted to be able to fight back if things got too rough, I wanted to be able to *move*. And why is it supposed to be sexy anyway? I'm bent up, awkward, my knees forced together by the way my ankles are tied to the chair legs, like some gangling, toe-turned pre-adolescent. I felt foolish, humiliated. I was surprised when the others didn't laugh at me. And then there's the discomfort, the abrasions and aches. It must be bad for you to be held in one position for so long, circulation slowed by rope-crushed blood-vessels.

Geoff's mood, edgy at the start of the shoot turned progressively fouler. Halfway through, he instructed MaryAnn to "mess me up". For a moment I thought he meant for her to beat me or cut me, but instead, she untied my hands, wrenched the coat off my shoulders, unzipped the back of my dress and pulled it all down to expose some flesh. When she retied my hands Geoff shouted at her to "Make the fucking knots exactly the same as they were last time. Christ, haven't you heard of continuity?"

In an odd sort of way it made the exposure of my breasts a little more bearable because the focus was not on me but on doing Geoff's bidding and trying to keep him sweet. As for me, I felt cold, I shivered despite the stifling heat of full-blast radiators and photographic lights. These were my breasts, they belonged to no one else, they are private, yet there I was allowing them to be displayed to these strangers and then to a million other strangers on the internet where they would provide friction for a thousand, hand-driven flesh-pumps.

No one said pphhhhaaaawwww. No one licked dry lips or drooled. Paulie grabbed them and pretended to bite them. Then out came his cock so he could pretend to do a deed, impossible in real life, but I groaned and moaned and pulled the right expressions and Geoff seemed satisfied.

"Was that enough story for you?" Geoff growled at me when it was done and I was rubbing cream into my rope burns. "Did you find your motivation? Huh? Layer upon layer of meaning and sub-text?"

"Sub-sex more like," Billy said and everyone chuckled, except me.

MaryAnn brought sandwiches and coffee then we were off again and this time I was down to my underwear, shoes on of course. I mean, what self-respecting kidnap victim would take off her heels when she was chained and gagged and thrown onto a bed like a partygoer's coat?

So what sort of book is this going to be?
Erotica, that's why I'm here isn't it? The Higgins Technique?
Well, it isn't working.
The women in those slim little books didn't complain about chaffed wrists and crumpled clothing. Their captors were not chain-smoking, unshaven, BO-ridden middle-aged men. Their chains were not cold and rust-stained and their gags tasting of plastic and dried saliva with buckles that caught strands of hair when they were tightened. They didn't see themselves as trussed and stuffed oven-ready chickens complete with pinkish-blue, goose-pimpled flesh.

An expose then, the sordid truth behind the brightly-coloured fantasy offered by the great god internet? But would it sell, would it be a moveable unit?

Tony

The sequel.
Undercover cop taken prisoner and in big trouble.
Good quality, good angles.
But...
Come on, come on focus. You're him, you're in control. She's tied to a chair, she not going anywhere, you can do whatever you want to her.

Feel it, go on, *feel* it.
She's gorgeous.
But I wish it was Rhea.

I wish she was the one tied to that chair, all poured into that tight, tight little dress and bundled in fur. I want to do that to her. I want to play rough and hard and I want to act out those stories with her. But she won't, she can't. That's what she told me, it would frighten her.

How many years have we been married, four, five? Second time for both of us of course. Who gets to our age with the same partner we had children by? I thought she would be different, and she was, at first, exciting, energetic, imaginative, in a straight sort of way. We rutted like rabbits for the first year or so.

We met at the swimming pool when we were taking our respective sons and daughters for their splash-and-scream lessons. I began to notice her, *really* notice her, after a few weeks, a quiet slim woman with short blonde hair, an elf face and big Audrey Hepburn eyes.

On the morning I mustered the courage to speak to her, she revealed that she and her ex share their time with their children exactly fifty-fifty. Me, I'm only allowed one weekend a month, half the school holidays and alternative Christmas and Boxing Days.

I'm an irresponsible parent apparently, not able to cope with my offspring between any ordinary Monday and Friday. Their new dad is a proper dad. He has his own construction business and built an extension on their house with his own bare hands. I bet he even made the bricks out of clay he dug up from his immaculate garden.

I'm a flighty, untrustworthy car salesman. I do okay, I sell cars and make enough to pay the mortgage and council tax and take us on a good holiday every other year (the Boxing Day year). I can't build extensions of course, and my garden is mostly lawn and decking. I can play a guitar, which I take with me to *The Crown* very Wednesday for the weekly open mic nite. Ten minutes I get, ten minutes of fame and blues.

We still sleep together, Rhea and I, still make soft, tired love.

But I want to throw her onto the bed and rip open her clothes and hold her down and bite her and slap her lovely, round little arse and tie her hands and lick her until she screams. I want her to pretend to be an undercover cop who's been found out. I want to make her shiver and blush when I threaten to do things to her. I want to chase her through the house and grab her and cuff her and drag her into the bedroom. I want her to scream and struggle and giggle and blush.

I don't want to hurt her.

I don't want to bruise or abuse her or beat her or strangle her.

I just want to take her into the story, I want.

I *want*.

I tried it once, grabbed her wrists and held them above her head and she went cold and told me to stop and cried and I felt terrible. I apologized and kissed her and eventually she nestled into me and said that it was all right but she couldn't ever do anything like *that*.

I promised I would never suggest or try or even mention it again.

But I can think it, imagine, pretend, when she's on night duty, out of the house.

I can pretend that the red-haired woman with her dress yanked down and her hands tied tight is.

Rhea.

The undercover cop, cover blown, chased through the house and finally caught before she can open the door and dragged back, hand (my hand) over her mouth, hot breath in my palm, and slammed (not too hard) face-to-the-wall and tied up and hauled upstairs to the chair where I can.

Do
Whatever
I
Want.

Geoff

John came to see me tonight. Shame he was too early for me to be properly stoned.

"New stuff, same old stuff yes?"

Didn't Khrushchev say something similar?

"I'm doing my best." How pathetic that sounded.

"We want a better story, different."

"So do I."

"Good old chap." He slapped my arm and grinned his crocodile grin. "What are your ideas?"

"I want the captive to fall for her captor. I want them to communicate and I want the woman to gain the psychological upper hand. I want Stockholm Syndrome, I want *The Collector.*"

"What collector?"

"It's a film, Samantha Egger."

"Forget collectors and whatever happened in Stockholm yes? These strips look nice but they're not…exciting. She's a lovely woman. Use her."

"I am fucking using her."

"I know, I know and pretty she looks all tied-up but is not sufficient yes?"

"Yes, fucking yes, yes, yes. So let me untie her and make a real bloody story out of this. It can still be hot and sweaty -" I know I'm winding the bastard up and it's dangerous. I can't help myself. "- but it can have a little depth."

"Yes, deeper is right. Deeper and darker. Good torture. Hurt her. Get Paulie to piss on her, I don't care, but is rare to get such a sweet-looking bird."

God save us from Russians who think they're Alfie.

"Punters, they like to see good-lookers get really hurt, yes?"

"I know, I know. I'll sort it."

"You sure you can believe in her?"

"She's doing the business so far."

"No, no, are you sure she is who she says so? We are a little worried she might be a police."

"She's not a police. Trust me."

He grinned and slapped my arm. "Of course I trust you, but be careful, yes?"

"Yes."

"And remember what Hitchcock said -"

"Torture the heroine, yes I know." Every-bloody-time.

Emma

Today I went into the dark.

I can't stop shaking and crying.

I don't think I can't talk about it.

But I have to.

I was already scared before I went into the studio. I couldn't find the Dictaphone, not right away. It was in my suitcase, where it was supposed to be, but buried right at the bottom under my clothes. It should have been hidden in a pair of thick socks rolled-up in my big charcoal jumper. I thought I'd been careful about that, religious almost. I must have forgotten to conceal it properly last night.

Everything else seemed okay, everything where it was supposed to be.

No one left the studio after we finished the shoot. I was even invited to stay for a drink and a tote on the communal joint. I passed it on, I can't let my guard down, I did have a drink though, but only one, vodka and coke. MaryAnn was pouring and she was as mean with the coke as she was generous with the vodka. I was exhausted and crawled back here to make my report then I must have fallen asleep straight away.

Does all this matter?

I'm rambling because I'm upset.

Because I'm broken into little pieces.

Okay, today. The dark.

They wanted me naked. MaryAnn told me when she brought my coffee and toast. She left a dressing gown for me. It smelled of washing powder, thank God. I showered, barely able to move I was so scared.

The dressing gown was made from a silvery-grey, faded satin material. It was cold and slithered over me when I pulled it on. I went to the studio barefoot. Once there I kept the dressing gown on for as long as I could.

"Come on Em, you gone shy on me?" Geoff looked even worse, the tremors more pronounced. He stank of cigarettes, booze and sweat.

I fumbled the belt and struggled out of the gown. MaryAnn took it from me.

And there I was, all of me, frail, pale and vulnerable. I shivered and felt awkward. I tried to hide myself with my arms and hand but it wasn't possible for long. I did not feel attractive or sexy. I felt small, weak, a mess. Images of shaven-headed, emaciated women being shoved into Nazi showers flashed through my mind, then a remembered photograph, glimpse during a schooldays visit to the Imperial War Museum, of similarly nude women being herded over a field towards a firing squad. One had carried a baby.

A baby,

Lilly...

I thought I was going to cry then, but managed to regain control.

They did some complicated roping first, Japanese apparently, it was excruciating and left me cross-legged on the floor, hunched forward, head bowed and shivering. Paulie waved a scarlet candle over me then drew back so that MaryAnn could smear imitation wax over my breasts. I had to writhe and scream. Writhing hurt. Screaming was easy.

They humiliated me and contorted me and all the time their faces were bland and bored and it was degradation by numbers. And, astonishingly, I became bored too, fed up with laying there unable to move, with being folded and twisted and pulled about. They made me crawl along on my hands and knees, tugged by a chain and a dog collar. They made me drink water from a bowl on the floor.

The room was grey and dirty and the world was grey and dirty.

But that wasn't what made me cry.

It was the cocoon.

And not even that, it was what I found in there, in the dark.

The cocoon was, essentially a one-piece rubber sleeping bag, zipped-up at the back. Once on it fitted tight and restricted all movement. Within seconds it was hot and clammy. I lay on the bed, unable to do more than twist a little and raise my head.

It was already a claustrophobic hell.

Then MaryAnn pulled the matching hood over my head and zipped it in place.

The hood had only two small holes for my nostrils. No other openings, no compromise or mercy. It clung to my scalp and pressed in on my face and suddenly there was immobility and utter, utter darkness.

I think they strapped my arms and legs as well but by then I was lost in the screaming, roaring black, by then I was in my coffin, a million tons of earth bearing down on its fragile wooden lid, by then I was smothered by nightmare, by a panic so complete it paralysed every muscle in my body, danced on every nerve.

I wanted to move, just to bloody, fucking *move*.

I wanted light, just a glimmer, a crack. I wanted sound, any sound other than the howl of blood through my skull. My bladder let go and I wet myself. The stink of it churned my stomach towards nausea.

Oh God, not in here, I'll choke…

Then I heard a sound.

A baby, crying for me, somewhere deep in that red-dark.

I wanted it to stop. But it cried on and on. I tried to move because the baby was desperate. It, she, Lilly, wanted me. Needed me.

But I couldn't get to her. I tried, God I tried.

Did she cry?

Did she cry out to her mother, who was asleep, arms wrapped about some lover she had picked up in a club? I was too drunk and fuck-tired to hear. I had what I wanted for the night, a faceless, brainless pile of muscle and cock to assuage the loneliness left by the departure of my beloved bloody husband? And why did he depart? Because he was jealous of Lilly apparently, because he "couldn't handle the way I had shifted all my affection onto our daughter." *Our* daughter. *We* made her.

He said that I wasn't the same, I was moody and obsessed. We didn't have any fun anymore. Surprise fucking surprise. So he walked out and never came back.

I was lonely, for God's sake, what was I supposed to do?

Silence.

I woke to it, head pounding, the walking penis's tattooed arm across my chest.

Silence.

She was supposed to wake me while it was still dark, demanding her five-am feed. But it was light and the time on my fumbled mobile phone was eight-twenty-three. I remember that time I will always remember that time. Thursday morning, 6th May, eight twenty-three.

I stumbled into the nursery, into that little room with its teddy bear wallpaper and mobiles and cot –

Blue, she's blue, her tiny mouth half open, her eyes half shut. Blue and limp and so very, very cold.

The brainless one stood around while I shrieked and howled and hugged the lifeless bundle of flesh and death that was my daughter.

She's crying now, God she's crying and crying and crying and I want it to stop - No, no I didn't mean it, no, don't stop. I don't want the silence. Not again. Jesus, please don't stop -

I writhed and struggled and I suppose that was what they wanted. I couldn't breathe, just through my nose. Every inhalation pressed the rubber over my face. And the universe was roar and crying and redness.

Then silence.

Like the silence that morning, utter, complete, unbearable, relentless silence.

Dead silence.

Tony

It was going so bloody well, the ante upped, hot wax and shibari, picture after picture of real punishment unleashed on the uncovered cop. God, she's suffering, she's helpless and she's having to take it because she has no choice.

And now this.

Okay so she's strapped and smothered and she can't move an inch. But I can't see her face or her eyes, I can't see her struggling. It's boring, it's like a bucket of cold water.

Bloody rubber suit. It could be anyone in there. It could be a bloke. God, that's done it. No use trying to get *that* thought out of my head now.

There's no story there.

Nothing.

Geoff

Em's got a tape recorder hidden in her room, a digital Dictaphone.

MaryAnn told me tonight, after the shoot. She was furious and more scared than I've ever seen her.

"I told you," she shouted. "I told you she was the fucking filth."

I tried to tell her that having a Dictaphone didn't mean she was a policewoman. But I couldn't make myself heard and, worse, I had no other explanation. Unless she was kinkier than the lot of us put together.

She had survived the cocoon hadn't she? She didn't look too good when we pulled the hood off but she had stuck it out. I think I fell in love with her at that moment. Most of the girls can only take five minutes. She did twenty.

The Higgins Technique

But her eyes…

What the fuck went on in there?

MaryAnn kept yelling at me to do something, but what?

I don't know what to do. I should confront her, threaten her, let her know she's in the shit. But if she is a copper she's going to call in her mates straight away and that'll be it.

"Have you ever been Inside?" MaryAnn seemed to have calmed down enough to actually talk to me.

No I haven't and I intend to keep it that way.

"Well it isn't all fucking Jacuzzis and colour tellies, I am never going back there Geoff." She was crying now but she wouldn't let me give her a hug. "I'll kill myself before I'll let anyone put me back in that shithouse."

We could make a run for it I suppose. Put the lovely Emerald Stone in the boot and dump her somewhere. If we trussed her up we could be a long way away before she got free or anyone found her.

There is another way, of course.

No, no I can't do that. Fuck me no.

Oh, I can pretend, I can tell a story, but I can't do it for real.

I need to talk to the others before I'm too pissed and stoned and tired. We're doing nothing wrong, a bit of soft porn, nothing worse than the shite they sell off the top shelf at the local newsagents. The law isn't going to be interested in a bit of play acting is it?

But what about the stuff I've done in the past? Is that what they're after?

Or is it the bastards who are paying me for this? They must be making good money out of these sites, money for other business interests that might be of concern to the forces of righteousness.

But she isn't a copper, because if she is she's the clumsiest bloody bit of undercover work I've ever seen.

Christ, what's the recorder for?

She's making her own fucking porno site. Is that it? Stealing my ideas, robbing my creative genius? Very funny. Christ I'm tired.

On more day. Something rough and imaginative tomorrow. Food, mud, nipple clamps. I don't know. I've run out of ideas. I've had enough. *The Collector*, then, yeah - no, because the woman dies in that film. Okay, she gets free, she beats the shit out of Paulie, he beats the shit out of her, they talk, yeah, she seduces him. All distressed

255

and ragged, she seduces him and they make fucky-fuck all weary and muddy and

I don't know.

I've run out of ideas.

I have to talk to the others. I have to talk to somebody.

Emma

I think I found the book in the dark yesterday. It won't sell, it'll hurt. But that is the only book I can write. It won't be top-shelf erotica, in fact it won't be erotica of any kind. It will be exorcism, cleansing, confession. It'll be self-mutilation, a carving out of guilt and soul.

I want to start it, now.

One more day.

One more shoot.

I'll grab the big and shapeless charcoal jumper and some jeans. I'll wear trainers. If they want leather corsets and rubber knickers they'll have to tell me. I'm cold and tired and I want to go home. They all had a big row last night. I could hear them downstairs, everyone shouting. I don't know how long it went on for because I fell asleep. God I'm sick of this.

Better get dressed.

A car's just pulled up. I'll keep the curtains drawn, stay in the dark. See nothing. It's raining again.

I'm nervous and frightened and tired and bored and I want to go home and I want to burn the book out of myself.

Lilly, that's its title.

Okay, it's half-ten, time for a shower and some face-paint.

Signing off. One more day Lilly.

I love you.

Far Beneath Incomplete Constellations
Alexander Zelenyj

Another bird-dream bloomed:

They were surrounded, he and his lover: trees reminiscent in some respects of the Black oaks he knew so well from childhood, dark-barked and robust; but wildly different, too, and imbued with the awesome capabilities of dream-logic: immeasurably more colossal, these, rearing higher than vision could perceive, their weirdly voluptuous bodies bending impossibly towards them where they stood in the centre of the circular moon-washed glade, stout verdant arms opulent with leaf and fruit the likes of which he'd never seen on any species of oak before. In the unimpeded lunar light, her face was clear where she stood at his side: her expression of excitement and joy for their forthcoming journey was a mirror of the emotions rampant in him, too.

Others were gathered there as well and, though he sensed they were of a friendly and vaguely familiar nature, he knew innately that he'd never actually met these individuals – nor anyone like them – before in his life. He strained his dreameyes to find them among the lunar-washed glade but always the surrounding foliage worked with the moonlight to cast deceptive and confusing shadow-speckles over the periphery of the clearing, where they lingered among the purple heather and wild grass, though certain details and attributes emerged: a plume of white flame held in the open hand of a shadow-shrouded figure; his neighbour clutching an immense alabaster jar high on the air before him; another figure holding aloft a lantern in one hand and in the other something which reflected the moonlight in a manner which served to deflect the illumination from the glowing taper within his lantern, keeping him obscured from sight amid this spectral lightshow; and another shadow-swathed individual clutched a long gleaming sword at his side, while the figure hovering like a phantom beside him held aloft a white-petaled flower the wan colour of the moon.

Despite these queerly-illumined details, it remained only he and his lover who were clearly visible, naked beneath the moon's full splendour for all to examine. Hands – of those convened in the forest reaching from the shadows, as well as the branches' knotted and leaf-bedecked fingers reaching into the hollow space of the dell – touched them all over. These embraces he sensed were of a hybrid variety, representing both fond welcome and the bittersweet pang of goodbye, with something like pride communicated to them for his and her achievement: finding one another in the great and treacherous vastness of the world.

Other less savoury touches touched them, too, though: no less tangible for their non-physical aspect, he felt the eyes of the envious burning into his own, resenting them their joy, their good fortune, their imminent escape from their earthly ranks to a better, unsullied place. These disgruntled ones could be discerned as restless shadows moving behind the greater shadowed crowd, skulking among the density of underbrush, their ill-wishing eyes furtively beholding the pair at the centre of the celebration. He saw his lover's narrow hazel eyes follow those furtive skulking shadows with trepidation. He squeezed her hand to assure her of their safety. Turning, she smiled for him, showing him her courage, though fear lingered in her gaze still.

In the distance, a sonorous murmuring, as of a giant grinding his teeth where he dreamed restlessly among the clouds.

The gathered revellers – and those sullen, moody watchers owning jealous eyes – turned together towards the west, eyeing the brooding sky: the lingering echo of thunder cascaded downwards to earth, and then the queer thought struck him that perhaps the clamour might have been some man-wrought instrument or happening of the present age which they all wished to escape: a descending bomb finding its target upon the earth – a sleeping house or speeding vehicle – or an explosion originating on the ground and erupting into the sky like some malefic fire spirit conjured to scorch the stars from their orbits.

He whispered his words into her ear, though all those gathered heard and rejoiced – clapping hands and cheering – in his eager bid for action: "Quickly, my love: we can beat the rain and the thunder! We can!"

She gave him a smile of confirmation. Before she could take his proffered hand though, the dream darkened, and a murmur of warning stirred among those gathered. Turning, he saw: a rogue among the throng, his umbrage greater than his fellow detractors, had stepped from the moon-shadowed foliage into the glade's centre. He was clad in a ragged, plain earth-coloured tunic and sandals, and wore his hair long and dishevelled. He stood with legs braced wide, barring their path with his feral eyes, his gash of snarling mouth, the long dagger gleaming in his fist.

In a display of chivalry he stepped protectively before his lover, facing their assailant while thunder renewed its grumbling over their heads, beyond the leafy roof. The man, crouching low, slunk towards them with his bright gaze of death and envy.

Suddenly she clasped his hand. The strength in her grip: he marvelled at it, sure and protective. He turned to her: her mouth smiled. Her eyes were fixed on his with determination. Love filled them, too – for him, and in this knowledge he rejoiced. He understood. He led her, the time for their departure arrived: they ran along the grass between the lines of their loved ones standing sentry on either side; some weeping joyfully, others clapping their hands in cadence to the steps she and he took upon the ground. They ran headlong towards their knife-wielding adversary advancing in defiance of their escape. Cries of encouragement rebounded from the dense thicket enclosing them, shaking acorns from branches even as the thunder boomed again in the west, doing the same, sending squirrels scrambling for their nests in abandonment of their late-day foraging and birds in bevies from theirs.

He felt her grip tighten yet more. Her little fingers growing stronger clutching his own, as if gaining strength through their embrace. Soon it was she who led their manic run. He followed in her wake. His heart bashed a song of joy behind his chest. They conjured a grass storm about them in their haste and vigour. Their collision with the death-dealing knife-wielder was imminent. He felt her pull away and upwards. He closed his eyes. He couldn't help the smile from spreading itself on his face: he felt his feet lifting from the grass. The cold breath across his bare leg was the keen edge of the blade slicing empty air, forever missing its opportunity to feed the old voracious world with his blood.

Goodbye, today: his dream-self thought this, and the relief flooding through him was like ecstasy as they rose up and up and up, like characters of myth ascending into their rightful and destined positions among incomplete constellations awaiting them like a final pair of celestial puzzle pieces. His lover's grip tightened and, with a remarkable strength he found that he'd always suspected her to possess, she drew him upwards to straddle her back. Now, though, he understood her altered nature: no longer petite of shoulder and narrow of waist, the girl was gloriously immense. Reaching for a handhold atop her arched back he realized he was gripping handfuls of silken softness: looking, he saw her coat of feathers. Again, he was less startled by the revelation than he might have been, as if he'd known all along the girl's potential for such amazing transformation. Her coat was brilliant, a vivid crimson which seemed to push away the night through which they ascended. A colour of rebellion among the darkness, a fire of celebration racing starwards. He smiled, he laughed, he roared with gleeful abandon while his heart hammered joyously at the awesome spectacle of which he was blessed to be a part.

Looking about him, he saw that they didn't fly alone: everywhere sailed the revellers, formerly occupying the forest shadows below and now transformed like she and borne aloft on great wings like hers. Like a fleet of gargantuan living ships, they arced with grace towards the stars. Their colours were likewise brilliant: fiery crimsons and icy blues and gleaming emeralds, a veritable rainbow assemblage, the great murder of avian-like beings rising into the heavens. His great joy escalated at the sight. He laughed again. He spread his arms wide, gripping his lover's sides tightly with his bracing legs. This gesture elicited an immediate response from her: a sexual ripple coursing through her silk-soft body which in turn aroused him: a violent pulse awakened in his loins, echoed with the hammering in his temples and a frantic quickening of his heart.

The rushing nocturnal air was glorious on his face. The million stars waiting overhead grew larger as they rose swiftly. He yearned to touch their silver beauty with his hands, to complete the journey and be among them, to know them and be cradled by them after all of the indifference and dissatisfaction he'd known below.

Then: a great stabbing traveled through him, like lightning stretching its electrical fingers into his limbs and extremities. His fingers and toes and penis crackled with it, his vision exploded with it. Slowly he grew aware of the focus of this pain. He stared downwards and found the immense stone arrowhead protruding through his chest, primitively-sculpted with jagged edges, heavy with his blood, ragged with his shredded flesh. He was struck dumb with the surreal sight of it – so simple, so crude an element interrupting his majestic flight – the deadly weapon and the evidence of its passage through his ravaged body. He started at the series of violent thundering thuds: looking, he saw a half dozen arrows embedded in his lover's wings and, even as he watched in horror, another bevy sliced among these. An agonized shriek erupted from the great bird's black hooked beak, a horn's wailing dirge across the mantle of the sky. The chorus of hollow thundering erupting about them he knew to be the other flyers falling victim to the same violence – soon their song of pain rang across the heavens, too.

He understood: assassins among the trees, secluded in aeries upon the earth below, their hateful, envious aim true, succeeding in their simple desire of preventing their escape into hallowed places after their time served upon the earth. His lover the she-bird beat her wings frantically in her immense pain, striving to hold them aloft, though their fate was already sealed.

He reached a hand towards the brilliant pole star pulsing overhead, watched it recede quickly, quickly as they embarked on their violent descent, reclaimed by that most ordinary and savage of worlds. As they fell he felt two new points of pain: along his shoulder blades, a heartbeat-pulsing, a violent ache as of his flesh and bone erupting in the nascent stages of an orgy of transformation, as if trying futilely to birth wings like those of the surrounding host; which might save him and his lover from the earth drawing them inexorably unto itself.

But they only continued their fall, like stars expired and energy-less, plummeting towards the nearest rock at hand.

He could feel her watching him with avid eyes where he was seated on the edge of the bed, stubble and fingers and subsiding erection glistening with her wetness. It was this intensity of her attention which had torn him from his post-coital dreaming: he turned away petulantly so that his face was pointed towards the tiny window, though he only stared vacantly into the middle distance, dazed from their rabid sex, discomfited from sharing the aftermath silence with her, resentful for her scrutiny pulling him forth from his reverie. Perhaps the vision would have concluded differently this time had she not disturbed it: he considered this idea briefly but knew, of course, that it wouldn't have.

The smell of their sex hung heavy in the air of the tiny room. Her books – both textbooks and the assortment of Japanese language paperback novels which made up the substantially smaller portion of her personal library which she'd brought from overseas – lay heaped about the room in crooked towers of varying sizes like some strange architectural schemata sprouting from the floor everywhere. The room's meagre assortment of furnishings – narrow bed; small wooden desk covered with papers and books and her laptop, open and humming a low murmur; and a single battered bureau that had come with the room – made him depressed. He closed his eyes to the wan sodium light of the single lamp fixture in the centre of the ceiling, and the stained walls, unadorned with pictures or posters or any other decoration which might serve to brighten the dismally austere squalor surrounding him.

From the opposite end of the bed came the soft sound of her stirring amid the nest of moist, crumpled sheets, freeing her small feet from the tangled fabric or wiping his semen from her thighs with an efficient hand.

Her name conjured exotic visions in his mind: Michi Samurakami, like a character of myth escaped from the ancient fairy-lore of her homeland and materialized like a miracle in his world. She was a student whom he'd met while waiting in the interminable line formed before the coffee shop in the student centre one early September morning just prior to the beginning of the academic day. The bustle of young men and women moving towards their classes had surrounded them, creating, conversely, a sort of bubble of closeness within which – in a matter of ten or so minutes – they had introduced themselves, chatted politely about inconsequential subjects, and grown to understand their mutual physical attraction towards one another. This attraction – intense, nearly violent in the way his appraisal of her that first morning immediately conjured vivid images of their copulation – he hadn't questioned, despite the unfamiliarity of his experiencing it towards a girl such as her. The overpowering nature of this attraction, he came to realize only much later was, in fact, the same aspect of the girl which he loathed.

They'd left the building together to wander the campus aimlessly for perhaps another thirty minutes before deciding – at his urgent and unsubtle behest – to abandon their morning classes and spend the time together. Perhaps she'd been impressed by his willingness to shun responsibility for her, abandoning his students without much deliberation at all. It was then she'd surprised him by inviting him back to her nearby shabby rooming house room for the first time, in this way bringing full circle a happening which he'd not long ago aspired to as often a possible with as many women (and as many of his students in particular) as possible, and which was evidently for her a wholly new – and therefore exceedingly frightening – experience. He'd felt a certain fear, too, having never been with a non-Caucasian woman and finding, in his unexpected, quickly-flowering attraction to her, that he'd never experienced something as fierce and all-consuming with anyone before in all of his unsatisfying, doomed-to-fracture relationships.

The rustling from beside him on the bed, he knew, was the girl kicking away the bed sheets entirely. Her smell came to him, her subtle perfume like cinnamon, mixed with her sex. The elixir of her stirred his senses. He sensed the beginning of arousal once again.

He considered their first time together: a violent tremor had seized her, running the course of her entire body as he held her in the room, kissing her mouth and neck and shoulders while he unbuttoned her shirt and slipped it from around her. He'd been successful in calming her during these initial embraces, if not his own anxieties, a feat which served to excite him in a way he'd never before then experienced – whispering soothing logic into her ear concerning the fortuitous or preordained circumstances by which they'd met, two people from opposite corners of the world happened to convene in a student centre in a long line of strangers; as well as the acceptable nature of what they were about to do, two lonely people who felt a rare and difficult-to-define connection. These things he whispered to her while admiring her delicate hands and arms with a pair of fingers tracing their curvatures, while wrapping his lips for the first time around each of her dark brown nipples in turn, while drinking in the overall fragile and unique look of this dainty girl relinquishing herself into his increasingly urgent affections, making her short emphatic cries while he revelled in the success of his casual duplicity.

They'd known each other for approximately one month, and he'd visited her in her home nearly every night in that time; hastening from his classes or abridging his office hours, followed by a reckless drive from the campus to this rooming house and this room in it which she rented for the simple reason that the funds bestowed on her by her family had been nearly exhausted by the high costs of tuition and textbooks, and what remained was enough to pay for nothing more elegant. Never before had he been so driven in something, neither academically nor socially. He'd considered the peculiar notion several days into their relations, while performing cunnilingus on the girl: it was as if he were possessed, by the physical shell of the girl, so incredibly, indefinably attractive to him, as well as by the idea of her representing for him some new, unexplored thing. And, after all this time of their inseparability, it was only of late that the reasons for his overwhelming attraction to – and paradoxical loathing of her – had begun to grow apparent to him.

He started at her voice – timorous, as delicate as the rest of her – disturbing the uneasy silence and his troubling meditations. "Maybe we can go to restaurant somewhere close, and eat dinner now? Are you hungry, Michael? It is almost seven o'clock." The idea of a human voice infiltrating the deep quiet that had settled over the room following their vociferous lovemaking seemed improbable. After what they'd done together it seemed as if every element of the world should be too weary to produce even the smallest of sounds. In the wake of the disturbance, he found himself shaken, unable to respond at all.

She'd been speaking to him more and more, a fact which threatened his uncertain peace in no small way. The past week she'd been relentless, in her quiet, timid way, in seeking to cajole him into reciprocating her small wishes and greater desires, this latter of which suffused each of the requests she made that they spend time together outside of their brief and frantic couplings. He mumbled something vague, the very sound of his voice epitomising the fragile armour of excuse-making. This gave him cause to consider the fact that he felt no difficulty in speaking to her while they were having sex; his voice a constant droning murmur while he spoke words he'd always wanted but had never been bold enough to utter with his other sex partners throughout the years.

Her accent, endearingly thick in the first days he'd known her – incredibly sexy still while she spoke to him as he fucked her, encouraging him to continue his own lewd soliloquies – now, in the aftermath of sex, unnerved him; in some ways, even repulsed him; so foreign to the sound of his own voice speaking the language, its timbre and inflection of the words she spoke. He flinched at it, was made discomfited by it, both by its sound as well as for what his reaction said about himself. And yet he felt a distant but growing sense of relief seep its way into him, too: this secret he kept – her, and their relations – belonged to him and no other. Neither his few professional acquaintances nor family knew the girl existed. Few strangers had even seen them together, being that he'd been successful in stifling her wishes that they take their relationship outside of the sex-room and into the social sphere of restaurants, as now, and bars and coffee shops and theatres and groceries and stores. He'd likewise managed to keep to a minimum the evening walks she enjoyed taking, through the abutting park and surrounding streets, unfrequented by much pedestrian traffic, though on the few occasions when he'd relented they'd encountered small groups of students from the nearby university, making him uncomfortable and embarrassed, as if he'd been found out in the midst of some shameful, morally wrongful activity. She'd asked him once, whether he was afraid of trouble arising from his liaison with a student, to which he'd readily assented only to be left stymied with her next simple question: "But we are adults, Michael, who care for each other – there can be nothing wrong in this. Am I right?"

In response to his silence now, her voice came again, plaintive: "Are you hungry, Michael? It is very late now. Maybe we can go to Emerald Tiger. It is my favourite restaurant to eat, and only few minutes' walk from here. I have not eaten dinner yet." He wanted to silence her but lacked the courage or cruelty or strength to do so. Instead, he only shrugged noncommittally and reached for his clothes scattered on the floor at his feet.

The girl was persistent today. "Please. Michael. *Please?* Why you not want have dinner with me? Why you always not do these things with me?"

"What do you mean? I don't know what you mean," he stammered, fumbling with his underwear entangled among the legs of his pants turned inside-out. Anxiety made jelly of his fingers, which he seemed unable to make work quickly or deftly enough.

He momentarily managed to extricate the garments, and was pulling his underwear on when her voice returned, a mournful beseeching in the anxious stillness. "I am hungry, Michael."

Where are the birds: this thought flew into his agitated thoughts, filling him with longing. Snatching his suit jacket from the edge of the bed he stumbled on uncertain legs towards the door, muttering over his shoulder, "I have term papers to mark. A mountain of them. Maybe next time. I'll see you soon. Tomorrow: I'll see you then."

Closing the door behind him, he caught a fleeting glimpse of her within: seated on the bed, naked still, her petite round shoulders and small breasts luring his attention, eyes watching him with an expression of wilful patience, as if her intention was to wait for him in exactly this posture until their next scheduled rendezvous, forsaking any and all commitments she may have to school, to work; using the bait of her nakedness to bring about his return, which she certainly knew to be the most potent means of ensnaring him again.

Then the door was shut, though the image of her burned in his eyes: her nipples like dusky coins, the thick triangle of her moist pubic hair which she unabashedly flaunted, her pouting lips and the ghost of their taste lingering on his own. He stood in the hall for a moment, fighting his growing desire to return to her and fuck her again, but soon enough forced his sluggish steps away and onto the moon-washed street where – despite his lingering arousal, the maddening tingling in his groin and fingertips and toes – he began to feel somehow cleansed.

A shadow darkened his warm yellow lamp-lit work space. Turning he found her owning the doorway to his office, hair newly auburned and eyes as piercing as ever.

"Michael, hard at work. This seems to be the version of you I've been finding of late." Her voice assured like he'd always known it to be.

He leaned back in his chair, squealing its frame. Feeling luxuriously at ease with this woman who'd once intimidated him in so many ways, he said, "Hello, Deborah. What brings you to my dark corner of the hallway?"

He examined her openly, a close perusal of her from top to bottom. He immediately remembered her during sex: the smell of her; her impassioned cries, boisterous but in an unsubtly calculated way, as if she'd decided long ago with some former lover on how best to articulate the physical sensations of having sex in the most suitably sensual way; the way she preferred riding him while only rarely allowing him to be on top of her, clutching his head to her breasts so that he'd suckle them as she came. As commanding in bed as she was out of bed. In recalling her in these ways, a great relish flooded his senses. He found that he was smiling, and judging from the uncertain and mildly vexed expression on Deborah's face, assumed that his enigmatic demeanour unsettled her.

Shrugging off his peculiar reaction to her she entered the office, sullying the room's smell of rich mahogany with her redolent perfume. She ran a finger the length of the bookshelf owning one wall, her words dripping with spurious weariness, "I'm finished teaching for the day, thank God. It's been a long one. I can't wait to get home, and have a long shower, and wash this day from me. And I'm *starving*. I could devour an entire menu whole. Have you eaten?"

He shook his head. He waited, enjoying the discomfited expression which stole over her when he neglected to make the overture she expected and hoped for. When she turned away from him to the book-lined shelf before her he said, "I've got to be somewhere this evening."

She didn't answer, only continued her perusal of the myriad books and academic journals cramming the shelves. Then, "We're not getting any younger, are we, Michael?" She'd said it in a wistful way while turning to examine the framed photograph adorning the wall, several years old, that captured the two of them, side by side with their colleagues in the English department, in attendance at a gala commemorating the retirement of a mutual friend. He understood the undercutting nature of the comment, though, being that she looked exceedingly good for her age (nearly a decade his junior with the looks of a woman younger even than this), aware of the grey in his hair and the crow's feet around his eyes and his increasingly distressing paunch of middle age. But he only smiled ruefully as he denied her. "Sorry, Deborah. I'm busy this evening, and every other this week." He felt a thrill in denying her in so veiled a manner, thinking of his secret life with the wondrous

Michi Samurakami, revelling at the visions of this clandestine liaison materializing in his mind while he spoke with his colleague.

"I see." Deborah straightened from where she'd blessed his desk corner with her buttocks. From before the doorway she asked him in a casual voice: "Who is she? A student again? Secretary? Which department have you invaded now?"

He only shrugged and offered her a quizzical expression he was pleased to note irritated her further. He examined her carefully, seeing only Michi Samurakami waiting for him in her bed, naked; different than Deborah in every conceivable way; his. He hadn't felt strong like this since his youth, long, long buried by the years.

"Well, there certainly is *someone*, Michael, for you to deny me." Her outward haughtiness may have been restored, he mused, but certainly her secret pride continued to suffer. He watched her exit the office in a stride certain to attract the interested eyes of faculty and students alike, then returned his attention to the papers drowning his desk, only to see her like a relentless apparition bent on driving him mad with her hauntings:

Michi Samurakami, naked and vibrantly wild in how she bent to his unrestrained will and whim and, in so doing, helped him to achieve what he'd never experienced with anyone else: true, *true* ecstasy.

She was waiting for him in the doorway later that afternoon as he ascended the filthy staircase of threadbare carpet and stained walls, standing partway into the unkempt outer hallway. Her face radiated its customary joy, as misplaced as ever, as if she waited for and expected much more from him than that which he ever gave her. He smiled curtly, sensing as he did so the inadequate nature of the gesture, its feeble insincerity when greeted by her own genuine exuberance. He came to stand directly before her, wearing a stern look of expectation, in a manner which firmly suggested that they enter the room together. She neither budged nor ceased her disconcerting, inscrutable appraisal of him, leaving him standing there nervously, drinking in her simple smell: soap and cinnamon and the faint underlying odour of her perspiration. It was a maddening odour, different from that of other women he knew – all of whom seemed always steeped in layers of differing cloying perfumes, as evinced only hours earlier by Deborah's malodorous appearance – as all things about Michi Samurakami were different from others. His progress into the room impeded, he was forced to speak to her.

"Should we – do you want to go inside for a while?" He knew, of course, that she knew his meaning, as she always knew his simple desires too well. He knew, also, of course, that her desires lay elsewhere at that moment.

Still smiling, she said in a voice airy and unperturbed, "Sun is shining today. Can we go for walk somewhere please?" He saw for the first time the bright floral-patterned handbag she wore slung over a shoulder; her bright green sandals and toenails newly painted a matching glistening emerald; her likewise matching green cotton skirt and clean white collar shirt he'd only ever seen her wear at school. She hadn't obeyed his usual wishes to await his arrival clad in nothing but her old bathrobe and pink plush slippers, the teasingly scant outfit which spoke to his innate preference for disrobing her in what he considered her "around-home" or "before-bed" outfits (in his lewd thinking, he likened this to the girl being in her natural habitat while he, visiting her, explored and conquered both her and her world).

He feigned a smile, sighed and, in the sigh, felt all of his great disappointment coalesce into a simple and robust fury directed at her for daring to delay his intentions and expectations with her. As he allowed her to close the door before them, his roiling emotions were overcome with another: and with this tremendous sense of loss filling him and making him nauseous, he could momentarily do nothing but follow her – with bowed posture and reluctant steps – into the sun, feeling quite as if she'd locked them out from the rarest of Paradises.

He wrenched the light shirt from around her shoulders, exposing her soft skin beneath with its abraded designs of fading bruises – encircling her bicep like a purple gauntlet, darkening her forearms, and blood blisters spotting her neck where his feral bite had found and drank of her – evidence of their previous night together; thinking as he did: this is my reward. Here it is. Here it is.

They'd only just returned to her room and already he was manhandling her the way he liked, the way she'd grown accustomed to and accepting of early into their relations. He sought to expunge the agonizingly uncomfortable hour past, and found that this was the only way to do so: wandering the streets of the neighbourhood and idling minutes away in the small park which abutted the building's rear lot. His discomfiture had grown the longer they'd remained in public, with the potential of encountering other early evening walkers who would see him with her, and judge him the way he might likewise judge a man he saw sharing the company of a girl like her. Once, a pair of students, a couple close in age, similarly Aryan with blonde hair and pale creamy skin, wandered past them where they shared a bench beside the narrow cement path which cut from one end of the park to its other. The smiles this young man and his lover had smiled he understood were benign, a well-meant pleasant wordless greeting, and yet it had birthed anger in him, and shame. He'd shrank from Michi Samurakami's gentle touch, become annoyed with the expression of disappointment that fell over her features; as if she was the more responsible of the two of them for this downward spiralling of their time together.

They hadn't spoken for many minutes thereafter, and when they had, it was he uttering a few conciliatory words to her because they'd drawn within sight of the rooming house and he feared her resistance to his desires underneath the pall of their dismal mood.

With a viciousness apparent to him even through his great lust, he peeled her sandals off each of her feet by carelessly stepping on her heels with his own shoe-shod feet, scraping her skin and eliciting a startled cry from her. A hard shove between her shoulder blades sent her sprawling across the kitchen countertop. She stood rigid, trembling in anticipation of him, allowing him to unzip her and tear the skirt from her legs. He could smell her excitement and her fear, this new elixir of her clouding out the kitchen around them.

"Fucking stay bent over," he seethed in her ear as she turned towards him, the inexplicable rage overcoming him again. She obeyed, letting him spread her legs further, her little feet clinging to the tacky linoleum while he stepped from his pants and underwear.

He fixed his gaze on her buttocks as he thrust into her, making her shriek. He felt them with his large hands, squeezing them and running his fingers along the cleft between them. He then turned his attentions to her breasts, pinching her nipples savagely and renewing her tortured ecstatic cries. He imagined her in the moment as he'd imagined her every time they'd been together: no girl, she, no student from overseas studying biology in a Canada she sought desperately to understand as she likewise sought to fathom him, too; no girl at all, more exotic a creature entirely, a cobbled-together gestalt beauty of various fantastical minutiae: parts culled from the rich myth of her culture, the wickedness of the folkloric oni sprite merged with the mischievousness of the fox mingled with the magical wisdom of a fairy spirit; overruled by that most ancient and beauteous of deities, the shape-changing avian goddess dwelling within the simple sensual shell of the girl. All of this which he was blessed to posses in every way: a slave to his every whim and will; for him to own and act out desires upon, however dark and perverse and depraved and shameful, however much he would never ever reveal them into the world and to the people he knew who lived unaware of the molten underworld of his mind.

Her cries then as ever were shrill, pained, and carried within them a profoundly alien quality; so utterly alien to the cries of passion he'd elicited from other women, whose sexual language always communicated a pleasure entirely divorced from true, unmitigated release; nearly inhuman, he reasoned, and it was through this logic, as ever, that he allowed himself to fuck her with perfect abandon, to speak the wanton words into her ears that he always did while in no way considering her feelings or what she might think of his most recent transformation from distant, moody man to brutal user of her amazing physical shell. "You... My... Little... Fuck... Animal... You're... Mine... All... Mine... Oh... My... God... What... Are... You... Doing... To... Me..."

It was then, not long after he'd fallen into the rapid cycle of pummelling her madly, that the divine-moment came in more profound a manner than he'd experienced it before, and the door to his ecstasy lay opened: he saw her wings unfurl from two apertures until then invisible atop the smooth curving hills of her shoulder blades; witnessed them bloom violently upwards in a surge of pastel emerald and brilliant crimson feathers which thrashed and fluttered a frantic wind into his face; the wind they bore was a hot one, a scorching gale that burned his cheeks and chest like a desert tempest, and sent a heated pulse throbbing through his erection. As her cries rose in volume and reciprocal bliss these wings beat a faster windstorm, urging bellowing cries from him, too, and quickening his journey towards his own orgasm like a rebirth into a new, unprecedented cosmology known to only a select and blessed few.

He awoke sometime in the bottomless miles of the A.M. He lay rigid, searching for what it was that had disturbed his slumber. He heard it coalesce from the indefinable pulse of the night, drifting into the sex-room through the ajar window beside the bed: music. A songbird's nocturnal hymn blessing the darkness, the moonlight, the stars like winter suspended in the sky. He thought faintly how misplaced the delicate song was among the ghetto of shabby houses and rundown tenements lurching into the street, like cold water seeking to cleanse a wound of irreparable damage and infection running amok.

 He smiled within the soothing melody of its sermon to the night, in weird rhythmic harmony with the girl's breathing beside him. A sense of peace stole over him, making him drowsy and luring him into dreams again.

*

They flew atop the roof of clouds, he the rider, she the great but delicate-boned creature beneath him, around which he clamped his strong legs tightly. Her transformation here complete: no vestige of her former form remained, that shell submerged beneath her new beauty: long-winged, razor-taloned, curved of beak, black-eyed with the moon reflected wetly in each immense and bottomless orb. Her plumage brighter than he'd ever seen it, a vivid crimson that fired the twilight through which they sailed, a beacon drawing the envious eyes of those whom they were leaving crawling far below in their small lives of little worth. Little bits of foliage and other floral debris drifted from his hair and from where they'd gathered among his mount's feathers when they'd burst through the dense forest roof, sailing downwards like confetti celebrating their remarkable ascension.

He spoke, without words, and she, of course, heard him in deep places.

I can live like this for the rest of my life. Like this, I want to live forever.

The mighty beating of her wings stirred a warm and reassuring breath of wind to swathe him: in its embrace, his recent troubled thoughts and self-doubts – remote now, barely credible at all – slipped finally away into darkness and freefall.

They grazed the constellations as they arced against the twilight's deep indigo sky, rising higher, higher.

But: a murmuring among the clouds, like a great voice of danger in the twilight. It grew and grew and then gave birth to a dozen gargantuan steel birds sailing forth from the indigo depths. Machines ugly in shape and brutal in purpose, the murder of bombers of a type he felt he'd seen before somewhere, perhaps in books or in documentaries chronicling one of the World Wars. They were gargantuan, blotting out the promise of the celestial light with a completeness that chilled him. Beneath their great shadow he felt all of his hope and peace crushed. These immense machines in turn birthed their children into the night: lines of bombs hatching from their bellies and arcing towards them on all sides.

Then, a great thunder roared in his dream, swallowing his peace entirely; smiting them down from their lofty ecstasy with its mighty bellowing, two frenzied fuck animals plummeting earthwards within a resounding dirge of agony.

He awoke sweat-bathed and with his heart crashing like thunder. He was delirious from the dream and confused as to his surroundings until the memory of his homebound drive returned, of collapsing into bed without thought, too weary from his time in the sex-room to attempt completing his lesson plans for the following day's lectures. He was gripping his erection. A pulse of excitement thrummed in its glans.

He stroked himself, slowly but building gradually into a violent manipulation of the member. He abandoned his efforts when the vision of her that had followed him from his dream – silhouetted against the sky, wingspan prodigious and feathers blood-red and soaring flight graceful – became too vivid, too maddening, making him understand the paltry and insufficient nature of his masturbation.

Throwing an overcoat around himself; snatching his keys from where they hung on a nail beside the door, heedless of his briefcase sent crashing to the floor from the tabletop in his haste, his cache of lecture notes scattering across the tiles; scrambling to his car parked in the driveway; racing through the deserted A.M. streets to the little rooming house on the opposite side of the city; slipping into her room using the key she'd given him as a show of her devotion to their relationship; startling her as he crashed into bed with her and lapped his tongue across her lips, cheeks, neck and, tearing wide her nightshirt, wetting her breasts; moving downwards to her vagina, lavishing his attention there until her dry lips grew moist.

Her cries grew quickly from frightened and alarmed to rapturous. In their clamour he felt himself lifted away.

He woke when dawn limned the window in red. As his sleep-dazed senses sobered, he felt her observation of him. He found her watching him from directly beside him, the lower portion of her face hidden within the crook of her bare arm. Her eyes were haunted and unwavering, and unnerved him. Though he couldn't see her mouth, her words fell clearly in the great morning quiet.

"I love you, Michael."

He felt somehow that he was being tested. That much more depended on his response than merely the girl's satisfaction that her feelings were reciprocated. Uncertain how to reply – confused with conflicting feelings of awakening revulsion and lust towards her naked beside him – he saved himself the only way that seemed possible. He clamped his eyes shut, hoping fervently that whenever he dared to reopen them the vision of her would be gone, only another dream fragment vanished into the ether of the forthcoming day.

*

It was following his awkward, embarrassingly slapdash lecture to a class of a dozen bemused graduate students that he'd decided to make of her an experiment: Deborah the challenger, disputing the reign of the mysterious Michi Samurakami. She'd found him brooding in his office and he'd relented to her unsubtle proposition – the second in as many days while visiting his office to pass the time with some small talk before her final class for the day – ostensibly a dinner date, which saw them return to his home and make immediately for the bedroom.

Of course, she failed to usurp his secret girl's mastery over his waking and dreaming life, despite her meaninglessness to him, despite his emotionless fucking of her. Despite her alluring body, long-legged, big-breasted, full-hipped. This he considered while examining Deborah's long slender calf gripped between his fingers, his erection growing limp inside her. She stared at him curiously, waiting expectantly, looking luxurious with her dark auburn hair billowing freely about her supple shoulders. When he pulled himself from her and moved to sit on the edge of the bed she mistook his silence for shame, and gave him her cruel words in a malicious effort at dealing his pride a killing stroke.

"It's okay, Michael. Don't fret about it too much now: it happens to all men, sometimes." The smile she smiled was spitefully pleased. She relished his would-be indignity.

She only ceased smiling when he said, "But it's you. Deborah: it's *you* that aren't enough for *me*." And he laughed at the expression of defeat and doubt that stole over her.

"You're pathetic." Her voice was a knife cutting through the darkness, though its aim was far from true. He only laughed with greater scorn and triumph. It was his turn to revel in her weakness. He found it felt exhilarating, wrecking her lifelong supremacy over him and all men.

"I'm leaving. Are you driving me or am I walking home all the way across the fucking city?"

"Yes," he told her. "You'll be walking home. You could never fly, Deborah. Not ever."

He rejoiced at her stunned eyes, the revulsion and alarm filling them. He glimpsed something like dread there, too, and he relished having birthed there. He watched her storm off, high-heels swinging dangerously in a vicious hand, humiliation altering her usual walk, devouring its haughtiness, her assuredness that the woman she'd always known herself to be was a godsend to all men.

Mostly, though, he felt only a great exhilaration at the idea filling him, that he stood at the edge of a mystery whose solution would yield him a fulfillment for which he'd always yearned but – until now – never come close to attaining.

He dressed hurriedly and remembered only when he was driving towards the enigmatic Michi Samurakami that he'd forgotten to lock the door to his house after him. He slowed, but sped onwards a moment after. If all went as he hoped, he would never return to simple rooms like these again.

Another vision like a revelation of the universe's secret potential:

A long line of them winding downwards from among the stars.

The glimpse was brief but delicious: a world un-guessed to most, existing within the fibres of the everyday but known seemingly to him and her alone.

He looked out upon it, squinting in the bright sunlight, for the sun shone perpetually in this place, though occasionally the moon, too, though always with just as much brilliance: a grand colony, a colossal mothernest housing them all:

Seraphs, or the closest thing to them to exist in the universe, or in any imaginable place or place beyond comprehension. Like some undiscovered Mesozoic stop-gap, or an un-guessed future step on the evolutionary plain which would see a marriage between avian and human matrixes to unveil a beautiful hybrid structure and physiognomy; a feather-coat lush and healthy, married to the basic bipedal human form, though its limbs much less cumbersome and unwieldy, boasting here a delicacy of bone structure, a buoyancy and aerodynamic grace wholly absent from the former; blessed also with wings and the dream-like capabilities of flight into furthest reaches: beyond cumulus-plains, past stratosphere, and into the furthest places between stars where Heaven or the closest thing to Paradise might lie. Weird-tailed, too, lush with feathers yet serpentine and long, muscular and coiling, as if flaunting some impossible antediluvian trait representing that point at which their evolution diverged yet further from origins begun equally with Archaeopteryx and ancient Stone Age man.

And she among them like a humble and benevolent queen: his little Michi-bird, air-dancing with a grace and aplomb beautiful to behold.

His dream-pulse quickened at the sight of her in her crimson glory, like fire licking the stars. His dream-heart thundered.

Perhaps he loved her after all.

*

"Michael?" from afar, muted as if filtering through a membranous wall separating the realm of deepest, deepest sleep from some far less sacred place.

No.

Revulsion began its measured seeping into him once more as, drawn forth from the dream-place by her voice of concern, he beheld the physical shell of her in the aftermath of their lust: the petite Asian girl with boyish hips and small breasts and slender legs, hair bedraggled, skin coated with a sheath of sweat that glistened in the moon-washed room.

He pulled himself out in time to shoot a residual burst of semen across her small buttocks, found that he possessed enough lingering lust to emit a final jet of ejaculate onto the madly fluttering wings themselves. He watched entranced as they folded in upon themselves, retreating into her flesh in a violence just as quick and startling to behold as their emergence, as if his semen were a murdering acidic agent urging their accelerated demise. He stared at her body while his senses, flooded with the madness of their time together, returned gradually to a more neutral state. The lingering vestiges of his latest dream-time faded. The squalid walls and tiles of the apartment returned.

Despite his encroaching lucidity, he yet entertained the mad notion that perhaps he'd truly witnessed the physical manifestation of transformation in her a moment ago. Maybe she was beautiful after all, despite the bewitching shell of her which he simultaneously worshipped and abhorred.

Then, in the moon colour and immense stillness, the girl's laboured breathing arrived in his awareness, drawing him fully awake. He realized the lateness of the hour, the frenzy of this most recent possession that had transported him so deeply into the bliss of their sex. In the aftermath of it, while they both dressed themselves by the moonlight, her voice came, small and pathetic with gratitude: "Thank you for eating supper with me yesterday, Michael. Maybe we will do this again sometime."

He winced at the words, and at what they revealed about them both: her achingly saddening manner of settling for whatever scraps of superficial affection he deigned to give her; and his own shameful and selfish and abhorrent ways. He looked to her, but quickly away: her smiling lips and eyes, victim of his deception, were difficult to behold with the feral energy of his lust temporarily depleted.

She followed him behind the wall of his closed eyes, though, smiling and smiling as if she were content, and this contentedness, it felt to him, was like a dangerous magnetic force luring his humanity forth from the its buried place within him.

He pulled his shirt over his head, desperate to be away from her unnerving presence. Seeing this, she whispered imploringly, "Michael. Please stay with me tonight. You do not have to go away. You always go away when you are finished with me." There was no accusation in her matter-of-fact voice, though he knew of course that she would be completely just in accusing him. Shaking his head in a futile denial of her claim, he muttered, "I don't know what you mean."

"Yes," she wore on, her voice now carrying a distinctly beseeching – and increasingly annoyed – note. "Yes, Michael. Yes you know my meaning. Please tell me, okay? I want to know from you – why do you like me? You always see me, every day, but you will not talk to me, ever. You come, and you go soon after we are together, and you never say very much to me. Why do you come? What things do you like about me? Do you... I... I need to know from you... Maybe do you...love me?"

A brief arrival of courage or boldness overcame him, despite the tremor of unease he felt upon hearing her words. In the softest voice of consolation he could muster, he said, "I don't. I...I don't love this part of you." He gestured a vague yet all-encompassing hand towards her. "This shell – I don't even...*love* it at all. I only love...*using* it. *Devouring* it. I'm sorry, but it's true. But what's inside...What's *inside* you: I'm under its spell." In the wake of this admission a great shame washed over him, tidal wave-colossal and surging without respite. Shame, and a kind of stunned resignation, because in that rare moment of honesty with the girl and with himself he'd for the first time allowed his true character to speak its voice. Disappeared was his elaborate world-making, evaporated into the ether of its own opulence.

He dared to look at her, unfiltered through the lens of his myth-making. She was frowning, pouting with a child-like audacity, while despair haunted her eyes. Sensing his appraisal she hid her face from him by engaging in a mock inspection of her bright bag resting on the floor beside her. Her perspiration-glistening body beautiful to behold, her strange eyes riveting, too, and frightening for the emotions they contained, as well as their quiet but unmitigated intelligence: the most exquisitely alien, unknowable animal he'd ever seen.

A moment later she was slipping into her vivid green- and orange-striped underwear while abstractedly watching the sky framed in the little window overlooking the street. Still looking away from him, she said in a nonchalant tone, as if meaning to sound offhand but the tremor in her voice revealing her teetering emotions, "You do not mean that."

He thought of the many people – all strangers – whom he would pass while en route from this girl's rat-infested apartment of squalor, through the city's downtrodden downtown centre where harried-looking businessmen and clerical staff mingled with the homeless and otherwise lost; and finally to his own reasonably upscale apartment on the east side of the city. He considered these nameless individuals, men and women of varying economic status and with differing physiognomies:

he didn't hate them, was not repulsed by them: he simply felt nothing for them. A hollowness, as if they could never hope to elicit emotion of any variety from him. He felt, he realized, dead inside.

Except when he flew in the dreams she gave him.

He looked again to the girl where she huddled naked on the floor at his feet, gathering her scattered clothing. Her little bare breasts gleamed in the ugly sodium light. Her little feet, emerald nail polish glossy and bright, were like pretty ivory sculptures. The rolling contour of her upper thigh becoming her buttocks drew his attention. Her small hands clutching her skirt before her small knees were a delicate sculpture of prayer, like a depiction of worship of their copulation. Her pale skin made him hunger for her anew, its smoothness like water to satisfy his insatiable thirst for her. He imagined the smell of her, and the cries she cried each time he visited her and used her as he needed, lest his hunger grow unanswered and inevitable madness overtake him.

He yearned for these aspects of her all over again – and to ascend along the pathway to elsewhere which she provided – but felt nothing more.

He reached a hand to her round small shoulder. Her warmth electrified his cold fingers. He left it there, squeezing subtly. She turned her eyes on him for the first time in many minutes – large, wide, crying, painfully hopeful – and in this way gave herself to him again.

He had her again. Straddling her he made her scream again. He held her ankles while fucking her and shooting his semen into her again. Slipping his erection from her he then crawled over her and inserted it in her mouth. She gagged. He watched her pleading eyes while saliva and semen dribbled from the corners of her mouth. He left her gasping for air on the bare floorboards, pulling his clothes on hurriedly and shambling, half-clothed, towards the door.

Amid her sobbing, cutting-words, slicing through the thick air with their pathetic fiction.

"You…like me. You *like* me."

The words came without thought. "Sometimes I think you might be an angel."

Her response came quickly, and with a certainty and gentleness which shocked him, as if she sought to deliver him a harsh lesson in the softest manner possible. "Maybe there is no such thing, Michael. Maybe you must accept me as who I am."

The words, brimming with a quiet desperation, stung his back as he hovered in the doorway. Turning and giving her his profile so that his words could be heard but so their eyes wouldn't meet, he murmured, stunned at the revelation he gave to her as if it was an epiphany to him, too: "I like…I love…I love your body. Every single inch of it. The taste and the touch and the smell of it. If I could, I'd live on it, and inside of it, so I'd never be away from it. But… But that's all you are. A perfect… A perfect shell. A perfect animal. But you're inhuman to me."

This was all the truth he could give her: she, to him, was the world, and though the world in which he lived was rife with the beauty of things to be touched it held no more than this. Beyond the dream of her, there was nothing but flesh. In the wake of this confession which she'd wrung from him the emotion blossomed violently:

He loathed her anew. He told her: "I hate you for this. For what you do to me. I don't want to be seen with you. I don't want a single person in the world to know about the things we do together. And yet I've never wanted something so badly." He was pointing to her. The vulgarity of the gesture became magnified when he realized he pointed to the dark triangle of her crotch. He then gestured angrily about the small room, signifying it, and the greater world of the everyday which it epitomised. "In all the world, of everyone and everything I've ever known, I've never wanted something so much. So much that it burns. So much that I want to devour it, eradicate it, because maybe if it's dead and gone forever I can find peace from it."

She watched him unwaveringly through her crying eyes. When she spoke, her voice was even and measured. "I know your word for this, Michael. You are…*racist*. This is you. You are *racist* against me. You hate me because you are frightened of what you do not know. And if you are racist against me then there is nothing I can do to change you. *You* must change. *You* must change or you will not find this place you always speak of." Her voice rose then into a pleading timbre which unsettled him. "It is a *beautiful* place, Michael, this place you dream. It is up to you if you wish to make it real place. You must believe me."

He knew in that moment, of course, that she was absolutely correct about him. His eyes saw her secret beauty, nearly tangible but

285

always eluding him, when he answered in a whisper, "I love your race." A tribe of curvaceous avian-like figures arced against the sky behind his eyes. The ghostly touch of feathers tickled his spine, was a fluttering breath against his neck. He felt nauseous, delirious in the aftermath of his sexual frenzy and satisfaction. He reeled on his heels, touching a hand to his temple. He heard himself say again, as if from a distance: "I love your race. What a magnificent tribe…"

"You need to see…doctor. You are sick." Quiet, subdued, less the whimper he'd half-expected from her than an angry and disappointed resignation. Then, "You made this place…It is only here." Her small hand, hollow-boned and graceful, touched her temple.

He shook his head. He smiled. He laughed. Tears welled into his eyes though he fought futilely to keep them within. "No: it's there." And he stabbed his own hand, stout-boned and cumbersome, towards the sky wheeling beyond the water-stained ceiling with its pathetic, weak light bulb. "Somewhere there, but so hard – so *difficult* – to find."

"I want place like this, too, Michael. But difference is, I want this place right here. With you, and me." She gestured about the room, towards themselves. "Together, we can find this place. But you cannot see it."

He shook his head with a viciousness born of the desperation to deny blasphemous untruths. He spat: "It's only – *only* – there." His hands, both hands, were raised over his head in revelation of the Heaven he knew.

She shook her head now, too, denying her beauty. "You make me like this, but I am only me."

His voice quavered with equal measures ecstasy and terror: "No: you're much more than that. You're everything I've ever wanted. You're like a…you're like a *dream*. A dream for me. I've dreamed of you my whole life…I've never felt comfortable – as at peace – around someone like I am when I'm with you…But saying it – those words – they sound so banal, so simplistic compared to how you make me feel, what you do to me inside…" He drifted off, confused anew with the conundrum of the girl he loved and loathed. Already he was growing aroused again. Already her breasts and legs and mouth called to him like food to a starving man. He amended his words to her: "When I'm with you I'm at peace. But only when...only when I'm using you...for sex. For...escape from... all of this..." Hearing the audacious vulgarity of the truths he'd revealed, he whispered, "Why do you...want me? Why do you want so much for me to love you, when I say things like this to you?"

The girls' voice was assured: "Because you found me, Michael. You were first – you were only – man to see me. No one else sees me. You were first man to speak to me. You were only man to make love to me. This means something. There is meaning in this. Do you see it, Michael? Do you see meaning?"

Briefly, fleetingly, startlingly, he looked and saw her as he dreamed her:

A headdress of elegant feathers adorned her, spilling its lush crimson assemblage – shot through with a rich chestnut – over her little shoulders; her chest feather-covered, too, the small hillocks of her breasts; her tender eyes revealing her secret name to him: Michi Samurakami his little birdgirl, his secret desire and treasure and gateway to better places.

Tears welled and washed the bird-queen away and when they cleared again only the girl remained, eyes stunned and wary, face bloodless and all-too human.

He gave in to his own desperation and fear when, with guilt stabbing him, he murmured the old refrain: "I'll come again tomorrow." Then, unexpectedly, like a sky long pregnant with rain and finally releasing its cargo, he wept. He wept from his great guilt, and from his thwarted lust, and he wept especially for the great confusion like a perpetual fog from which he could never emerge, despite always glimpsing a vague tremulous evidence of light and revelation in the uncertain distance.

Perhaps she pitied him his madness. Maybe she was merely as afraid of her own loneliness as he was of his. Her voice was tiny, drifting to him through his sobbing as if from another room, another, much more distant time.

"I should not see you again. My family...if they knew of these things you say, they would forbid me to see you. But I think tomorrow – tomorrow when you come to visit me – tomorrow you will love me.

I hope you will... I hope tomorrow you can love me. Because you saw me, Michael. You found me and saw me. And I hope tomorrow you can love me."

He moved towards the door, nearly tripping on his own feet in his haste to be away form her and the enigma of her riddles. Her voice stopped him. Imploringly: "You are right: there is a place. Michael: there *is* a place."

He made the mistake, as he always did, and turned to her. She was standing in the room's centre, naked. Her shock of dark pubic hair slick with his semen. Her breasts perfect and beckoning. He wanted her. He loathed her. He felt suddenly like crying again, as if the contrasting emotions vying for supremacy within himself were too great and he, caught between them, had no recourse but to give in to his great turmoil and confusion and collapse entirely.

Finally, he left her, without goodbye, easing the door closed like a whisper behind him.

Her weeping, as ever, was the song he would remember most: from behind the door he heard it faintly. He felt it inside, too, as a lingering prickling of guilt behind his chest. At least in this he knew that he possessed some lingering shred of humanity.

A final and desperate experimentation: he bought himself a prostitute later that night but even someone like this – nothing more than a physical shell used for fucking by the loneliest of men – offered no gateway for him.

Only the disheartening reality of the woman, wan-skinned and ugly beneath the small motel room's diffused lighting, giving him ineffectual fellatio while he examined her with growing curiosity and disgust, as if she were a rare animal displayed within a zoo's observatory enclosure: her seeming engrossment in the task at hand, the voluble, moist sucking sound, the uninspired, wholly perfunctory groaning she emitted, muted for the shaft filling her mouth; until eventually the woman grew perturbed and removed his shrivelled, flaccid penis from between her lips and eyed him questioningly; and when he offered her no response nor reason for his detachment from her fondling, muttered an indignant-sounding, "It costs the same, man, whatever we did tonight."

Her breath was rank, an obnoxious mixture of morning-breath and alcohol and penis-smell. It wafted up to him like air from a furnace burning garbage, while she fidgeted with her bra, her naked breasts sagging before him like a pair of giant pale marine life forms beached atop her tumid belly. He thought of birds, and how flight was impossible within the suffocating net of this room. He placed a crumpled bill on the night table, and left the woman to slip her giant repugnant breasts back into the cups of her bra.

He was turning to leave but stopped himself, hand on the doorknob. Facing the woman he said, "Wait. Will you... Will you help me understand something?"

The prostitute eyed him in her wary, arrogant way. "I don't know what you mean, man."

He approached her, came to stand directly before her where she sat on the bed's edge. He removed his wallet from his pocket and the robust wad of bills bulging its leather slot. He threw it across her lap. Her expression changed from guarded to stunned to excited to wary again. She said in her voice of practiced bravado, "What do you want to do, man?"

He confessed, "I want...a lot. I want a lot more from you than I've asked for so far, if you have it in you to give. Will you help me? I need for us to try to visit a place, together."

The woman said nothing. To her expression of unease and confusion, he made his proposition clear. "The money is yours. Let me do what I need to do."

Fear stole into her eyes. She eyed him cagily. She examined the bills fanned across her lap, traced their edges with her fingers. Resolution usurped the fear in her gaze. She surrendered herself in a voice feigning composure, loud but wavering, true to her role in the many-cogged intricacy of the universe he sought to understand.

"I'm all yours, hon'."

*

Walking listlessly down the street, he considered the results of his experiments with the whore. How it had proven one fact without doubt: no woman, not even one utterly devoid of personality, nor even owning a name, could elicit escape for him. A desperation seized him, and quickened his steps through the dismal streets, as the magnitude of his conundrum became apparent: how would he ever be able to come to terms with Michi Samurakami, whom he worshipped and abhorred in equal measure? How could their dream-flights be made real, and ensure his escape from his perpetual frustration and dissatisfaction like a cancerous growth stealing his joy each day passing? Would he ever understand her true mystery, beyond the tantalizing and agonizing sense he had that he was halted firmly at the edge of this knowledge?

He flexed his fingers, mired in the woman's residual fluids, crackling within their dried veneer. The pungent stink of her lingered, too, hanging about him like an ominous cloud beneath which he nearly swooned.

He understood then that his Michi-bird – and the dream birthed by her – must die, if he was to survive the madness looming over the world from which he could only secure a dream of escape.

Merely the sight of the building through the misting rain conjured in his mind the kingdom held impossibly within its walls, and he felt himself growing aroused, and hopeful once again for eternal escape into its fabric.

Turning into the small lot and nestling the car it into its regular slot between the large grey metal dumpster and the Dodge Dart on the other side made him think of him putting his penis in her vagina. Stepping onto the rain-wet parking lot concrete, his penis hardened, springing from where the waistband of his underwear had held it fast so that its head now pressed with a violent heat into his abdomen. Entering the building, all of the sounds from its various occupants – voices speaking, arguing, the tinny electrical jabbering of a television and radio, a dog yipping – merged into a meaningless and insignificant droning which barely registered on his ears at all; while the familiar stale air and uncertain lighting and unsightly stained carpet all worked together to remind him of the girl, and her body, and those parts of her body which he was to devote all of his frenzied attentions upon.

Reaching her door at the summit of the creaking staircase, his felt his breathing quicken and a bevy of butterflies become unleashed in his stomach. The failed experiments of the evening behind him were trivial, nearly forgotten beneath the promise of the wonder forthcoming. Nearly delirious with lust for the girl within the room, he paused before her door, eager, tense. Casting a cursory glance about the hall to ensure he was alone, he unzipped his pants, eased his swollen penis into his hand. He stroked himself, squeezing his testicles, too, his nose touching the door wood, the smell of the room beyond wafting to him from beneath the door: the familiar scents but with some indefinable new ingredient mixed there, too. The lingering supper-smells of noodles and chicken fried rice, her subtle scent of rosemary, the unsavoury smell of the room itself, perennially musty and stuffy with old air; and this new smell, metallic and cold and – beyond these vague aspects – utterly beyond his ability to define.

He continued stroking himself, slowly and gently, rubbing his penis head against the cold door wood while imagining her breasts in his hands, her nipples gripped between his teeth, her wings exploding from her body like proof of the Heaven he'd found in her but which denied logic every time he imagined the girl while away from her and the madness she birthed in him.

He started: from the opposite side of the door he discerned her low, murmuring voice: "You are right: I am not able to save him. He is not prepared." The words, though he heard and understood them clearly, carried an unmistakeably peculiar aspect, an indefinably unfamiliar intonation, a foreign inflection overriding the Asian accent with which he was so familiar; as if the girl's voice were being translated through the filter of an alien throat unaccustomed to the language it spoke.

He knew not what the words meant, though he assumed they were spoken in relation to him. Something in the statement's inherent sentiment of condemnation seemed appropriate in defining him in relation to her. A fleeting sense of indignation arose in him, but quieted quickly – he was accustomed, after all, to resigning himself to his faults in her eyes.

He recoiled then: another voice, in response to her, neither masculine nor feminine but rich with both sexes, husky yet carrying a subtle soprano timbre, as well as the same indefinably alien aspect as hers, only notably more pronounced: "So few are. It is a wonder madness hasn't devoured this child from his time spent with you."

Jealousy mingled with terror in his heart. Confusion flooded his senses. The girl's universe contained only him. Who was this invader of the divine sex-room? Who dared sully its dirty floorboards and the conduit towards Heaven this tiny but limitless space represented for him? The bronze apartment key was in his fingers and his heart thunder in his chest and his blood a river pounding in his ears as he steeled himself to confront the intruder, to vanquish this defiler in order that his secret existence and the promise of his future peace might be saved.

But when he slipped his key into the worn lock and himself inside the dingy room beyond, his eyes rebelled: the small space was crowded with them, its squalor mocked by their strange grandeur, like a far-future alien society's theatrical interpretation of the Roman empire built within a framework and stage neither magnificent nor ambitious enough to contain it. Their numbers seemed to push the flaking walls and ceiling away, to plunge through the trembling floorboards, threatening the collapse of the building, perhaps the entire neighbourhood and city beyond.

He sought to speak but words would not come. Only his mouth agape, eyes spellbound by the vision of them: many were helmeted, heads encased in headgear similar to that which he'd glimpsed – moon-speckled and shrouded in the camouflage of purple heather growing wild – in his dreams. Large, by turns angular and aerodynamic, mechanized and stylized, seemingly utilitarian but remarkably ornamental, as contrasting as every other aspect of them. Their array of arms both entranced and puzzled the eye: a pair of long steel-bladed spears, their pointed tips perforating the water-stained ceiling, were held in the massive silver-gloved fist of the same individual who wielded what appeared to be a rifle filched from a future epoch of conflict, its peculiar hand-grip entwined sensually about his gloved fingers like a living appendage; beside him an individual clutching a curving scimitar catching the moonlight through the window, reflecting also the electric crimson eye radiating forth from the bulky rectangle of metal adorning the left shoulder of another, its purpose as mysterious as the individual's veiled multitude of eyes glimpsed as a piercing array of blue jewels beholding him from beneath the silver steel cap he wore. Another figure, insect-helmeted and gargantuan with steel shoulder-guards like rolling hills, his invisible gaze through the weirdly intricate, tightly-grilled latticework of his helm felt as a resolute and burning touch, clutching in his left hand a large mirror within a frame sculpted from a deep red wood or jasper. A figure crouched before him, head enshrined with a queerly-lit amber globe of glass, holding in one hand a three-thonged whip, while from the wrist of his other hung a silver-golden wreath like a colossal jewelled bracelet. There was a significance to these details of dress and adornment, Michael sensed, though he knew not what it might be.

    Their skin gleamed, silver and wondrous and shot through with a powdering of golden dust glimmering in the gloom, as if through a marriage of dust particles from a moon and long-expired sun. The nearly spectral aura which this created hung over them all, those armour-adorned as well as those clothed in what appeared to be ceremonial robes, long and flowing and rich and patterned with woven exotic symbols like ancient hieroglyphs to his uncomprehending eye. They exuded an imperviousness he admired and envied, knowing he could never possess such rare beauty merged with indomitable strength.

    A baroque elegance defined them too, though, seen in their florid headdresses and wild array of pageantry: the long flowing cloaks worn by some, the feather-plumes sprouting from the helms of others and flowing over their shoulders, down the lengths of their backs, the ornate jewel-studded gauntlets encircling their wrists, the great glimmering stones hanging from their necks and reflecting one another's magnificence in rose- and emerald- and violet-coloured glass eyes. Some sported an antique finery, cuirass and breastplate and pteruges overlaid with fine tunics, while others simple robes of an archaic aspect, inlaid with gold and silver designs, at odds with the strange mechanized nature of certain of their armaments: the pulsing lights organized in a vaguely hexagonal design upon the chest-plate of one; the thick black ridged tubing connecting the rifle-like weapon slung over another's shoulder to the gargantuan smooth-skinned metal cylinder like a silo strapped onto his back; the mirage-like shimmering orbs hovering about another's head, their purpose as unknowable as the intricate webs of steel cylinders encircling his hands, like great and terrible mechanical arachnids feeding upon his extremities.

He felt in that instant his craven nature, his paltry strength in a universe where such might and beauty and un-guessed mystery existed alongside him. These were warriors, he knew instinctually, of the mightiest order, and scholars too; theologians, sages whose knowledge and erudition and culture knew no equal anywhere, owning all the wisdom possible to acquire in the infinity beyond the atmosphere of the tiny, tiny Earth. Each of them potentates owning this knowledge, rulers all, governing all those beneath them in an endless spectrum of possibility. He felt his once-vaunted professorly status shrink alongside them, mite-like before their cornucopia of wisdom.

He blinked and their numbers seemed to have swelled, threatening more than ever to tumble the walls of the sex-room, to tear through the weak brick and mortar of the tenement and set the night afire with their otherworldly brilliance. Their ranks stirred now, too, as each shifted in place to focus their attention fully upon his insect's presence intruded into their midst, their uncanny array of arms and accouterments and regalia making of them a motley but perfectly conjoined assemblage that entranced his eye and owned his heart in spite of the colossal fear enveloping him while in the presence of ones as awe-inspiringly beautiful as they.

Despite their radically alien quality – this beauty of so startlingly profound a nature that it seemed from moment to moment as he gazed upon them as if it might in fact transcend it and arrive within the equally enthralling realm of the grotesque – despite their possession of so rare and startling a beauty, they were yet familiar to him; yet he became overwhelmed with an uncanny and powerful affection towards them. They appraised him with jewel-like exquisite eyes of contradiction: neutrally judgemental, equally sympathetic and condemning, hard but munificent. He'd never looked into eyes like those, utterly inscrutable, but then he realized that he had, every day since he'd first met her waiting in an endless, unmoving line of unremarkable people so much less fortunate than he.

And she among them now, on bended knee upon the groaning floorboards as if in obeisance before them though her splendour surpassed theirs: his Michi-bird. Now, though, her beauty lay exhibited in the most profound way: her sleek limbs soft of feather, the pair of silver-dusted wings, arched and radiating a consummate power, unfolded fully from her back like the sails of some great galleon of the future. And her eyes: oh, the familiar ache filling those mournful black orbs as she beheld him stumbled into the midst of their gathering like a new speck of dirt tracked onto a gleaming golden floor, like a flea leapt blasphemously upon the pristine rostrum owned by an angel army convened in their secret stronghold.

He knew not how long he stared, enthralled and speechless before their beauty. Bathed in their appraisal, a vista of scenes materialized in his mind's eye, and himself at the centre of each:

He was a child of twelve years, squatting at a keyhole and marvelling at the scene within the room beyond, in which his father and mother stood naked in room's centre, the fingers of his right hand lost amid the thick black hair of her groin while she leaned her head back and groaned with a pleasure he yearned to know. It was the rarest kind of moment for him to have witnessed: his mother would be alone forevermore only months later, never to remarry after the sudden death of her husband, housebound and unhappy until her own death from cancer three decades later.

The vision vanished and was replaced with another: waking in his bed when he'd still been in University. Running a hand across the naked girl asleep beside him, remembering her promise of devotion made during sex only hours earlier. She loved him, and was prepared to marry him once they'd graduated at semester's end. He was the man with whom she wanted to make her life. He'd believed that he loved her, too, yet knew in that moment of observing her asleep, serene, vulnerable, delicate, that she deserved a man who reciprocated these feelings in as complete a way as she'd given herself up to him. Ending their relationship of two years – while seated across from one another on his bed with the dawn sun reddening the walls – had been difficult. She'd wept through the soliloquy he gave her, in which he bended the truth so that she'd feel loved while taking the brunt of the blame for the way things had turned out for them. He wasn't ready. He needed space, and time to learn what it was that he wanted. Her name had been Sarah. It was three more years before she was finally married, to the man she'd once overlooked – a fellow student and mutual acquaintance – so that she could be with him.

Sarah's ashen face of distress disappeared, replaced with much more recent history: he was straddling Michi Samurakami in her human form, penis filling her mouth while he filled her with his semen. Her groaning, pained but blissful as she rejoiced in this love he gave her, seemed to fill his ears, the room, the world more brightly-lit beyond the darkness of his dissatisfaction and flowering obsessions.

This sex-room moment disappeared and a fragment of dream-scene materialized in its stead, an amalgam of the place of Paradise to which she'd taken him time and again, though only ever ephemerally: astride the girl in the glory of her final transformation, winged and mighty soaring against the beckoning constellations.

Finally, this vision too was evaporated into the ether, leaving the incredible reality of the creaking room and the magnificent assemblage gathered within it, silent as they beheld him.

He turned his eyes to the girl with her entourage surrounding her. He winced beneath their light. Tears streamed from his eyes. He remembered his fruitless attempts to replicate with others the ecstasy which only Michi Samurakami could provide him. The memory of the infidelities bloomed a great guilt in him, and his failure a deep shame. He confessed to her, tears upon his cheeks: "She had no wings. The whore had no wings, and I looked deep. Oh, my Michi-bird, I looked so *deeply* for them but, in the end, there was only you. I should have known. I should have known." His hands he held high on the air for the host's judgement, blood- and semen- and feces-encrusted.

She gazed upon him with a great pity in her obsidian eyes. The entourage surrounding her surveyed him, too, though their appraisal was a colder one, detached and scientific. It chilled him while her eyes burned him. A scalding touch he knew well, though never in so potent and concentrated a degree, as if through entering the sex-room on this most vital of nights, he'd unwittingly stumbled into a portal leading to the very face of the sun.

He sensed the message within it all, some immense truth partially exposed. He sought to fathom it. He felt himself exploring along its periphery. He wept, in his confusion. Still, he failed to understand it.

Through it all, her new-voice cutting tremulously through the great clamour like a thread needled through armour:

"I cannot save you, Michael. You are not ready. I hope that what knowledge you may have gleaned has not hurt you so much that you cannot find some joy in the life you will live."

He heard the sorrow filling her words. Her eyes bewitched him, more slanted than he remembered them and more bottomless and wild, too, more cherub-like her face, more pronounced the colossal wings flowering from her shoulders as if filled with a gale's wind.

He looked from her to his erection gripped in his fist and to her again. There was logic in the gesture, he sensed, though at that moment even it lay beyond his comprehension. Acting instinctually he began to masturbate. Struggling to waken the hot fire to jet from him and into the world where it could exist alongside those convened before him. He stroked himself with growing ferocity. Pain seared from his loins. His member and testicles ached with it. The beauty of the host filled him. Her splendour owned him. He sensed but couldn't catch the elusive thing flitting through his reeling consciousness: a thought, some idea, a path long and long and winding and winding but worth the walking for the blindingly bright but unseen destination waiting at its end; a path nearly-formed but made invisible by the fire-lust boiling between his thighs and threatening to set him afire, a shell of molten blood and flaming flesh.

Then a violently divine light erupted silently into his eyes. It silenced his volcanic thoughts. It quietened the world around him even as he understood the futility of adding his semen into it. Blinded, he felt himself descending floorwards, and then he felt no more.

When his eyes cleared from his dreamless slumber, he was first and foremost uncertain about time: how many seconds or minutes or hours or more may have passed. The light was gone, another dream-scene vanished. Looking to his shrivelled flaccid penis dangling from his open pants he found that he'd ejaculated onto himself. Judging from the extent of the dark, soiled fabric, it had been a prodigious amount of semen, and noting the thickness of its consistency he knew he'd come recently. It was only then, after understanding his post-ejaculatory state, that he examined his surroundings:

The room he didn't recognize, though he felt a certain familiarity with its spare design, a kind of affinity for its bedraggled, shoddy appearance. Alarmed, he scrambled to his feet, making for the door. There, though, he halted, heart smashing, breathing pent-up, held by the sudden compulsion to remain in the room. To examine more closely the dirty bare walls, the ceiling with its water-stains in the shapes of continents never before mapped, and the spartan furnishings of ancient bureau, small work desk, and bed; to the bedside he crept and looked long into its dishevelled folds, its sodden sheets and chaotic blankets, its un-laundered pillows and cloying smell of sweat and sex and cinnamon wafting to him.

For a moment he'd stood on buckling legs, seeking to orient himself. Fear of amnesia evaporated when he remembered the route home, and soon enough he found his way there, weary, frightened and confused as he toppled into his bed, desperate for sleep to come and take away his great uncertainty.

In the days that followed, he grew to engage in a peculiar ritual:

Every night, long past midnight, he would drive to the rooming house, and let himself in with the matching key he'd discovered in his pocket. This wee hour because he'd relished the kinky notion of finding and surprising a possibly new tenant with his arrival and – insofar as his fantasy unfolded – seducing her (it was always a woman who roomed in the fantasy) to his every desire. But every time he slipped his key into the well-worn copper keyhole and entered he found the room as barren as when he'd first awoken in it. In fact, no other tenant ever roomed there, despite the commonplace murmur of voices from behind the other closed doors of the little decrepit building. Never a window yellow with lamplight when he watched furtively from the street below. Only the meagre furnishings of bureau and dresser and bed – never made, the bed, but remaining always and forever in the dishevelled state he'd first found it, as if it were a sculpture meant to represent some human trait or quality – these permanent fixtures of the room. He went to the window always, seeking clean air to clear his spinning thoughts, and there he saw, and was surprised to find them there, as if the discovery was a new one every time:

Upon the floorboards below the window, a variety of feathers which stirred mockingly at his approach. Each night their colour grew more faded, and their lushness more threadbare and balding until nothing remained of their original uncannily vivid crimson and emerald and indigo and golden and silver hues, only a hoary, lifeless and ragged gathering stirring idly, like ancient cobwebs, at his approach. He would stare at them. He cried for them. He yearned to witness the flight they'd once been capable of, while wondering at the nebulous sorrow the thought birthed in him.

Turning to the sky framed in the window, and seeing its clear expanse of stars beyond the trees, he shook his head in futile denial of the great loneliness that awoke in him, and could do nothing, of course, but weep and weep more.

A new era had begun for him on the night of his inexplicable awakening in the dingy room. It was a period he grew incrementally thankful for each day passing, for the world which had seemingly opened for him then.

This he considered while the girl – a slim student fresh from Africa whom he'd found in the school pub, poring over notes for a first year English class, her accent deliciously thick – kissed him fiercely. His lips bruised hers. His teeth bit her neck. His strong hands crushed her tiny breasts, first overtop the orange cotton shirt she wore and a moment later through her bra and then along bare flesh when he yanked the undergarment down so that each breast spilled from its little cup.

The epiphany had arrived in him that he now possessed the wicked power of greedy deceit as he never had before: and so he'd approached her, and impressed her with his academic credentials and flattered her with his avid interest in her physically, as well as those subjects she chose to bring up in their hour-long conversation before he'd succeeded in luring her, tipsy from the pitcher they'd shared, to his home.

She pulled away, keeping her fingers encircling his erection so that he would know she still meant to allow him to have her. His eyes cleared momentarily of their lustful frenzy. "What is it?" he gasped, fingers still pinching her hard sharp nipples.

"Will you tell me again? Tell me again: do you like my body?"

He was nodding. He was smiling. "Oh yes I do," he was saying over and over again as he twisted her erect nipples to make her cry, and then pulled her skirt to fall about her ankles. He didn't heed her plaintive requests their entire ten minutes together – he was engrossed in owning her. At some point while fucking her he chanced to look out the window and became mesmerized by the first stars awakened and hanging like something sacred in the tapestry of the western sky. Something in them unsettled him and he returned his attention to the girl beneath him. She felt right. She felt perfect in the sex-moment, much like the other women he'd been with in the past several months had felt while he'd fucked them, too; after the tedious game of wooing them, during which his secret anxieties and self-consciousness troubled him, and he questioned the things he said and the way he perceived himself in relation to others. She – this exquisite, strange, and unknowable girl of foreign descent – was the polished faceless slate of delicious mystery he needed most in the world to make himself feel secure.

In her ecstasy she spoke with abandon, thoughtless and impassioned. "Oh, I love you, Michael. So much, I love you."

His words came without thought: "I love you, too. Oh yes."

A peculiar thought arrived in his mind then: *I once knew your sister* – he thought this as he raised her buttocks a degree higher while continuing to fuck her. In another time, in another world: *I knew your sister.* Even as he thought this, he realized the falsity of it: this girl, sexy and alluring and in ecstasy of him, was merely a girl, but no more. Her cries grew more shrill and pained as he fucked her. In their ecstatic agony he cocked an ear, listening intently as he sought to hear another kind of voice living within her own – the idea of a violent wind came to him, though he knew not why; a wind as if from a million wings beating together as one, as if in single-minded, rapturous celebration of his endless moment lost in the bliss of her – but heard nothing.

He pulled his penis from her a moment later, startled at its limpness. Desperation seized him, and he turned the girl about to sit on the edge of the bed. Kneeling before her he urged her to lay back, legs spread. Placing his head between her thighs, he slipped his tongue into her vagina. Closing his eyes he found the path opened to him again, after too long being denied ingress: a portal, through this girl, to the only paradise he'd ever known, evanescent, but wholly renewable with her and any other woman he could convince to love him.

The gentlest of touches, feather-light and teasing, grazed his naked shoulder as he pleasured her, and traced a delicate design the length of his back in its descent towards the floor far, far below. He shivered, but maintained the slow, circular-moving rhythm he'd established unabated. If this was all the Paradise he was ever to know, he would keep it, and revel in it, and grow dizzy with transient joy while engrossed in it.

The new dream was always a brief journey but it had grown to hound him relentlessly, always recurring in the very same way:

Waking from slumber he was startled to see: a million points of light frosting a cold glow in the endless blackness. Dazed by the sight of the naked starscape stretching infinitely, humbled and frightened by it, he lay there a moment seeking to understand his situation, seeking familiar designs among the frosting lights.

When no constellations coalesced from the million light-points, a great terror consumed him. He scrambled to his feet to discover himself located on a small rough-hewn rock, approximately as wide in all directions as his bedroom. He reasoned that it was an asteroid, or meteor or some such cosmic detritus drifting through the space miles. And he, like a wildly misplaced flea, was unaccountably trapped upon it.

He shook everywhere at the realization of his hopeless plight: he was blessed or cursed with an atmosphere of life-preserving oxygen and gravity holding him rooted to the rock. He had this gift-curse of a sustaining atmosphere upon the spheroid, but nothing else. He crept with trepidation to the edge of the rock in various places. Peering carefully over its ragged lip, his stomach reeled:

Nothing. Nothing and nothing and nothing.

He crawled back to the centre of the rock, and there he sat in a heap, and wept. Never before, in waking or dreaming life, had he felt so profound a sense of abandonment. Some time later – he couldn't be certain exactly how long for time felt queerly protracted, surreal, a false idea beneath the weight of the naked stars – a trickle and a splash reached his ears. He turned at the miraculous sound, and was amazed to see a small pool of milky water several feet from him which he'd inexplicably failed to notice upon his initial examination of his surroundings.

He scuttled to it, feeling the cold breath of the universe licking at him every inch of the crawl, blighting the foolish shred of hope sputtering in him at the discovery.

The pond surface was stirring subtly, as if some invisible hand had recently disturbed it. He eyed it wondrously, warily. He stared and he stared and at some point in his beholding of it he understood that it was not water at all, but a prodigious amount of semen gathered in this crater upon this drifting rock upon which he was imprisoned. Revulsion came over him at the epiphany, and soon a kind of horror stole into him, too. Then, he discerned something beneath the semenline: a dark amorphous shape resting in one place, as if floating, or mired in the viscous liquid like an ancient creature preserved in prehistoric amber.

The desperate hope reawakened in him at this possible clue to his quandary. He reached a hesitant hand beneath the gently undulating pond surface. The semen was hot, a freshly-spilt ejaculate filling the crater. He watched as a series of reluctant ripples widened from where he'd plunged his arm into the thick mire of it. Tears came to him then, though he knew not why. They washed the semen away and made his efforts difficult, but momentarily his eyes cleared and he saw that the semen-pond was still once more.

Searching about, he closed his fingers around the dark object embedded within. He withdrew his hand and stared: between his sticky, dripping fingers he clutched a bluebird. It was like any bluebird he'd seen back home, which called from the Black oaks in his yard or visited the wooden birdfeeder he kept below his bedroom window. Its tiny body was black with wetness, heavy and sodden. Its white crest was sullied a filthy grey, too. It was dead, of course, and radiated an intense cold as if he gripped an immense ice cube, despite the hot bed from which he'd withdrawn it.

He wept anew. He could do nothing more nor less. The cold breath of infinity surrounding him lapped at him like a black ocean eroding a stone, chilling him deeply. His tears took the vision of the bird away and – despite the certainty of doom overhanging him like a pall – his dream-self felt an infinitesimal relief at this small mercy.

Upon waking from the dream, while the young woman dozed naked and spent in his bed beside him, the great loneliness assailed him anew. And with it, another bludgeoning thing swept over him, too, as it did in the aftermath of sex with the woman – and every other person he'd lured into relations with him throughout the past months – every time: the certainty that he'd lost some very profound and meaningful thing, beyond the transient intimacy of the last body he'd devoured in his bed, far beyond anything so mundane as the everyday pains and pleasures and satisfactions he knew.

Wrapped in the cloying, suffocating fabric of this certainty, he crawled from beneath the single sodden bed sheet. He looked for the girl's feather upon the hardwood floorboards – frantically, desperately he scrabbled about, searching with a nausea churning his belly which was his escalating fear and regret growing like an epiphany in his heart – but found nothing as ever, only their soiled underwear and the deceiving moonlight drenching the room like a dream he could never fully fathom.

Lussi Natt
Andrew Coulthard

The Approach

As Tom wandered along the uneven track toward the cabin, his heavy bags wrenched at his arms. Why did he always have so much luggage with him?

For some reason he paused on the rutted track. His eyes roamed across the snow-dappled tundra to where something pale was moving, an arctic grouse he assumed. But it wasn't, it was a distant figure; white shawl drawn tight about her shoulders; black hair like a cowl. She was moving away from him and rapidly disappearing from view. Now that was unusual out here, he reflected. Especially at this time of year.

That night he dreamed he was in the stand of birch behind the cabin. He ran his hands across the flaking bark and his fingers caught on long fibres of dark hair, as if an animal had brushed against the tree. It was just like wool caught on a fence, only it wasn't wool it was human hair, glossy and strong. Then he glimpsed her, the woman from the moor. With a half grin and shadowed eyes, she turned from him and vanished.

Only a solitary birch remained where she'd been and strands of her dark hair fluttering in the breeze.

Calling Home

- Hi Anna. How're things?
- Yes, everything's alright.
- Sure?
- Yes.
- Are the kids playing up?
- No, they're fine Tom...Stefan won't do his homework.
- Do you want me to speak to him?
- No, no it's okay. He's playing on the Xbox at the moment;

I've allowed him half an hour. He's promised to get on with it after that.
- What's up then?
- Oh, nothing, you know what it's like.
- Do you want me to come back? I'll get the first train, I could be there tomorrow.
- No, you've got to do this, I understand, it's just...have you had any ideas? Done any writing?
- When's your mum arriving?
- Oh Tom, don't remind me...

After the call, Tom went into the kitchen and made himself some coffee, pouring the steaming liquid into his steel thermos. That'd keep him going for a bit.

He thought about Stefan: twelve years old, just a kid, but his hulking body growing out of control. He didn't communicate anymore and Tom was lucky if he got a civil word out of him. They'd become strangers to one another and it'd happened almost overnight. The two of them had always been so close, but it was as if the boy was retreating from him, drawing back inwardly. Where once there'd been laughs, fun and co-operation, his son now treated him to silent scowls and folded arms, extending on bad days to stamping, shouting and door slamming. Maybe he should be more patient with the lad, get away with him, do something they both liked...except Stefan didn't seem to like anything these days apart from comic books and video games.

Perhaps, if he could just find *it* again, the thing he'd lost, the facility that had been effortlessly his when he was younger. But who was he trying to kid? He couldn't even really remember what *it* had been.

"You can't swim in the same river twice 'cause the river's always flowing," he mumbled sadly. But didn't that sound more like *it*? More like the sort of thing he'd once have thought or said? It did. And maybe he didn't need to step into the *same* river again anyway. All he needed was to step into *a* river, *any* river. He'd dried out over the years and now he was going to do something about it.

Tom raised a chipped coffee cup to panelled walls coated in scratched pine print. "Here's to the finding of rivers!" he called.

There was a loud thud from the bedroom. He jumped, almost dropped his coffee and ran to investigate but at first glance nothing seemed amiss. The room was as it always was. Old, iron frame bed, worn blankets and ancient horsehair mattress; walls clad in more plastic imitation pine; dirty floorboards in need of a good sanding; the stubby pine wardrobe, with its dark patina, built by some half-remembered ancestor. All spic and span, nothing out of place.

He walked to the window. Ugly windows, he'd always thought, like the whole damned cabin. Yet despite the lack of beauty there'd been so many happy times here, when he'd still been in his element.

With a struggle, he managed to recover some faint sense of the pleasure and excitement he'd once felt here. That had been during his first time in Sweden of course; long ago now. Back then, he'd thought of it as the thrill of the Nordic wilderness…he'd been a bit of a romantic in those days.

Being here used to give him a deep sense of relaxation. It wasn't just the cabin, it'd been the whole place – the lake and the surrounding lands. Now, however, he felt more or less nothing. He must be pretty far gone.

Tom peered out at the lake through some sort of muck that was smeared across the glass – probably bird-shit.

The bedroom provided the only view of the lake because of the odd angle at which the cabin had been positioned. A proper cabin, a modern one, would have had a huge open plan kitchen and living area with a gigantic window overlooking the lake and low hills beyond. Not this one. The kitchen window backed onto a birch thicket, the only windows in the tiny living room were made from two portholes purloined from an old beached steam barge and they looked out onto the flank of a steep-sided knoll that marked the end of the track.

The lake itself wasn't particularly large, just a couple of kilometres in circumference – more of an irregular oval than a circle. A skin of grey ice coated its waters today. It looked spongy and weak, though it was probably quite thick. He wouldn't walk on it he decided.

Tom's attention returned to the dirty smear. It wasn't bird-shit, but some other sort of liquid and it was still running. Curious, he put on his boots, laces dangling free, and stepped out to investigate further.

The air was still and silent outside and, today at least, the cold was entirely bearable. He didn't notice anything odd as he approached the window from the beach but then he saw what he assumed was a clump of ice at the base of the cabin wall, wedged between the rocks. It was spotted with blood.

Tom drew a sharp intake of breath as he realised what he was looking at. It was a dead grouse or ptarmigan; he could never remember the difference. The locals called them *Ripa*. They were popular game birds but this one was far from appetising, its head a bloody pulp. What on earth had happened?

He glanced up at the window pane and back at the dead bird. Steam was rising from its crushed skull. It must have flown into the window and at a hell of a speed too. But why?

When he was a kid, he'd lived in a house with an open living and dining room. From the front of the building, you could look through the living room window and see straight out onto the estate behind the house via a window in the back wall. Birds often mistook his home for some sort of tunnel and regularly crashed into the front window, breaking their necks. One day his father had put up a partition wall blocking the view and that had been the end of it.

He put a hand on either side of the window and peered in through the smear. It still made no sense. The window was small, the glass thick and the room shadowy beyond. Short of wanting to batter its way into the building, why would the bird have done this? Maybe it was short-sighted or mad, he reflected.

Creating

The notebook screen glowed before his unfocused eyes. The white desktop background and the shadows of the cabin contrasted sharply. It gave him a sense of comfort, as if he were looking at his therapy lamp, the light source that helped him keep his seasonal depression under control during the deep Nordic winters. He'd forgotten to pack that lamp, somehow.

Tom nodded forward, half-sleeping checking himself just before he fell too far. Time for bed and he hadn't found anything yet; first full day down without result.

He'd really tried, but every path he'd set off on soon dried up. He'd let his mind free-wheel for a while, written whatever came up, but nothing resonated. As he became more desperate, he'd even written about the grouse. He imagined it with bottle-bottom glasses on; maybe he could try a children's story, he'd reasoned: *Gary Grouse and the Optical Illusion.* It had been a very stupid idea.

Disturbed Sleep

Tom woke up with a start, disorientated and uncomfortable and yet in very familiar territory.

He lay back panting, his heart racing. These were the same old feelings of anxiety: disquieting, unpleasant and completely inexplicable. His breathing began to settle but uncomfortable rushes were still passing up through his trunk and swirling around in his head. When at last they subsided, a residue of glum wakefulness remained complimented by little waves of despair.

It had been a while since his last bout of insomnia and he hadn't expected one now, not up here where he used to sleep so soundly. He sighed. He hadn't brought his sleep CDs with him. *Fuck, no lamp and no CDs either!*

Well that was that. He had to leave tomorrow; get back to his family and the preparations for Christmas. This trip had been a big mistake.

Amongst other things, sleep disturbances had dogged Tom all his life. Over the years different experts had put it down to various causes ranging from diet, stress and lack of exercise to more deeply rooted and insidious things. But truth be told, he'd never really accepted their expert opinions.

He closed his eyes again, allowed his mind to "reach out and probe his being", as the CDs generally suggested. He repeatedly bunched up his shoulders and relaxed, tensed every muscle in his body for as long as he could then let go on exhalation. After that he counted backward from one hundred in threes, visualising a path leading into a leafy valley.

Nothing worked. Tom sat up with an angry grunt and hurled off his quilt. He knew this situation only too well. There was no way he was getting back to sleep for a while.

It was freezing in the bedroom, though it shouldn't have been, not with the heater on. He moved over to the ugly grey metal box below the window to investigate. Yes, still on – one of those stupid 1970's wall-mounted things that all older cabins had and which invariably meant big electricity bills.

He rested his forehead against the windowpane. *So cold.* When he heard noises from outside though, he forgot his frustration for a while and listened. It sounded like faint splashing, as if something big was floundering about in the water. But the lake was under ice, probably metres thick and nothing could be out there at...he checked his watch, it was 02:15. Tom peered out of the window, but could see nothing through the frozen smear left by the dead bird. The splashing continued. What the hell was going on?

He stumbled into the kitchen, fumbled for the light switches; *kitchen light on.* Shit, the light was blinding and now he wouldn't be able to see a thing out there. The outside lights were what he really needed, not these. He found the right switch; *on.*

Back at the window again, he thought he could make out something large, non-descript and white, flopping around some way out on the ice in the weak rays from the cabin's external lighting. Or, no, wait a minute...there was a *hole* in the ice; he could see water splashing and the big white thing thrashing around in it. In fright he pulled on his fleece, his padded windproof, hat and gloves and snatched up the heavy torch.

Tom stepped out into the shaft of light from the cabin door, gasping as the cold hit him. From his nose, he felt the telltale pinching that told him his mucus membranes were freezing. At least twenty-five below, perhaps colder, he reckoned. *Mustn't stay out here long.*

He waved the beam of the torch back and forth across the ice. The village was miles away. Was this a suicide? Where the hell was the man? He couldn't see anything but ice.

'Hello!' he called. 'Hello, where are you? Do you need help?'

He was shaking, his teeth chattering. He had to get properly dressed; he couldn't be out here like this. Tom glanced back at the cabin. The door was still open; oh shit! He'd have to close it or what little heat there was would be gone; it was probably too late already.

The outside lights were positioned on the corners of the cabin and gave off less light than they might have done. He shone the torch out onto the ice again; nothing but ice. Maybe if he got a bit closer to the edge of the lake. He glanced back at the open door, torn.

Just a quick check Tom, somebody might be dying out there.

He stumbled across the rocky beach to the lake edge, clumsy in his unfastened boots. The torch beam scythed across the dull ice, sweeping back and forth across the place where he was sure he'd seen the hole, only now he couldn't find it. The lake's grey skin was blank and featureless without even so much as a fissure. Where was the breach? He listened intently for a time. Silence. Tom felt a grim sense of disquiet descend over him; the person must be dead.

Then he heard movement; it was coming from somewhere to his left. He spun in that direction. A dark shape loomed toward him, footsteps dislodging rocks and gravel at the waterline. Tom swung up the torch, startled and shone it directly into the face of the man as he bore down on him. The face he glimpsed was pale and stiff with unspeakable rage. Unseeing eyes stared through him and past him, the jaw was set, the brow drawn into a stony ridge.

'Hello...' was all he could manage in a pathetic voice before the man struck him. Tom was hurled to the rocks. He landed heavily, sprawling onto the ice, the torch flying from his grasp. His assailant passed him by and continued, never deviating from his path. Without the torch, Tom couldn't see him anymore, but the sound of footsteps carried back as the man stomped further on his way.

Christ, what the fuck is going on out here? What was that all about?

Tom was shaking. He got to his hands and knees. All he wanted now was to get into the cabin and lock the door behind him, but he was too afraid of what would happen if he made a sound and drew attention to himself.

313

The torch was several metres away further out towards the centre of the lake, its beam pointing away from him. Tom wanted it. He needed it to see his way safely back to the cabin; all too easy to trip on unseen rocks and stuff.

Tom hadn't fancied the ice much before, it had looked porous, a sure sign of weakness. Now he was out on it though, it felt rock solid, but he couldn't decide if he wanted to risk going further out. Solid ice here didn't mean solid ice there. Where was the hole he'd seen? That guy was there somewhere too, wasn't he, if he was still alive? He needed to move, though, the night air was rapidly sucking the last heat from his body.

Tom crawled a few metres further from the shore, at all times listening for sounds of protest from the ice, but there were none. The ice was so perfectly smooth and hard that if he didn't know better, he'd suspect it was frozen all the way down to the lake bed.

At last his trembling fingers closed about the icy metal shaft of the torch. Then he summoned such courage as he could and shone the light out over the lake one last time. There was no sign of a break in the ice; not anywhere.

'Shit, this is crazy. Get back to the cabin, lock the fucking door, have a hot drink and get warm. Then get the hell out of here and back home tomorrow,' he told himself in a voice that sounded more like his father's than his own.

Tom was back on the beach and hurrying toward the open door when a hand reached out from the murk and grasped his arm. He yelped in fright and spun about, raising the torch like a club. But in his panic he overbalanced and stumbled backwards falling heavily onto the rocky beach.

Tom's quaking torch beam revealed a slight figure leaning over him. It was a woman, wincing against the light. Her face was lined and pale, her tangled, black hair streaked with grey. She was dressed in white – a sort of thick overcoat over white robes, maybe a lab-coat or hospital uniform of some kind.

'Are you alright?' she asked. 'Please, your torch is hurting my eyes. Let me help you up.'

Her Swedish was accented. She looked a bit odd, but friendly, reaching out to help him. Tom took her hand; it was very cold to the touch.

'Who are you?' he asked breathlessly.

'Katja,' she replied.

Katja; unusual name in Sweden these days. Maybe she's foreign, he thought. 'Are you local?' he asked before realising what a stupid question it must seem.

'Er, not originally, but I have been in these parts for some considerable time.'

'I see,' Tom said trying to be polite, though he didn't see at all. 'Look, er, did you witness what happened here?'

'Yes,' Katja replied.

'That man...'

'The Shorewalker,' she said simply.

'The Shorewalker? He's called the Shorewalker? Is he ill? Some sort of psychiatric thing I mean?' Tom asked while slapping and rubbing his bruised arms in an effort to warm up.

'He is...lost, he cannot find his way. He must walk the shoreline because he cannot reach the other side.'

'He can't reach the other side? All he has to do is keep going round the lake, it won't take him more than twenty minutes. Bloody weirdo attacked me. Are you his doctor?!'

'No, he didn't attack you; you just got in his way. He is bound to his course and cannot change it,' Katja continued.

'Bound to his course...he looked blind, I mean his eyes sort of stared straight through me,' Tom continued.

'He is bound to his path,' she repeated as if this explained everything.

'Yes, well, look I'm freezing, you must be too. It's the middle of the night, I'm going inside. There's coffee, hot chocolate? It's dangerous to be out on a night like this without the proper...'

'No, no, I cannot accompany you.'

'Right,' Tom said turning away towards the cabin. 'Well, I'm getting inside and by the way there was something on the ice, in the water in fact...' But when Tom looked back to question her about the man in the lake she'd vanished.

He swept the beach with his torch beam: *nothing*. Then he thought he heard a sound from the direction of the birches behind the cabin, just a little sound, like that of ice straining and cracking underfoot.

He shone his torch in that direction, where it danced across the ranks of pale, slender trunks. That was it, last straw. Tom rushed inside, slammed the door and locked it.

He put some water on; he'd make some soup, coffee, anything to warm up. Then he grabbed the quilt from the bedroom and the old, thick, woollen Swedish army blanket from the armchair and swathed himself in them. He lit candles, lots of them, always a good way to raise the temperature.

It was 05:30 as Tom thumbed through his timetable, sipping at a big cracked mug of coffee. There'd be no sleep for him tonight. He found what he was looking for: Lantvägs bus no. 746 left from the stop once a day Monday to Friday at 09:45. It was roughly a three kilometre walk to the dilapidated wooden shed that served as a bus shelter and a forty-five minute ride after that to the village. The daily Stockholm train departed at 11:00. He'd make it no problem.

At some point though, Tom drifted into slumber. When he awoke, it was to a grey mid-afternoon. He'd slept in.

Call 2

- I'm telling you it was out there. Something was there!
- And there's nothing now?
- No, nothing, no hole...
- But if it's that cold the ice will just refreeze; you know that Tom.
- Not even a ripple or blemish though, there'd be something Anna. It was a bloody big hole.
- Then you must have dreamt it. It was just a nightmare.
- I didn't, there's grit and dirt on my clothes where that Shorewalker nut pushed me over. It *happened*.
- Tom, darling, nobody lives round there, not for miles, you know that.
- Well maybe somebody has moved here or something. I don't sleepwalk, when have I ever done that?

- I don't know, perhaps you've started. Maybe this is something new. You said that you'd had one of your turns...
- Look, Anna I...
- Tom, why not use it? Write this down; see if it gets you started on something.
- Anna, darling, I just want to get out of here, come home. I could get a taxi into town, maybe stay at the Hostel...
- It's winter Tom, the Hostel's closed. Everything's shut once hunting season's over.
- I want to come home.
- I know, darling. Look, come home tomorrow. If you have problems sleeping tonight you can use the phone as an alarm clock in fact use your own phone to wake you up, you didn't forget that too did you?
- No, I have it.
- Spend today writing.
- What about?
- I don't know, about what a great wife you've got.
- I don't have what it takes anymore Anna, it's gone, I don't know where; I just know I've lost it. I made a mistake coming here.
- Look, I'll see you tomorrow night. It'll be alright. There are lots of other things you can do.

Lussi

As Tom was peering moodily through the window a figure appeared from nowhere. He stiffened, a jolt of fear running through him like an echo of the night before. It was a woman, Katja he assumed; it certainly looked like her. She came from the left, from the direction of the birches behind the cabin, and was wandering down to the edge of the ice keeping her back to him.

Today she was much better dressed for the conditions. White clothes again, though this was proper winter wilderness stuff. In fact it looked almost military, like some sort of camouflage. The thick, white weatherproof material was streaked with grey lines and black dots making it resemble speckled snow or birch-bark. Her hood was up, sensibly, but her glossy black hair flowed out from either side unchecked.

He didn't know what to do. It was daylight still, but the confusion and strangeness of the previous night hadn't left him. She might be dangerous; you sometimes heard about some very odd people in the out of the way places of the north – and speaking of which... He searched his limited view for any sign of the Shorewalker, but to his great relief found none. Maybe he should keep out of sight until she went away again.

He waited. She stayed where she was. Time passed.

Tom, this is stupid. Get a grip on yourself. It's just a woman, out for a walk. Maybe she's planning on fishing. Face it, face her. Get it over with.

He dressed properly: thermals, fleece, thickest jacket, hat and gloves, boots properly laced. He put the folding lock-blade into his pocket and zipped it up, but it felt bad there, what was he going to do with it? He removed it again, putting it back in the drawer where it had resided since Grandad Sten's time. Then he took a deep breath and opened the door.

She spun about at the sound of the door, startled.

'Hello, just me,' he said, waving and trying to look friendly.

She stared at him, eyes wide.

'Katja?' he asked. Something was wrong. She looked different today, younger.

'Katja?' she repeated, a question in her voice.

He slowed, stopped a few feet from her. No grey in her hair, her skin softer, pinker, no lines. She *was* younger, this wasn't the same woman.

'Sorry, I didn't mean to startle you, I mistook you for someone else,' he explained, raising his hands.

'Katja?' she asked again, her dark eyes glittering. Then a change came over her face as if she had suddenly understood something. 'Oh, Katja, yes. You thought *I* was Katja.'

'Yeah, well only from behind, I'm sorry. Is she a relative of yours?' Tom asked. The woman seemed to think about this for a while before nodding. 'Right,' said Tom. Obviously another *unusual* character, he decided.

'I'm Tom,' he went on, removing his glove and extending his hand. She took the proffered hand as if unsure what to do with it. Her skin was warm, not icy like Katja's had been.

'My name is Lussi,' she said a little self-consciously.

'Lucy, that's an unusual name in Sweden, but you sound like a Norrlander, you must be from round here. Are your parents from somewhere abroad?'

"Well they usually say something about Sicily, but actually I go much further back than that,' she said, an inscrutable look darting across her face.

'You go back much further than Sicily? I see,' but he didn't. She wasn't making much sense. Maybe they'd opened a low security lunatic asylum in the area since he was last here. 'Er, well, anyway, I'm sorry that I startled you.'

'Yes, you've already said that,' Lussi replied and smiled.

'So I did, sorry. Do you live nearby?'

'Yes, quite near,' she replied.

'I didn't think there was anything for miles around here. There didn't used to be.'

'No,' she agreed.

'Still, there've been a lot of new holiday chalets built on the other side of the village, near that ski place. It's about the only thing that's thriving in the area now the forestry has gone. Or have they been building things around here too?'

'Yes,' she said simply and smiled.

Tom smiled too, feeling self-conscious suddenly. 'Look I'd invite you in, for coffee I mean, but I know that Katja said...'

'Sure, coffee would be nice,' she interrupted and began to make for the cabin.

Coffee

'Anna? Her whole family are from round here, or they were. I mean back then there was enough work in small places like this. But they're all gone now and the old ones have died off.'

'Like the man who built this cabin,' Lussi agreed.

'Yeah, Sten, my wife's grandfather. He was quite a character,' Tom said pausing to remember that stony-faced man of few words. 'He used to work the strips of forest the family owned. They had quite a lot of land back then. This was his retreat, by which I mean it's where he went to get away from whatever it was he needed to get away from...'

'His wife, his family,' Lussi said smiling.

Tom snorted. 'Anyone would think you knew him,' he said.

'Yes,' Lussi agreed, her eyes sparkling.

'Anyway, his wife, Lova, hated the place.'

'It is ugly,' Lussi said.

'Yes, very, though I think she hated it for other reasons. I used to have quite a soft spot for it myself,' Tom chuckled. 'Have you seen the places they've built up by the new ski resort? Now they're beautiful. Well...'

'Good name though,' she interrupted.

'Good what? The ski resort?'

'No, here.'

'Oh, that was Sten again, Birke Sjöbo, *the birch dwelling by the lake*. Wait a minute though, how do you know what it was called? You can't read the sign anymore out there, the paint's all flaked off.'

Lussi smiled mysteriously. 'You can read it if you already know what it used to say.'

Tom didn't know what to reply to that. Perhaps the locals still talked about Sten and his hideaway; they probably did. Lova always claimed Sten wasted his time and their money fishing, bird-watching, drinking and making dubious improvements to the cabin. But there had been all kinds of rumours about the old man once. Even well after Tom's arrival, people still speculated about what he'd got up to when he was here and he certainly came out whenever he could, even when he was very old.'

They continued chatting for a while. Tom found himself telling her about why he was there as he prepared coffee. The 1960s coffee cups rattled as he set them down onto the battered tabletop. 'So I suppose I shouldn't let it bother me so much. It's probably all just a bit of a mid-life crisis, or something like that. Silly really; I mean, we do OK, I have a pretty good life, but recently, I don't know...it's not enough anymore.'

Tom found himself staring at one of the cups. He'd always considered them hideous with their period brown and orange blobs overlaid with black line patterns, but only now did he realise how chipped and worn they'd become. 'Old stuff, this. Typical holiday cabin things I'm afraid,' he began to explain.

Lussi took up her cup turning it in her hands to scrutinise every detail as if she'd never seen anything like it before. 'Old?' she asked.

'Yes, probably been here since the mid-sixties.' He fetched the coffee thermos, milk, crisp-bread, margarine and cheese. 'No cookies, I wasn't expecting company. But help yourself to what there is.'

'Cookies?' she repeated softly. She glanced at the food and then at him, a look of discomfort on her face. 'Sorry, I can't,' she said.

'Can't?' Tom looked askance at his meagre offerings. 'Can't say I blame you there, actually,' he agreed.

'No, no, it's OK, I just...can't,' she repeated and then shrugged, smiling. There was something about her smile that bothered him. He thought it pretty, he thought *her* pretty, but also unsettling.

He busied himself again, but found himself looking more carefully at his guest than he had. She hadn't even removed her jacket, even though for once it was pretty warm in the cabin. Hard to say what she looked like underneath all that arctic military gear, but judging by her face she was slim enough. Then something occurred to him. 'Diet?' he asked uncertainly.

She smiled and repeated the word softly: 'Diet.' Her eyes took on a faraway look.

'Sorry I'm not making sense, I mean, you know, the food. You didn't want any. I thought maybe...'

Lussi didn't reply. Instead she began to sway her head languorously from side to side, her eyes half closed. Alarm bells were ringing, oh no, he'd been right; she was a nut after all. What on earth was she doing?

Lussi ceased moving her head. Instead she bunched up her shoulders, straining every muscle before relaxing again and stretching her arms before her across the table. Tom's sense of unease was growing and yet he found himself mesmerised. 'She's like a cat, all *willowy*,' he thought to himself.

'Willowy? No, not willow, *birch*,' she murmured.

Tom felt his face colouring. He'd been thinking aloud and yet he could have sworn not. 'Sorry. Putting my foot in it...what do you mean when you say birch though?'

Lussi watched him her dark eyes glittering. 'Diet,' she whispered.

This had gone far enough. 'Look, I'm not sure really what...' he began, but Lussi swirled up from her seat, eyes full of something that both excited and terrified him. She glided closer, pressing herself against him, the military jacket rustling like leaves in a breeze.

'Diet, is important,' she whispered her face close to his. 'What we consume, we become. What do you feed upon Tom?'

Tom was paralysed, her face so strange and yet compellingly attractive, hovered just inches from his own. He wasn't listening to her. Her scent filled his nostrils; an odd and powerful aroma. He liked it, had never smelt anything like it – or had he? Familiar and unfamiliar, attractive and yet there was some faint trace that wasn't entirely agreeable. She drew a deep breath and exhaled into his face, filling his nostrils with the odour of vegetation: plants, earth...somehow more winter than autumn, overpowering and disarming.

Images of dead grasses tumbled through him, speckled with tiny, yellow leaves, dusted with frost. He was filled by them. And then he was falling.

Call 3

When Tom awoke he was in bed and it was dark. He stirred sluggishly a little uncertain where he was. Then he tried moving properly, expecting discomfort for some reason, but pleasantly surprised to find none. Quite the opposite in fact, his limbs were supple and strong. He pulled back the bedclothes and almost sprang to his feet. He had something to do. He needed to find something he'd mislaid. It was near at hand, he was sure of it.

There was a sound from outside the room. At first Tom didn't recognise it. Then he was running for the door, fumbling for the light switch.

- Hello?
- Tom? Is that you?
- Yes.
- Tom, it's Anna. Where are you?
- Anna...yes that's right...
- Tom, are you alright? You sound like...have you been drinking?
- I'm in the cabin. You know that, you must know that, you've just rung me here. What did you mean by asking where I am? I'm in the cabin.
- Tom, it's after twelve.
- Yes, you woke me. I was dreaming, I think.
- Tom, darling, you were supposed to be coming home. The kids waited up for you, for hours. I've been phoning your mobile all night. I thought you were coming back today.
- Yes, you're right. I thought so too. I must have...something's happened.
- What? Are you hurt?
- No, no, I feel really good. Just, I'm a bit bleary-eyed, just woken up. Anna, I think I might...there might be something after all. I'm going to try one more time.
- You mean writing?

- Maybe, I think so, I'm not sure.
- Shit Tom, why didn't you phone? Stefan was disappointed, Klara was really disappointed. She started crying when you still hadn't appeared and I sent them to bed. What am I going to tell her in the morning?
- I don't know; I just felt so tired. I think I was having a quick nap, but you know how it can be sometimes, when I haven't been sleeping. It takes me by surprise, catches up with me.
- You should have phoned us to let us know.
- Look, I'll call you in the morning, I...Anna? Anna?
- Yes, call me in the morning.

Tom sat down at the table. He was wide awake now and it was after midnight. He'd slipped his day around; he knew the pattern only too well. If he was going to do any work, he would have to do it now, during the night and if he was going to travel home tomorrow he would have to stay awake. Because once he nodded off again, nothing would wake him.

Dreaming of the Other Side

Leaves rolled up about him in competing vortices, crackling with energy. But they weren't dangerous; they just made it hard to see very far. Dense banks and shoals crashed into one another, glittering swarms swirling by like ocean breakers. The air was filled with their chatter. They were birch leaves, of course. Cascades of gold pieces: tiny ragged autumn leaves that had been shed before the ice came down.

Tom wandered among them, thrilling to the energy they imparted as they washed over him. He couldn't see the land around him; it was all a mystery except when he glanced upward. There he sometimes glimpsed the banded colours of a northern winter dawn/dusk. Flocks of blind grouse were sweeping across the sky, but Tom knew that they wouldn't reach their destination. And that was the tragedy of it: they would be lost, wasted.

He thought about the Shorewalker and the leaves parted, revealing the lake, and the fells beyond. It wasn't winter here or maybe it was, but there was a light to everything of another quality, as if perhaps from within. It was a soft, warm light, but whether evening or morning he couldn't tell. Perhaps it was both.

He began to move toward the lake when the Shorewalker appeared. Tom stopped. He knew instinctively it would be dangerous to proceed. The Shorewalker wouldn't veer from his path, he couldn't see, but if Tom got in the doomed man's way...

Looking out over the lake, the other side came into view. It appeared to be just the same as usual, yet here among the leaves he sensed, no, he *knew* that it could not be reached. There was something there, part way round, something invisible that would stop anyone who tried to pass it. Somehow the Shorewalker couldn't get past it either. Whenever he reached that point, he would just find himself back at the beginning, always on this side, trapped in some weird loop.

And how the other side beckoned!

It had changed. Not that it looked any different, but somehow, in some very significant way, it was. He scrutinised it for a time, checking off little features of the shore line, the flanks of the mountains, the skyline and the peaks. The other side looked just the same, but it *felt* different. And now he knew that the other side was the place where he would rediscover all that he'd lost. And he wanted it.

The phone was ringing. Tom sat up, he'd been asleep, hunched over his notebook. The screen came into view. Black; it had probably switched itself off hours ago. But now the phone was ringing.

He struggled up. It was still dark outside. What time was it? His watch showed 6:15 am.

- Hello, it's Tom...
- Hi, are you awake? I thought I'd check.
- Anna?
- Yes, I'm on early this week remember. You sound tired darling, make yourself some coffee.
- I was asleep. I fell asleep at the computer. I feel like somebody has been dancing on me.
- Oh Tom, have you been working on something? That's great!
- Er, yes, actually, there is something.

- But that's fantastic. You can read it to me when you get home.
- I'm very tired.
- Of course, but you'll be able to sleep on the train won't you? The kids are looking forward to seeing you. Stefan said he wanted to play that game with you, you know the one you used to do together on the X-box, the one with all the monsters?
- Yes. Look, I might stay for another day or two after all.
- But I thought you wanted to get home? I thought you were uncomfortable up there?
- Yeah, I know, but maybe I just needed to give it a chance. Anna, I might have found something.
- Well what about the sleepwalking and the ghosts on the ice and all that?
- I know, but I think it's OK now. You were right, it was probably just one of my bouts of insomnia. Maybe I did sleepwalk...
- Tom, are you alright?
- Yes, yes I think so, really I think so. Coming up here was a good idea. It isn't always as easy as we want it to be, but maybe I *can* reconnect, Anna. You know, I didn't realise how much I miss it.
- When will you be back?
- Soon, really, I promise. Look tell the kids I'm missing them too; tell Stefan we'll take out every boss in the game when I get back.
- I'll call you, shall I?
- OK, yes, of course. I'll call you too.

The notebook sparked into life and his desktop came into view. Plain background, few icons, no files open. He checked the most recent word file, but there'd been nothing new since *Gary the Grouse*. Tom started up his word-processor and began writing. Not until deflected sunlight shone through the living room portholes did he pause.

*

Tom looked up, surprised, blinking. What time was it? He found it hard to focus on his watch. That had been a present from Anna, one Christmas or other, or had it been a birthday? Didn't matter. *Shit*, he felt tired, his neck and shoulders were killing him.

He got up and paced the room. He needed a break, definitely! But he didn't want to leave what he was working on, not even for a few seconds. There was so much there, so many ideas and they all slotted together – or rather he was uncovering them and aligning them somehow...it was like so many beautiful strands for him to weave into a marvellous coherent whole. If he let go of them for even the shortest time, they'd be beyond his reach, fading and drifting away like breeze-borne smoke. Then all he'd be left with was the little he'd so far brought into being through the medium of words: a thing partially-realised and only half-gestated. And he wouldn't be able to save it, it would die in his hands: a cold, grey non-descript stillborn; its intended destiny squandered.

'Oh boy, Tom, you wanted it back and you've certainly got it!' He laughed aloud, despite himself. It'd been so long, that he'd almost managed to wipe out any recollection of the obsessive quality of creation. All this time, his preoccupation had been with rediscovering how to connect to the source, the molten rivers within him. In his eagerness, he'd forgotten how hard it was just to remain connected; how much toil and pain such symbiosis involved. But, shit, was it back now! He was in the river, bracing his back against the current and the mysterious waters both enervated and seared him.

He found himself at one of the portholes. The light was different today, it was sunlight! How apt. He glanced again at his watch, able to decipher the face this time. 10.25 am. Incredible. He'd been working for hours, no wonder he was tired. And today was sunny. God he needed the sun. Much as he wanted to sleep, he would have to go out. Maybe there was some good blue sky to be had and if not, even sunbeams through a chink in the gloom would be medicine to him.

He opened the cabin door to be greeted by a wall of light. Intense white-gold, flowed from the low sun to strike the lake and set it on fire. Tom found himself wandering out into the haze, drunk on light and suddenly he was back in his dream. Somewhere out there, the Shorewalker marched back and forth, never making the other side, somewhere across the frozen waters lay the *other side*. Not the ordinary, everyday 'other side' of course, not the one you could see and easily reach. This was an alternative other side, with qualities all its own, the one the Shorewalker yearned for.

    The light was turning his vision blue and green. The smooth ice shimmered until it almost seemed as if it was no longer there. Instead, little waves sculpted a dynamic mosaic of shattered glass, dancing in radiance.

    A presence moved in the glare, he sensed it and when her hand took his, he wasn't at all surprised. She whispered something, at first pulling gently away or perhaps wanting him to follow her. But he couldn't hear her; the light had saturated all his senses.

    'You should go. Now is not a time for you to be here,' her voice quiet but insistent penetrated the nimbus, creating ripples and coronas of its own.

    'Why,' he murmured dreamily. 'Why, when I am finally rediscovering what I've been looking for, when I...'

    'But you mustn't stay. For your own sake, get away, get back to what you know,' she rejoined. 'Take with you what you have and make do with that.

    Damn it, what did she mean? Her words wormed their way into him, lessening his euphoria. Where was she? He couldn't see her at all, yet her hand was there in his and he liked the feeling it gave him. Her slight fingers were neither warm nor cold, he was soothed by their touch and his sense of them became a focus in the light.

    Tom led her toward the cabin, turning his back on the burning lake. Inside, in the cheerless cavity of the kitchen as his eyes struggled to adjust, she released his fingers. He was near blind, his vision a welter of blue and green hallucinatory effects, but he knew she was still there and she gradually came into view just a few paces distant, a figure both indistinct and dim.

    'I've been...disconnected from myself, from something important to me; very important. How can I explain it?'

    'Shush now, you don't have to,' she whispered.

'You know, once upon at time, just *being* was enough. Life was that good. That was the *river* I submerged myself in, the waters of my... oh dear I'm afraid I'm getting this wrong, missing the mark. Words just can't, you know, capture it. Have you any idea what I'm talking about Lucy?'

'Lucy?' she asked.

'Yes it is you, isn't it? Or is it Katja? It's one of you, I can see that much,' he said squinting and coming closer to her. The woman before him reminded him of both Katja and Lussi and yet the more he peered, the more he realised she wasn't either of them. This new one was different again; not as young as Lussi or as old as Katja.

'How many of you are there?' he wondered.

'I am Rondan,' she said.

'*Ronda*? Aha. Ronda. That's another unusual name for Sweden. Not that there's anything wrong with odd names, but three in a row? Your parents must have been very inventive or different or straight off the boat from the old country. I mean, you are sisters, aren't you?'

'Sisters,' she repeated softly, which Tom took to mean *yes*.

'So, Katja will talk to me but she won't come in here and drink my coffee. Lucy's fine with coffee, but she refuses to eat my food. What won't you do?'

'There's nothing,' Rondan breathed and took a step closer to him. Then Tom sensed that strange conglomeration of aromas and odours again, all of them natural, many agreeable. He became quiet drawing in long, slow breaths, letting her scent affect him deeply, just as before. His vision cleared, his body relaxed, images and feelings tumbled and coursed through him.

'I smell apples, flowers, plums, herbs. There are hints of the air on open moorland, pungent green notes. Animal scents of game and venison mixed with pine trees, resin and woody odours like the smells of new growth and sap; freshly sawn logs. Yet also, faintly, vegetal odours; the dampness and rot of boggy places...' he murmured.

'From which the roots of us feed. That which we consume....'

'...we become, yes, your sister Lucy was on about that,' Tom responded, his voice drowsy. 'Most people would say *we are what we eat*, though I've never liked the expression. It always irritated...'

'Shush Tom. Nourishment arises and we consume and transform it; new buds, new branches, new strength and beauty. You have all you need now, will you not leave? Go, there is still time...

'Yeah, the bus hasn't gone yet or I don't think it has at least...but wait a minute, it must have, it's late morning, the bus goes at...'

'Let us take back this place, it was ours before he came,' her voice was less insistent than before.

'But, I don't want to leave,' he said, sadly. 'This is beautiful, I want to be here. I want to feel this. I want to feel...'

'You will be changed by it, Tom. He was.'

'Who was? Who are you talking about?'

'Tom, please' she said her face close to his.

He wrapped his arms about her and drew her to him. Their bodies fitted snugly together as he knew they would; cold wind across open moorland soughing through the vegetation; sunshine and ice; shifting shadows in woodland; bubbling streams; the drop of water in cavernous spaces. And in the heart of it all, they were together, tiny and as one.

'You mustn't,' her voice was barely audible.

He kissed her, she responded. 'I want to reach the other side,' he whispered.

'Yes,' she sighed. 'Yes.'

Dark Night

The knowledge of what had taken place hit him the moment consciousness returned. Tom groaned and opened his eyes just a slit onto night.

Had it really happened or had he dreamt it, he wondered, almost hopeful. In response, impressions of tightly entwined bodies drowned out the darkened room. He put up his hands to fend off the images but was struck by a powerful wave of sensations and feelings whose intensity left him stunned. Beautiful and terrible: it must have happened.

Even as the dry voice of his rational mind was cursing his stupidity and denouncing his sins, he yearned for her. His breath caught in his throat, his stomach lurched; his skin reached out like tiny hands all across his body, begging to interlock with her again.

Love, sorrow and the pain of the passionate: I never thought to experience this again. And it's yet another thing I'd more or less completely forgotten about. What have I been doing all these years?

The phone rang. Tom sighed more deeply.

- Hello.
- Hello darling, it's Anna. How's today gone?

Tom looked at his watch. 7.25 pm. OK, yes, she was right, another day had gone. What had happened this morning had happened and it couldn't be undone. *Just pick yourself up, dust yourself off and move on.*

- Yes thanks, OK.
- You don't sound too sure.
- Well, everything has its ups and downs, you know.
- So, not so good today?
- Yesterday was a good day. I really got going on something. Today, well...
- Well what?
- Do you know when you look back over something you've done? You know, something that seemed fantastic when you did it, then...
- Oh, you mean like when you used to paint all of those lovely pictures and then rip them up a week later because you said they were shit?

Her voice was stone cold, it shocked him. She couldn't possibly know, could she?

- No, not that exactly...of course not. Anyway, Anna, those pictures *were* shit...
- You were the only one who thought so and even you loved them just after you'd painted them.
- Yeah, OK then, but this is writing. It's different...

He felt annoyed. She never let up about those stupid bloody paintings. She didn't understand and anyway they were his to do with as he pleased.

- So you haven't wiped the hard-disk or thrown the laptop into the lake yet?

Now she was laughing and he relaxed a little, though the sound was a distant thing that left him otherwise unmoved. He wished he could share in it, but he couldn't enjoy anything right now. There was a gulf of his making between them.

- Tom? Are you still there?
- Yes, sorry. Tired and a bit down.
- When are you coming home?
- I don't know...soon. Tomorrow, or maybe the day after.
- It would be good to know. Mum's arriving tomorrow, remember. I could do with the moral support.
- Of course. Look this trip has given me a lot. The excitement has settled a bit, that's all. Things are getting back into proportion. At least I've found out that I can still produce ideas. There's plenty for me to work on when I come home. I probably just need to digest it for a while, you know, to produce something a bit more balanced.
- Aha. So when will you be back?
- I think there's maybe something I'd like to do. I haven't completely decided yet.
- What?
- I might like to take a walk around the lake, perhaps get up to the nearest peak. If I do that, it'll be tomorrow.
- And will you come back the next day?
- If I decide against the walk I'll come back tomorrow, but otherwise the day after, yes.
- Are you sure?
- Yes, this time I'm sure.

He made himself something to eat: tinned pea soup, crisp-bread, water to drink. He wanted coffee, but if there was to be any chance of him sleeping later on, he knew he shouldn't.

As he ate, Tom found himself thinking about his infidelity. His recollection of it was both powerful and vague. He was moved by it, and not just with feelings of guilt, yet when he tried to picture Ronda his memory became indistinct and fleeting. In some strange way, it was like trying to see at night: he caught glimpses from the corner of some inner eye, but when he tried to look directly, the glimpses began to fade and the harder he tried to focus the less he could see. Her features ought to have been indelibly etched into his memory, but not even impressions of her body or the magic of her physical proximity were entirely clear in his mind. All that remained was a blurry enigma and some powerful, hard to define feelings.

*

Tom was on the beach when he heard the splashing again. Very clearly this time.

'Get away Tom, get away from here,' she said. But who had said it? Katja? Lucy? Ronda? He had no idea.

He was squinting out over the ice into darkness. The illumination from the exterior lighting was weaker somehow and didn't reach even as far as it had the other night. He needed more light, he needed the torch, yet he hadn't brought it with him? Why? None of this was making any sense. He shouldn't be out here, anyway.

Tom turned back towards the cabin, but the thrashing from the lake was intensifying. What was it? Then his probing hands found the torch, tucked away in one of his deeper jacket pockets. Good thing! The beam lanced out across the ice, and now he saw it.

Way out, somewhere near the centre of the ice there was a breach, a big one too. And something was in the water, some large, featureless pale thing. It could have been an overweight man, maybe; hard to make out the details, though. More like a floundering, white seal.

'Tom, get out of the way, he's coming! Get away...' It was one of the women again. She must be very close but he couldn't see her, even though he shone his torch beam every which way, even into the birches.

Tom turned back to the mystery in the lake and froze. There were trees on the shore, three birch trees, old and rotten, with hollow trunks and an air of decay about them more like wet autumn than deep winter. His heart was pounding in his ears. The thing in the water was screaming out wordless cries and he wanted to help but the trees stood sentinel between him and the lake, evenly spaced at the very water's edge.

'He's drowning,' the woman's voiced declared, without passion, without any inflection at all.

'Then shouldn't we try to save him?' Tom pleaded desperately.

'No, he asked for it. It's what he wanted,' the woman replied. The voice sounded like Lussi's.

'Lucy? Where are you? Show yourself. We can still do something for him.' The man was struggling less now, his white bulk more beneath the water than above it. 'Please!' Tom shouted.

'You have to get away Tom, he's coming. He'll be here any moment.' That had been Ronda, he was sure of it. He whirled around searching the beach with his torch beam, but there was still no sign of anyone, just the rotting trees by the water's edge. Then he heard footsteps crunching along the edge of the ice, heavy and rapid. He knew at once who they belonged to.

Tom acted without thought, heading for the lake, his need to escape the Shorewalker overriding any fear he felt for the three birches. Somehow he was convinced that the Shorewalker could no more follow him out onto the ice than reach the other side. He'd be safe there.

But he'd underestimated the trees and as he neared them they silently compelled him to slow. And the air of decomposition that had previously been no more than a hint grew so heavy that he gagged.

Poison! They're trying to get me with poison gas! The thought was so ridiculous that normally he would have laughed. Not now though. His head swam and his eyes were streaming so much that he couldn't see. Tom felt himself begin to topple and cast out a hand to find something, anything to which he could cling, but there were only the trees. His fingers brushed across the parchment surface of bark. It was the middle one: *Lucy.* The thought came unbidden. He swayed again and grasped harder at Lucy's trunk until with a crack his fingers plunged through the thin, dry surface into putrid humus beneath.

Ugh!

The stench of rot was overpowering now. He released her and fell again but before he struck the ice, fingers like iron rods seized him. There was terrible strength in those hands and somewhere through the veil of his tears he sensed a face pale with rage in which blank eyes were set.

*

Tom woke up with a cry. He was in darkness, wet, cold and shaking.
- *Where am I?*
- *I'm in bed!*
- *Really?*
- *Yes, in bed.*

His fingers reached for the lamp switch. Light on, bedroom much as always, blankets hurled onto the boards in a heap and his damp sheets furled about him.
- *A dream, it was just a dream; or was it?*

He clambered out of bed, staggering to the window, but Tom's gritty eyes could not penetrate the wall of blackness outside. Then he made his way into the kitchen, because he had to be absolutely sure. His trembling hand rested briefly on the door handle, fear vying with the need to know. The door swung open and as the cold air hit his slick body, he gasped.
- *Madness! You're insane. You'll freeze to death for sure this time!*

His torch beam lanced back and forth across the beach and far out onto the lake. No trees along the water's edge, no breach in the ice, no sounds of drowning.
- *It was just a crazy dream.*

He closed the door again, noting how light and flimsy it seemed tonight. Anybody wanting to break into the cabin would make short work of it. An image of the dead ptarmigan arose in his mind.
- *Anybody except Gary the Grouse that is.*

Tom dressed and wrapped himself in blankets, he was shuddering uncontrollably and his breath plumed in dense clouds of vapour. As he made his way back into the kitchen he passed the front door and double-checked that it was locked. His fingers smeared a thin layer of frost that had formed on the inside of the door. He had to heat the place up, get warm. There was still an option he hadn't yet used, one that, when it worked, was far superior to the pathetic electric heaters.

He rummaged around in the kitchen cupboard, digging out tattered yellowed newspapers, small strips of card and packaging and other items of makeshift tinder that they'd collected over the years. Was there any wood though? They hadn't taken care of the place properly since old man Sten had died. Yes, there at the back, the good stuff.

Tom pulled forth half a dozen sections of split birch log and went into the living room with his haul. There he began to prepare the flaking iron stove, carefully laying a fire as he knew it should be done. Once he was finished, he drenched his handiwork in the remnants of a bottle of lamp oil, just to be on the safe side. Then he pulled up the best armchair and lit the fire. It caught straight away.

He settled back into the chair with a shivery sigh. He didn't want to be here anymore and just wished he could go home – or rather he wished he was already there without having to go through the discomfort and tedium of a journey. But for now this was the best he could do and tomorrow would be a better day. Maybe he would succeed in trudging off to the bus stop and make good his escape, but more likely he'd sleep in and then need time for a slow laborious pack and to get himself sorted out.

The fire really took hold, crackling and popping with fierce intensity. He fed two more pieces of firewood into the stove before closing the sooty glass hatch. There was a problem with the old potbelly, the main reason they didn't use it that often; the flue was damaged. Sometimes smoke leaked out into the cabin. It didn't always happen, but when it did, it meant sore eyes and a smoker's cough the next day. They'd meant to have it fixed or replaced, but it only happened occasionally and they weren't here often nowadays, especially in winter. He eyed the blackened metal pipe leading up into the ceiling with suspicion, but there was no sign of smoke. It was going to be alright.

Reality

Tom awoke to gummed up eyelids and laboured breathing. He didn't feel like he'd slept at all, but he knew he had to get up. He forced his eyes open. They hurt and no wonder, the room was hazy with smoke. *Oh of course, that had to happen didn't it!*

He cleared his throat of what felt like the residue of a hundred filterless cigarettes. His chest was tight and raw, like bronchitis. Great, and he was planning on walking round the lake and up into the hills today. No chance.

He checked his watch. It was mid-morning, but it still looked as if it was very dark outside. A trip to the porthole confirmed his fears. No sun. A pall of dense cloud lay like an iron lid over the land, turgid and unmoving. It'd be night well before 2pm. Maybe he wouldn't make it to the other side of the lake, never mind up the hill.

During a miserable breakfast of crisp-bread, aging milk and the last curled rinds of sweaty cheese, Tom reflected on all that had happened since his arrival. He thought a lot about the sisters, but found he couldn't picture them clearly today, not even Ronda. They'd become somewhat like a fading dream. Of the previous day, he recalled intense sunlight and creative euphoria, but there was no guilt, in fact almost no memory of his encounter with Ronda, as if the events had taken place many years before or perhaps not at all.

Did it really happen?

He stopped chewing, surprised by his own question. The more he concentrated, the less he was able to disentangle the reality of his visit from lurid dream. The crisp-bread was sawdust in his mouth; his body and mind hurt; the day was murk and his mood was plummeting because he needed his therapy lamp. All of that was real; but the sisters, the drowning man and the Shorewalker?

He shook his head, bemused. Then something else occurred to him. He turned on his laptop. There, on the desktop was a new file: *Into*

Bewilderness. Tom snorted; pathetic title! Well, that could be changed. He opened the file and began reading. It was all there, everything, from his arrival and the strange encounters to his lovemaking with Ronda. He'd made it all up. Tom laughed, nervously, relieved to an extent, yet this was way too intense...even weirder in a way.

It meant the trip *had* been a success, he'd reconnected, definitely, there was no question about it. But the dreams and ideas had nearly swallowed him whole. Still, he was well and truly back in the river and that was what he'd wanted. Now all he had to do was to keep from drowning.

Final Calls

- How are you?
- Better, much better in fact.
- I'm glad to hear it Tom, I was getting a bit worried yesterday. I know your highs and lows and when you swing like that...it's like you used to be, you know, before...
- I know and you're right. I didn't quite see it, but I do now.
- You've been taking your...
- Yes, of course, I didn't forget those. *Damn, no he hadn't, he hadn't been taking his pills!*
- No I know you didn't forget them, *I* packed them for you myself. I was beginning to wonder, though, you sounded so down yesterday.
- Really, it's OK. I'm fine. Much more balanced, you know. What goes up and all that. The important thing is that I've found, you know, *it* again, really.
- Really?
- Yes, Anna there's no doubt. I've reconnected, somehow in some important way. And after the high and yesterday's crash I'm feeling balanced, even on the plus side.
- Plus? Not too much on the plus side though?

- No, no, in a good way.
- That's great Tom.
- Yes, I feel good. And I've written loads, you know.
- Oh that's fantastic darling. I look forward to reading it when you get back. Tomorrow right?
- No doubt this time, I'm really looking forward to getting back. I've already packed.
- Wow, that's not like you.
- No, I know, but I don't want to leave anything to chance tomorrow morning. No more delays, I'm coming home.
- You could come home today, you know?
- But there's only one train and I've already missed the bus.
- No, not on Thursdays, I was paying the bills last night and did a spot of surfing. Extra train on Thursdays. Extra bus too, though you'll have to run.
- Oh, no, no running for me today Anna.

After the call Tom sat for a time in the living room staring into the blackness of the cold stove. Was that it then? He'd forgotten to take his tablets? He chuckled, a dry clucking sound, but inside he felt as cold and dead as the ashes in the grate.

The only thing he'd reconnected with on this trip was his illness: no creation without mania, no euphoria unless his ardour was then quenched in bitter wells of melancholy. His creativity *was* an illness, that's what the doctors had tried to teach him. It'd been a brutal lesson and one that had left him shattered. Worse still, part of him had never accepted their verdict, a part that always believed that he knew better.

Luckily, when he'd first been told, Anna had been there for him. Nowadays it was all too easy to underestimate how much that had meant. Later on, when he was better and they'd found an even keel together, they'd had the kids and for years their lives had brimmed with purpose and duty. But no matter how much he had to enjoy, he could never shake off the nagging feeling that something was missing. Family life and moderate professional success just weren't enough for him.

He wiped away tears. The kids were getting bigger, they had lives of their own and needed more space than they used to. Anna was so tired when she wasn't working. They didn't travel anymore, didn't climb the hills as they once had. That's where the idea for this trip had come from, a last ditch attempt to prove to himself that the intensity and vision existed independently of all the dross; connect to the best without enduring the worst. And now he was in pieces all over again.

He'd lost a lover of sorts, not Ronda, not really – 'someone else' from way back. What had Lucy said? We come from Italy but we go much further back than that. Well, that's how it was, in a manner of speaking.

*

Midday was very dark, practically dusk. He wasn't up to it physically or mentally, but something about the prospect of being outside in the biting cold appealed more than waiting out his last day in the mausoleum air of the cabin.

He trudged first to the knoll. He wanted to get up to high ground, have a proper scout about and the hill beside the cabin was the closest high ground there was. He might make it a little way up the mountain on the far side of the lake before the fading daylight forced him back, but if not, this would have to do.

The slopes of the hillock were exposed in places, the steep angle denying the wiry vegetation any purchase. He scrabbled upwards as best he could, the ribbed and stony earth as hard as bedrock beneath his fingers.

It was tough going and more than once Tom paused to hawk up a gobbet of phlegm, courtesy of the faulty stovepipe. But after a few minutes of panting and cursing, he made the rounded summit and, after catching his breath, he began surveying the surrounding landscape. Even from this short distance, the cabin looked tiny; a battered shed beside an overgrown stand of saplings.

He shook his head, smiling, the building really was ugly. Sten had assembled a peculiar mismatch of leftovers from older houses to create a genuine, real-life blot on the landscape. Yet when seen in context, embedded like a tiny wart in the rolling tundra, its significance paled beside the grandeur of its surroundings.

The land was a patchwork of darkest browns and greys streaked with lengthy snow-fields where the contours dipped into sumps and troughs. Then there was the grey sheet of the lake. On its far side, a small cluster of whale-backs rose. Erosion had smoothed away their drama, giving them a harmonious air.

Tom had loved those hills once. He'd wandered them back and forth, up and down the ridges, conquering their hunched peaks. He and Anna used to picnic in the crooks of their slopes, by small springs and among stunted arctic birches.

'Years ago now,' he breathed.

He let go of memory, rotated slowly, eyes scanning the murky land, looking for signs of habitation, anything at all that might suggest new buildings, a house a trailer or some sort of camp that hadn't been here before. But there was nothing, just as he'd known there wouldn't be. A new building might have given some credence to the sisters as living breathing entities, but now he knew for certain. Nobody wandered the tundra for miles in temperatures of nearly thirty below.

Before setting off around the lake, Tom decided to take a look at the birches – not that he expected to find anything there, but he wanted to be thorough. He approached their silent rows with some slight nervousness and paused briefly on the threshold before squeezing in among a labyrinth of dappled trunks and knee-high dead grasses.

He'd only forced his way a few paces before he sensed something ahead of him in the shadows. Tom paused, his heart hammering in his chest.

'Ronda?' he croaked.

There was an explosion of movement directly before him. Something huge and pale burst up into his face, its calls like those of the drowning man in the lake. Tom screamed and stumbled backwards, falling among the slim birch trunks, his body wedging there painfully.

There was a beating in the air like wings and the calls, no longer moans or cries, resolved themselves into those of a bird. He swivelled about and caught sight of the Ptarmigan as it swooped low over the lake. Moments later, its receding form angled upwards, following the contours of the hillside until he could no longer follow it against the sheets of snow on the higher slopes.

Tom laughed. 'And that one was for *Gary the Grouse!*' he called out.

On his feet, he inspected himself for injury but, short of a few bruises, there seemed to be nothing wrong. He steadied himself on the trees. Ahead of him, there was a tiny glade where the bird had been roosting and seeing it again after so many years prompted a flurry of memories. He moved a few more tentative steps into the space and his eyes picked out some unlikely shapes around the roots of one of the larger trees. He found two greying cylinders entangled with grasses and spotted with old leaves. Tom recognised them at once, they were beer cans.

Anna and he used come here to this very spot during those first summers, back when her father, Ole had still been alive. Everyday had followed the same idyllic pattern for him then. Late morning would see him struggle out of bed and grunt his good mornings before shuffling down to the lake for a swim. The others had almost always been up for hours already and Anna's mother, Kerstin, would be preparing lunch by the time he dried himself off.

In the afternoon they would go for walks, pick berries or mushrooms if it was the season, walk the hills or maybe drive into the village for provisions. Then in the evenings, which this far north were as light as day at that time of year, they'd sit out long into the night, eating and drinking until their voices had become a drowsy murmur in the gloaming.

Her father would nod off first, his nut-brown, shiny head nodding forward onto his chest, and then Kerstin would bundle him off to bed while Tom and Anna remained in the old canvas, wood-framed deckchairs. Within minutes, Ole's snores would echo from the bedroom, but her mother was a light sleeper and so he and Anna would sneak away. Sometimes they would scale the knoll to watch the light play along the horizon, but more often they would come here to the heart of the birches to make love.

A smile touched his lips as he remembered Anna back then; so much younger, her half-naked body smooth and pale, her hands braced against the tree trunks as she leant forward. He used to wait until she was ready, until she glanced back over her shoulder at him, her lips splitting into a grin of invitation drawing him closer.

It had been here too that they'd scattered Sten's ashes, spreading them around the glade one summer night, each toasting his memory with a can of beer, probably those that were still lying at his feet. They never came back here again after that. It didn't feel right, she'd said. He'd agreed, of course.

Tom backed out of the glade and made his way out of the birch thicket. As he left the trees, something snagged on his fingers. He paused to examine it and found several strands of dark hair entwined about his index finger. There were more on the flaking bark, but Tom had learnt his lesson.

'Oh no you don't! No Birch-girls today thank you,' he called out over his shoulder.

The walk around the lake was uneventful. At first Tom paid little attention to his surroundings, a jumble of fragmentary thoughts, memories and feelings filling his head. There was a sense of departure in the air, of final farewells. He'd come here to rediscover something, but in truth he was saying goodbye to cherished illusions, to the happy past and all its memories and to this place. Once he left here, he would never come back.

He finally directed his attention outward, to a colourless landscape. The lake was grey smooth ice without ripples, fissures or breaks. His booted feet crunched along the edges with a sound like the Shorewalker himself, a thought that made Tom smile. And there were no mystical forces stopping him from getting to where he wanted to go either. On the other hand, the day was so grim that his resolve to get to the other side was fading. He could push himself, but why should he? What was there to see over there that he hadn't seen before, especially on a day like this? The excursion had lost its meaning; the land was dead, the fire was out. But he persevered for a while.

By the time Tom had forced himself halfway to the other side a wind was picking up and he could feel the pricking of powdery ice granules on his face. Soon he could see tiny particles swirling and rushing about the surface of the ice. He wondered what the weather forecast was. He hadn't switched the radio on since his arrival. Shit, if a lot of snow fell tonight he might not make it along the track tomorrow and the busses might be off anyway. Well, that settled the matter. He was going back to the cabin, sod the other side.

Lussi Natt

The stove was roaring. He'd searched the flue before building up a new fire but couldn't find any sign of a breach. Well what the hell, his eyes and lungs were already wrecked, but he was going to be warm tonight.

There was something good for dinner too, something he'd been saving; a tin of meat and vegetable stew, it was lamb according to the label. Tom didn't normally hold with tinned foods but he'd picked this up on a whim to make a change from all the soup he always ate up here. He even had a litre carton of some cheap red wine with him, just in case, and tonight felt like the right occasion. It'd be a tasty farewell feast.

He placed himself before the laptop for awhile, but to no avail. He was going to work on these ideas, of that he was convinced, but they needed time to incubate first.

By late afternoon, he'd already eaten and was sitting drowsily before a well-stocked blaze, a coffee mug of wine in his hand. He'd opened all the inside doors, between the living room and bedroom, planning to get the whole place warmed up before the fire burned down. Then at bedtime, he'd close the doors, hopefully shutting out any late night fumes.

For the first time since his arrival, Tom felt at peace, both with himself and his situation. He looked forward to tomorrow, especially tomorrow night and being home, but there was no hurry.

He'd just drained his cup and allowed his head to nod forward onto his chest when he heard her voice.

'Come on then sleepy head, we have to get you cleaned up!'

Tom snapped into wakefulness with a jolt. Had he taken his

tablets? Yes, he was sure he had – this morning, exactly as he should. He rose to his feet, went into the kitchen to his bag. Yes, there, today's dose was gone. He must have been dreaming.

Tom checked the bedroom, just in case, not bothering to turn on the light. It was lovely and warm. What time was it? 6pm. Bit too early for an early night, but soon. He would sleep the whole night through and wake up refreshed and alert at some ungodly hour tomorrow. He'd not miss his bus.

'Ah there you are! Come on, we have to get you ready!'

Tom whirled round. She was standing in the doorway, a silhouette against the lighted kitchen.

'Who?'

He sensed rather than saw her smile, but she was too shrouded in darkness for him to make out any details.

'Now you're hurting my feelings! Have you forgotten me already?'

'Lucy?'

'Lussi will be along later,' she said softly.

'Katja?' he asked weakly, knowing that it wasn't.

'You know who I am, *Tom*,' she chided, her voice becoming harder.

'Yes,' he whispered. 'Yes, I know.'

'Right then, let's get you prepared,' she said stepping into the room and closing the door.

He felt for the light switch, but she placed her hand on his. 'No Tom, don't. It's better this way.'

'It is?' he asked.

'Yes, darling, believe me, for both of us,' she said, taking his hands and placing them on her bare skin. His breathing quickened and he found himself leaning towards her, the glorious blend of her perfume enclosing him.

'Ronda...' he breathed, his head falling onto her shoulders and her body clove tightly to his.

'Råndan,' she corrected. 'Or Råhanna if you will.'

They flowed together, their slick bodies glistening in the darkness. 'Like this, we're both of the land and the lake...we are of the river and are one with its silver waters,' she whispered – or had it been him?

After their lovemaking, as he lay in a dream of light, she washed his body, something which felt oddly appropriate to Tom. His eyes rested beneath heavy lids shutting out the visions of one world to contemplate a vista of glowing lands, stretching off into the inner distance.

'I'm not ill,' he said 'it's real.'

'Yes, Tom, it's real,' she whispered back at him.

*

Tom woke in the armchair. The fire had burnt low to glowing banks of embers and an occasional lazy flame. For a few heartbeats, the last vestiges of his dream stayed with him and he found himself reaching out for her.

'Ronda?' he murmured hoarsely.

He was uncomfortable somehow, in fact he was wet. Tom came to more fully. There was blood on his shirt, he was covered in it! He sat up, shit; it was everywhere, on the seat on the floor... Then he saw the coffee cup. His wine! He'd fallen asleep and spilt his wine. *Aw hell!* Now he needed to get changed, he'd been planning to wear these things tomorrow. And the armchair, it was old, but how was he going to explain it to Anna...but then they never came out here now, did they?

Tom changed clothes and stocked the stove again, using up the last of the firewood. He wandered into the bedroom and put on the lights. The bed was unmade, but only because he hadn't fixed it that morning. He stooped low and sniffed the sheets, part hoping, half fearing the scent of her musk. But he found only the faint odour of his own sweat. He'd dreamt it, *of course he had*, but it had been a good dream. This might be a good sign. Even with his medicine, his mind was trying to tell him something and, as long as the message was so agreeable, he wasn't going to complain. Let dreams and visions come. Just so long as he could tell the difference, he'd be fine.

He peered out of the window. The external lighting was on and he saw now that a lot of snow had fallen since his walk, but it looked as if it had stopped. Damn, he'd forgotten to check the radio forecast. Still, it didn't look too deep, maybe a few centimetres. He'd be OK and they'd have the ploughs out already. He'd get his bus, he'd get home.

He suddenly realised he could just about make out the contours of the hills, as if the sky were paler than inky blackness somehow. Now how was that possible? He decided to take a quick look, a last night-time excursion. For once, he prepared himself well. Warmly dressed, he made sure he knew which pocket the torch was in before slipping out and quickly closing the cabin door again to keep as much of his precious heat as possible.

As usual, it was shockingly cold outside, but snow cover changed things. His eyes could make out more of the land and see further, his footsteps were muted. For want of a better expression; it was nicer.

He wandered down to where he thought the lake probably began, no longer certain thanks to the snow, and stared out over the open expanse. As he left the immediacy of the cabin, the vast sky came into view presenting him with its solid glittering vault. It was the best starry night he'd seen in years. God, he wished Anna was with him for this!

He was still reeling from the wonder of the canopy above him when he heard the sound from the ice. Several distinct cracks were followed by the slopping of water. No surely not, he wasn't asleep now!

Nervously, he drew forth the torch, shining it in the direction of the sound. There was something there, something black. It could be an animal, though definitely not his drowning seal. There were far more wolves in the north these days, maybe one was prowling about out there, yet he could see that whatever was lying on the lake was completely still.

Tom was afraid again, but this time he was angry too. This wasn't supposed to happen! It was his last night here and he'd already resolved what was going on: he'd found a bit of creativity, been a bit ill and was having some dreams. He didn't need this, he didn't believe it.

He glanced about him, the sky forgotten. His torch beam raked the birches and the cabin, glaring into every fold and crevice in the snowy beach. There was nobody about and no unexpected birches by the water's edge. 'Fuck this,' he snarled and set off onto the ice. He was more afraid than he wanted to admit, but his anger kept him going. It was time to sort this out once and for all.

As he approached the dark object, it became increasingly apparent what it was and Tom began to slow. Somebody had made a hole in the ice, a perfectly square hole, about 1.5 metres square, the sort that Norrlanders used when they went swimming after a sauna. The sheer unlikelihood of such a thing stopped him in his tracks. The ice had been perfect when he went for his walk, flawless. No sign of any new buildings, which meant the nearest habitation was a good twenty miles away, so who could have done this and when?

He glanced back nervously towards the shore. No trees or strange women there. Everything was very clear in the snow-reflected glare of the cabin's external lights. In fact it was far darker where he was, but he was afraid to go back, afraid in case someone or something appeared there to cut him off. And anyway, would he even be safe in the cabin?

There was a faint sound behind him, perhaps just the creaking of the ice, but Tom spun round toward the perfectly square aperture to be certain. His torch beam fell full on the towering figure of a corpulent, older man, not twenty paces away. The folds of his worn, soiled working clothes glittered with frost and his eyes were like those of a dead fish, thickly coated in a white film. His pale face and bald head glistened in the torch beam.

Tom staggered clutching at his heart. He couldn't breathe! He knew those slack, dead features, knew them only too well; it was Sten, Anna's grandfather.

The figure raised his right hand in a wooden gesture, clumsily indicating that Tom should approach, but one more glance at the blind eyes and open mouth was enough. Tom bolted for the shore and the safety, he hoped, of the cabin. Behind him Sten gave a long, wordless, gurgling cry and set off in thudding pursuit.

Even before he had covered half the distance Tom saw three figures emerge from the birches, moving sinuously from the shadows to the light. Well to hell with them, he was going to get to the cabin and if they tried to stop him, he'd kill them.

'Slow down Tom, it's OK,' Ronda called to him from the shore. 'He can't follow you.'

Perhaps it was because he was desperate, but Tom found himself slowing down a little. He glanced over his shoulder only to find that Sten had stopped chasing him and was trudging slowly back towards the hole in the ice.

'Darling it's alright now. Come back to us and I'll explain,' Ronda called. But when he next looked toward the beach it was empty. Tom whimpered. He looked for Sten but he too was gone. He shone his torch about the lake but couldn't find the hole either.

Tom hung his head. Tears ran down his cheeks and along his nose as he walked slowly back across the ice. He was mad, there was no other explanation. And it wasn't like before either, this time he'd completely lost his mind. He would call Anna, tell her the bad news, ask her to get help for him. Maybe they could pick him up tomorrow and take him in. He didn't want to travel alone, not with all this weird shit going on.

He made the shore and tramped the short distance to the cabin, anticipating its warmth. But the door was locked. It couldn't be, he hadn't locked it and it didn't have a latch, you had to actually turn the key. He hadn't done that. The keys, where were they? He began searching his jacket, his trousers, everywhere, but he didn't have them. Had he brought them out with him? Maybe he'd dropped them?

Tom turned back to the lake retracing his footsteps, eyes glued to the intense circle of his torch beam on the snow. The only footprints were his, but there was no sign of the keys anywhere. He was at the water's edge, did that mean he would have to go all the way out there again. He wouldn't, he couldn't, but if he didn't get into the cabin he'd die out here.

The Shorewalker was already behind him unexpectedly when Tom heard his footsteps. Suddenly a pair of arms had encircled him from behind, pinning his own to his sides in an unbreakable grip.

He screamed and struggled as hard as he could but he could hardly move let alone break free.

'Help!' he yelled, his voice carrying out into the night and echoing from the nearby fells. 'Somebody help me! Please!'

There was sound and motion nearby. A woman, smiling face, dark glossy hair reared up before him. She was one of them, but she looked so strange, clad in a long, flowing, white robe she wore a crown of candles on her head, woven with grasses and birch twigs.

'Ronda...' he gasped. The woman nodded up the beach toward the cabin and Tom strained to see where she was looking. 'Ronda!' he yelled. 'Help me please!'

The Shorewalker wrenched him round to face the cabin. Two figures blocked his view, each a halfway thing between an ancient stunted birch and a naked human female. They quivered and creaked, their bark flaking.

'Ronda and Katja say *hi*,' Lussi said directly into his ear.

Tom was about to pass out as the Shorewalker spun him back toward the lake. Something was happening out there. Groaning and splashing came from a hole in the ice where a large shape thrashed and shook, slowly sinking from view below the ice.

'Why, why are you doing this,' Tom gasped.

'We want to help you,' Lussi said her eyes widening in earnest as droplets of wax fell from the candles into her hair.

'Then let me go, please, just let me go home to my family,' he pleaded.

She shook her head sadly. 'It's too late for that now Tom, much too late. But don't worry you won't end up like him,' she said indicating the drowning thing in the lake, 'or him for that matter,' she added nodding toward the Shorewalker. 'We like you and we're going to help you. You're going to the other side.'

'But you don't have to help me, I can go there myself,' Tom reasoned.

'You didn't get there today did you?' Lussi argued in a happy voice while she rummaged in her robes for something.

'No, but I didn't want to, tomorrow I could...' Tom stopped. Lussi had produced a long slender knife, which she was pointing at him. The tip glittered, very close to his face.

'Lucy, please, I don't know what you think...'

Lussi flicked her wrist and Tom's field of vision shrank. At the same time his left eye burned with pain.

'You won't be needing that anymore,' she said. 'Or that!' she added and Tom was plunged into darkness. Where his eyes had been there was only fire. Somewhere nearby somebody was screaming, but he couldn't decide whether it was him or the drowning man.

The Shorewalker still held him and he felt their hands on him as they stripped him of his clothes, slashing at the material with knives when it wouldn't give way of its own accord and cutting him in the process.

Then he was propelled out onto the ice, hurled bodily into a sprawling heap, spinning and sliding away from the shore. The ice numbed his bare skin, preparing him for water so cold it seared his flesh.

He wasn't completely sure when ice gave way to water. Neither did he know whether he'd fallen into Sten's cut or if the ice had simply parted to swallow him up at their command. He struggled for a while, but the life was already ebbing out of him even before the ferocious cold enveloped him.

Tom sank, drifted, faded. He slid deeper and deeper, drawing water into his lungs, turning them to ice until at some point he had been reduced as much as he could be without disappearing altogether and there he remained, hovering on the very cusp of non-existence.

*

How long he remained in suspension was impossible to gauge, it could have been mere minutes or many years. At some point however, timelessness gave way to change and, after an eternity as ice, he became aware of the waters about him again. They were becoming warmer. And there was something else too. A glow, indistinct and faint but growing in intensity.

Soon there was no question about the light. Tom began to struggle toward it, his body lighter than he remembered. He moved easily and rapidly toward the surface, spiralling upward and yet, suddenly, his feet struck the bottom. Pleasant sensations as his toes sank into soft sand. He moved forward, the light growing and fragmenting, forming a glittering cage that flowed and shifted about him.

Tom broke the surface of warm waters and rose into a haze of gold. Before him, the other side beckoned.

Author Biographies

Nina Allan
Nina Allan's fiction has appeared in the magazines *Interzone*, *Black Static* and *Midnight Street*, and in the anthologies *Subtle Edens*, *Never Again*, *Strange Tales* from Tartarus and *Best Horror of the Year Volume 2*. Nina won the Aeon Award in 2007, and has twice been nominated for the British Fantasy Award for best short fiction. Her first story collection, *A Thread of Truth*, is published by Eibonvale Press. She lives and works in London. Nina would like to thank her good friend Chloë Mavrommatis for the loan of her childhood memory of 'the door to anywhere,' which provided the original inspiration for this story.

Gerard Houarner
Gerard Houarner works at a psychiatric center and sometimes writes. His latest work includes *The Oz Suite* from Eibonvale Press and *A Blood of Killers* from Necro Publications.

Rhys Hughes
Rhys Hughes is the author of many books. He has a fondness for aardvarks, cakes, rhomboids, tea, melodies, limes, lutes, stars, toucans, drums, novels, hope, ginger and mountains; but he dislikes sarcasm, violins and butter. His website can be found at: http://rhyshughes.blogspot.com

His book *Tallest Stories* is due from Eibonvale press late 2010.

Brendan Connell
Brendan Connell was born in Santa Fe, New Mexico, in 1970. He has had fiction published in numerous places, including *McSweeney's, Adbusters, Fast Ships, Black Sails* (Nightshade Books 2008), and the World Fantasy Award winning anthologies *Leviathan 3* (The Ministry of Whimsy 2002), and *Strange Tales* (Tartarus Press 2003). His published books are: *The Translation of Father Torturo* (Prime Books, 2005), *Dr. Black and the Guerrilla* (Grafitisk Press, 2005), *Metrophilias* (Better Non Sequitur, 2010), and *Unpleasant Tales* (Eibonvale Press, 2010).

His blog is at: http://brendanconnell.wordpress.com

David Rix
David Rix founded Eibonvale Press back in 2004 with its/his first book, *What the Giants were Saying* – a highly bizarre novella of creativity and wind turbines that received some very positive reviews. A second book, a collection of linked tales called *The Book of Tides,* is due for publication by the end of this year. See www.davidjrix.co.uk for more information.

Allen Ashley
Allen Ashley has been short-listed for a British Fantasy Society award every year for the past six years. Allen is a widely published writer, editor, lyricist and poet. A passionate advocate of the short story, his most recent collection *Once and Future Cities* (2009) is still available from Eibonvale Press. Check out his web site at www.allenashley.com

Jet McDonald

Jet McDonald is a writer, musician and storyteller. His fiction has been published in *Subtle Edens - An Anthology of Slipstream Fiction* and is due to be published in the forthcoming *Catastrophia* in Sept 2010. His work has also been included in "The Idler" and *Paraphilia Magazine* and his novel *Automatic Safe Dog* is due from Eibonvale Press later this year. He is a member of spoken word collective *Heads and Tales* and in 2008 won the Missouri Review Audio Fiction Award for his contemporary spoken fiction. He has performed his stories and music at festivals across the UK including Glastonbury Festival and the Hay on Wye Literary festival. His freaky folk band *Jetfly* have been aired on BBC 6 radio and toured nationally with four albums. More information about his literary and other pursuits can be found at www.jetfly.org.uk. As of May 2010, Jet has embarked on an overland cycle tour to India.

Douglas Thompson

Douglas Thompson's short stories have appeared in a wide range of magazines, most recently New Writing Scotland, Ambit, PS Publishing's *Catastrophia* anthology and *Albedo One*. His first book, *Ultrameta*, was published by Eibonvale Press in August 2009, and hailed as "a new form or literature for a new century" and "a modern classic" by *Sci-Fi Online*. His second novel *Sylvow* will be released by Eibonvale in August 2010. The idea for the *Blind Swimmer* anthology was dreamt up by Douglas, David Rix and Andrew Coulthard in Douglas's living room, while hungover the morning after his first book launch.

www.glasgowsurrealist.com/douglas

Terry Grimwood
Terry thinks he can sing because no one boos him when he does his turn at the local Jam Nite. He plays harmonica as well and, as a college lecturer, tries to turn recalcitrant students into electricians. Oh, and he writes. Published in the likes of *Nemonymous, Midnight Street, Murky Depths, New Horizons* and *Bare Bone*, Terry has also written and Directed three of his own plays, started up the very occasional Exaggerated Press and brought out a collection of his short fiction called *The Exaggerated Man* (available from Amazon). His novella *The Places Between* is due out from Pendragon Press in September 2010 and his novel *Bloody War* will be published by Eibonvale later this year.

Alexander Zelenyj
Alexander Zelenyj is the author of the short fiction collection, *Experiments At 3 Billion A.M.*, published by Eibonvale Press, and the short novel, *Black Sunshine*, published by Fourth Horseman Press. His fiction has appeared in a wide variety of periodicals, including Underground Voices, Euphony Journal, Inscape, Revelation, Amazing Journeys, Freefall, and Front & Centre, and anthologies such as Terminal Earth, Way Out West and Columbia and Britannia. He lives in Windsor, Ontario, Canada, prefers basements, and often spies peculiar murders in the night sky. Visit him at www.alexanderzelenyj.com.

Andrew Coulthard
Born in Hartlepool, raised in Helensburgh, then pushed beyond sanity in London, Andrew Coulthard has lived in Stockholm since 1990 with his Swedish wife Kristina and their two children. He runs a business training company and every now and then indulges in a spot of translating for good measure. Andrew is currently working on a collection of short stories and putting the finishing touches to his novel, *Nemo's Labyrinth*.